THE
SPANISH SACRIFICE

BOOK 6 OF THE ONE HUNDRED YEARS OF WAR SERIES

JAY PERIN

Publisher's Cataloging-In-Publication Data
(Prepared by Cassidy Cataloguing Services, Inc.)

Names: Perin, Jay, author.
Title: The Spanish sacrifice / Jay Perin.
Description: [New York, New York] : East River
     Books, [2024] | Series: One hundred years of war
     series ; book 6
Identifiers: ISBN 979-8-9882648-1-1 (paperback) |
     979-8-9882648-0-4 (ebook)
Subjects: LCSH: Ex-presidents--United States--
     History--20th century--Fiction. | United States--
     Politics and government--1989---Fiction. |
     Petroleum industry and trade--History--20th
     century-- Fiction. | Heirs--Fiction. | Sacrifice-
     -Fiction. | Murder--Fiction. | Man-woman
     relationships-- Fiction. | Extortion--Fiction. |
     LCGFT: Political fiction. | Thrillers (Fiction) |
     Historical fiction.
Classification: LCC PS3616.E7443 S63 2024 | DDC
     813/.6--dc23

The characters, names, businesses, places, locales, events, and incidents are either the products of the author's imagination or referred to in a fictitious manner. Any resemblance in either the book or the promotional material to actual persons, living or dead, or actual events is purely coincidental.

Editor: Chase Nottingham
Cover: www.ebookorprint.com
Maps and illustrations: Murat Bayazit
Video (book trailer): Nauman Gandhi
Special mention: www.GetCovers.com

www.EastRiverBooks.com

To the One They Called God;
To the Best of Men;
To That Goddess of Knowledge;
To the Chronicler.

Table of Contents

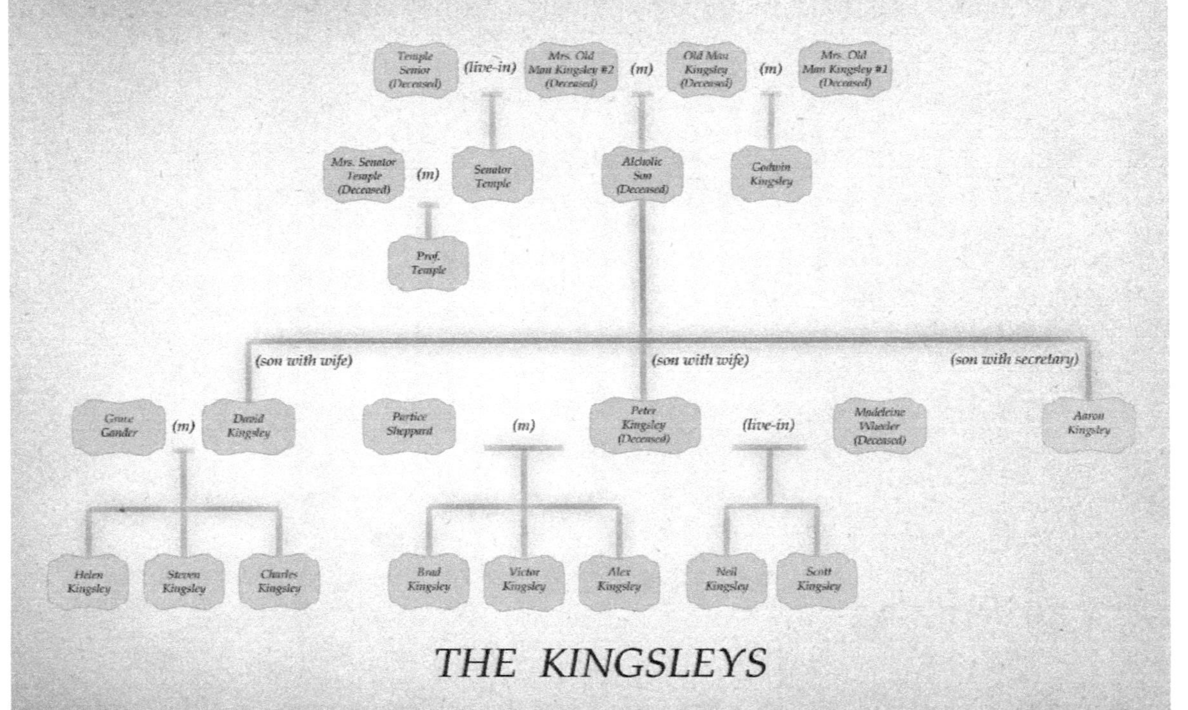

Temple Senior (Deceased)
(live-in)
Mrs. Old Man Kingsley #2 (Deceased)
(m)
Old Man Kingsley (Deceased)
(m)
Mrs. Old Man Kingsley #1 (Deceased)
Mrs. Senator Temple (Deceased)
(m)
Senator Temple
Alcholic Son (Deceased)
Godwin Kingsley
Prof. Temple
(son with wife)
(son with wife)
(son with secretary)
Grate Gander
(m)
David Kingsley
Partice Sheppard
(m)
Peter Kingsley (Deceased)
(live-in)
Madeleine Wheeler (Deceased)
Aaron Kingsley
Helen Kingsley
Steven Kingsley
Charles Kingsley
Brad Kingsley
Victor Kingsley
Alex Kingsley
Neil Kingsley
Scott Kingsley
THE KINGSLEYS

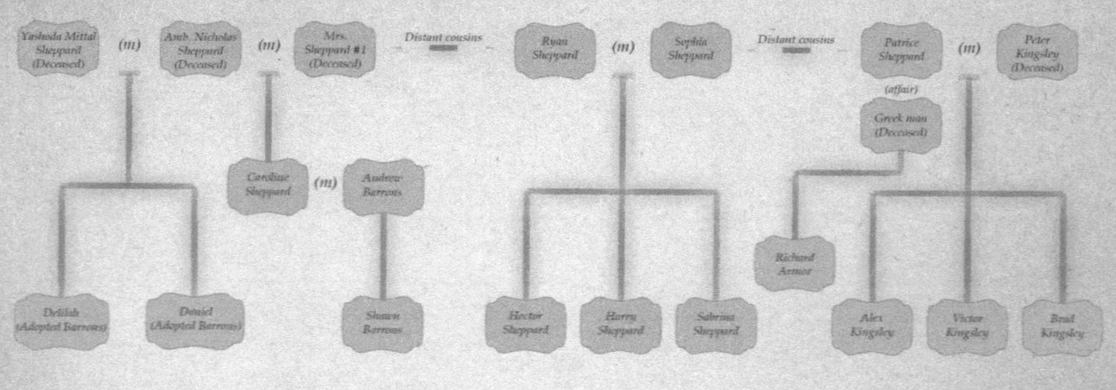

THE SHEPPARDS

Part I

Chapter 1

July 2000 (2 ½ years after the end of the exile)

Green-wood Cemetery

Brooklyn, New York

Rain—loud and unrelenting—battered the city as it had done the entire month, shaking green leaves loose from the trees in the graveyard. A minister stood in front of the group in the clearing, all of them sheltering under umbrellas as the eulogy was given.

The tarred road running through the cemetery was only a few feet to the right of the ongoing service. The occupants of the parked Cadillac still couldn't hear the words of the cleric over the rolling thunder. Didn't matter. Temple couldn't think beyond why. Every one of the black-clad mourners would be asking the same question. Why was a soul with so much promise taken from them?

Mounds of wet mud hid the freshly dug grave next to the clergyman. The casket rested on the other side of the burial site.

"It should've been me," Temple whispered, warm tears rolling down his cheeks. His shoulders shook. "It should've been me."

The secret service officer in the next seat shifted, wrapping an arm around the elderly politician. A box of tissues was offered.

"It should've been me," Temple said again.

He was ninety-five. He'd lived a full life, done everything he wanted to do. It was time to give an accounting to his maker. Instead, the war Temple declared led them all to this day.

Statesmen like him talked about rules of conduct in righteous conflict, but the beast inside the human was territorial, recognizing only himself and his own. There was only one rule he followed— kill or be killed.

Flute music started outside, Noah Andersen playing "Amazing Grace." There was none of Noah's usual finesse. Weeping openly, he kept having to pause the song. The women went on sobbing. With a heart-rending cry, the mother collapsed onto her knees. The brothers, the beloved... how would they carry on living?

A shadow at the periphery caught Temple's eye. The man who was rumored to have done the killing. He was staying behind the trees, out of sight of the bereaved.

Fury balled into a hot and hard knot in Temple's chest. *"I need to go there,"* he said. The words came out garbled as they often did thanks to the bullet he took to the brain more than a decade ago.

The secret service officer next to him glanced upward as though he could see the pouring skies through the roof of the car. "Mr. Temple... sir..."

Inclining his head in the direction of the killer, Temple said, *"I want to talk to him."*

His cane wasn't of much use on the muddy ground. Supported by one of the officers, Temple walked unsteadily behind the backs of the mourners and approached the killer. Two more secret service officers accompanied the former president, one of them keeping him dry with an umbrella. The fourth one remained in the car.

Temple was never very tall, and age took a few more inches from him. Looking up, he stared hard at the killer. A second passed, five seconds, ten. The killer didn't look away, didn't hide his guilt and his regret.

Temple didn't give a damn. When push came to shove, the man sacrificed an innocent to protect corruption. He would do it again. The remorse wasn't over the blood he spilled but about the dishonor he brought upon himself. About no longer being able to have pride in himself as a warrior.

A finger stabbing the air, Temple said, *"You will die... soon. And you'll remember the one you killed at the moment of your own death."* His mother would soon weep over his grave even as a mother was weeping now.

It didn't matter how the words weren't clear. The killer understood them, accepted the judgment.

He could run, but Temple would make sure he paid for what he did. They would all pay.

Chapter 2

Two years ago, late March 1998

(almost 2 months after the end of the exile)

World Trade Center, New York City

Seagulls flapped their way across the blue sky outside the South Tower. Inside the main conference room in Barrons O & G's corporate headquarters, all was quiet and pleasantly cool. The honks and shouts from the streets wouldn't reach this high up.

A good thirty minutes remained before the scheduled board meeting. Standing next to the pristine white column, Harry kept half an eye on the view through the glass-paneled wall as he perused the copy of *The Wall Street Journal*. Market expectations from Pfizer had skyrocketed after the FDA approval of Viagra, the drug for erectile dysfunction.

Folding the paper back, he sighed. It was no use. He couldn't focus enough to read even the comic strip.

The skyline outside kept dragging his mind to the past. *Twenty-four years*, Harry mused.

His seventeen-year-old self had waited in trepidation in a similar hall when the Barrons office was located in the Flatiron Building. Lilah was on her way up, and Andrew Barrons was preparing to deliver an ultimatum. He wanted her twin brother as heir, but Dan wouldn't agree to be adopted on his own, and Lilah had already rejected the idea in the days after her parents' demise in a plane crash.

For her, the Sheppard clan—Harry's family—was her own, but the self-centered bunch struck a deal with Andrew. They wouldn't stand in the oilman's way when he presented Lilah with a stark choice. Agree to an adoption, or there would be no help for the bankrupt Sheppards.

A shift in the air, the scent of her perfume. Young Harry didn't dare turn around and face the hurt and the fury in her hazel eyes when she learned of the betrayal. Instead, he limped to the windows to stare at the gleaming towers of the recently built World Trade Center.

Even knowing her life was being bartered, Lilah couldn't bring herself to abandon the Sheppards. Sacrificing her pride, she capitulated.

Neither she nor Harry knew at the time how many more sacrifices would be demanded of her in the years to come. Neither imagined how Lilah would eventually be dragged to the military court in Cuba where she was assaulted, her clothes torn, her bloodied body exposed to lust-filled bastards. Neither realized a decade-long exile was waiting for her.

Soon, Harry reminded himself in the here and now. The exile was over, and a just war would soon begin. The business empire stolen from Lilah would be back under her control, and she would destroy it.

"Harry," a voice called from behind.

He turned from the window, throwing a questioning glance at the two men in business suits. Dan, Lilah's twin, sported dark hair and eyes like many other Sheppards, including Harry. Add to the mix the light-brown skin of his part Indian, part Irish-American ancestry, Daniel Barrons was considered a handsome fellow by the tabloids.

Next to Dan was Andrew's biological son, Shawn. The sandy hair and brown irises were probably inherited from Andrew's long-dead first wife. Like Harry, Shawn was not a board member. He was not even a regular shareholder, having been cut off a long time ago. Shawn Barrons showed up only to get justice for his sister.

"Andrew's on his way up," said Dan, glancing briefly at the secretaries going back and forth with files and folders. "We'll start the conference in ten or so minutes."

Tossing the folded newspaper onto the table, Harry nodded. This time, the oil driller was going to be the one ambushed by those he trusted. Starting with Andrew Barrons, all those who tormented Lilah would face justice.

#

Half an hour later

Harry took one more sip of warm, creamy coffee before setting the mug on the coaster. Right ankle propped up on the other knee, he maintained a casual attitude as he studied the men and women seated around the long conference table. Every damned board member of Barrons O & G was present, and all were leaning forward, listening intently to the speaker. Andrew, the CEO, was at the head, Dan on his left. The Barrons heir was standing, explaining to his audience in measured tones what to expect in a potential corporate war with the Kingsleys.

"Not taking a side is not possible under the circumstances," insisted Dan. "Yes, we could end up being in the network's bad books for a while. Yes, a clash between the businesses will cause problems in the market. All the companies, including Barrons O & G, will suffer losses. What we need to remember is the magnitude of harm to the oil sector and the global economy if we let *status quo* continue. We need to remember what Steven Kingsley did in Cuba. Moreover, he shot someone in full view of the guests in a casino in Vegas."

"Cuba was a long time ago," boomed Andrew. The man was in his seventies, his formerly brown hair now stone gray and wrinkles around his blue eyes. Yet his tone carried the same strength, the assumption of how others would fall in line. "As for the Vegas shooting... law enforcement decided it was self-defense. Besides, Steven's been a good steward of the network all these years."

"Absolutely," Dan agreed without missing a beat. "Perhaps the cops are right about Steven not doing anything wrong in Las Vegas. We can also acknowledge he hasn't made any major errors as the network's chief executive. Cuba still needs to be addressed, long time ago or not. Steven pulled a bait-and-switch on his own cousin—Brad Kingsley, my sister's husband—to get them into trouble with the American government. Lilah and Brad were on the run for nearly ten years thanks to Steven."

"Rehashing old stories is a waste of time," Andrew declared. "If you're determined to do it, let me remind you Steven couldn't have done what he did to Brad if Brad himself didn't cooperate."

Dan inclined his head. "You're right. Brad might have been conned by Steven, but we do expect the CEO of an entity such as the network to be alert to potential problems. To exercise caution in his professional life. However, we're still left with the uncomfortable yet undeniable fact that Steven deliberately led the Kingsley brothers into the deal with Iran. Maybe military intelligence knew Brad's basic personality; maybe they didn't. Maybe they didn't realize he wouldn't recognize the nuclear trafficker. *Steven* fully well knew Victor and Alex and Lilah would've cottoned on to what was going on. He still let the operation continue without involving any of the people who might have called a halt to it. Why?"

Murmurs went around the table.

"Your objection to Steven Kingsley hinges on your faith in Brad," pointed out Andrew, a mild flush on his cheeks. "How do we know for sure he didn't in fact recognize the trafficker? Even in your sympathetic interpretation of the episode, Brad was negligent. He should've talked to the senior executives in his company before considering a deal of such magnitude. Those executives happened to be Victor, Alex, and Lilah, the same three who would've recognized the nuclear trafficker. It was Brad's choice not to involve them."

"Andrew," called a stooped gent.

Harry recognized the fellow. Eighty-nine with three former wives and a current one in her forties. Several children, all of whom occupied various executive positions in his business. He was someone on the list Harry made using the financial tracking software built by his sister. If some of the details on the old fraud were to be leaked, his ex-wives could sue for the false info he presented in divorce proceedings. His holdings could end up being divided between three very angry ladies. The government wouldn't be very pleased, either.

Dan started cultivating the elderly businessman shortly after the events in Cuba. A dinner here, a golf game there... it took time, but they agreed how exes who were already loaded didn't need more millions in their bank accounts.

"Your point is well taken," said the old man, nodding at Andrew Barrons. "Then again, so is Dan's. We cannot afford to ignore the tactics Steven used to become CEO of the network. For God's sake, we all read the transcripts from the military interrogation in Cuba. What his brother did to Lilah... Steven and his friend... what's his name?"

"Armor," supplied Harry, speaking up for the first time. "Major Richard Armor, JAG Corps lawyer."

Every eye in the room turned toward Harry.

"Yes," said the elderly board member. "Neither Steven nor this Major Armor said a word to stop the assault. Lilah—the CFO of the network and *your* daughter, Andrew! If they could do it to someone like her, what else are they capable of? Brad might not be as competent as we would like, but at least he's not a criminal."

"Yes, my daughter," said Andrew, a trace of impatience in his tone. "Unfortunately, I cannot let personal feelings get in the way of what's good for Barrons O & G."

"Your attempt to be objective is appreciated," said yet another board member. "It *is* important to note how Steven's leadership has been good for the members of the network purely in terms of money. However, some types of private behavior suggest a man cannot be trusted in public life. Steven's activities certainly qualify as such."

Andrew's surprise was evident. Across the table from Harry, Shawn smiled a little. A few years ago, he'd accompanied Dan on a trip to Brazil to meet said board member. Armed with info from the girls of Eden, the strip club, the brothers had waited in the hotel lobby until their target sauntered down, sated from his encounter with a seventeen-year-old boy.

Shawn had been barely out of his teens, too, when he was booted from his position as the Barrons heir simply for being gay. Most board members supported the action, including the supposedly devoted family man now speaking to Andrew. Shawn had zero qualms about using the intel to make the hypocrite toe the line.

Blackmail—neither Dan nor Shawn gave a shit how it could blow up on them. Still, Dan had issued warnings to several board members how attempts to dispatch him or Shawn to the hereafter would automatically trigger the release of critical documents to the press. Evidence of certain businessmen's bad behavior would be all over the media.

More members spoke. They brought up how as the new CEO, Steven engineered the ouster of Harry from chairmanship. There was no evidence of the Kingsleys framing Harry, but rumors abounded. Once he was kicked out of his leadership position, Steven assumed the title of chairman as well. The court had since admitted to the grave miscarriage of justice, declaring Harry innocent of all charges. So why couldn't Steven be given the boot and Harry restored to his former position?

The Barrons board didn't realize it, but if Harry were to return as chairman, he would use his clout to help Lilah destroy the network. The oil empire could not be allowed to continue as a shadow government over humanity, its rich and powerful rulers deciding the fate of every man, woman, and child on the planet. Andrew, of course, didn't know about Lilah's plans, but he kept raising objections to any action against Steven.

"The choice is not necessarily between Brad's incompetence and Steven's criminality," Dan eventually said. "Let's take one step at a time. I believe most of us can agree Steven should not be the

CEO or the chairman. Only then does it become a question of deciding on his replacements."

His audience glanced at each other. "True," muttered a woman. "Barrons could get a turn at leading the network."

"Why not?" concurred one of her colleagues. "Financially speaking, we're on par with or bigger than other well-known names in the oil sector."

With an audible ptchaah, Andrew said, "What Steven did to my daughter was not enough to convince the network to kick him out nine years ago. It certainly won't be now, so how will Barrons get a turn at leading?"

The woman who spoke before inclined her head toward Harry. "Mr. Sheppard is going to court about the chairman position. A reasonable judge could order the board to take action against Steven Kingsley. The chairman's office will return to Mr. Sheppard, but the CEO title... Mr. Sheppard was actually proven innocent. Brad Kingsley was only pardoned, which means Barrons has cause to challenge him for the chief exec's office."

"The court!" said Andrew. "Who knows how long it will take before a verdict? Who knows if Harry will actually win? And I don't want Barrons to be on the losing side. The people present here are not gullible. Do I need to spell out what happens to losers after a war? Our best bet is to stay out of the mess."

"Talking about gullibility," Harry cheerfully took up. "The network's board members aren't exactly chumps. If the officers of the Barrons board see potential advantage in ousting Steven, the rest will, too. Which means a succession war if Steven does get canned. Right, Andrew?"

"Uhh?" Andrew frowned, clearly confused by the seeming support from an unlikely quarter.

"Merely clarifying what to expect," said Harry. "If Barrons decides to throw support to Brad—or me—in a corporate war, it should be with full awareness of potential consequences. We'll be outnumbered and outgunned, with a good chance of gaining nothing even if we win." He paused for a second. "Nothing except the knowledge we did the right thing by the network, by the oil sector, and by the people of the United States. Steven Kingsley must not be allowed to continue as chairman and CEO."

"Agreed," said the elderly fraud who was the first to speak up. "Sorry, Andrew. I'm with Dan on this."

With each vote cast, Andrew's expression grew more puzzled, his cheeks more flushed. The men he expected to side with him automatically, those who could normally be counted on to put their greed above any sense of justice, now chose to support Lilah. Oh, yeah. Blackmail might be a dirty weapon, but it was quite effective on this crowd of selfish bastards.

As the board filed out half an hour later, a red-faced Andrew muttered, "Eight to four. The exact two-thirds needed to override a chairman's veto."

Digging into his blazer, he took a pill bottle and popped something into his mouth. From where he was sitting, Harry couldn't see the label.

Andrew glanced to the left where his chosen heir was seated. "Do you expect me to believe all those people were suddenly outraged by what happened to your sister?"

Dan said nothing, meeting his adoptive father's stare with one of his own. Next to Dan, Shawn also stayed silent, a smirk twisting his lips.

"What's your next move?" Andrew asked through clenched teeth. "Kicking me out of my own company?"

"I don't want your company," Dan said, his tone steady. "I never did. If none of it ever happened... Papa and Mama's plane crash, the adoption... I would've been happy doing my own thing. When my parents died, I was grateful to you for taking in me and Lilah. I still am. You were our brother-in-law. Family. The offer of a role in your business was simply an opportunity which came my way. Still, if Shawn objected, I would've declined. He'll verify our conversation on the topic. After I heard what you did... how you and the Sheppards sent Lilah to Libya..."

Andrew jerked back in his chair.

"Yeah, I know," Dan said bitterly. Andrew's ploy to get Lilah out of the way so he could start introducing Dan to his social circle was what put her in the Sheppard home on a fateful night so long ago. "Harry told me. We both learned about it relatively recently. I thought about walking out right then and there. Trust me... I would've. Except I *need* Barrons now." Which was more or less Lilah's reaction after she heard. Only, she hadn't been as shocked as her twin. "Rest assured, though," Dan went on. "There's no danger of any internal revolt, provided we agree on how things function from here on out."

If Harry were a better man, he would've left the Barronses to their drama, but he was relishing every moment of it. Swiveling his chair slightly, he cast a glance in the direction of the Flatiron Building where the old Barrons office used to be.

Phase one begins, Harry said to his past self, the seventeen-year-old watching the Twin Towers of the World Trade Center go up. The war was on.

Chapter 3

A week later, April 1998

Long Island, New York

"bin Laden?" Lilah echoed the gray-suited fellow who'd shown up at Temple's residence to debrief her. There was a colleague with him, an athletic-looking woman with her blonde hair in a high ponytail. Both were seated on the couch across the coffee table in the library. Lilah's lawyer, Grayson Sheppard, remained alert in the chair next to hers.

Three months had passed since the exiles returned to American soil. The Kingsley brothers had already been interviewed by the CIA. Alex and Victor's prior activities when they were with the military made the U.S. government very certain they got help from the same criminal elements once used by intelligence operatives. The feds didn't care that the fugitives went to known terrorists for help. Inside info was what the intelligence brass hoped for.

Local terror groups stopped cooperating with the U.S. military at the end of the Cold War, and intel was needed on new safehouses, routes, the hierarchy within various extremist organizations, and their potential targets. Alex explained it had been almost a decade since the exiles faced off with the Afghani radical called Yasser Afridi, but the spy agency still wanted all the data it could collect. They learned that Lilah was present during Alex's initial meeting with said *jihadi* as she was the only one of the fugitives who understood Arabic. Hence, the arrival of the two officers at Temple's home where she was staying.

"To be honest, Afridi and his friends spoke mostly in the local language," said Lilah. "He talked with Alex in English. I caught only a couple of sentences here and there in Arabic. Alex must have told you already."

"Yes," said the CIA man, his tone impatient.

The female officer had yet to speak, and her eyes were darting around the airy room with its polished wood furniture. A leather jacket in dull red—Lilah's—lay discarded on the reading table by the large windows. The fragrance of potpourri mingled pleasantly with the smell of the books lining the shelves. Miniature models were arranged alongside the tomes—replicas of ancient edifices, ships in bottles, cars, bikes, airplanes. It was Temple's way of keeping himself engaged after a bullet took away his ability to read and write, to communicate in whatever way.

The former president and his friend, Noah Andersen, were not present at the conference. Nor were Lilah's guards or Temple's security detail.

"Captain Kingsley made it a point to remember the names you picked up at the meeting with Afridi," continued the visitor in the gray suit. "The captain did admit he was forced by circumstances to inform the rest of you about what he did during his time in Pakistan."

Lilah stayed silent, not confirming, not denying.

Grayson, her elderly lawyer, cleared his throat. "My clients signed a legal agreement with the CIA. None of what they reveal to the government about their exile can be used to prosecute them. Alex's alleged disclosure of confidential information to his family would be covered under the contract. Moreover, he would have discussed—if he did at all—any prior encounters with Mr. Afridi only because lives were at stake. Circumstances as you said."

"I'm not trying to mislead Mrs. Kingsley into giving away... this is not a setup," said the fellow from the CIA. "I was merely trying to say Captain Kingsley's military experience in the region was only part of what made him memorize the names. Back when he and his brothers and you were executives in the network, the government would've kept you updated on terrorist activities which could impact the market. al-Qaeda began functioning around the time you... er... found it necessary to leave the country. Mr. Kingsley... Mr. Alex Kingsley recalled communicating with the state department about this particular terror group just prior to the events which led to your exile."

"We were told to watch out for bin Laden and his crew," Lilah acknowledged.

The female operative coughed. "Captain Kingsley mentioned—to us—keeping track of news reports on their activities during your exile. I assume you did as well."

Lilah nodded, noting the hint of an accent.

"Vast majority of the American public hasn't heard of al-Qaeda," said the male officer, face tight and eyes grim. "The bastards behind the World Trade Center attack all had links to the group. We lost eighteen of our men in Mogadishu thanks to them. Five Americans and two Indians in the Riyadh truck bombing. Nineteen more at the Khobar military complex. Even so, there are some in our government who refuse to get their heads out of their—" He cleared his throat. "The Soviet Union broke up, and some people seem to think we've won forever. No new enemies to fight. They're not taking bin Laden seriously, but he's serious all right. He and his pals have declared *jihad* on America."

"Holy war," Lilah murmured.

"Right," said the woman across the coffee table. "Any information on the group could come in handy in determining their capabilities and intentions."

"I get it," said Lilah. "Believe me... I'm not withholding info. Alex would've explained that we didn't get anywhere near Afridi's village—the terrorist camp, I presume. We couldn't afford to." The jihadi financed his activities with cash obtained from trafficking women, and Lilah was likely on his list. "What I heard from him were only those two names—bin Laden and Abdullah Azzam. Afridi didn't seem to agree with bin Laden's priorities."

"Azzam was one of the founding members of al-Qaeda," muttered the male officer. "He was in fact assassinated over different priorities. It would've been right before your encounter with Afridi. There's a high chance bin Laden arranged the death."

"If you know that much, you clearly have people on the inside," Lilah pointed out, frowning. "Much closer to the leadership of the organization than we ever got. So why are you here?"

"If we can stop even one bomb from going off—" started the man.

"Ms. Kingsley," called his female colleague. "The public might be blissfully unaware of bin Laden and his kind, but you... lemme tell you about my parents. They were lucky to move to the States from Bamyan—Afghanistan—but they do have family back in the old country. They know better than anyone else... my mother has told me stories... trust me when I say it's critical to put a stop to the damn bastards now. They're already escalating. Who knows what they're planning next? The United States cannot afford to ignore any detail about al-Qaeda and bin Laden, no matter how trivial. Gathering information is our only intention. We're not trying to trap you into saying anything incriminating."

Lilah contemplated the duo for a few moments. "Alex would've given you the general location of where we hid and the route we took. Not sure how much it will help, but I'll give you my version. There's also a friend of mine who has a knack for sketching out routes."

The gray-suited officer said, "We have our own experts—"

"I will only work with people I trust," Lilah stated. "In any case, the CIA should be fine with him—Petty Officer Harry Sheppard." Harry never divulged details of the clandestine work he did for the government, but he certainly didn't get his Medal of Honor for routine missions. And he always, always, always used maps to plot strategies when they were building the oil network. He would be able to make some sort of a guide from Alex and Lilah's descriptions.

"Noted," the male officer said in capitulation. "Regardless, your cooperation is much appreciated."

"In return," Lilah continued as though he had not spoken, "I want access to the records CIA has on what happened to me and the Kingsley brothers in Cuba."

"You want…" started the female operative. "It's not poss—"

"Make it possible," instructed Lilah. "Or no deal. As you said to me, criminals need to be stopped before they escalate. In my case, the escalation already happened, and I'm trying to clean up the mess they left. Any evidence I can present against them could help."

"The CIA does not take sides in private matters," objected the woman.

"Since when?" Lilah laughed a little. "The FBI's concern about the activities of the executives of Peter Kingsley Company was supposedly what triggered the sting operation against my husband and his family. American authorities then used the bad blood between cousins to arrange a military interrogation. Is the CIA distancing itself from the FBI's tactics? If so, I'd like an official statement. It could help us in court."

"Using an existing situation is different from putting a thumb on the scales for one side or the other," said the male agent.

With a nasty smile, Lilah said, "Allow me to point out that putting a thumb is exactly what the U.S. government did—*knowingly*—when Kingsley Corp was brought into the picture to take control of the network in case Brad were to be charged. The authorities did not limit themselves to representing the American public."

"There were extenuating—" the female officer began. "Ma'am, you're a lawyer, and you obviously have your arguments ready.

Regardless of who was right back then, you're a civilian now. Not even a defense contractor. We cannot share such info with civilians no matter how rich or well-connected."

"Yes," said Lilah. "I'm a civilian. No matter how rich or well-connected or how many defense contracts someone gets, a solitary individual is not left with many options if governmental entities decide to go on the attack for whatever reason. I learned that lesson... the Kingsley brothers learned the lesson when we were hounded out of our home and business with the help of the military. Yet here you are, asking me to take your word for it that what I share with the CIA won't be used against me. Yes, there's a legal agreement, but a bigger legal agreement called the American constitution existed when I was arrested. My rights as a citizen were still ignored. So yeah... this trust you're asking for? It has to work both ways. I want all the details of the mockery of an investigation which led to our arrest, and you'll have to trust me that the only place I'll use the info is in a court of law."

The two visitors exchanged glances, saying nothing.

"Take my offer to your bosses," Lilah suggested. "I will also need some sort of documentation of our agreement with your supervisors' names on the paper. Call it insurance." She got to her feet. "Sorry I have to cut this meeting short—previous appointment with friends." Gesturing toward the chair where Grayson Sheppard was seated, Lilah added, "Please send any contract to Gray. He'll review it from my end."

Chapter 4

A few minutes later, Lilah shrugged into her red leather jacket. The floral shirt and jeans would do for dinner with her schoolmates. A couple of hours with people who knew her only as the old Lilah, the one before everything changed in her life. She needed this.

Grayson still stood at the library window with Noah Andersen next to him. Thankfully, the former attorney general had stopped dying his hair the silly jet black, letting it go completely silver. Same as Temple, Noah was in his nineties, but he walked with the gait of someone a couple of decades younger. He still golfed at the local course, declining the use of carts, and the sharp green eyes easily penetrated the façades put up by people.

Suede booties hardly making any sound on the carpeted floor, Lilah joined the two elderly lawyers for a quick peek outside. The intelligence officers were trudging through the foggy drizzle to their waiting car. Raindrops pattered on the stone-paved path across the lawn, creating a pleasant rhythm. Tall trees with cinnamon-red bark bordered the yard, hiding the home from public view. Beyond the trees was a high wall with a main gate and a small side entrance. The officers would have to drive around the house to exit.

"There will be redactions in any document they give us," Grayson mused. "I doubt we're going to find anything useful."

"Perhaps, but we have to try," said Lilah. As the visitor's vehicle disappeared around the corner, she let out a soft breath. The request from the CIA had rekindled hope in an idea she'd almost abandoned. Or rather, a variation of it.

"Well," said Grayson. "I suppose we shouldn't leave any stone unturned. Let's see what the agency comes up with."

"Worst that could happen is they refuse," agreed Lilah. "I'll give them our route map regardless."

"But they don't need to get their hands on it right now." Grayson chuckled. Turning away from the window, he added, "I'm going to say hello to Temple before heading home." The former president would be in the workshop next to the garage, tinkering with his models.

Only when Grayson's back disappeared down the hallway did Noah ask, "What are you up to, Lilah? Grayson's right. There's going to be zero usable info in any papers we get. You're not pissing off the CIA with delaying tactics simply for the sake of it, I assume."

"You assume correctly," Lilah stated, going to the couch to grab her purse.

Grayson was the lawyer for all the exiles, so she couldn't confide in him with the expectation of secrecy from Brad and his brothers. Noah was different. His official role in the legal team solely as Harry's lawyer meant he was under no obligation to divulge info to anyone other than his immediate client and the authorities. Lilah could disclose to Noah anything that did not break the law.

"We can't ignore any opening to bring our numbers up in the network's board," Lilah went on. Thanks to Dan, Barrons O & G would vote with Brad. Which still left their side at a ten-eight disadvantage in the eighteen-member board of Peter Kingsley Network. "If we present evidence of malfeasance on the part of the Kingsleys, more members could swing to our side. However, there won't be any *direct* evidence against the Kingsleys in military or intelligence records. Not about them trapping Brad."

"Godwin's shrewd," agreed Noah, padding to the bookshelves lining the wall on the right. Picking up a paperback, he leafed through it. "With experience at leaving no tracks." The Kingsley patriarch was the mastermind behind his grandson Steven's evil schemes and perhaps the only man who managed to hoodwink both Temple and Noah for a significant length of time. "So why did you ask for the records?"

"Names," said Lilah. "I want the names of the people who signed off on the Cuba plan for Godwin."

Noah turned to stare, book in his hands. "If a third party were actively involved in plotting the Cuba episode, he might have kept lips zipped initially but not after the assassination attempt on

Temple. At that point, the instinct would've been to cover his own behind in the event the Secret Service came knocking. Not to mention how the Kingsleys don't leave loose ends. Our third party would've feared for his life. There's also Harry. After you and the rest left on your exile, official sources were under orders not to communicate with him, but his name would've been the first to occur to anyone with anything to fear from the investigators or from Godwin. A whistle-blower, an anonymous tip... there was nothing. Or it wouldn't have taken Harry nine years to get a pardon for Brad."

Shaking her head, Lilah said, "There were at least two government officials we know about who were involved in the entire plot."

"General Potts," acknowledged Noah. The Kingsley hanger-on had left his position as dean of West Point at the time, going on to be the head of army intelligence. Major Potts, the general's son, still worked for the CID. "Unfortunately, both Pottses hid behind national security mumbo jumbo."

"Right," said Lilah. Opening the purse in her hands, she took a quick glance at the contents. Cell phone, wallet, her new pistol... all the essentials for a night out. She snapped the handbag shut. "What I'm getting at is even the Pottses would've needed some assistance somewhere. Steven and gang were expecting to find planted evidence in my computer, so someone did the planting. The raid had to happen afterward, so someone in the team coordinated with Steven to decide on the date. Someone sent the investigation reports to Godwin to help him formulate arguments against us."

"Either of the Pottses could've done it all," insisted the former attorney general. "Neither will snitch. Well, the senior Potts definitely won't, and father and son function as one unit."

"Noah." With a small huff, Lilah slung the purse on her shoulder. "I'm not looking for a smoking gun. Not anymore. I mean... Harry and I tried that with the Amber story, too."

Amber Barrons, Andrew's cousin, was part of an earlier attempt at a partnership between the Kingsleys, the Barronses, and the Sheppards. She died before the wedding could be scheduled. Correction: she hanged herself. There were a few people who demanded further investigation into the tragedy, but the noise soon died down. Then, Godwin wrote a hefty check to Amber's parents. Why, if the Kingsleys truly had nothing to do with her death? The hush money was the only blemish on the record of the esteemed public servant.

"Temple was already a senator at the time," Noah said. *"He* was the government official helping Godwin then."

"They did a good job covering up what happened," accepted Lilah, her fingers gripping the backrest of the couch.

Only when Lilah was attacked by a criminal at the network's first board meeting did Temple realize the Kingsley patriarch never had any intention of letting her live to learn *realpolitik*. Before the former president could put a stop to Godwin's scheming, the Kingsley brothers were tricked into an unsavory business deal and forced to run.

Both Harry and Noah were convinced Amber's tragic demise was the secret Temple would've used to fend off Kingsley interference in the plans to get presidential amnesty for Brad. For his efforts, the politician ended up in the crosshairs of an assassin. The bullet which pierced his skull didn't kill him, but he was left unable to communicate in any meaningful way. Unfortunately, Temple never revealed what he knew even to his old friend and confidante, Noah Andersen.

Noah glanced back toward the bookshelves. Behind one of them was a steel-doored locker where Temple's personal documents were stored, including his writings. "After Temple got shot, I went through every one of his journals for info about Amber. I read every piece of paper in the locker except his father's logbooks, which wouldn't have mentioned the girl. He died before she came into the picture."

"And you also got nothing," brooded Lilah.

"Nothing at all," said Noah. "Whatever the truth behind the poor girl's death, it was bad enough for Temple to never put it in writing. He didn't dare. I also talked to his secretary. She was with him a long time. Again, nothing. The support staff... the incident didn't make headlines, so a clerk or a telephone operator wouldn't have reason to remember. Not decades after Amber's suicide."

Lilah nodded. "Which brings us to what I was saying. The Cuba incident *was* all over the papers. If the CIA gets us the names of the people involved, we could ask their staff a few questions. Circumstantial evidence, but it could add up."

"A clerk who transcribed a report, a secretary who took a phone call," conceded Noah. "Problem is the approach still boils down to the Pottses, father and son. If a secretary printed a report, it would've been for General Potts, not Godwin. Trust me... the general's loyalty toward the Kingsleys is unshakeable. When he needed help, only Godwin was around. Moreover, Potts and Andrew Barrons had a falling out back when Brad and Victor and the rest were boys. Temple's told me the stories, and I've watched General Potts in action over the years."

Lilah knew there was bad blood but hadn't been interested in the details. "The general holds Andrew's behavior against me?"

"He's never said so in my hearing," admitted Noah. "However, his actions at critical junctures suggest... if not animosity, at least an active indifference toward you. General Potts will not snitch on Godwin for anyone, least of all a Barrons. The one higher priority in Potts's life is his son, and Major Phillip Potts happens to be Steven's friend."

Lilah gestured with her hand. "Perhaps we should give the general a choice between his son and Godwin. We really need something, Noah."

"Believe me... I get it." The former attorney general groaned. "Ten-to-eight in the board in Steven's favor even with Barrons on our side. Two-thirds majority will be needed to oust him. How can we call for a formal vote until there's a reasonable chance of winning?"

If a vote were to be held this evening, both Harry and Brad would lose. Steven would continue to be chairman and CEO. Without Harry's clout as chairman, there would be only one remaining way for Lilah to bring about the network's destruction. An antitrust investigation against the monstrous entity, which Brad and his brothers would not agree to. Nor would any of the network's member companies. Not at this time.

"Steven's got support in the board because of backing from his friends and family," pointed out Lilah. "Everyone knows it. And some of us understand Godwin's behind Steven's schemes."

Noah, Harry, Lilah, Daniel... any number of people could tell the Kingsley brothers the truth about their grandfather. The five men would still find excuses for Godwin's behavior and ditch the person who dared open their eyes to the patriarch's actual role in the saga.

"At this time, there's no way to discredit Godwin or change his mind," went on Lilah. "The other people who prop up Steven—General and Major Potts, Major Armor—if they're not going to rat out the Kingsleys, could we get them out of the game some other way? Perhaps force Godwin to sacrifice one of his pieces? It could weaken Steven to some extent."

Noah stilled. "Not sacrifice." Blinking rapidly, the old lawyer continued, "Perhaps we could get the pieces to lose heart in the game. Psychological warfare is a legitimate part of military operations."

"Propaganda."

"I mean psy ops on a more personal level."

"Unreliable tactic," Lilah mused. "Too dependent on the target." She sighed. "But like Gray said, we can't leave any stone unturned."

"We can't," Noah agreed grimly. "I hope Harry has better luck with Gateway. We simply cannot risk asking the board to vote until the odds improve, and an antitrust investigation will be even more difficult to arrange."

It wasn't long before Lilah learned they would have little choice in the matter.

#

Dinner with friends turned into a wine-and-chocolate session in one of their apartments. It was close to noon the next day when Lilah's car drew up to the door of Temple's Long Island residence.

"Please take a break," she said to her two guards as she exited the vehicle into the safety of the walled yard.

Perhaps her tone could've been less abrupt, but the private security firm was retained by Brad. None of the brothers anticipated needing bodyguards within American borders. The political attention surrounding the expected corporate war meant high likelihood of the feds getting involved in any untimely deaths among the former exiles or their supporters. Steven wouldn't dare attempt any direct attacks.

Not the case with Lilah. Brad was apparently concerned about the danger to his estranged wife from associates of the criminals who accosted her over the years. The men he hired to protect her were legit enough. Except they couldn't be trusted not to snitch. Lilah didn't have a choice of firing them or replacing them without that, too, being used as evidence of potential infidelity. Fortunately for her, within the confines of Temple's home, the private agents were forced to follow orders from the Secret Service.

Instead of going straight to her room for a nap, Lilah made a detour to the workshop next to the garage. Temple would've been concerned when she didn't show up for breakfast. He seemed to find peace in seeing her alive and well.

A secret service officer was present in the workshop, making conversation with Temple's valet as he helped the former president tinker with one of his models. At Lilah's entry, the elderly politician looked up from what appeared to be a miniature Rolls-Royce.

A look of relief going over his face, Temple said something, but it was incomprehensible. In the last nine years, he managed to learn only a few words. The salt-and-pepper hair had turned completely gray in the time, and his form was ever-so-slightly stooped. He didn't need his cane to walk inside but never left the house without it. The blue eyes showed signs of his advanced age.

There was a clock on the wall behind the retired politician, the seconds needle jerking rhythmically. *Time,* Lilah thought, settling herself on a stool with her purse on her lap.

Fears and desires shifted in importance day by day. Circumstances morphed; allegiances decayed. Time did change people. *Most* people. Not Brad or his brothers.

Nine years after the Cuba incident, and Brad still clung to his insecurities. He still believed himself to be the wronged party in their marriage, accusing Lilah of favoring his brother Alex. When the pardon finally came through, Brad went to Noah Andersen to see if there was a way to permanently relinquish control over the network to Steven. Not the ownership of the company nor the dividends from the stock. Merely the control. Brad would do it only to spite Lilah and to thwart her supposed ambition.

The former attorney general put a stop to Brad's plans with a reminder about the pre-nup signed by him. Lilah couldn't be fired from her position as CFO of the business—Peter Kingsley Company—unless there was evidence of gross incompetence. Signing over permanent control meant she could be fired by Steven, who wasn't bound by the pre-nup. She could go to court to protest the roundabout breach of the marriage contract and demand compensation in the form of more shares. A divorce initiated by Brad would also give her more shares as per the contract. If one or more of Brad's brothers threw support in her direction, Lilah could even end up with enough stock to appoint herself CEO.

A stretch of an argument. Oh, Brad's brothers flouted his orders now and then to help Lilah, but to actually take her side and cause him material loss? No way. Still, the possibility worried Brad enough that he abandoned the idea of surrender and was cooperating with the plan to fight Steven.

The marriage was long over, but Brad was stuck unless he could produce evidence of infidelity and break the pre-nup. Infidelity! Lilah shook her head. She was stuck, too. Unless she wanted to risk him telling Steven to keep it all, Lilah had to continue in her role as—

"You're home," someone commented. Noah Andersen beckoned to her from the door to the garage. "I was waiting to talk to you. A call came from Kingsley Corp. Steven's father is sending an emissary. The family would like to see if there's another solution besides all-out corporate war. Some possibility of compromise."

"What?" Lilah laughed. "Steven doesn't want any sort of compromise. This is only a delaying tactic. Maybe he's afraid Harry will somehow get Gateway to switch, too."

"Wait," said Noah. "There's something else. I also heard from the CIA director while you were out. Your request on records pertaining to the Cuba incident triggered a conversation between the director and the energy secretary. The secretary wasn't in the picture when it happened, but your return caught his attention. He was already reviewing the same records and had contacted Steven with questions about the network's stability. Impact on global economy and so on. Well... the powers-that-be are not happy with the answers they got. The current administration is proud of their record on the economic front, and they don't want anyone destroying it in the home stretch. There's already talk about a potential tech crash, so imagine trouble in the oil market on top of it. The secretary apparently didn't say anything to Steven on what he planned to do. Which is where my conversation with the CIA director ended."

Lilah gestured with her hand. "And?"

"I contacted an old friend in DC," Noah said. "By then, one of Harry's former colleagues had also called him. Rumor has it a couple of senior civil servants in the energy department suggested a deadline after which the government would intervene."

"Intervene how?" Lilah asked, confused. An investigation into monopolistic practices as she wanted? Without being prompted? It was hard to believe. Few lawmakers would dare such an aggressive approach without at least some members of the network calling for it first. The alliance was that powerful now. If the members took a united stance against the idea, they could retaliate by sending the economy spiraling into a deep hole. Which would put reelection into doubt for the people's representatives.

"My contact didn't know for sure, but a couple of possibilities come to mind," said Noah. "None of which bodes well for either side. I expect Steven got the same intel, so he wants to talk. No question it's a delaying tactic. He wants to get past the deadline before pulling some new trick to keep everything."

"When *is* the deadline?"

"December 2000."

"Perfect timing," Lilah noted grimly. "It puts us just past the next presidential election in the U.S." To escape government intervention, the warring parties would remain on their best behavior until then. The delay would protect politicians up for reelection from a market crash until America went to the polls. Once election day was behind the nation, the lawmakers would intervene. "So if we don't win a board vote, there's now a cutoff date by which we have to convince everyone—including the American government—that antitrust action is the only way forward."

Part II

Chapter 5

More than a month later, mid May 1998

(2 ½ years to deadline)

Leon, New York

"The Barronses, the Sheppards, the Kingsleys," listed Harry, hoisting himself onto the hood of his new Toyota. The wait outside the historical society office was likely to be more than a few minutes, and a warm and sunny spring morning was not to be wasted within a closed automobile.

Alex was already seated on the car. No, he had draped himself across the windshield and the hood as though preparing to nap. And why not? It was peaceful.

The street they were on was currently empty of other vehicles. The terrain was very different from Manhattan, with vast yards and thick-trunked trees surrounding hardboard buildings. A large American flag fluttered in front of the edifice which housed the Historical Society. There was none of the constant honking, no angry voices. Chirping insects and tweeting birds did set up their own lazy orchestra, the occasional humans passing by adding to the music.

"The three original businesses of the network," Alex muttered, eyes still shut.

"Yup," said Harry. "Barrons O & G will vote with us. The Kingsleys will stick with Steven. Which leaves Gateway from the three founding members."

There was perhaps one opening to persuade the Sheppard family enterprise to withdraw support from Steven. In the years Harry was in prison, his brother, Hector, had consolidated power. The board members almost invariably nodded yes to Hector's diktats. If he were to speak against Steven, albeit under duress... the other option was to discredit Hector, thus turning Gateway's attention to Harry.

All three original members of the alliance remained part of the eighteen-member board of Peter Kingsley Network. If at least two out of three opposed Steven Kingsley's rule, more of the network's board could be convinced to support Harry's reinstatement as chairman, thereby paving the way for Brad's return.

Which was what took Harry and Alex on the seven-hour car ride from Manhattan on the eastern side of New York State to the town of Leon on the western side. Unfortunately, it was beginning to look like a futile undertaking.

"Maybe Liam will succeed where you failed," mused Alex.

Liam Luce, brother to Harry's ex-wife, was currently inside the historical society building, talking to the solitary occupant. "Let's hope so," Harry muttered, twisting around to glance at the entrance.

Wind gusted briefly, scattering yellow daisies all over the lush landscape. A bunny scampered across the road. Beyond the streets, beyond the cluster of buildings stood bluish-green hills, wispy mist floating across the peaks. The Enchanted Mountains as the locals claimed. Driving down early in the morning, Harry had spotted silhouettes of barns, men calling out to each other, a braying donkey or two.

"Shit," he murmured. "This place is beautiful. I wouldn't mind living out in the country someday."

"Mountains and farming communities are not your thing, dude," responded Alex. "You're a man of action."

"Not forever," said Harry. He wasn't about to give up his guns or his blade—the Ari B'Lilah currently strapped to his ankle—but slowing down? Oh, yeah. "I think I'd like being close to nature. Not farming. Horses, even cattle. When this is all over, maybe I'll go into something like the witness protection program and live on a ranch where no one can find me."

Alex laughed. "And play your saxophone for the cows and the goats?"

"Possibly." Turning back around, Harry swept a hand to indicate the scenery. Fittingly, there was a new sound, the distant clip-clop of a horse. Otherwise, the surroundings remained as serene as before. "Imagine the peace and quiet. It would have to be somewhere warm all through the year, or—"

"Or?" Alex prompted, finally opening his eyes. When Harry merely shrugged in response, Alex continued, "Warm or not, doncha think the quiet will get too much after a couple of months?"

The hoofbeats of the faraway horse got louder, faster. Peering down the tarred road, Harry said, "I'm sure I'll find something to—"

A buggy appeared.

"What's..." Alex, too, sat up to check what was going on.

The horse-drawn cart barreled toward them, the driver a mere lad wearing a straw hat over his bowl-cut blond hair. Not an unusual sight in Leon where the majority of the residents were Amish. The very conservative religious sect rarely used any kind of technology, including automobiles.

Harry frowned. The carriage seemed to be heading toward the car. If the driver didn't pay attention, a collision would—

"Whoa," Harry shouted, heaving off the hood and diving to the yard next to the building. His elbow hit something sharp—a small rock—sending electric pain zinging down to his fingers.

Yelling, "What the hell!" Alex, too, tumbled to safety next to Harry.

Swerving at the last minute, the buggy continued hurtling down the path. Small clouds of dust rose from the creaking wheels.

Footsteps pounded down from the society office. "Are you all right?" yelled a skinny fellow. Looming over his shoulder was the familiar blond head of Liam Luce, the same question in his gray eyes.

"Yeah," Harry said, hauling himself up and brushing off bits of grass and mud from his tee.

"Kid couldn't be more than fourteen, fifteen," Alex commented, also standing. A wood chip was stuck in his dark hair. Brown eyes narrowed, he stared in the direction of the disappearing cart. "Guess you don't need licenses to drive buggies."

Liam snorted. "Or they really don't like him here," he said, tilting his head toward Harry.

"Dude, are you sure you wanna hang around this town?" Alex asked. "After the last ten years, Sabrina won't appreciate it if I get myself run over by horses."

"Here lies William Luce," said Liam, voice somber, "killed by a cart. No way."

Harry chortled. Sabrina would kill him—her own brother—with her bare hands for letting Alex die. Not to mention Verity, Liam's sister and Harry's ex-wife. His *first* ex-wife. Which was important because there were only two such women by his count, but the media named eight thus far, along with an absurd number of girlfriends. Also, a couple of boyfriends. Harry was currently in pursuit of one of the ladies who made the list of Mrs. Harry Sheppards.

The rest didn't matter, but this one said something which caught the attention of someone Harry trusted. He needed to know, to see for himself how much of what she blurted to the tabloid reporter was true. Then, he'd ask her for help getting the Sheppards—his own family—to see reason. Gateway's support of the war declared by Lilah could hinge on the outcome of this visit.

The skinny fellow from the Historical Society was glancing at the three men in turn, confusion writ large on his face. He was dressed in a gray suit, not Amish apparel.

"May we talk inside?" Harry requested. After what the society official witnessed, he was not about to share info without being given at least the bare bones of the story.

#

A few minutes later, the skinny fellow blinked at them from across the desk.

"We're looking for someone," Harry began. "An Amish lady. She might be twenty-nine, thirty now. Name's Jorah."

Sitting up straight, the historical society official considered his guests for a moment or two. "May I see your driver's license?" he asked.

Sighing inwardly, Harry complied and prepared to be shown the door yet again.

The first instance had been shortly after daybreak when the three men got to the address near Leon—a homestead within a few feet of Conewango Creek. The minute Harry showed his ID, the man of the house politely informed his visitors how the Amish didn't believe in violence even for self-defense. They wouldn't be facing his hunting rifle, but nor would they gain anything by loitering.

The second stop was the post office. The sole employee—a bespectacled woman with gray in her hair—had been all smiles until Harry introduced himself. The experience was more or less the same at the village market. It was Alex's idea to look for the Historical

Society, perhaps in the next town. They would know of families which settled in the area more than a century ago.

"Look," Harry started before the society official could kick his visitors out. "I get it. People around here believe I'm an S.O.B." He gave a brief rundown of their experiences thus far. "But don't you think it should be up to Jorah to decide if she wants to talk to me or not?"

"Most of us are aware of what the poor girl went through because of you," said the official. "We've also heard of your... er... rather colorful history." With a sigh, he sat back. "I'm acquainted with Jorah's father; he's the gentleman you would've met at the farmhouse. He reacted as any father would under the circumstances, but the Amish believe in forgiveness. You can be certain he will eventually regret not allowing you to have your say."

"So help us," Liam urged. "If you can tell us where to find Jorah..."

"I do know where she is," the official admitted. "But..."

Motherhood out of wedlock was a big no-no for the Amish. When the girl got pregnant, the family was ready to drag the culprit to the altar for a quickie wedding. Unfortunately, the lady wouldn't say a word about the father except to admit he was someone outside the community.

Her punishment was shunning. Weeks of social ostracization, during which she was forbidden even to eat at the same table as church members. The girl—she was barely above the age of consent at the time—still refused to contact the father when the baby was born. She refused to give the child up for adoption. Unlike some others in the sect who found themselves in similar situations, Jorah—which meant first rain in Hebrew—lucked out in having parents who understood how young people sometimes slipped up. Instead of disowning her, they merely sent her away to stay with a cousin, a childless widow of fifty-some years. Mother-son duo continued to live with the same relative, helping her around her chicken farm.

The kid was now eleven and tall for his age. Eleven long years during which his father—Harry Sheppard, according to tabloids—never showed up.

"I... uhh... didn't know about the child until recently," Harry assured the historical society official. "Or I would've made arrangements."

Alex shifted in his chair, but Harry ignored his brother-in-law's discomfort. What was said to the official was not untrue. The first Harry heard about young Samuel or his mother was from the one man in the Sheppard family business who could be trusted. Talk among the employees and the timing of the birth clearly pointed to the actual perpetrator, but blame was laid at Harry's feet, instead. He was here to enlist Jorah's support in the war against Steven Kingsley, but Harry did want to know. Why him?

"What's done is done," Harry continued. "I'd like to talk to Jorah. There's the matter of my responsibilities toward her and the boy."

Chapter 6

In less than half an hour, the three city-dwellers were glancing around a spacious and airy living room clearly constructed with a large family in mind. When the widow and her now-deceased husband moved in, they wouldn't have known how destiny decreed something else. Like it did for Lilah.

Pinching the bridge of his nose briefly, Harry continued to study the surroundings. Windows were set to maximize light. For whatever reason, there were two clocks on the wall to the right. Gas-powered lamps, a couple of deep couches, rocking chairs... no signs of electricity. One of the chickens in the yard outside fluttered to the windowsill, pecking on the glass pane in greeting.

"Good morning," a trembling voice said from the inner door. A small white cap covered her brown braids, and the clothes were typically Amish—long-sleeved gown in solid blue reaching all the way to her black shoes. Guilt was clear in the light-green eyes, along with a hint of fear, but she didn't look away from the visitors.

"Jorah?" Harry asked.

The young woman nodded, as did the lady of the house who stood right behind.

"Please sit," he requested.

Perching on the edge of a chair, Jorah straightened her shoulders as though preparing to take whatever punishment coming her way. Her cousin was on one of the couches, sharp gaze watchful and bony hands folded over her plain white apron. The lady would be sixty-five now according to the report Harry got.

For a few moments, there was only silence... except for the clocks ticking on the wall. Jorah fidgeted a few times, darting a glance or two at her relative.

It didn't take much longer. "I'm sorry," the young woman said.

"Why me?" Harry asked.

"Because I didn't..." A sob, quickly stifled. "I didn't want Samba to..."

"Start at the beginning, my dear," instructed the cousin, tone firm but not unkind.

A tear trickled down Jorah's cheek, followed by more. "All I wanted was to ride in the car," she whispered.

Already knowing the outline of what must have happened, Harry listened to her story.

Dante—Gateway's COO—had come to Harry with his concerns about Hector, the elder Sheppard son. On paper, Ryan—Harry and Hector's father—was still CEO of the family business, but Hector ran the show now. He'd made his dislike of Alex and his brothers clear. For decades, Hector's loyalties remained with the other half of the Kingsley clan, to the point of vacationing with them. Until recently, Harry had believed Hector merely used the breaks to get drunk without worrying about his wife or work.

Sometime twelve years ago, Hector went on a trip with Charles Kingsley and a couple of women to a winery in Western New York. It wasn't far from Leon.

"Twenty miles," said Jorah. "Maybe."

The travelers stopped at the grocery store in town to ask for directions.

"I saw the Porsche parked outside," Jorah said. "Silver color. I'd never seen a real one before. Only in magazines at the store. It was so, so beautiful. I couldn't stop looking."

She was still gawking at the car when the travelers exited the shop. The seventeen-year-old admitted she knew the route to Forestville, having driven her buggy there many times to supply produce from her family's farm. Jorah was thrilled at the prospect of riding in an actual car. A Porsche! It was a sedan, not a convertible, but the automobile was still magnificent. The trip would take less than half an hour, the blond man assured her. Someone from the winery could drive her back.

Jorah didn't like the look of the second fellow. Snickering all over the place and teetering about. The blond man seemed decent enough even though he was rather abrupt and smelled fruity. They all did, including the two women. Alcohol, as the Amish girl realized only much later. Her father never drank, and she never encountered anyone who imbibed among the people she knew.

"I *wanted* to go, so I..." Jorah took in a shuddering breath. "The women were there, so I told myself it would be fine."

Pulse racing in excitement, she climbed into the back seat of the sedan. The off-key singing of the group was easy enough to ignore when the scenery flew past at a speed she'd never imagined. It was so glorious that Jorah was tempted to shout into the wind.

She caught only one name during the entire ride—Hector. The other man and the two women seemed to defer to him.

The group—including Jorah—was shown to a suite in the winery. Thrilling adventure at an end, she'd been waiting self-consciously in the living room for the promised van driver to show up when the blond visitor ordered her to help him bathe.

"I was so shocked," Jorah mumbled. "I thought maybe I heard him wrong, but he said it a second time. He got angry when I said no."

Her objection didn't matter. Her pleas fell on deaf ears. Her screams as she was dragged into the bedroom were ignored.

"I never got to the bathroom to... to..." Jorah whispered, her shoulders shaking violently. "He never... never took... my clothes were still on me. It felt like a long time, but... maybe only a couple of minutes, but it hurt so badly. I thought I was going to die."

When it was over, the man told Jorah none of it would've happened if she did as she was told in the first place, which was to help him bathe. He claimed he hadn't been looking for sex. It was merely punishment for her disobedience.

"He told me I could leave," she recounted, her voice almost inaudible. The trembling ceased, the girl now shrinking into her chair. "My dress wasn't torn, and there was only a little blood... under my skirt. No one would see."

Except she didn't know how to return. There was one community phone used by her church, but if she called...

"Everyone would know," Jorah said. "My family... my sisters... there are seven of us. They would be humiliated."

Sick of her sobbing, the assaulter finally did ask the winery staff to have her driven back to Leon. She managed to stay silent throughout the ride. Confused, scared. The woman who drove the van didn't say anything, either, except to comment she was quitting if the damned bastards did end up buying the establishment.

Back in the safety of her home, Jorah's silence continued, but she'd never been much of a talker for her family to notice. "I washed and washed and washed," she said, "but..." The tiny stain seemed to stay on her thighs. In the room she shared with two of her sisters, Jorah asked for God's forgiveness for lost chastity. If only she hadn't been so fascinated by the outside world. If only she never stopped to look at the car. If only she didn't succumb to the temptation of a ride.

A couple of months passed before Jorah realized everyone would understand soon enough what she'd done. Her sins would be—

"*Sin?*" Liam bit out. "The only damn sinner in this—"

The cousin cleared her throat, putting a stop to Liam's outburst.

Thoughts whirled around Harry's mind, a heavy weight settling in his chest. "Go on," he said to Jorah.

She glanced at her relative, and the older woman nodded permission.

Disbelief, horror, questions. The girl didn't reveal the identity of the father only partly because she couldn't. All she knew about the horrible man was his first name—Hector—and the possibility of him buying the winery. The other reason was that the church would insist Jorah marry him, and she didn't want to. Yes, her refusal would also count as a sin, but she didn't want to. The God she adored was said to be kind, and He would understand. She hoped.

When her parents sent her away, Jorah was relieved the questions would stop. Still, she scoured every local newspaper, searching for news about a change in the winery's ownership.

"Nothing," she said. "There was absolutely nothing."

Until the summer of 1992.

#

Jorah's son, Samuel, was five and had started school when she came across an article on a certain Harry Sheppard's sentencing. On the cover of the same tabloid were pictures of his parents and the rest of his immediate family.

She recognized the blond man immediately. "I was shocked at first," said Jorah. "Afraid of... I don't know... just afraid. I ran to the school and got Samba—my son—and went home. In the morning, I went back to the store and got the magazine."

The Sheppards were clearly rich and powerful, but one brother was an assaulter and the other a murderer. No, the Amish girl never wanted her son hearing the truth about his conception. She also hoped he'd never, ever run into the family of the man who created him. It didn't matter that Samuel—Samba as she called him—kept asking about his father.

"I ripped it up," Jorah said. "The magazine, I mean. But I couldn't stop. Every time I went to the store for groceries... I don't know why I kept looking for news about you. Maybe I was afraid one of you would find out about Samba."

Articles about the astonishing number of women Harry was supposed to have courted, something about a military medal, stories about him taking a bullet for a lady friend. He was adamant he was framed for the murder of his former father-in-law. The children of the deceased—Liam and Verity Luce—were public in their support of the man accused of killing their father.

The more Jorah read about the younger Sheppard son, the less convinced she became of his evil nature. Perhaps she *wanted* to see something positive in the blood flowing through her child's veins. Samba was getting more and more insistent she reveal his father's name. Poor boy was mocked every day about his missing papa. In school, by his playmates, everywhere.

"The year Samba turned seven..." Jorah went on. "The riot in that place... the prison... everyone was talking about it. About you, Mr. Sheppard."

Even the policemen—*especially* the policemen—were singing Harry's praises for saving a correction officer's life and preventing the escape of some really bad men. Within months, he was nominated for yet another medal.

Once again, Jorah begged God for forgiveness, this time for a sin she was about to commit rather than for past transgressions. Calling Samba to her side, she pointed to the article about the convict who was nominated for the Medal of Freedom. Young Samuel's father had made mistakes in his life, but he was still someone the child could be proud of.

"I thought it was a way out," the Amish girl said miserably. "I mean... you were in prison, so how would you come to know? And you were in fact kin to my son." Inclining her head, she acknowledged, "What I did doesn't make any sense now, but it really seemed like a way out at the time."

Samba was to keep his father's identity a secret, Jorah told the boy. But within days, the entire Amish community in the county heard the name—Harry Sheppard.

Holding folded hands to her face, Jorah said, "I didn't expect Father to..."

Her parents saw a ray of hope for their lost daughter. They telephoned Sing Sing and asked to speak to the famous prisoner. The poor couple didn't get anywhere, of course. The staff would've dismissed the caller as yet another attention-seeking idiot claiming to be Harry's girlfriend/wife/mother of his child. Or perhaps a tricky reporter looking for a scoop.

No, Jorah didn't know how news of the call got to *The Big Apple Reporter,* but Harry could guess. The proprietor of the yellow paper—Eugene Bishop—was part-friend, part-problem for Harry. Bishop had visited the prison a couple of times during the mission to prove Harry's innocence. The sonuvabitch would've kept an ear out for talk, and the staff at Sing Sing wouldn't even have realized what he was up to.

Bishop confronted Jorah's parents at their farm, but the confused family could only repeat what they heard from their older daughter. The couple retained enough presence of mind not to reveal Jorah's whereabouts, but Bishop cornered her at the school her son attended. The reporter wanted specifics. When did she meet Harry? Where? Why didn't he acknowledge the child?

"I didn't know what to say," Jorah admitted tearfully, her hands wringing the fabric of her skirt. Was Harry in New York around the time Samba was conceived? Or she'd be exposed as a liar. Was he married then or between wives?

She already knew the name of the correction officer saved by Harry—Regina Berra. Without pausing to think, Jorah blurted to the journo that Samba was in fact Harry's son with Regina, his supposed third wife according to gossip columns. Jorah was merely fostering the boy in secret on account of the officer's job and Harry's imprisonment.

From the other end of the couch, Alex coughed. Liam shifted in his chair.

"Officer Berra is mixed-race," Harry said. "Her father is white and mother black. I presume Samba can't pass for having a black mother."

"I didn't know at the time she is black," Jorah said.

"Oh, what a tangled web," her cousin murmured from the second couch.

"Samba looks like..." Jorah continued. "Like... maybe a little like you but not much. And he has blond hair."

Bishop pointed out this major discrepancy, but Jorah was stuck by then. She continued to insist Samba was a Sheppard.

Eugene Bishop returned to New York City and reported the unbelievable tale with his own embellishments. The article suggested Regina Berra had indeed met Harry long before the murder which sent him to prison. Something about a fistfight between him and her bear of a father in the Cattaraugus State Forest which was only twelve miles from Leon. When the bout was over, Harry apparently managed to impregnate the officer. Regina threatened to slice off Bishop's balls for the ridiculous article, but the tricky bastard always worded his fables carefully and never left room for legal recourse.

Still, the story made Jorah's parents hopeful that their daughter's life would get back on track. Harry would hear about his son and would contact her. She would finally marry the father of her child even if he didn't happen to be Amish. The family kept hoping, even praying their gratitude to God when they read about Harry's exoneration.

There were of course no calls from New York.

"Which explains the reception we got in town," Alex muttered.

The elderly cousin nodded. "Jorah told *me* everything. We prayed together about it. We prayed for you, Mr. Sheppard, that the

Lord protect you from all evil. In the end, I agreed it would be best if Jorah did not talk to anyone else, but..."

The damage was already done. Poor Samba was taunted even more. It didn't take long for the lad to start getting into fights, which complicated his life further. The boy obviously didn't know why his young mother disclaimed maternity, albeit only to the reporter. Samba stopped communicating with her except for minimum interaction on unavoidable topics such as money for essentials. He was furious at everyone and everything.

"Did you consider taking him to a therapist?" Liam asked. "Maybe tell him the truth in a safe setting? We can even get DNA testing for proof."

"No," said Jorah, shaking her head. "I will never... I don't want him to know how..."

"But—" objected Liam.

"If it gets to that point, we will," interjected the cousin. "But it hasn't."

"Speaking up is the best way to stop such criminals," insisted Liam. "Your church can say what it wants, but this is 1998. The world has changed. Women have the freedom to—"

"Then, allow Jorah to exercise her freedom, sir," said the cousin. "She doesn't want to talk about it. Also, the world hasn't changed as much as you claim. You city folk pretend to be all supportive, but you're judgmental, too. Look at you... you're already judging her faith in the church. You think we're misguided. Uninformed. You think of yourselves as our betters. Well, sir, there's only one who's superior to all of us. Only He has the authority to tell Jorah how she should live her life, and you're not Him."

Liam flushed. "Sorry," he mumbled.

"I was worried people would judge Jorah for what that man did," continued the older lady, her tone calmer. "Some would be full of sympathy. Neither side would give Jorah the chance to put it behind her. So I agreed with her decision on how best to deal with the earthly evil she was unfortunate enough to confront." The woman turned to Harry. "Mr. Sheppard, whatever I read about you says you won't get our Jorah into trouble for a mistake she made out of fear. I hope you can find it in your heart to let things be. You don't have to admit to something you didn't do, but if you simply don't say anything... it will be good for your brother, too, if none of it comes out. I can also promise neither Jorah nor Samba will make any financial demands of your family. I will continue to provide whatever they need."

"Is he in school now?" Alex asked. "Ahh... does he drive a buggy?"

Harry threw a sharp glance at his friend. They were both considering the same idea. The blond boy who tried to mow them down earlier with his horse cart. An eleven-year-old who was big for his age could pass for a lad in his teens. Word of Harry's arrival would've spread rapidly, and Samba could've heard about it on his way to school. The lad could well have made a rash decision to attack in retaliation for the years of neglect and humiliation he suffered.

"Most of our boys are taught how to drive a buggy," said the cousin. "And yes, Samba uses one to get to school. Unless Mr. Sheppard is in fact planning to acknowledge the boy as his, you will need to leave before he returns. Samba will not take well to open rejection."

"Is there a photo of him we could see?" Harry asked.

"No," Jorah said. "It's against church rules to pose for pictures. The reporter—Mr. Bishop—wanted to take one, but I couldn't allow it."

A miracle. The tabloid owner showed some semblance of journalistic ethics and published his report without any images of the boy. Unknown to Jorah and her parents, the story got to Dante, the COO of Gateway. His first inclination was to laugh it off as one more imaginary tale about Harry. And yet... an *Amish* girl and her family doing this for attention? Members of the community weren't exactly the sort to pull such stunts. Despite the possibility of being taken for a con artist or a mentally disturbed woman, Jorah remained adamant her son was a Sheppard. Bishop didn't simply narrate her claim; he placed her words in quotes. Somehow, it carried the ring of truth, at least to Dante's ears.

Well... Harry was not the only Sheppard male of the age to procreate. The family reproduced at a prolific rate, and he was merely one among dozens in his generation within the extended clan. His own parents proved to be more judicious than their kin and popped out only two boys and a girl. Which didn't make Harry the only male even in the small group. There was Ryan and Sophia Sheppard's firstborn, Hector.

Dante knew Hector owned a winery in the Amish-heavy area of New York State. Gateway kept meticulous records, and it wasn't difficult for Dante to look through Hector's travel itinerary from twelve years ago. There was also Hector's wife who walked out on their marriage around the same time.

By then, Dante's investigation caused some employees to hint at gossip among the junior staff about Hector. His drinking was known to all, but he never misbehaved with female personnel. However, those of his underlings who had the misfortune of seeing him inebriated told a different story. He suffered no delay in satisfying his needs. Most of the time, it was not an issue. Money, power, a well-kept physique... a no was rare, but it was never tolerated.

Hector didn't seem to care about consequences. For one, he and his estranged wife didn't have children to fight over, and their pre-nup protected his business holdings. For another, he always picked women who were unlikely to open their mouths about it after. Circumstances were invariably such that Hector could argue the sex was consensual. Like a young Amish woman who volunteered to go with him to the winery.

Which meant Jorah wasn't going to give Harry the leverage he needed over Hector to sway Gateway's support. Nor would Samba's existence discredit the elder Sheppard son in the eyes of the law.

"All right," said Harry, standing from the couch. Alex and Liam also got to their feet. "I merely wanted to hear the truth."

"Now you know," said the cousin. "What are you planning to do?"

Harry shrugged. "Nothing. As you asked, I won't deny any of it. Unfortunately, I cannot publicly claim Samba as my son without raising further questions. Nor am I in a position to do so because of other matters I need to attend to. Fatherhood involves responsibilities, and I... Samba would have expectations I cannot fulfill. Jorah, you can still choose to make it official. Put my name on his birth certificate and so on. As for financial help... I understand your feelings about my family and my brother in particular, but the fact remains Samba is entitled to support from the Sheppards. I'll make sure he has it."

"Thank you," said the widowed cousin.

Harry inclined his head. "Thank you for the prayers on my behalf."

#

Driving their way out of town, the three men remained silent for long minutes, none of them even glancing at the landscape whizzing by. Harry kept his hands on the steering wheel, his brain on the steady hum of the car engine.

"Blackmailing Hector won't work," Liam finally offered from the back seat. "Not without Jorah's cooperation."

"No," agreed Alex. "Gateway will continue to support Steven."

"Wasted trip," Liam mumbled.

Harry glanced at the rearview mirror. "Not necessarily."

"Dante offered to visit them," reminded Liam. With a loud honk, a truck overtook the sedan and sped away. "He could've handled plain old financial arrangements, which was all we got done."

"I still needed to hear the story straight from Jorah," said Harry.

"Why?" Liam asked.

"Because eventually, we're going to face off over the network," Harry said. "The Kingsleys, the Sheppards, and the Barronses are going to end up battling each other, including my brother and me."

"Dude," called Alex. "Yeah, we lost our potential hold over Hector, but we're still negotiating with Steven and the rest. Bit premature to decide it's going to fail."

Liam groaned. "Here we go again."

With prospects of a favorable board vote dimming, Alex and his brothers would be content with a power-sharing arrangement with their cousins. They'd already tasked Harry with finding a compromise. Lilah let them believe her opposition to a diplomatic solution was only because she wanted the network completely back in her hands. They didn't have a clue about her actual plan— destruction of the monster structure built on her back.

After her return from exile, Lilah had informed her twin of her objective. Both Dan and Shawn agreed with her. The network needed to go. Those like Liam who were merely looking for justice weren't told about the entirety of Lilah's plans. None of them would be opposed to the notion of dismantling the structure, but an inadvertent leak would prove disastrous. If the network's board members heard what she intended to do, they would all turn to Steven to stop her. Not one would volunteer to give up the clout which came with such an alliance. The Kingsley brothers wouldn't, either.

Unfortunately, the five men remained reluctant at the idea of hauling their grandfather and uncles and cousins to court even to get their own damned business back, let alone destroy the network. Hence, the negotiations.

Harry inclined his head toward Alex. "Peace is always preferable to war of any kind, even corporate. However, we need to prepare for an eventuality where the enemy we face might be our own flesh and blood. In my case—my brother, the other Sheppards who work for Gateway, the people I used to call colleagues. And when I look Hector in the eye, I need to remember Jorah. Alex, you will see your grandfather, your uncles, your mentors, your cousins. You cannot forget even for a moment who they are. What they're capable of. Consider our visit to Leon as groundwork before the actual war."

"The Kingsley situation is different," argued Alex. "I can't blame Grandfather for Steven and Charlie's doings."

Left unmentioned were the disagreements Alex and Harry had before on Godwin's involvement in the whole saga. Alex wouldn't want to talk about it with Liam listening, and the debate would be meaningless in any case, with both sides sticking to their respective points of view.

"Misplaced blame is not helpful," acknowledged Harry, "but we can't deny Godwin was at least unwittingly a part of Steven's schemes. Remember it well when you come face-to-face with the Kingsleys."

Part III

Chapter 7

A week later, late May 1998

Central California

"Family," Alex agreed with his brothers' assessment of the importance of the upcoming reunion.

It was damned hard to focus when—a shadow moved at the periphery of his visual field. Alex whirled around, but the shadow had already vanished into the hustle and bustle of the shooting range.

"At the end of the day," Brad continued, "family's all you can rely... Alex, anything wrong?"

Alex held a hand up. "I saw someone," he said to the other four men.

Turning a three-sixty in the wide passageway, he noted the familiar sights and sounds of the range. The hour was relatively early, but several members were already at the row of indoor booths, destroying targets lined up along the sparse grass outside. Low hills loomed behind.

A couple of instructors walked briskly past, both wearing shoulder holsters over black shirts emblazoned with the logo of the place. A group of nervous-looking individuals followed a jeans-clad woman into a room. Newbies, likely, arriving for their first lesson. The constant reports of guns being fired... the chatter of staff and visitors... the mild breeze... not a piece of paper out of place.

No one was paying undue attention to the group of five men whose mugs had been splashed across the papers recently. Most Kingsley males were on the tall side, and Brad, Victor, and Scott inherited their father's brown hair and blue eyes. Alex got his mother's dark coloring, and Neil was blond and blue-eyed like *his* mother. Except for Brad with his stubble beard, all brothers were clean-shaven. The man who invited them to the range might be advanced in years, but he would also be easily pegged as a Kingsley.

"No one's sticking out," Victor said, scanning the area.

"Not to me, either," said Neil. "But this ain't exactly my turf." Neither the surgeon nor his twin brother, the astrophysicist, were trained to spot danger. Brad got his degree from West Point as did generations of Kingsley men before him, but he never saw combat.

Alex rolled his shoulders. "No," he insisted. "This is the third time today I've caught... three times in the ten minutes after we got out of the car, and I haven't been able to pin him down. He's good."

"I trust your instincts," Brad said, tone steady and refined as always. "Keep an eye out—"

"Alex, my boy," called a voice full of paternal warmth. At the other end of the row of booths stood Godwin Kingsley.

"Grandfather," called Alex, sprinting to him. Laughing exuberantly, they greeted each other with hugs, Godwin planting a kiss on Alex's forehead.

As the other brothers followed, Alex studied the changes in the old man. The silvery-white hair was tied back with a leather thong as always, the short beard neatly trimmed. Age hadn't caused his tall form to bend though he was a few months older than his stepbrother, Temple.

Still, there were many more wrinkles than Alex remembered. The skin on Godwin's hands appeared thin. Fragile. How many years did he have left? Alex's heart squeezed hard at the thought.

Gray eyes moist with tears, Godwin welcomed each grandson with a hug and a kiss. Cameras flashed, clicks joining the gunshot sounds from the booths.

Of course there would be some press presence. Godwin had wanted to see his grandsons before Kingsley Corp lawyers showed up to talk to Brad. Both sides hoped to avoid the media altogether by arranging the reunion far from New York, and the Kingsley family owned a vacation cabin in this Central California town. Still, after one or two inquiries from newspapers, the former supreme court justice decided it would be better to have a few trusted journalists documenting the meeting rather than risk an unruly crowd stalking him and the former exiles.

"It's good to have you back," Godwin said, holding Brad by the shoulders. "I didn't know if I would live to see…"

Murmurs of sympathy rose from the watching crowd.

Alex frowned. Only a couple of the men wore press badges. The rest… the suits, the holsters, the alert attitude… there were almost a dozen guards. Harry had mentioned something about Steven hiring protection for the former justice, but a dozen men?

"Why so much security?" Alex asked. "Everything all right, Grandfather?"

Releasing Brad, Godwin shook his head as though in exasperation. "Steven insisted. He… ahh… had concerns."

"Concerns?" Alex echoed. He blinked. "About…" About them.

Understanding dawned on the faces of his brothers, followed by anger. "Sonuvabitch," ground out Victor.

Throwing a meaningful glance at the watching journalists, Brad pushed the rounded glasses up his nose. "Grandfather, please assure Cousin Steven he can trust us to see to your protection when we're around. The five of us are your family as well."

One second, two seconds, three—Godwin inclined his head. "I wouldn't expect any less of Peter's sons."

Alex almost wished Brad hadn't tried to defuse the situation. The media wasn't going to be fooled by his spin and would report exactly what was suggested. Steven just told the world he believed his cousins to be dangerous. How they could even do physical harm to the family patriarch if he stood in their way. If it weren't for what Brad said, either Alex or Victor could've plainly declared what they thought of Steven's little trick. *Very* plainly.

"Brad," another familiar voice called. A man of average height detached himself from the crowd behind Godwin, coming forward with an extended hand.

Gray hair, brown irises... Alex smiled widely at his former teacher. "General Potts," greeted Brad. "What a surprise."

The general laughed. "When Justice Kingsley mentioned his trip here, I asked to tag along. I wanted to see how you were doing. Our last meeting—"

"Cuba," said Scott. The twins didn't go through the military academy, but they knew of the Pottses' close association with the Kingsley family. "You were... umm... part of the interrogation."

The pleasant look vanished from the general's face. "Yes," he said shortly. Turning back to Brad, the former dean continued, "You and your brothers are dear to me, but I had a duty. Like the justice, I was forced to support what happened in court. No relationship can outweigh loyalty to the nation for a soldier."

"I'm aware, sir," Brad said. "You've always supported the right side... will continue to do so. Getting a pardon is fine, but I hope to prove to you and the rest of the world I never intended to do anything wrong. Once my name is cleared, I hope to have your endorsement again."

Potts nodded in obvious approval. "You're a good man, Brad. You don't hold any unnecessary grudges toward people for simply carrying out their responsibilities."

"Let's switch to more agreeable topics," interjected Godwin. Placing a hand on Victor's arm, the Kingsley patriarch continued, "You're home now. Back in the family fold. The manager of the range has arranged private brunch in the club restaurant for our group."

Alex let out a surreptitious huff of relief. Godwin didn't expect them to gather at the vacation cabin, the same place where the spat between the cousins took the first deadly turn. Brad, Victor, and Alex were ambushed by Steven's assassin, which eventually led the patriarch to call for a division of family assets. Alex didn't feel like revisiting unpleasant memories today.

As Godwin turned to walk toward the restaurant, Alex spotted yet another familiar face in the group behind. "Brad," Alex called, keeping his tone soft. He inclined his head slightly to the left. "Look."

Victor was strolling ahead with Godwin and wouldn't have heard what Alex said, especially not above the sounds from the booths. Brad, Neil, and Scott peered in the direction indicated. A woman with a camera, Godwin's guards, and—

"Shit," muttered Neil. "What the hell is Charlie doing here?"

Their last encounter with Steven's criminal little brother had also been in Cuba. For the crime of assaulting Lilah, Charles was given a mere slap on the wrist by the military all thanks to his connections. According to Harry, Charles was also responsible for the death of Lupe Valdez, the strip club owner who helped the exiles, but there was no proof.

There was the other one—Jack Drummond, Helen's husband—who was literally Charles's partner in crime, but

Drummond was kept away from Kingsley events these days. Alex hadn't known about the history between the politician and Lupe until after the exile. Drummond showed up in Beijing to attack Lilah, but he paid a price for it, unlike Charles. The feds were now aware of what a violent bastard Drummond was, but actually pursuing a case against him wasn't possible at the moment because it would be the word of fugitives against a congressman's, albeit a disgraced one. Still, the press had connected the stories of the exiles' travels to Drummond's unfortunate experience in China. Rumors were aplenty, which explained why Steven didn't want his brother-in-law front and center.

Blue eyes blinking behind glasses, Scott stared at Charles standing not ten feet from them.

"Keep walking," said Brad. "We came here to see Grandfather. There's no need to acknowledge anyone except him and General Potts."

Charles, too, seemed to be avoiding his cousins. Nodding politely at a smirking journo, Brad gestured at Alex and the twins to move along.

"We're going to brunch," Scott stated as he fell into place next to Alex. "With Charlie."

"Apparently so," murmured Brad, looking straight ahead at the exit where Godwin and Victor waited. "We cannot make a scene in front of the media no matter what. Steven's trying to create the impression we're the bad guys. Unstable."

The stock market would come to the conclusion. So would the network's board and governments around the world, including the one in DC.

Striding toward his grandfather, Alex watched Charles out of the corner of his eye. The idiot and one of the security officers were marching alongside, Charles talking. The man who'd been spying on the Kingsley brothers earlier knew what he was doing. No way it could've been Charles. Not unless he managed to grow a whole new brain in the nine years Alex had been on exile.

As before, Alex did a three-sixty while walking, making a quick study of the Kingsley entourage and the few pressmen around. A couple of the reporters looked puzzled, and a security officer or two returned Alex's visual inspection, but there was no one who stood out. So who—

"Shit," Neil said. "Wait until Victor finds out about Charlie."

"Alex," called Brad. "Get Victor aside and let him know. We don't want any scenes."

"Right," said Alex, turning back. They were only a few feet from the door. "I'll—"

A sudden movement invaded his visual space from the right. One of the booths... black shirt with the gun club's logo... an instructor. A rifle went up.

"Down!" shouted Alex, bounding to the exit. Arms flung to the sides, he shoved Godwin into the ranks of his guards while tackling Victor and bringing him to the ground.

Something whizzed by. Alex didn't know how he managed to see it in the commotion, but it was the bullet meant for his brother. Confused silence from the crowd... shock... a grunt from Victor. Alex hit his head on the doorjamb, sharp pain radiating across his skull. Screams, shouts, thundering feet— "Victor," bellowed Neil. "Alex!"

"What the..." Heaving Alex aside, Victor scrambled to his knees.

Alex hauled himself to a sitting position. "Grandfather?" he called, heart thundering. "Brad, Neil... check if he's okay."

#

"Accident?" Alex bit out.

"Yes, sir," the manager said stoically. The restaurant staff stood at a polite distance while their boss—a heavy-set gent with a completely bald head—updated the visitors on the shooting incident.

The former supreme court justice and his entourage, including Gen. Potts and Charles, were the only guests in the club restaurant besides the Kingsley brothers. Godwin and the general were seated with Alex and the rest. Charles was still sticking close to the security officers. One of the guards in fact had the look of a Kingsley. Probably a distant relative, roped in to keep the criminal out of trouble.

Through the square-paned windows, Alex could see cops going in and out of the range. The reporters had raced each other to town as soon as they were allowed to leave. Thank God for cell phones. Alex managed to contact Sabrina before the news hit the screens.

"Probability of accident..." Scott blinked a couple of times, appearing to calculate. "...is not high."

"I assure you," said the manager, "the instructor who fired the gun is a law-abiding fellow. Retired police sergeant with exemplary service record."

"He pointed the rifle straight at Victor," snapped Alex. "Safety was either off, or he took it off. Then, he pulled the trigger."

Stance stiff, the manager said, "Mr. King... *Captain* Kingsley, I shouldn't have to tell you how safeties can malfunction. The instructor has acknowledged it was stupid to point it in someone's direction. He says he was in fact demonstrating to a new member how such behavior was not allowed."

Victor snorted. "And his chosen target simply happened to be me." Stabbing a piece of steak with a fork, he brought it to his mouth. Victor wasn't pale or shaking or sweaty. His slitted eyes went to the only other occupied table in the restaurant, where Charles was seated. The moment the manager was out of earshot, Victor asked bluntly, "Grandfather, why is Charlie here?"

Brad had yet to say anything, but the same question was on his face as he took a sip from the champagne flute. Hell, on every one of their faces.

Godwin sighed. "I get what you're thinking, but it's unlikely. Steven and Major Armor were scheduled to meet with the Saudi ambassador, and they decided it was best to keep Charlie where he could be seen. The guards..."

It was Neil's turn to snort. "They're babysitting him? Wish Steven got this idea in Cuba. At least Lilah would've been spared."

"Yes." Godwin gestured at one of the servers and asked for more coffee. Eyes on the steaming beverage being poured, he continued, "Neil, your concern for your sister-in-law is admirable. However..." With a nod, the patriarch dismissed the waitress. "Steven's fear was not about his brother's misbehavior."

"Huh?" said Neil.

"Victor," called Gen. Potts. "You made a threat against Steven in Cuba. You said you would break his thigh."

Victor snarled. "Damn right, I threatened him. The S.O.B. asked Lilah to give him a lap dance! How would you have reacted?" A second later, he added, "Sir?"

Potts inclined his head. "As your grandfather said to Neil, your loyalty to your brother's wife is admirable."

Across the table, Brad's face tightened.

"Regardless," continued Potts, "Steven's worried about Charles. About your plans for him."

"They *should* be worr—" started Victor.

Holding up a hand, Brad said, "What my brother means is we're going to use every *legal* means possible to get justice. The army chose to let Charles go with an other-than-honorable discharge, but my brothers and I will not allow the network's board to forget what happened. Our cousins will get the punishment they deserve. Nothing more... nothing less."

Chapter 8

Later in the evening

"No one with a press card was allowed in the restaurant," Alex said into the phone, toweling his hair dry with his other hand as he walked to the window of the hotel room. A second thick towel was wrapped around his waist. It was strange being a guest again after spending most of the last decade as an employee at the tourist resort in Goa.

Alex shook himself mentally. He was back in the United States.

The Pacific Ocean roared gently against sandy shore only a few feet from the four-star establishment. A familiar figure was strolling along the beach—Brad, with the dog he adopted in Goa darting in and out of the frothy water. The scene made Alex smile. Unfortunately, he didn't have the time to join his brother. Harry wanted every detail of the morning's incident.

"Could one of the waitstaff have overheard when we talked about Charlie?" Alex continued. "Sure."

"And they could talk to the media," mused Harry. "Which is precisely what Steven wants."

"He's trying to make it seem like we're the ones to worry about," Alex agreed. "What about you?"

"Me?" Harry asked. "It will be difficult for Steven or anyone else to point fingers at me for the time being." After Harry's eight-year sojourn in prison for a crime committed by someone else, the narrative had shifted big time in his favor. There was no proof Steven did the framing, but yeah, there were doubts. Whatever he and his mates said about Harry could even work against them if the authorities decided it was yet another stunt to drag a hero veteran back behind bars. Not so the case with the Kingsley brothers. "Remember," Harry continued, "Brad has only been pardoned. Not exonerated. We cannot afford to let anyone create more questions about him or the rest of you."

"Thank God for Grandfather. He told us what Steven's up to." At Harry's silence, Alex asked, "What, dude? Don't tell me we're back to Lilah's old theories about my family."

In the years the Kingsley brothers were on exile, Harry never mentioned Godwin's name to the media as one of the culprits. Alex had hoped it meant... both Harry and Lilah truly believed their own claims. Fear was all it was, but they were targeting the wrong person.

Harry sighed. "Look, if only for your sake, I hoped I was wrong. At least in the beginning. Unfortunately, Godwin's name keeps popping up in every episode, starting with the tribe in Argentina."

"We got suckered in Argentina," Alex said, turning away from the window and going to the mini fridge to grab a bottle. The damp towel hung around his neck. "Damn oil scout." The explosives he supplied were rigged, something Alex and Harry realized only months after the incident.

What the two men believed were smoke bombs caused a massive chemical fire, wiping out an entire Native American village. Of the handful who survived, the chief of the tribe—the machi— was one. Her pregnant granddaughter was injured by Alex's bullets, later dying in childbirth. Time had dulled his horrific memories of the fire, but every now and then—the boy would be around the same age as Alex's son, Michael. Until Lilah left with the Kingsley brothers on exile, she'd been keeping track of the kid, making sure he didn't suffer at least financially. Alex hadn't asked specifically, but Lilah would've remembered to hand the responsibility to Dante, Gateway's COO, the only outsider on their side who knew about the event.

Alex took a swig of ice-cold water. He needed it. The dead girl's husband who arranged the massacre was killed, but his demise didn't take away Harry and Alex's responsibility in the matter. Still, they didn't do it on purpose.

"You and I are not exactly chumps, and we still fell for the scout's shit," Alex continued. "So how is it difficult to believe he lied to my grandfather, too? For God's sake, Mr. Temple was involved. For you and Lilah to be right, Temple, the sitting American president, would have to be behind a grand conspiracy to get you killed. He's on *our* side today."

"Even if I buy your version of the story, how do you explain the rest?" Harry asked. "We both know the particular rapist wouldn't have shown up at our first board meeting without solid assurance he'd be safe from me." Col. Parker was the one responsible for assaulting a teenaged Lilah in Libya, a fact known only to Alex besides Harry and Lilah. Except Harry believed Temple and Godwin knew as well and that they arranged the confrontation in Panama. "Then, Cuba happened."

"Parker showed up because it was his last chance at getting you out of the picture altogether," Alex said. "As for Cuba... tell me something. What would you have done in Grandfather's position? He used to be a supreme court justice. Military intelligence contacted him about possible treason by his own family. What do you think he should've done differently? Hell, Lilah is a lawyer herself. How can she not see there was simply no other option for him?"

"There *were* options," Harry insisted. "Yet Godwin chose to argue against you. He wouldn't stop even after it was clear what happened to Lilah."

"It's easy to judge someone from transcripts," Alex said. "Grandfather must have been heartbroken, but he agreed to be a part of the investigation for the sake of the nation. Then, he heard what Steven and Charlie did. It took a couple of minutes to recalibrate."

"And now?" Harry asked. "Why is Godwin still with Steven?"

"C'mon, Harry. Do I have to explain to you what fiduciary duty means?" Godwin was the president of Kingsley Corp. Except in cases of illegality, he was obligated to support the company in its decisions. "And don't start on me about him quitting, either. He can't. Grandfather is the head of the family. He will not leave Kingsley Corp until he dies."

"Not bad for a spin," Harry said. "If we get to a legal face-off, let's hope a court shows more objectivity."

A shudder went through Alex's insides. If they were forced to go to court, attorneys from both sides would present their cases. Steven's version of events would be ripped apart in a heartbeat. The former justice was well-respected, but a sharp lawyer could still do serious damage to Godwin's reputation. The man who'd stepped up as father-figure to his orphaned grandsons would be attacked by the same grandsons. That, too, in the twilight of his life.

Alex guzzled more cold water straight from the bottle. "I know my family. All right? Take my word for it, dude. The only people to blame here are Steven, Charlie, and the other son of a bitch—Armor."

"Family or not, your heart has to be in the fight," Harry said, tone steady. "Or else get ready to lose and live under Steven's rule."

"I'm in it to win," Alex said, collapsing into a chair by the window. "But I'm not going to forget they're still my blood. My father didn't give a shit what happened to me and Brad and Victor. Grandfather... Uncle Aaron... they were the ones who cared. Steven's mom... he's her son, but she never did anything to hurt us."

"Wasn't she at the interrogation?"

"Because the investigators involved the entire family in the sting to make it believable," Alex countered. "You know it already. Aunt Grace was not a part of any conspiracy. She's not the type."

"But she never said a word until the end," Harry pointed out. "Until it appeared Charlie would get into trouble."

"Not all of us can be you, Harry."

"Uhh?" Harry laughed. "I'm not sure how to interpret it."

"After everything you did for us? The rest of your family is with Steven, but you don't give a crap whom you go up against when it's the right thing to do. I couldn't ask for a better friend. My brothers and I could not ask for a better partner. Only, remember what I told you before Cuba. Don't mention any of the shit about Grandfather to my brothers." They would never believe it and would cut Harry out in a heartbeat no matter what he'd done for them.

Tone softening, Harry said, "Yes, I remember our conversation. *You're* still putting up with me, though. With Lilah, too. I can't thank you enough for what you did for her in Goa. Not many men would dress up like—"

"Yeah, yeah," Alex said. "No need to thank me. Lilah is also family."

"Nevertheless, you have my gratitude," said Harry. "Let's get back to the gun club incident. Something fishy about the setup. The instructor who shot at Victor was in full view of everyone else. Let's say you didn't spot him, and Victor got hit. How did the shooter plan to get away?"

"I suppose he would've continued to bank on the claim it was an accident."

"Still, why would a police sergeant with a spotless record gamble with potential jail time?" mused Harry. "Prison could happen even in cases of accidental deaths. Also, with the amount of media attention on both sides, would Steven be dumb enough to pull this stunt within the United States? Let's say he didn't stop to think. His buddy Armor ain't stupid. He would've advised Steven not to risk it."

"Go on," said Alex.

"Victor was talking to your grandfather at the exit. Correct?"

"Yes."

"You were already on your guard when you spotted Charlie. Then, you saw the rifle pointed in the direction of the door. You assumed it was meant for Victor."

Alex sat up and set the empty bottle on the side table. "Grandfather? But why would Steven shoot at Grandfather? For one, without him, they'd lose. For another, he's a former supreme court justice! Every cop in the county... maybe the FBI... more so than with Victor."

"Yes, but what if the bullet was never meant to hit the target?" Harry asked.

Alex blinked. "If it didn't... if I didn't..."

"Your actions made it clear how your first thought was Victor was the target. If no one realized what was happening, what was to prevent Charlie from claiming your grandfather was miraculously saved? Even if the instructor said it was an accident, the journalists watching would've been left with the impression our side just tried a hit on one of the most revered figures in the country. The incident, coming right on the heels of Steven hiring special security for

Godwin, would've hammered a certain image of you and your brothers in the public mind. Your cousins would've made sure of it. Yes, we could argue how it was their doing, but a narrative once set is difficult to change."

"Bastards," ground out Alex. "They're willing to go to... shooting at Grandfather! We're hiring someone to take a closer look at this instructor." Spotless record or not, there had to be something in the fellow's background to prove motive.

"We'll do our own investigation," Harry agreed. "But chances are neither we nor the cops will find anything to point to Steven. He and his buddies would've taken care not to leave loose ends. Since no one was killed, the DA will close the case after a week or two."

"Damn," said Alex.

"Let us chew on it some more," said Harry. "Steven must be worried after what happened at the Barrons board meeting. Desperate men make desperate choices. What if he eventually decides it's worth it to pin an actual death on Brad? We cannot allow another Will Luce situation where some innocent bystander becomes collateral damage."

Chapter 9

A week later, June 1998

New Castle, New York

The Barrons residence had not changed much since the garden party so long ago when Alex met Harry and Lilah. The home was as grand, as roomy and tranquil as Alex remembered. The settee and chairs were clearly antique, and above the large fireplace hung a portrait of Andrew and his wife, Caroline.

Age had given Andrew a bit of girth and glasses on his aristocratic face. Lilah's half-sister remained the impeccable hostess she always was, unruffled by the sudden arrival of close to a dozen guests. Caroline and Dan shared the Sheppard coloring of dark hair and eyes, and there were eighteen years separating them, which meant society had forgotten she was in fact his sister and not mother.

"Thank you for asking us here for this meeting," Harry said, nodding at Andrew before settling himself in one of the chairs.

The rest of the group was already seated. Most of them, anyway. Liam was not in town and would be updated later. Caroline was at the door to the room, talking to the butler. Strangely, Lilah stayed put in her spot next to the window, viewing the beautifully kept garden. How long had it been after her last visit? According to Sabrina, Lilah hardly maintained contact with her half-sister and brother-in-law.

"Since we've decided to go through with this..." Andrew started, voice as loud and ringing as always. "...we should plan to win. Daniel..." Andrew inclined his head toward his adopted son. "...persuaded the board to go along with Brad, but the market still sees me as the chief executive of the business. Without my presence front and center, it will be difficult to convince the network's board that you have full support from Barrons O & G. Likelihood of failure will go up. If you fail, you will take my company down with you. I do not want to see it happen in my lifetime." Andrew sat back and glanced at each of the men in turn. "Let me make it clear: I still think this is a bad idea for Barrons. Unfortunately, I see no way of getting us out now, so the only option before me is to make sure we win. Which is why all of you are here. It's important to make a public show of unity."

Everyone in the room stared in silence at the gray-haired oilman, including Temple who couldn't have understood what was said thanks to the brain injury. Then, Noah chuckled. He, too, sat back and crossed his legs. "Always the businessman," said the former attorney general. "I shouldn't have expected anything less from you."

Light-blue eyes wary, Andrew scrutinized Noah for a few seconds before turning to Brad. "Two-thirds majority is required to remove a chairman, which we don't have. Steven only needs half of the board plus one—which he has—to remain in his position. A vote will go against us. Still, we should go prepared. Evidence of weakness on our part will cause harm when we eventually go to court. We should also look at the finances. How are we so far managing?"

"Personal finances are fine," said Brad.

Alex marveled at the equanimity with which his brother answered. Andrew Barrons's refusal to help had a great deal to do with how long the exile lasted. He—and others—made sure the Kingsleys brothers and their allies were left without the resources needed to fight the enemy. The cash situation had changed since the pardon. Steven still wouldn't release dividends from Peter Kingsley Company. However, the five men and their supporters had other assets they could now access without fear of authorities.

Money, unfortunately, wouldn't bring back lost relationships. News of Victor's wife filing for divorce during the exile had made it to India through tabloids. His son, Gabriel, had no connection whatsoever with stepmom and moved in with Alex's wife and son.

Since then, Alex had been worried about his own marriage, but there was no need. He was one lucky S.O.B. to have someone like Sabrina in his life. Their home in Long Island was now crowded with Michael, Gabriel, and Hema, Lilah's former intern. The girl whose parents harbored the Americans in India was also arriving in New York soon. Given the circumstances under which the exile ended, there was risk of the local mafia targeting the young lady to exact revenge, so Alex asked her papa to send her to the States.

Brad was staying with Victor in his old apartment in Manhattan. The twins rented a two-bedroom in the same building. Lilah would remain a part of the team, but she made it clear her marriage to Brad was over, and she'd continue in Temple's home. The Hermitage, as some in the press had taken to calling the former president's residence after Lilah moved in. The name gave everyone a chuckle.

"But sir," Brad continued, "my brothers and I are hoping to avoid going to court. The second round could work—negotiation."

Andrew ptchaaed. "Brad, numbers matter in negotiations, too. Ten-eight in the board, and it's our best-case scenario even with the lucky break of getting your brothers' uncle in there." Neil and Scott's uncle used to work for the Kingsleys, but the fellow moved on to a different oil services company years ago and climbed his way up the corporate ladder, making it to the C-suite. His membership in the network's board as his employer's representative was not something planned by Harry or the Barronses. The driller continued, "You've been in the business long enough to understand what—"

"The law firm we hired is excellent," interjected Grayson. He remained personal attorney to Lilah and the brothers for now but would not speak for them in corporate dealings.

A former protégé of Temple was the man picked by Harry and Noah to represent their side. The lead attorney's specialty was antitrust law, which meant he was used to defending structures such as the network from the government, and his team included men who knew contract and corporate regulations inside out.

"The legal team will remind the ten board members who remain opposed that a corporate war would result in consequences regardless of who won," said Grayson. "Some of those ten opponents could decide to abstain, which means Steven won't have his half plus one in the board."

"Stalemate," commented Scott.

"Correct," said Grayson. "We won't win, but Steven won't, either. What would happen next is a big unknown, but the government intervention we're all worried about might be the result. The possibility will force Steven to negotiate."

"The strategy hinges on one or more members on Steven's side defecting or at least decamping," Andrew pointed out. "Unless, of course, someone here has tricks up the sleeve to change minds like you did with the Barrons board."

"No tricks," said Harry, "which is where you could help, Andrew. I've been working with the lawyers, but you're the senior-most businessman among us. Your voice will be heard by the men on the board. Steven has Godwin and General Potts. My understanding is Godwin will be the one overall in charge on their side. Which reminds me... *we* should also have a commander in chief. He should be on the frontlines at the negotiations, along with the lead attorney, and keep track of our overall strategy. Not the five brothers or me since we don't hold official positions in the network. I suggest an executive from among our eight supporters."

"It will tell the other side we're functioning as one unit," concurred Andrew. "Each company should have a role to play in our dealings. Diplomacy is unlikely to work under the circumstances, but there's no harm in taking a stab at it before we go to court."

"I propose Dan as the commander," said Alex. "Currently, Barrons is the biggest company on our side, and he's Lilah's brother."

"Why not Andrew himself?" asked Victor. "He's the chief executive. Shawn is another possibility."

"Me?" Shawn sat up. "I don't work in the oil sector. You have my full support, but I won't be a good pick for the job."

"I was thinking your presence would link us to the new economy," Victor explained. "Information technology and so on. You wouldn't be left on your own. All of us will be there to help." Throwing a glance at Dan, Victor added, "You'd be great. Merely tossing some ideas out there."

Dan inclined his head.

"Thanks for the vote of confidence," said Shawn, "but I agree with Alex. Dan's the best man for the role. He organized the eight supporters you currently have."

"He's also been studying the situation since you and your brothers left on exile," Andrew said to Victor. "Dan can handle the operational aspects while I focus on talking to other CEOs in the network."

"Any further thoughts?" Harry looked around the small group. "Good. Dan it will be."

"I'll let the board know," said Dan. "All contact with them and with the Kingsleys should go through me. I am talking about business discussions, not personal, but if something comes up when one of you brothers meets your family, I'll need to be notified."

"Which brings me to something important," Harry said. "We should review what happened at the shooting range. When the enemy changes tactics, we must recalibrate accordingly."

"Critical," agreed Andrew.

"Absolutely," said Noah.

Alex glanced at his brothers. The same worry was on all their faces, fear of what their friends and well-wishers were about to say.

#

Voice halting, Scott gave a summary of what happened in California.

"Steven's never going to change," said Victor, "but he won't dare try to kill us at this time. And none of us will blindly buy what he says and get into trouble like we did with the Cuba episode. So he's trying to frame us in the media."

"Victor," called Harry.

"Sadly for Cousin Steven," Victor continued, "we have our own friends in the press."

"Victor," Harry called again.

"Let's do a couple of interviews," Victor suggested. "Put it all out there. I'd like to see how—"

"Listen to me, my friend," Harry said. "Don't underestimate Steven. If his scheme in California had worked, you five would've been seen as problem children. Washington's already getting heartburn."

"Except they're blaming Steven for it," Neil said. "Not us."

"Yeah, you escaped taking the fall for what he did," agreed Harry. "This time. What happens the next time? There *will* be a second attempt soon. Maybe a third one. Imagine a few such near-misses in an election year. Imagine the economic instability. Imagine the public reaction. Yes, the network is powerful, but once market volatility becomes a reality, politicians will try to save their own asses by attacking the entity responsible. The board will attempt to prevent such a scenario by voting out the culprits before the instability gets to a tipping point. All of you—me included—would be permanently barred from having any sort of decision-making authority in the oil sector."

Scott raised a hand as though in a classroom. "Even if the... umm... instability doesn't get to a tipping point, Steven will get leverage from the bad press over the accidents. We will lose support in the board."

"Exactly," boomed Andrew. He seemed about to continue but went into a fit of coughing. Signaling the rest to carry on, the oilman dug out a pill bottle from his pocket and put something under his tongue. Harry stared at Andrew with a small frown. Neil, the surgeon in the room, was also staring, and Mrs. Barrons, looking mildly anxious, gestured at the butler.

"Let Steven try again," argued Victor, drawing the room back to the topic under discussion. "He didn't expect his first 'near-miss' to backfire."

"Yeah," agreed Neil. "As Victor said, we can put out our version of events. We could end up peeling off more support from them, instead."

Andrew glanced toward Neil but didn't say anything in response. There was a half-groan from Dan as he took a cup of water from the butler and handed it to his adoptive father.

"What's wrong with their idea?" demanded Alex. "Chances are at least fifty-fifty of us coming out on top."

"The outcome of any strategy depends on multiple inputs," said Harry. "Not all of those inputs will be yours, Alex. The other side also understands the chances of their tactics backfiring. If Steven, Armor, and the rest see the scales tilting toward us... the more support we manage to swing, the more worked up the enemy is going to get. It won't be long before Steven finds a thug willing to take a few years in prison for a supposedly accidental death in exchange for a nice chunk of cash. No matter who ends up dying, Brad and the rest of you will be held responsible."

"Killing a bystander merely as part of propaganda?" Alex asked. "Hell, it's not allowed even in actual war."

"We both know it happens." Pinching the bridge of his nose, Harry added, "Laws of war are important. Necessity, proportionality, humanity, honor, distinction between civilians and combatants... which of the principles of conduct in a just war has Steven shown himself willing to follow? Remember everything he and his friends did to Lilah. Remember Will Luce. Remember Lupe."

Victor hissed. "But if Steven tries something similar this time, the FBI..."

"...will investigate," completed Harry. "However, we don't know who the enemy plans to sacrifice. Need not be someone high-profile. Another victim... another knife wound... another gunshot... or some other method altogether. Once the media groundwork has been done in the U.S., the crime could even happen outside the borders. What I can guarantee is Brad will be blamed. We cannot even rule out the possibility of the target being Brad."

Alex shifted in his seat. His brothers were exchanging glances.

"Steven's main target has always been me," agreed Brad.

Harry nodded. "Push him enough, and he might just risk it. Let's say it doesn't happen. Let's say you win back the network before Steven attacks. The cycle of strikes and counterstrikes will not stop until either you or he ends up dead. It won't matter even if you sign over your rights, lock, stock, and barrel. Steven will continue to see you as a threat."

#

"So what's the solution?" Alex asked.

Huffing out a breath, Harry said, "Let's review our options. As things stand, we won't win a board vote. Diplomacy doesn't have much chance of working when one side is intent on killing the other. Also, as Andrew said, we don't know if any of Steven's supporters can be persuaded to abstain. Third possibility is a court battle. I'm suing the network for wrongful termination. If I win, I could somehow convince the board to bring Brad back. He himself could go to court. Unfortunately, there's little to no chance of us winning since the network is a private entity and entitled to fire officeholders. Then again, an open airing of what Steven did to you five and Lilah could force a second board vote.”

“No one is allowed to lie in court,” Scott said. “Right? Steven will have to admit everything he did.”

“Don’t be naïve,” Andrew said brusquely. “Witnesses lie all the time.”

“Maybe,” acknowledged Scott, “but *Lilah* could tell everyone what Charlie and Armor are like. There are the transcripts from Cuba, but it will be different when she talks about it. The board might reconsider its stance once the public hears what actually happened.”

“Yes.” Harry blinked a couple of times. “However, the process will be long and uncomfortable. Media... politicians... commentary on the entire Kingsley family and not just Steven and Charles.”

“Excruciating,” Alex mumbled. A clever lawyer could twist Godwin’s role in the military court into something nefarious. It would certainly help the exiles’ case if one of Steven’s main supporters went down, but Alex and his brothers would rather lose everything than hurt the old fellow in the last days of his life.

“Right,” said Harry. “Once again... when Steven sees things going badly for him, he will retaliate.”

“Nothing will change until Steven’s completely out of the picture,” said Dan. “He will keep plotting to get Brad... get all of us. How many attempts have there been so far?”

“The only way out seems to be to get rid of Steven,” mused Shawn. “But I assume *we’re* not planning an assassination.”

Harry hesitated for a second before responding. “There’s a fourth possible strategy. Remember how we dealt with Sanders? He was also not above violence, but we disabled him. Wiped out his military capabilities so he could never mount an attack again.”

Everyone in the room was leaning forward, eyes fixed on Harry. Even Lilah turned from her scrutiny of the gardens to listen to him speak.

Brad pushed his glasses up his nose. "Which in Steven's case means..."

"Kingsley Corp," said Harry.

Part IV

Chapter 10

A week later, mid June 1998

Upper East Side, New York City

Richard didn't consider himself a coward, but delivering bad news to the Kingsley patriarch was not an easy job. Until earlier in the day, Steven had managed to avoid answering questions from the network's board by citing the ongoing investigation of the gun-range incident. The cops had barely concluded it was an accident, and the calls started again, this time with warnings on how such coincidences couldn't be repeated.

Then, a call came when Steven was in the boxing ring at Hector's gym. The pallor on Steven's face when he hung up made it clear what was coming. He might be CEO and chairman of the network, but his grandfather ran Kingsley Corp which was the business entity in charge. When Godwin issued his summons, immediate compliance was advisable. Anyone tempted to disobey merely needed to remember the punishment meted out to Brad's wife. And whoever failed at a job was required to give an accounting as Steven was doing right now.

Neither Richard nor Steven was invited to sit, so they remained on their feet in the middle of the former supreme court justice's home office. Steven's uncle, Stanley Gander, was also present, the man's slight form fidgeting at his nephew's side. The old justice stayed in the leather chair all through Steven's ramble, fingers hovering over the chessboard on the large carved desk. As he frequently did, the patriarch was playing himself.

"Steven," Godwin finally called, tone quite gentle. "How is it possible you don't understand the concept of overkill even after all these years?"

"You wouldn't have considered it overkill if it worked," Steven argued.

"But it didn't, did it?" Godwin asked, eyes still on the chess pieces. "Somehow, nothing ever does with you. Imbecile!"

Stanley Gander flinched. On Steven's other side, Richard took a deep, angry breath.

Face darkening, Steven said, "With all due respect, Grandfather—"

Godwin held up a hand. The white pawn was moved closer to the black king. Richard was no chess prodigy, but he understood the game well enough to know black would be checkmated in two short moves. "How did you come up with the idea?" Godwin asked. "When I first heard what you did, I should've asked. It didn't occur to me at the time. What made you think of it?"

"Uncle Aaron called my father about the extra security for you," Steven explained. "They got into an argument. Uncle Aaron said something about nobody believing Brad would attack you."

"And you immediately set out to prove him wrong." Sighing, Godwin straightened. "Aaron..." The patriarch rocked back in the leather chair.

When nothing more was forthcoming, Stanley stuttered in his southern accent, "D-do you think he went to David on purpose? Then, tipped off Alex?"

Godwin shook his head. "Aaron's my son. We disagree on several matters, but he won't plot against me. Not actively. Still, he's kept in touch with Andersen. I believe also with Harry. Either of them would've picked up on the possibilities behind the extra security. A comment here... a small warning... enough to send Aaron to David. Harry would've reminded Alex to keep an eye out for trouble, which he would've done in any case."

Steven hissed. "Still, it did start with... I wish you would... Grandfather, why can't you fire Uncle Aaron from Kingsley Corp? My father said he's talked to you about it several times."

Godwin looked up at his grandson with a sardonic glint in his eye. "What? And leave myself at the mercy of loyal relatives like you and your father?"

Steven flushed. "If blind loyalty was what you wanted, you could've left Kingsley Corp any day and joined Cousin Brad."

But then, Brad's missus would've been a thorn in the patriarch's flesh. As the CFO, she controlled the money, and her con man friend maneuvered the five idiots into following her orders. Working through Steven was easier for Godwin, which did give the former a small amount of clout in the equation.

Waving a hand, Godwin brushed off the comment about familial devotion. "Aaron wouldn't be an issue if you could manage to keep your ego in check. And your impatience. If you had come to me with your ridiculous idea, I would've told you not to do it. The timing was not right." When Steven failed to respond, Godwin nodded. "You anticipated I would say no. Which is why you didn't tell me. I don't expect you involved Mr. Armor, either, because he would've said the same thing."

Richard stayed silent, but Steven did hatch the plan on an impulse, informing his friend only on their way to the meeting with the Saudis. By then, it was too late.

"Listen to me carefully, son," said Godwin. "The media is withholding judgment for now, so I don't foresee a major crisis so long as you don't put on a repeat performance."

Which perhaps explained the absence of the usual display of towering rage. The contempt was obvious as always, but the spine-chilling anger was missing.

"My concern is the instructor," Godwin brooded. "You'd better hope he doesn't trace the cash back to you somehow."

"He won't," assured Steven. "As far as he knows, one of the thugs my cousins managed to piss off wanted payback. Easy money without actually having to kill anyone. What I find hard to believe is the idea that Harry and/or Andersen simply hoped I would do what they wanted. And they assumed Alex would know where to look?"

Laughing in derision, Godwin heaved himself up with his hands on the edge of the desk. "Do you know what Harry was doing the last eight years in Sing Sing? I can tell you what I would've done in his place. He's been studying us... our personalities, priorities, patterns, potential responses to situations. Harry got *you* to kill Luce's murderer. Thanks to the DNA *you* handed to the police, Harry's been exonerated."

"If I didn't, Rich would've been identified by the damn killer," Steven snapped. "*He* would've been in prison."

"Your friend is a free man," acknowledged Godwin. "The price you paid for his freedom is the safe return of your cousins. We can all thank you for finding ourselves on the verge of yet another tussle over the network."

"Sheppard doesn't need to study my priorities," Steven said. "I'll tell him myself. I'll tell you, too, Grandfather. There are some people in my life I consider important. It's not a long list, but Rich is in there. His safety comes before Kingsley Corp, before the network."

Yes, Richard thought. His loyalty was returned in full measure by Steven.

Godwin inclined his head. "Harry clearly knows this. He simply waited for the opportunity to play you a second time for the fool you are. He got the perfect partner in Alex. Ask your friend Armor if it was a surprise to him how Captain Alex Kingsley spotted a threat and defused it in a matter of seconds. Thanks to him, your senseless plan fell apart. Sometimes, I wonder how you and Alex could both be my grandsons."

Visibly gritting his teeth, Steven stated, "You wouldn't have said this if it worked."

"Steven." Godwin huffed. "You run the network well enough, so how can you fail to see the timing was wrong? The government set a deadline of December 2000. They didn't give us this long a break—more than two years—out of the kindness of their hearts. It was solely to make sure neither side misbehaved until after the next presidential election."

Rumor had it DC then planned to force term limits on senior executives. The CEO of Peter Kingsley Company was automatically CEO of the network, but the clause needed to be renewed every twenty-five years. Of course, the member companies could change the status if they got enough votes to counter the chairman's veto.

The authorities would normally have to prove unlawful activity before they could intervene in the operating structure of a private undertaking like the network. However, DC could simply make a strong suggestion about democratizing the oil empire, and board members could decide to throw their own hats in the ring before the twenty-five years were up.

What the civil servants who ran the nation didn't seem to understand was how succession needed to be done in an orderly fashion. Not by force. Or it would cause chaos. Market instability. Or they knew it would happen after the elections and therefore didn't care.

If someone started trouble *before* the election, the reaction would be swift and strong. Economic meltdown would lead to public panic and problems for politicians when they faced the voters. Some bright mind would come up with the idea of a takeover as bureaucrats invariably imagined themselves capable of running a business enterprise. Other governments would of course object, but Washington could exert enough financial muscle to make it happen. The board members would see what was coming and punish the side which created trouble to try and stave off an officially sanctioned coup. Then, they would go after the politicians who caused difficulties for the American empire.

If Richard had known about the gun range plan, he would've advised Steven against it because of the risk involved. But if it worked, Brad would indeed have been facing questions.

"Harry conned you into acting without thinking," said Godwin. "Thanks to your stupidity, I'm sure some board members are reconsidering their support. Secondly, your cousins were ready to negotiate. We could've come to some kind of agreement with them. The government would back off, too, once there was no question of instability. We could've maintained control over the situation until another opening presented itself. *After* everyone's guard came down."

"I'm not sharing power with Cousin Brad," Steven said immediately. "Not with the whiny, sanctimonious idiot. His brothers did the hard work, and he lost it all on a dice roll. I'm the one who was in charge for the last nine years. I built the network into what it is today. No way I'm going to give up any of it."

"Now, you won't have to," said Godwin. "Lilah doesn't care to share power with you, either. Nor does Harry. Only Brad and his brothers are willing. The incident at the gun range gave Harry the perfect excuse to talk those five out of a peace deal. Oh, he'll make a pretense of it for public consumption. If the board still votes against their side, he'll drag us to court."

"So?" Steven asked. "The network is a private entity. A court won't overturn the board's vote. And I'm not worried about Sheppard giving us the Sanders treatment like we heard. Their side doesn't have the resources now to drive us out of business as they did to Sanders."

"The threat of Sanders treatment—as you call it—is yet another ruse," Godwin said. "Harry is using the idea to scare Brad and the rest into agreeing to take legal action. Once we're in front of a judge, everything about the episode in Cuba will come under public scrutiny. Lilah will force everyone present at the arrest and the interrogation to testify under oath *in front of the media.* The family name—"

Steven snorted. "The family name! Grandfather, even the board members who support me sometimes act as though I'm a criminal. Andersen and Sheppard and their media friends sing Brad's praises, but the fact remains he gambled with national security. So rest assured... the family name is already black enough. What you're worried about is your own reputation."

Throwing a quick glance at Godwin, Stanley put a hand on his nephew's shoulder. "L-let's talk about—"

"The reputation and the goodwill I carry come from decades of hard work," ground out Godwin. "Generations of Kingsleys worked to make the business what it is. Fools like you and your brother will destroy it all. The family was cursed the day you were born."

Shrugging off his uncle's hand, Steven chuckled without mirth. "You said the same thing when Charlie and I were boys. In front of the entire family! Guess what? Brad ain't getting the chance to watch us get humiliated again. He won't be allowed back into the family or the business. I don't give a shit if we end up in court over it."

For a moment or two, Godwin simply stared at his grandson. Then, he huffed. "I'm going to ask you one more time to set aside your ego and exercise some patience. If Harry does show up to talk peace, call his bluff. Make him follow through. A legal battle will not be limited to the courtroom. Once Lilah takes the stand and tells her story, every politician in the country will be on the air, offering opinions on you and your leadership. Even if a judge rules for us, we could end up losing the next board vote because of political pressure."

"The last time I agreed to share, Brad got half of the family business." Steven snarled. "In a few years, I was forced to bow and scrape before the new emperor of the oil sector. Not happening again. I get what you're saying about maintaining some control, but please understand my side. I'd rather go down fighting than simply surrender to an incompetent idiot like Brad."

"Justice Kingsley," Stanley tried. "Let them bring us their p-p-peace offer. In the meantime, we should get ready to go to court. Our attorneys are good. We're also lucky to have you, sir, to lead our side. And Major Armor. General Potts will also speak for Steven."

"I believe our chances are more than reasonable," Richard said. "Brad's gone with a—"

"Andersen's choice for an attorney," snapped out Godwin. "Antitrust lawyer. I'm familiar with the man's work. He's one of the best there is, and his team includes some of the finest minds practicing contract law and corporate governance and securities. There's nothing we can throw at them they wouldn't have anticipated already."

"Even the best can only work with the material they're given," said Richard, "and the law is hundred percent in our favor. Problem is the nature of the war we're fighting. As you said, it's only partly legal. Most of it will be political." Looking away from the former justice, Richard called, "Steven, public perception *will* matter, and Mrs. Kingsley could turn out to be a big problem."

"Precisely," said Godwin. "You had a hand in creating the problem, Mr. Armor. You and Steven and Charlie. Now, the story of the assault has taken on near-mythical proportions."

"However, opinion is divided on Mrs. Kingsley," Richard said, choosing to ignore the jibe about his involvement. "We have our supporters in the press, too. Our PR team is also top-notch. They will continue to work with the media."

"Feminine tears are a powerful weapon," Godwin said. Walking around the desk, the former justice went to the photographs on the damask-covered wall to the right. "The network has the power of money, and it will end up being seen as a lone woman battling an evil empire. She will cut a sympathetic figure."

"We have no way of stopping a shrewd attorney from telling the story to a judge," Richard said. "But there's a difference between a third party reciting the details and Mrs. Kingsley putting on a show in the courtroom in front of TV cameras. What we need is a way to keep her out of sight."

"How?" Steven asked.

"Something we need to figure out," Richard admitted.

Turning from the black-and-white pictures on the wall, Godwin smiled. "Too bad."

Huh?

"Huh?" Steven echoed out loud.

"Too bad Mr. Armor was not born a Kingsley," Godwin commented as he frequently did with Richard. There were also times the old fellow ridiculed his servant's son for not matching up to the aristocrats around him. "Intelligence is, sadly, an uncommon quality, but you have plenty of it. I should tell your mother. She must be proud."

Richard resisted the urge to roll his shoulders and show discomfort. At least Godwin never mentioned Richard's new bride. She was a quiet woman who didn't have anything to do with the Kingsleys, and Richard preferred to maintain the distance.

Walking back to his chair, Godwin gestured the other three toward the exit. "Refusing peace talks outright is not an option, so speak with the legal team and make arrangements. Mr. Armor, see if you can get Steven to change his mind. A diplomatic solution remains our best option. If not, we'll be ready to face Brad and the rest in court. Steven, leave your cousin's wife to me. I'll make sure Lilah doesn't say a word about what happened in Cuba. Nor will her lawyer."

Chapter 11

Later the same night

Shadows loomed ahead of Patrice. The path through the Kingsley garden was lit well, but there were always the recesses a normal human couldn't see into at night. Where a predator could conceal himself if he so chose... behind the dark silhouettes of the trees on either side, in the thick shrubs...

There it was again, a shuffling sound to the rear of her. Patrice pivoted on her heel and stared back the way to the garage above which was the chauffeur's apartment. Crickets, distant honks from the street outside... no human voices. No one came around the corner to assure her all was well, that she was scaring herself for nothing.

Running back to the garage was out of the question when the stalker waited along the path. Even if she shouted, there might be no one to hear. Richard's adoptive parents—the chauffeur and his wife—had been in the tiny kitchen at the back of their apartment when Patrice left.

She didn't even get a chance to talk to Armor, Sr. in private. Richard's fate was not a priority for any of the others who knew the secret behind his birth. If Godwin decided to put all the blame on the outsider... Patrice needed to act fast, and she needed to ensure Richard's father's cooperation. Before the Kingsleys decided to silence her permanently.

Patrice took a deep, shuddering breath, and the floral fragrance seemed cloying all of a sudden. She *wished* she'd brought the new cell phone Sabrina got her. Something... some way to get to safety... Aaron's wing was around the corner of the mansion, but the main entrance was directly ahead.

Not waiting to think twice, Patrice wheeled around and sprinted as fast as her sixty-five-year-old joints would carry her. Electric lamps burned above the massive front door.

Air whooshed out in gasps. Her lungs burned. She couldn't tell if the stalker was following.

A step up, two steps. She was at the door. Looking over her shoulder, Patrice raised a hand to jab at the bell.

Before her finger hit the button, light spilled out through the opening door. "Aunt Patrice?" came Steven's surprised voice.

Stumbling, she swiveled to face the Kingsley scion. "Steven... I... ahh... I..."

The ancient butler employed by Godwin was with Steven.

"Are you all right, ma'am?" asked the man standing right behind the butler. "You look..."

Patrice would know Richard's slightly impatient voice anywhere. The blond hair, the ice-blue eyes. She almost wept in relief. He could escort her to Aaron's wing. No one would dare attack her when... unless of course the stalker were in Richard's pay. Could he have arranged it? Was he so far gone into evil that he would kill her for Steven?

"I'm fine," Patrice said abruptly, willing her voice to stay steady. With the back of her hand, she wiped the sweat from her cheek. "Just... it's warm outside. I came here to... umm... I needed to speak to... to..."

For the life of her, Patrice couldn't remember the name of the butler. She'd interacted with the fellow many, many, many times in the years since she married Peter.

She made a vague gesture toward the old retainer. "...to you, sir. About... umm... arranging a memorial service for Peter."

"Memor—" started Steven, confusion in his eyes.

"Well, I meant to have a commemoration on the twenty-fifth year of my husband's passing," said Patrice. "Our grandchildren would've had a chance to learn something about their history. Unfortunately, my sons were forced out of our home a year before the ceremony could happen. So we're having it now."

Steven had the grace to flush.

"Of course, Miss Patrice," the butler said with remarkable aplomb as though it was quite normal for her to run into the house late at night with strange requests. He stepped aside for her to enter the building.

As she brushed past Richard, Patrice asked in silent despair, *Did you do this? Did you now decide to do away with the mother of your enemies?* He wouldn't know the blood he spilled was his own.

There was a fourth man in the room, a guard she'd previously noticed hanging around Charles. Patrice would've guessed he was hired to keep Steven's criminal brother out of trouble, but he had the Kingsley coloring. Some relative she never met before, probably.

"May we discuss the service after Mr. Steven and Mr. Armor leave?" requested the butler. "I would prefer not to call someone away from their break only to lock up."

Patrice nodded and counted mentally until her pulse slowed, steadied. She was safe. For now. There were things for her to do, tasks she'd left very late. They needed to be taken care of before the stalker made another attempt.

Without further chitchat with Patrice, Steven and Richard stepped out into the garden. "Yuri," Steven said, nodding at Charles's minder before walking off.

A Kingsley named Yuri? Patrice shook her head mentally. The name of Charles's babysitter/guard was none of her business.

A moment later, Richard turned. "I'd recommend carrying a gun when you walk around alone at night," he said to Patrice. "There's a range downtown where you can take lessons."

She almost smiled despite the circumstances. In the years between her wedding day and Maddie's reentry into Peter's life, he'd taught his wife how to shoot. Patrice was not a crack shot by any measure, but she could point, aim, and pull the trigger without having to think about the steps. However, there was the small matter of her disliking guns.

"Thank you," she said out loud. "I'll consider it."

Patrice waited until the men were far enough down the path to the gates before signaling the butler to close the door. A stern glance at Charles's minder—Yuri—sent him scurrying to the interior.

"I'm sorry," she said to the butler. "There's no memorial service, but I didn't know what else to say. I... ahh... I heard something in the garden. Maybe it was a stray cat or something."

Come to think of it, it *could've* been a stray animal. Vagabond felines didn't give two hoots about the private property sign at the front gates. Or perhaps a rabbit or two wandered in from Central Park. The possibility should've occurred to her before she made a fool of herself.

"It's quite all right, Miss Patrice," said the butler. "Better safe than sorry. I'll ring for one of the kitchen staff to accompany you to Mr. Aaron's wing. Let me also alert the judge's security. They'll make sure all the windows and doors are locked."

#

It took less than twenty-four hours for Patrice to confirm that she had indeed kept her secrets for far too long.

The quarrel at the dinner table was still going on. Nine years! Patrice had lived in Aaron Kingsley's apartment at the family mansion for almost a decade without having to stare at Steven's parents over her evening meal. It was Grace Kingsley—Steven's mother—who invited herself and her husband to dine with Aaron and his lady friend. Patrice would've made herself scarce, but Aaron insisted on both sides hearing his point of view.

The media called him the illegitimate Kingsley, the third of the sons of the alcoholic half-brother shared by Godwin Kingsley and Mr. Temple. Aaron was tall like the rest of the men in the family but thin, with signs of aging in his brown hair and gray eyes. The widow he was seeing—Judith—was right next to him, munching on a banana.

Staring at David—Steven's doting father—Patrice muttered in her mind, *Blind in life* and *attitude*. A childhood illness had taken most of David Kingsley's eyesight, and his wife had to wear thick, dark glasses for her migraines. Neither could see beyond their son.

"Oh, for crying out loud," Aaron griped at his brother. "He's my father as much as yours." They were talking about Godwin, the man who brought them up, not the alcoholic who contributed his genes. "I won't embarrass him or this family by going to the media."

Clumsily sitting forward, Grace called, "Aaron, both David and I know you have everyone's best interests at heart. You won't talk to the press, but if the issue gets to a court..."

"You'd better remember you work for Kingsley Corp," interjected David. "And I'm the CEO."

"Threats, brother?" Aaron asked, hurt evident in his voice. At his side, Judith hissed and tossed the banana peel into a bowl. "Why am I surprised?" mused Aaron. "You didn't remember Peter was your brother, either. Or how could you allow his daughter-in-law to be assaulted in your presence?"

The pale skin showing beneath Grace's dark glasses turned red. "It shouldn't have happened," she murmured. Steven's mother showed some semblance of a conscience, albeit nine years later.

David kept insisting his son did nothing wrong in the entire saga. "How can you be so sure Steven was behind everything?" demanded David. "It could've been Richard or Major Potts."

A frisson of fear went through Patrice's heart. The Kingsleys *would* place all the blame on Richard.

"Enough!" said Aaron. "I know it was Steven because he's been nothing but trouble from the time he was old enough to talk."

Grace mewled in acute distress.

Aaron huffed. "Sorry, Grace. I love all my nephews, including Steven. I want all of them to be happy."

"You expect us to believe it?" asked David, bitter anger in his voice. "After what you just said? You won't even acknowledge me as the head of the family."

"Father's still alive," Aaron pointed out. "Until he passes, he will remain the Kingsley family head."

"So?" Shaking a finger at Aaron, David stood. "*I* am the oldest in our generation and the CEO of the company. If you want a place in the family, you *will* treat me and my sons with respect."

With a short laugh, Aaron stood as well. "The CEO spot in Kingsley Corp always went to the best man to lead the company.

Not the oldest son. You wouldn't have been CEO if Peter didn't leave."

"How *dare* you?" David spat.

Aaron wouldn't relent. "Moreover, you got appointed *acting* CEO because Father kept hoping Peter would return. We never changed your title on paper."

Startled, Patrice glanced from one Kingsley man to the other. This was news to her. But then, it was irrelevant when Godwin actually ran the show.

Watching David almost shrink into his clothes, Aaron sighed. "Listen to me, brother. For once in your life, please listen to me. Talk to Steven! There won't be any Kingsleys left for you to lead if he goes down this road. We'll all be either dead or in prison."

Unless they sacrificed the chauffeur's son, instead.

Chapter 12

Next week, late June 1998

Upper East Side, New York City

The Frick House, which now held the art collection bearing the name of the same philanthropist, was not far from the Kingsley residence. Both Gilded Age mansions could boast of hosting magnificent art, but the Frick was open to the public.

The museum library was Patrice's favorite place with its floral frieze, low bookcases, paintings on the walls, and ornately decorated ceiling. She always visited this room when attending a meeting of the benefit dinner planning committee, so no one would wonder why she wandered in here today. Given the early hour, it was empty of other guests, but...

"I don't want anyone to ask questions about why you showed up here," Patrice said to Harry.

He'd clearly been at the gym when she called and had just as clearly left without bothering to change. Military PT clothes in an art museum? Anyone who saw him would deduce this trip was an unplanned detour specifically to meet Patrice. Not a chance encounter.

"You're worried about your sons." Harry continued to walk around the chamber, pausing briefly to peer at the giant image hanging over the fireplace. "I'm helping them. You asked for an update. Which is all a third person needs to know."

"Yes, but..." Patrice made a helpless gesture with her hands. "We're talking about..."

"The question of whether we're discussing Richard will come up," Harry agreed, his interest apparently tweaked by one of the vases in the room. "Godwin will not worry unless he sees Richard changing his mind about Steven."

"Do you think he will?" she asked, already knowing the answer.

There was an inaudible mutter from Harry. Back still turned to her, he said, "Aunt Patrice, you're Alex's mother. I can't lie to you outright, and you'd catch on quick if I tried to patronize you. Truth is Richard's an active participant in Steven's schemes. They were equally involved in every attempt to kill Alex and the rest. The gossip about Lilah? The tabloids started it, but—"

"I know!" Patrice held up a hand. "Believe me, I know. It's just... I have a hard time saying it even to myself. The son I gave birth to turned out to be a monster. He's trying to eat my children... my other children... but I still can't give up on him." Bitter tears spurted, blurring her vision. A half-sob escaped. "I'm sorry. I don't mean to..."

Shoulders heaving, Harry abandoned the flower vase which had caught his attention and resumed pacing. "No, *I* should apologize for upsetting you. You're already in a difficult situation. Which reminds me... Aunt Patrice, the Kingsley home is no longer safe for you. Please consider moving in with Brad and Victor. Alex said they already asked. I do get why you wanted to stay with Aaron all these years, but..."

"It's the only way I can keep an eye on Richard," she said.

"I understand," Harry said, "but at least take someone with you when you go out. And carry a phone. You said the security guards didn't find anyone in the garden, but it doesn't mean there was no stalker."

Patrice nodded. "I'm not going anywhere alone until this whole network issue is settled. Harry, I was thinking about the negotiation idea. What do you hope to achieve? Even if Steven agrees to some kind of a deal—which is a big if—he's not going to change his ways. My sons won't be able to live in peace as long as he sees even a small chance of a win over Brad."

"No," conceded Harry.

"So you do understand," Patrice muttered. "Why are you letting my boys do this, then?"

Hands in the pockets of his camo shorts, Harry stopped pacing and turned to face her. "Like you, they have conflicting loyalties. None of them can see beyond their bond with Godwin."

"No," said Patrice, holding up a finger. "My sons *are* like me, but I didn't keep my secret for so many years because of loyalty. Let's call it what it was—fear. I married Peter to be close to my baby, but once the others were born, I didn't want them to know. I didn't want *Richard* to know. I didn't want Peter's boys to somehow lose their place in the company if it came out that they had an illegitimate half-brother. Brad, Victor, and Alex are not stupid. Neil and Scott are bright young men. They don't see Godwin for what he is because they don't *want* to see. They're afraid of losing their family, their identity, like they lost their father years ago. Fear, just like me."

Harry inclined his head, not saying anything in response.

"And you know what?" she asked. "I'm afraid even now. I'm afraid of what's going to happen to my sons because I didn't tell them the truth. I'm afraid of what's going to happen to me if I do tell the truth." Patrice pressed her knuckles to her teeth, but a sob still broke free. "Last week, I was afraid of Richard. I didn't know if he would... he would, wouldn't he? If he thought it would help Steven."

There was compassion in Harry's eyes, but he continued to stay silent.

Taking a deep breath, Patrice composed herself. "There's no more time to waste. Not for me and not for Brad, Victor, and Alex. They have to move past their fears. Harry, tell them I want them to forget this silly idea of negotiation and go to court."

"I've been trying, but..."

"Listen to me, please," said Patrice. "The only way to end this non-stop fighting is for the Kingsleys to be defeated so thoroughly that they have no way of standing up to fight again. Crush them!"

Harry smiled. "You're back."

Patrice frowned. "What?"

"The tough woman I met at the Barrons garden party," Harry explained. "You told me off that night. You said you'd walk away from the alliance if it looked like anyone would cause problems for your sons."

"Did I?" Patrice shook her head. "Instead, Lilah got into trouble because of the network. It will continue to be a problem no matter what. If there were a way to destroy it all... let's say some court decides the network is against the constitution or some such. Yes, there will be significant difficulty in the beginning—the stock market, the economy—but won't it be better in the long run to not leave doors open for criminals like Steven?"

A hint of respect in his eyes, Harry said, "You're very wise, madam."

"Wisdom came very late in my case," Patrice said. "I just hope it's not too late for Peter's boys. You tell Brad. Tell him I did not raise him to be a coward. Tell him and Victor that they need to understand right from wrong. Ask Alex to do what Lilah says. If they listened to her before... tell Neil enough is enough. Scott already understands. He's a smart boy. Tell all five of them not to come back to me unless it's with news that they're putting up an actual fight against the Kingsleys. Destroy the network if possible. If not, at least get it back."

"What about Richard?" Harry asked.

Suddenly drained, Patrice closed her eyes. "Tell him the truth," she murmured. "It's time."

Part V

Chapter 13

A day later

San José, California

Being Alex and Sabrina Kingsley's kid did come with a humongous advantage—access to the Barrons brothers. Michael had hijacked the chief's chair as he always did when visiting Uncle Shawn's consulting company. On the television at the other end of the glass-walled suite was a familiar face, talking about Toyota's new car called Prius.

"Mass production of hybrid vehicles is a welcome development," Harry stated, his voice more or less the same as it sounded in person. "Earth doesn't have infinite resources. At the same time, we cannot ask the average Joe to pay a premium for..."

Inside the room, none of the four people present paid much attention to the exchange happening on screen. Michael had heard the arguments before.

The miner in West Virginia and the factory worker in China would want to feed and clothe their children before saving the planet. Hospitals needed to stay open. Food had to be transported. Cheap fuel literally meant life to the world's poor, and concerted effort was required to make non-fossil energy affordable and readily available.

Member companies of the network invested in wind and geothermal and nuclear and so on. Barrons O & G financially supported several labs around the world working on fuels straight out of a sci-fi movie. Dan even mentioned solar winds once. Gigawatts and gigawatts of energy harvested from the upper atmosphere of the sun!

Yeah, finding alternative sources of energy was mission-critical, but there was a more pressing matter on Michael's mind at the moment. Keeping his eyes on the letters and numbers scrolling down the monitors on the chief's desk, Michael reached for the TV remote. Across the room, the screen blinked off.

Shawn remained where he was, standing next to the windows on the left as he talked to the wild-haired chick. Not giving a shit about any of it, Gabriel stretched out his giant form in the chair to Michael's right—earphones on his buzz-cut dark head and Discman on his lap.

Reaching sideways, Michael turned off Gabe's CD player.

Gabriel's light-blue eyes snapped open immediately. "Hey!"

Michael squinted meaningfully toward the windows. Tara, the girl whose family offered refuge to the exiles in India, had arrived in New York only the week before. She was immediately dragged along on this trip to California to meet one of the network's board members—Neil and Scott's uncle.

"... please, please, please." Voice light and clear, Tara entreated as she hopped from foot to foot. Like the boys, she was dressed in a tee and shorts and sneakers. Dark curls bounced around her head, and the tip-tilted dark eyes glinted as though she were planning a prank. "I know you're busy, but please help me set up this... this..."

"...CAD," Shawn finished for her, laughing. "Computer-aided design."

Sitting up, Gabriel removed his earphones. "What?" he asked in a low tone.

Leaning closer to his cousin, Michael muttered, "She wants someone to show her how to use design software."

Gabe shrugged. "So?"

"So?" Searching his mind for a valid objection, Michael threw half a glance at the girl. "So... so... why can't she ask Ma? It ain't difficult to install, and Ma lives in the same house!"

"Maybe Tara doesn't know about Aunt Sabrina," Gabriel whispered back.

A distinct possibility. Michael's ma had been stealthy for years about her interest in digital technology. She seemed to get some sort of thrill out of operating in secrecy.

"Whatshisname would've helped," countered Michael.

"Uncle Alex wouldn't know what the hell CAD is," Gabriel pointed out.

True, but Michael's father treated Tara like she were his own kid, even to the extent of calling her champ. Champ! Michael's ma, too, acted all cheesy about the chick, like she finally got the daughter she always wanted. The other Kingsley brothers, Hema, Lilah... all of them luuuurved Tara and bragged about how fearless she was during an encounter with some bad *hombres* in Goa.

Gabriel snorted. "Bro, you're just pissed she went to Uncle Shawn instead of you."

"Me? What are you..." Annoyed, Michael sat back. "You're an idiot."

"Yeah?" retorted Gabe. "I'm not the one who already has a girlfriend."

"*Girlfriend!* You *are* an idiot. I don't give a shit about this chick."

Merely shaking his head in response, Gabriel returned the earphones to the prior position and stretched out again.

Michael turned his eyes back to the monitors on the desk. He did not care about some girl who turned cartwheels in the basement on Saturday instead of practicing her self-defense skills like "Maestro Alex" ordered. Michael certainly did not care... er... that way. He was plenty busy already without adding complications to his love life.

Besides friends and school and his plans for West Point, there were the boxing and wrestling and shooting lessons. Flute sessions with Mr. Andersen. Not to mention the ongoing battle with his ma over his intention to get a motorcycle license in a few months when he turned sixteen.

"Ready to go, boys?" asked Shawn.

Go? Michael frowned, then remembered. Shawn had promised a pre-release look at the iMac. Tomorrow, the boys would go on a road trip to San Diego to visit Gabriel's former foster mom and his old friends from the *barrio*. Which reminded Michael of the extra-special treat coming up. The soccer world cup! Without any annoying non-adults of the female persuasion.

While Michael was planning out the entire summer in his head, Gabe hauled himself up and threw a casual glance at Tara. She had her foot propped on the edge of a chair to tie her shoelaces. Bending down to Michael's level, Gabriel murmured, "Chick could kick some serious ass with those legs."

"C'mon," urged Shawn, gesturing the kids toward the door.

"Gimme a second, Uncle Shawn," Michael called out from his chair. "I... uhh... lemme close what I'm working on." For good measure, he moved the volume slider on the Winamp window. "Tom's Diner" blasted out.

The other three started, Gabriel leaping back a foot or two. Looking mildly puzzled, Shawn instructed, "Turn it down, Mike."

The decibel level was lowered immediately. "Sorry," said Michael. "Accident. I'll meet you in the lobby in a minute."

He needed the minute... or two... maybe ten before he stood. Or the rest of them would see how much he didn't care about Tara that way.

Erika, Michael reminded himself. His sweet, beautiful, *trusting* girlfriend. He wasn't gonna cheat.

Besides, Tara acted like Michael didn't exist half the time. Not to mention his father and uncles. If they realized what was going through his mind... blood was supposed to be thicker than water for the Kingsleys, but he didn't intend to test the theory where Tara was concerned.

On his way out of the room, Michael snorted at his own stupidity. Blood! Power was what mattered to the Kingsleys. He would never forget the day Major Richard Armor marched into the castle in Panama and ordered his underlings to slam Alex Kingsley's face into the wall. All with silent consent from the elders in the clan.

Someday, Michael promised himself. Armor would pay for what he did. The trip to Europe for the soccer world cup would only be the beginning. Oh, yeah. The Kingsleys would pay.

Chapter 14

A week later, July 1998

Long Island, New York

Pinning the last photograph to the corkboard—that of the Kingsley sidekick called Armor—Lilah straightened. "I believe we got almost everyone in the three families," she said to the ladies with her.

Hema was one of the few people around Lilah whose allegiance remained undivided, to the point the young woman went on exile with her former boss. Lilah could trust Hema with secrets she mentioned to hardly any others. As for Sabrina, her entry into the

Kingsley family as Alex's bride changed the outcome of the family's plot against Lilah.

Sabrina was distracted tonight, though. Her bright-green gaze kept darting to the open door, but the conversation in the library could not be overheard from this side of the house.

When an attachment was built next to the garage for the former president to work on his models, a studio apartment was added on top for a live-in nurse at some point in the future. The place was cozy, with the door opening into the sitting area, a kitchenette to the far left, and bathroom to the far right. The sleeping nook was next to the window on the right. At the foot of the bed was Lilah's workspace, which included a small desk with a computer on it, corkboard hanging on the wall above. No separate entrance. The Secret Service would find it easier to protect a building with a limited number of access points.

The security at The Hermitage couldn't be beat. It was the only walled property allowed on the block, and both main and side gates were always kept locked. Any documents—digital or paper—that Lilah left in her room would be safe. None of her enemies could dig through this particular abode for intel, and no one could plant evidence.

Safety aside, Lilah was glad she accepted Noah's invitation to stay there. Her childhood home in Brooklyn lay empty, but she didn't relish the idea of living alone with only memories for company. Unfortunately, the defenses in place at the former president's residence made it impossible to eavesdrop on the discussion going on in the library.

"Alex had better tell me what they decide," Sabrina said, irritation evident in her clear voice.

The only surprising part about a Kingsley emissary contacting Dan was that it didn't happen immediately after the huddle in the Barrons home. Panicked by Harry's suggestion, the five brothers would of course have called their beloved grandfather. Chances were Godwin remained in wait-and-watch mode until the cops closed their investigation into the California shooting. Now, the family needed to put on a show for the network's board that they were serious about peace talks.

Brad and his brothers were present at the meeting along with Noah and Harry, but none of the rest could make it to Long Island on such short notice. Dan and Andrew would listen on speakerphone.

"If not Alex, Harry will update us." Lilah had declined to attend for reasons she didn't bother explaining.

Staring at the corkboard with pictures, Hema made a face. "Weird," the Nepali girl said, wiggling her fingers toward the black-and-white photographs at the very top. Godwin Kingsley's father flanked by images of his two wives. "He looks so normal."

Tucking a blonde strand back into her braid, Sabrina glanced at the board. Her frown gave way to a smirk. "Considering the rest of his family, he probably *was* the most normal."

Lilah nodded gravely. "He merely stuck his ill first wife in a mental health facility, then divorced her to marry an actress... Mr. Temple's mother." The former president's father, also a politician, watched the world from the fourth snapshot on the top.

As the other two women snickered, Lilah adjusted her reading glasses. Contact lenses were fine, but she preferred to ditch them in the evenings.

The second row on the Kingsley side was occupied by Temple, Godwin, and the half-brother they shared, the one who sired the next generation. General Potts found a place at the same level, too, though he was several years younger than the rest.

With a felt-tip pen, Lilah drew a circle around Godwin's face. "President of Kingsley Corp and head of the family. Steven's commander in chief. As of now, we don't have any weapons which would work on him."

There was a last snapshot to the left of Godwin. A blonde teenager in a polka-dotted two-piece swimsuit laughed at the camera, a string of beads around her neck. Andrew's cousin, Amber Barrons.

"I snooped around on Classmates.com about this Amber girl," said Sabrina. "Not one bite so far. No chat rooms from anyone in her school, either."

Lilah shrugged. "We knew it was a long shot."

A long while ago, she'd asked Shawn about Amber's untimely demise, framing the tale as delicately as possible to avoid implicating the Barronses. He and Andrew might be on the outs, but they were still father and son, and Lilah didn't want the wrong parties being alerted about the investigation. Yeah, Shawn was a mere infant when Amber died, but she was staying in the Barrons mansion at the time. Employees could've talked in his hearing as he grew older. Shawn admitted to appropriating the dead girl's amber beads, but he knew only as much as anyone else. He claimed the beads were a way of keeping alive the memory of a life cut tragically short. Dan on the other hand never even heard about Amber until Harry mentioned her.

Hema pointed to the third and fourth generations. "I know most of the rest." The three sons of the dead alcoholic, their significant others, Temple's estranged offspring. Following them were the warring cousins on the two sides and their spouses, with Major Armor's image pinned next to Steven's. The newest generation of Kingsleys—Victor and Alex's two boys and Steven's three-year-old daughter—made up the bottom row.

"Last but not least," muttered Sabrina, her eyes on the piece of paper pinned to the left of the Kingsley brothers. "You, Lilah. I wish we'd used an actual photo."

Lilah threw a quick glance at the magazine clipping. She never brought any snapshots of herself from the brownstone in Brooklyn and didn't want to use the two or three stills of her in Temple's collection. "Femme Fatale!" screamed the headline visible below the image. The sleaze rag had plenty to say about Lilah's appearance. Her height of five feet eight, her figure, the blue-black hair and hazel eyes, the supposedly sexy huskiness of her voice... the tabloid even commented on her blue lotus perfume. There were also the usual cheap shots about Lilah's love life.

"The people I care about know better," she said, keeping her tone steady. "The rest don't matter, so let's focus on our energies on our psy ops strategy." In quick succession, Lilah drew four more red circles on the board. "Steven's little brother and brother-in-law. Both need to die as painfully as possible, but they're merely pawns. General Potts and Major Armor are the high-value pieces. Of the two, Armor's going to be the bigger problem because he's in it mainly for his pal."

"And he hates Alex and the rest," brooded Sabrina. "Still, there has to be *something* we can use as leverage against Armor. Everyone has weaknesses."

#

As Hema returned to Sabrina's home next door to work on college admission forms, Lilah continued to stare at the corkboard. If not Amber, what Noah said about the Pottses could—

"We need to take a different approach," Sabrina said suddenly. "To psy ops, I mean."

"Go on," Lilah said.

"The women," explained Sabrina. "I wonder how Steven's wife feels about what hubby is up to. Does she even know what's going on? What about Mrs. Major Armor?" According to Noah, Steven's best buddy/lawyer recently got hitched.

Grimacing, Lilah said, "We can't blame the wives for the men's behavior, but the women are old enough to understand what's happening. They're either fully supportive or at least turning a blind eye."

"Knowing something in the abstract is different from having it shoved in your face."

Lilah sighed. "Sabrina, they're not going to help us. Steven's mother was right there in Cuba. She didn't move a single muscle until it looked like Charlie would get into trouble. Same for Steven's father."

Not completely correct. David and Grace Kingsley then read the note Temple sent to Godwin at the military court. The missive forced the former supreme court justice to back down, and his adopted son and daughter-in-law surrendered so quickly afterward that it was almost comical. The only possible reason Lilah could think of was the Amber story. Did Grace and David know what happened to the girl? Were they involved? It was unlikely Godwin would've gone to such lengths to protect the couple. Maybe they were protecting *him*, thus safeguarding their son's interests.

"Mommy and Daddy were afraid something would happen to their family," Sabrina said, lips curling into a wicked smile.

"I don't like that look on your face," said Lilah. "What are you suggesting?"

"The ladies should know Kingsley history, doncha think? What those boys do in a family squabble. Alex and his brothers are also Kingsleys. If they decided to retaliate in kind... Steven's missus should at least worry about the possibility. Armor's wife, too."

After a few seconds, Lilah muttered, "They might do something useful if only out of self-interest." Arranging a conversation would be tricky, though. Forewarning would allow mental guards to go up.

No, the women needed to be caught by surprise, the message hammered in before they even realized what was happening.

"Besides, the two of them were living it up while I..." Eyes wide and bright with strong emotion, Sabrina admitted, "I didn't sleep through a night all these years. There wasn't a single morning when I didn't force myself to open the newspaper. I was scared I'd see news about Alex... about you... about everyone else... I was afraid of one of you dying somewhere and me never knowing."

"Sabrina," Lilah whispered, her heart breaking. "I'm so—"

Holding up a finger, Sabrina said, "Don't you apologize. I know exactly whose fault it was. Yeah, Brad was an idiot to believe the gossip about you and Alex and jump into a deal with the Kingsleys. But Alex should've told his brothers to kiss his rear end. Instead, he enabled the behavior. He and I will duke it out once everything else is settled. We've got to if we're going to remain married. In the meantime, let's talk to Steven's wife and the major's. If they ignore us, we've lost nothing. Even if we get through, you're right that they won't help us directly. But one or both could slip up and do something out of fear. At the very least, they could make life miserable at home. Even if they simply suffer in silence... yeah, they're grown women. We can't blame them for what Steven and Armor did, but the ladies know. After what my boys and I went through because of the Kingsleys... what they did to *you*, Lilah... the stories they planted..."

The gutter press speculated constantly about Lilah's equation with all Brad's brothers. A sizeable chunk of the respectable media called *her* an enabler—even a Stepford wife—for not filing for divorce from the man who caused a national security problem, albeit unwittingly.

"Crazy!" Sabrina went on. "Armor instigated an assault on you, and people believe..."

That Lilah was once involved with the fellow, that she was still pining for him. There were in fact some columnists who framed the assault as fitting reward for her rejection of a low-born paramour.

"And Steven's wife is okay with it all," Sabrina said grimly. "Armor's, too. Or they're pretending to be unaware. Lilah, isn't there at least a little part of you that wants to get back at them?"

"More than a little," Lilah admitted, her mind on the details of Operation Kingsley Wives. "Trust me, I want those four to die crying in pain—Steven, Charlie, Armor, even Steven's uncle. Unfortunately, payback is a distraction we can't afford. The goal in any game should be to..." She blinked. An idea sprouted.

"...take out the king," a rich, deep voice completed from the hallway.

#

Sabrina jumped. "Harry! You scared me."

Leaning sideways against the doorjamb, Harry continued, "Checkmate. Right, Lilah?"

"Checkmate," she agreed. The familiar mix of pain and pleasure squeezed her chest at the sight of her best friend. His dark hair was disheveled, and the jeans and tee and sneakers had clearly seen better days, but Harry's coffee-colored eyes were bright with anticipation. He was holding a small cardboard box for some reason.

"What happened at the meeting?" Sabrina asked.

"The emissary was sent by David Kingsley," Harry said in response. "Not Steven or Godwin."

"Ahh," said Sabrina. David had no real authority in Kingsley Corp or the network. Any genuine peace offers would've come from the family patriarch or from Steven.

Lilah nodded. "So this meeting definitely was for the benefit of the network's board." And of course, the emissary would've been on the lookout for information—hints of Harry's next moves.

Brad and his brothers were open books to their grandfather, but the enemy would be desperate to find out what Harry was thinking, planning. Lilah didn't need to hold Harry's hand through the meeting, and the five brothers were sure to refuse guidance from her, so she didn't bother attending.

"The emissary did offer a formal conference," Harry said. "Not with Steven himself... with the company lawyers. Andrew said he would send his personal attorney."

Lilah bit back a smile. The message would get to Steven and Godwin. Andrew Barrons was not a supreme court justice or an army general, but he possessed both money and clout in spades. The network's board would see him taking the negotiations seriously, but only as much as the Kingsleys did.

Straightening from his casual position against the doorjamb, Harry sauntered into the room to stare at the corkboard. At six feet four, he towered over his tiny sister. There was the faint whiff of his usual sandalwood cologne.

Tucking the small cardboard box under his arm, he peered closely at the family tree on the board. He tapped on Major Armor's photograph with his index finger but didn't say anything.

"What?" Sabrina asked, glancing from her brother to Armor's image and back.

"Hmm?" Harry shook his head infinitesimally. "Simply thinking about the crisscrossing connections. Lilah, you didn't include the general's son. Potts, Jr. has also been helping Steven."

"I couldn't find a picture," admitted Lilah. "Of him or of Mrs. Armor... the major's wife." There were no photographs of Phillip

Potts with any of the Kingsleys, and the fellow seemed to have avoided appearing in the media.

"We shouldn't overlook Junior," Harry warned. "He's good at what he does—clandestine work for the CID." Calls between the U.S. Army Criminal Investigation Command headquarters and a prison in India had been intercepted, leading Harry to the exiles before hired killers could do away with Lilah and Alex. Potts should've been in boiling hot water for it—except there was no record of the caller being him. The prisoner purported to be on the receiving end of said calls was not cooperating. "From what I hear, Major Potts is also involved in counterterrorism operations."

Lilah asked, "Counterterrorism? al-Qaeda and bin Laden?"

Harry's brows drew together. "Yup. What d'you wanna bet the major is aware the CIA talked to you? Sure, you have a promise of immunity on what you reveal to the government, but..."

"I'll be careful," Lilah said. It didn't pay to ignore anyone, let alone an enemy who possessed a knack for staying under the radar and was familiar with the world's most dangerous criminals.

A smoky baritone voice called Sabrina's name from down the hallway. Alex.

"Coming," she called back, adding, "I'd better go," to the other two in the room.

Alex and Sabrina were busy to say the least. Shenanigans with the network aside, they were dealing with fifteen-year-old Michael. The boy's behavior toward his dad was best described as intentionally unfriendly interspersed with moments of yearning for fatherly approval. There was also sixteen-year-old Gabriel, Victor's son. He didn't even glance at his old man before stating quite firmly he would continue to stay with his actual family—Michael and Sabrina. Hema's presence was a buffer, forcing the lads to moderate their attitudes, but there was a new wrinkle.

Young Michael did not seem happy about Tara's arrival. Oh, he was not overtly rude to the girl, but the teens barely said two words to each other. Yup, plenty of drama in the household to keep Sabrina occupied.

"I'd better leave, too," said Harry, reminding Lilah of *her* personal soap opera.

There could be no alone time for her with any of the men in her acquaintance, except her brothers. She treasured every minute spent talking to Dan and Shawn, but Lilah couldn't allow herself the reprieve of bantering with her best friend without a third party being present. They took care to be circumspect even on the phone.

Brad never harbored doubts about Harry, and anything nefarious suggested by the enemy would be refuted by the years of respectful behavior on the former SEAL's part. However, the first hint of impropriety from him or Lilah, and Brad would challenge the pre-nup in court.

Holding out the box in his hands, Harry continued, "Here... I got this from Brooklyn. A late housewarming gift. Thought you'd like to decorate this place with something from your childhood. You know... something to remind you of back when."

The glint in his dark eyes... Harry was either nervous or up to no good, neither of which boded well for Lilah. "Tell me what's inside," she demanded.

"Nothing that will get you into trouble," Harry promised. "But don't open it until I leave."

The suppressed mirth in his voice... Lilah's bad feeling became a worse feeling. Frowning ferociously, she snatched the box and pried the lid loose.

Inside, the glass reptile coiled itself tighter.

For a second, Lilah simply stared at the lizard. When she looked up, Harry's bright gaze was pinned on her, daring her to attempt payback. Sabrina was looking confused.

"Argh!" screamed Lilah. Heaving the box high, she hurled it at Harry.

Guffawing, he sprinted into the hallway. She gave chase, but he was already in the main house. His laughter echoed back as he raced down the stairs.

Sabrina followed, muttering about crazy brothers.

It took Lilah and one of the secret service officers a good ten minutes to locate the poor glass lizard and deposit it in the garden. She didn't offer explanations as to how the creature found its way into the house.

Later, Lilah sat at her desk and continued to make notes on her newly hatched plan. Inquiries had to be made on the itinerary of a couple of high-profile attendees at a certain sporting event in Europe. Favors needed to be called in to arrange an incident.

Lilah set her pen down. It was no use when she couldn't stop sputtering. The year she turned fourteen. Hormones had hit her and Harry hard, adding a crazy new layer to their friendship. Exciting, frightening feelings. The stupid boy reacted by playing pranks and by being as annoying as he possibly could. He thought it would be great fun to give her a lizard for a birthday gift. Oh, she'd made him pay. He apologized a thousand times before she relented.

On another spurt of laughter, Lilah removed her reading glasses. Tapping the desk with the earpiece, she asked, *Are you courting me again, Harry?*

Part VI

Chapter 15

A few days later, July 12, 1998

Paris, France

Neural networks were amazing but unpredictable. Enjoying the warm breeze drifting around the rooftop restaurant and the view of the Eiffel Tower, Temple smiled at the two boys across the table. They were waving their arms about and belting out "The Cup of Life" with all the vigor of their youthful selves. As always, the secret service officers kept an eye out for potential problems.

Other diners didn't seem annoyed by the clamor. *Au contraire,* most of the guests were singing along.

A few lines from one song... Temple was gratified his ability to decipher spoken language had improved as much. All thanks to the two lads who were constantly in and out of his home, filling the silence with their chatter and antics. Also thanks to them, he learned how to spit out a thought here and there.

Noah, too, kept talking to Temple, updating him on their war plans. Flying to France in the Barrons corporate jet with Michael and Gabriel was also Noah's idea. Something about it being good to get out.

Temple had nodded acquiescence, reminding himself for the millionth time to be careful about Shawn Barrons. There was no way for the former politician to completely avoid Shawn, but it needed to be very clear to the enemy how no communication was going on. If a day came when Temple was able to articulate the secret behind Shawn's birth, it would mean the end of Godwin Kingsley.

The Kingsley patriarch had gone as far as to order an assassination attempt on a former American president. Shawn was merely a businessman. If he turned up dead somewhere... Temple had already failed the mother. He couldn't fail the son, too.

"Yeah!" thundered Gabriel, drumming on an upside-down plate with his cutlery.

Startled out of his musings, Temple clapped. Hoots and cheers went around the terrace restaurant as the boy held his spoon and fork high in the air.

"You know," said Michael. "We could go to..."

Temple lost the rest of what the lad was saying.

"Hello, sir," said a voice.

Looking up, Temple smiled at Lilah's brothers. A couple of others he knew were with the men. One was Harry's friend from back in Libya—a Bedouin fellow who invested in oil. What was the name? *al... al... al-Obeidi!* There was also the lawyer who interned with the then-senator from New Jersey. The gent's specialty was antitrust law.

"Temple," called Noah, glancing briefly toward the boys who were now shoveling scrambled eggs into their mouths.

The former attorney general said something in low tones, only part of which Temple caught. "...Spain... conference... important."

Struggling to respond, Temple said, "Dan... meeting..." He sighed. Neural networks were indeed amazing—when they chose to work.

Setting his napkin aside, Noah stood and signaled to the boys. "Let's go. Lilah will join us at the stadium."

Lilah? Temple held up a finger. *"Hold on a minute now,"* he tried to say, but the words came out mangled. What was Lilah doing at a soccer game in Paris when there was a business meeting under way in Spain?

Chapter 16

A little after 9 PM

Stade de France

"Madame," called a male voice, the accent upper-class Parisian.

From the private terrace attached to the Barrons box, Lilah glanced behind. So did the former president. Noah's eyes remained studiously fixed on the teams battling it out on the grass, while Amy—Dan's girlfriend—and the two Kingsley boys yelled themselves hoarse for Brazil. Dan and Shawn were already on their way to Barcelona, accompanied by the lawyers.

"A message for you from the bar," the tuxedoed headwaiter said to Lilah. "Your friends have arrived."

"Merci," she said, rising from the chair. Her two bodyguards of course followed while the secret service officers stayed put.

Sauntering down the corridor, Lilah flicked her gaze at the mirror on the wall. Light-cotton midi with tiny daisies printed on crimson background, silk scarf in an intense chili red wrapped around her head and neck, block-heeled sandals in tan. The last item in her battle gear, the big, black-framed sunglasses, dangled loosely from her fingers.

The bar area glowed from pink and purple-blue lighting, but the room was dark enough for Lilah to go unspotted. Very French accordion music played overhead while men and women enjoyed drinks in the air-conditioned coolness. On the giant television screen behind the counter, the game played on mute.

"Malbec, please," she requested one of the bartenders. The guards wouldn't imbibe while on duty, so she didn't bother offering.

Settling the goblet on the countertop, the waiter poured wine. His eyes darted meaningfully toward the small crowd gathered in the near-right corner of the room. There was a woman dressed in peasant costume, studying the palm of someone from her audience. A fortune teller.

"Here you go, *madame*," said the bartender. "Enjoy!"

Drink in one hand and sunglasses dangling from the other, Lilah made her way to the high table near the fortune teller. Steven's wife was impossible to miss. Her big, blonde hair, the straight-backed posture—she was swaying in place to the music and clearly didn't give two hoots if anyone stared at her impressive curves. *Very* impressive. Her companion almost disappeared by her side.

Titling her head to one side for a better view, Lilah studied the second woman. The yellow cardigan and floral skirt suited the small brunette. Her excitement as she waited for her destiny to be foretold was clear in the way she fidgeted.

Rosa Valerie Armor, known to family and friends and her readers as Arvi. Her husband, Major Richard Armor, was a few years older than the Kingsley brothers, which put him close to fifty. Arvi was only in her early thirties. The one detail Lilah's research unearthed besides what was publicly known about the history teacher/novelist was how Arvi was fascinated by oracles.

The fortune teller looked up and met Lilah's eyes for a moment before glancing away and asking Mrs. Steven Kingsley for her palm. Oh, yes. The women were about to hear the scary truth about the future waiting around the corner.

Slipping on her glasses, Lilah joined the crowd.

#

Yes, it was rather silly, but Arvi's little hobby wasn't harming anyone. Even after her wedding to a man who was comfortably off, she was careful to stick to her assigned budget on her monthly trip to the psychic in Corpus Christi.

She loved to travel, too, visiting historical sites in different cities, but this venue where the idle rich gathered was not her idea of a good time. Still, Richard wanted her to get to know his best friend's wife, *and* it would provide material for Arvi's next book. Especially the guards. Her bodyguard romances always sold well. Arvi could hardly believe her luck when a gypsy woman also showed up.

"All right," Steven's wife said to the seer. "Tell me something about my past. Then, I'll see if I want to believe your predictions."

Rolling her shoulders to the overhead music, the fortune teller smiled. "Ahh... a skeptic. You wish to test Zolda, yes?"

"Is it really your name?" someone called from the crowd.

"What's in a name?" retorted Zolda, stopping the swaying to peer at the young man who asked the question. "A rose by any other name..."

The crowd laughed at her witty allusion. The two Kingsley bodyguards stood by, amused looks on their faces.

"Go ahead," said Steven's wife, not distracted even for a second. "What do you know about me?"

Zolda sighed. "You're an open book, *madame*. A powerful husband who loves you, a daughter... three years old now. Apple of her father's eye. Happy marriage."

A slight hush fell over the crowd as everyone waited for a response. "You could've guessed this much," Steven's wife finally said. "Or maybe looked me up before."

"Even the age of your daughter?" Zolda smiled again, her eyes darting toward Arvi. "All right. How about I study you and your friend together? Your auras are linked."

An expectant mutter went around, and Steven's wife acquiesced with a slow nod. Clasping the two proffered hands, the seer stared unblinkingly at the women in front.

One second, two seconds... five... ten... Arvi began to get worried the lady had gone into a trance or such.

"Fighting," Zolda finally murmured. "So much fighting. What for? Some men don't like to lose, do they? No matter what they have, they want more. They want what belongs to their brother."

Arvi bit her lip in confusion. Richard was adopted. He didn't have any brothers or sisters. The stories about the Kingsleys... they *did* fight. Some of the rumors about Richard himself... he'd said most of it was simply gossip, part of the ongoing PR war with Steven's cousins. Richard came up the hard way in life, and trust-fund babies like the Kingsleys considered him an interloper. They used the media to discredit him.

Steven was an exception, a man who saw beyond the fake boundaries of class and money. His wife wasn't uttering a word in protest, though. The sheen of sweat covered her face.

"Women's tears," continued Zolda. "Men start the wars, and their wives are left to cry. Yesterday, it was someone else; tomorrow, it might be you."

Arvi gasped.

Snatching her hand back, Steven's wife said, "Enough! What kind of shit is this?" She swatted away Arvi's hand as well and looked around. "I want to speak to the person in charge. Where's the manager? I want to ask... this con artist was certainly not hired as entertainment."

"No, she was not," a female voice said from behind, the tone husky yet somehow smooth.

As one, the crowd turned to stare at the woman in the red floral dress and silk scarf, her face hidden by dark glasses. Setting her wine glass on the high-top table, she took a couple of steps to reach Arvi's side. There was glamor in the way the mystery woman moved, seduction in the fragrance surrounding her.

"But tell me," she continued, "which part of what Zolda said is untrue? Steven did cheat his cousin—his *brother*—out of his property, didn't he? Mrs. Armor, you're new to the... I suppose to the family... so perhaps you don't know. The major commanded his subordinate, Captain Charles Kingsley, to strip a woman naked and drag her to the courtroom."

"Wh-who..." Steven's wife stuttered. "Who are you?"

Arvi's mouth was dry. She couldn't bring herself to ask *any*thing, and her feet seemed frozen in spot.

The guards were on alert, but they wouldn't get involved unless there was actual danger. Unnecessary intervention would invite bad press.

Lips quirking, the mystery woman asked, "What's in a name?" There were no laughs from the crowd this time, only nervous titters and puzzled questions. A couple of camera flashes came from the periphery. "If you don't want to hear your fortunes from Zolda, let *me* take a shot. Steven is a Kingsley, and the family history is full of blood feuds and vendettas. Major Armor is not a part of the clan, but he's as involved as Steven in all their crimes. Guess what? Steven's cousins—Peter's five sons—are also Kingsleys. What Steven did to them, they will return five-fold. Stop what's happening if you can. Before it's too late."

"Manager!" shouted Steven's wife. "I want the manager. He needs to... someone needs to call the cops!"

As though there had been no interruption, the mystery woman said, "You asked for my identity." The dark glasses came off, and her mouth curved up.

Arvi couldn't look away from the electrifying face before her. The tendrils of blue-black hair escaping the scarf, blazing hazel eyes, perfectly carved features... the force of a thousand thunderbolts radiated from the smile.

"Lilah," said the stunning woman. "Lilah Kingsley."

The power-hungry temptress Richard had been linked with.

Chapter 17

The burly fellow immediately behind Steven's wife took a step forward. Without turning to look, Lilah held a hand up to stop her own security from responding. The message had hit home. A brawl between the two sets of guards would be overkill.

Swallowing hard, Steven's wife said, "Harassing other visitors is not acceptable no matter who you are. France has laws against it, I presume." Whirling to the men assigned to protect her, she said, "We should make a citizen's arrest and call the police. Everyone here saw what she did."

Arvi Armor was still staring silently at Lilah, the dread in her eyes now tinged with some other emotion. The crowd continued to gape at the tableau.

"What are you waiting for?" Steven's wife demanded, frowning at the guards.

"Ma'am," muttered one of the men, his gaze going to someone behind Lilah.

"He's telling you it wouldn't be smart," said Noah's familiar voice. "Not with the Secret Service watching."

No one stopped Lilah when she pivoted on her heel and joined Noah and Temple. Michael and Gabriel were with the former president's security detail. Zolda—former employee of Lupe Valdez in her Berlin club—would be escorted to safety by one of Lilah's guards. Zolda's real name would remain a secret known only to Liam and Harry.

Walking back to the Barrons box, Gabriel said in an awed tone, "That was goddamn awesome!"

"Pow, pow, pow, pow," agreed Michael, bouncing on his feet and making jabbing motions with his fists. "And they're down and out!"

Lilah laughed. "I'm amazed the plan actually worked." Even with Mrs. Armor's interest in seers, there had been no guarantee the women would want their fortunes told. But then, a regular conversation with them was impossible. The ladies would've walked away as soon as they realized who they were talking to. Even if they stayed long enough to hear the words, mental walls would've been firmly up. Now— "Let's hope they think about what I said."

The overhead music changed to something snappy, and the boys of course had to do a slo-mo *Reservoir Dogs* walk. Lilah laughed again, remembering the toddlers they'd been when she left on exile. Gabriel and Michael, the matched set of angels. Here they were, trying to look all bad to the bone.

When she turned to make a comment to Noah, the two elderly men were a few paces behind. There was a thoughtful frown on the former attorney general's face.

The moment the boys were within sight of the game, they ran back to their chairs, shouting, "What did we miss?" at Dan's girlfriend.

Sliding back into her own seat at the private terrace, Lilah questioned Noah, "What? You don't think I got my point across?"

"Magnificently," said Noah. "Not a huge win, but we never know what small detail counts at what critical moment."

Lilah gestured with her hands. "Go on."

"Mrs. Armor's reaction seemed more personal than fear and general hostility."

"Steven's wife was doing all the talking," Lilah pointed out.

"Yes, and her friend was staring straight at you. Could be jealousy. Resentment."

"Of whom?" Lilah asked. "Me?"

Noah smiled without amusement. "You're supposed to have been the love of her husband's life."

"Gimme a break," muttered Lilah. After a couple of seconds, she asked, "Enough for her to keep the major away from us?"

"Perhaps," Noah said, the perturbed look lingering on his face. "She could also put up roadblocks in *our* path. Major Armor is a dangerous man, and we don't need his wife to add to the problem."

"Armor *is* dangerous," agreed Lilah, "but I'm more worried about his and Steven's reaction to Dan's trip to Spain."

Once the Barrons jet landed in Barcelona, Dan and Shawn would drive across the northern part of the country to a town called Muskiz. The oil refinery located there was not affiliated with the network, and the management was involved in a feud with Steven. Dan planned to join a presser held by the executives while Falcon Papazian—the exiles' lawyer—stuck around and made notes on the situation.

All very straightforward. Except the family of a disgraced American politician had connections to the area. Jack Drummond—the rapist who showed up in Beijing on Kingsley orders—was the son of a former financier who was rumored to have laundered piles of cash for a European crime syndicate. According to Harry, one of the methods used was liquor sales in tourist hotspots across the continent, including this region which saw heavy traffic during the famous bull run in the summer.

When Dan heard, he almost gnashed his teeth in anticipation of a confrontation. Lilah, not so much. If only the Kingsley brothers had simply killed Drummond in China or just allowed him to escape as Brad wanted. Instead, they humiliated the enemy and ruined his career, *then* let him go. Drummond would be out for revenge, and Lilah's twin would be considered prime target.

"Someone's going to alert Drummond about Dan and Shawn being there," Lilah brooded. "Armor and Steven will hear about the press conference before it even happens." The worry wasn't only about her brothers. Those who helped them could also end up in Kingsley crosshairs, including Saeed al-Obeidi who joined them on the trip.

The concern in Noah's eyes increased exponentially.

"Mr. Andersen," Michael called. "Did you get a chance to talk to Ma?"

Startled by the sudden intrusion of normalcy, Lilah glanced at the boy. He and Gabe were staring hopefully at the former attorney general. Amy—Dan's girlfriend—laughed, holding her straw hat to her red hair.

Noah groaned. "Not this again." Turning to Lilah, the elderly lawyer explained, "They want me to talk Sabrina into letting them join Dan after the game."

"Uncle Dan won't mind," said Michael. "Pamplona's only a couple of hours from the refinery."

"We'll check out the town this year and do the bull run next July," Gabriel said, fidgeting in excitement.

"The bull run?" Lilah asked ominously. "Are you *trying* to give Sabrina a stroke? She won't agree."

"Why not?" wheedled Gabe.

"It's dangerous," said Lilah.

"You just said there could be problems if Armor and all of them hear about the refinery," Michael countered. "But Uncle Dan's going, anyway."

"That's quite different," Lilah said. "Dan's an adult." The men and women who managed the refinery were adults, too, she told herself. They'd know what they were getting into no matter which side they picked. They would be careful. As the boys sulked, Lilah added, "Bullfighting is not for kids. A bunch of men surrounding a young bull and killing it for public entertainment."

Grimacing, Dan's girlfriend said, "Like an animal sacrifice."

The Spanish Sacrifice. Lilah didn't know why the words popped into her head, but she couldn't stop thinking about it the rest of the evening.

Back in the hotel, she went in search of the gym. Thank God, there was a Muay Thai bag. Kicks, knees, punches... kicks, knees, punches... Lilah ordered herself to snap out of it, to shake off the unease. What Amy said merely triggered the memory of a chess move Lilah had used off and on. She'd intentionally sacrificed pieces to gain tactical advantage. Nothing to do with the looming showdown over the oil empire.

Part VII

Chapter 18

The next night

Corpus Christi, Texas

"No, Ma," Richard insisted into the cell phone, breath coming in huffs as he jogged along the shadowed North Beach toward the blue-lit form of USS *Lexington*. The old aircraft carrier now served as a museum, and tourists were partying on the shore to Latin music despite temperatures which hovered in the eighties. Skirting the crowd, Richard continued on his way. "What happened in Paris *was* different," he contended. "Brad's wife is not merely the woman he married. She was... *is* a partner in his company. How was I supposed to leave her out of any argument over the network?"

Arvi worked at Texas A & M. She had nothing to do with the oil business. Steven's wife never even visited the Kingsley office. Attacking them was unquestionably out of line.

Richard's ma continued to rant about Steven being bad news. She fretted over the gossip about her son and Mrs. Brad Kingsley. "I don't know how I manage to look Miss Patrice in the eye—"

"Tell her not to bother you anymore," said Richard. "End of story."

Which, of course, set his ma off again.

The restaurant—Blackbeard's On The Beach—was in sight. He couldn't wait to grab his customary beer. No, not beer. He needed something stronger tonight.

"Ma," he called. "Forget the gossip for a moment. After what happened with Arvi, it should be clear *Miss* Patrice's sons are not gonna show us the same consideration you show their mother. Tell Justice Kingsley you're quitting and move into the apartment I got you. The building already has security, and I will hire extra guards to keep an eye on you two. Besides, you're both more than old enough to retire."

"The judge's guards keep us safe," she dismissed. "And yes, we *are* old enough to retire, but how are we supposed to live in peace when you—"

"But..." Richard interjected as he walked through the doors of the noisy restaurant.

"Major," called a familiar server. "Your friends are waiting for you."

Richard frowned. Steven was back in New York, and the one other man Richard counted a friend was Major Phillip Potts. He, too, was not in Texas.

"But what?" Richard's mother asked on the phone.

"Over there," the server pointed across the room, balancing a tray with his other hand.

Peering through the crowd, Richard blinked. Someone he never expected was chilling it in a chair by the windows, drink in his hands—Dante Maro, the COO of Gateway. The server taking his order moved to the side, revealing the second occupant of the table. Alex Kingsley's bosom buddy, card sharp and swindler extraordinaire, Petty Officer Harry Sheppard. The con man glanced across the room and grinned as he recognized Major Armor.

"Gotta go, Ma," Richard said. "I need to take care of something." Snapping the phone shut, he strode toward the enemy.

#

"What do you want, Sheppard?" Richard asked the moment the server was out of earshot.

Spearing fried calamari with his fork, the trickster said, "Major, Dante and I came all this way only to talk to you. Least you could do is sit before barking at us."

A muffled snort came from the other man.

Richard gritted his teeth. "Least I can do is let you walk out of here without—"

Sheppard held up a hand. "I apologize. Major Armor, I'd like fifteen minutes of your time to discuss a matter of critical importance. We didn't think calling you for an appointment would work, so Dante and I waited here for you to show up. Yes, I did have someone check into your routine... as I'm sure you and Steven have done to the rest of us."

"Please sit, son," requested the COO.

Maro was nowhere old enough to address Richard as son. Still, Gateway's COO was known to be a straight shooter.

Sheppard sighed. "This is your home turf. You've been a regular at this restaurant for years. Dante and I are not idiots to attack you here. There's nothing for you to fear."

Baring his teeth in a snarl, Richard said, "I'm not a woman, either, to fall for your scare tactics. Tell whatshername to stay away from—"

"No," agreed Sheppard. "You're a warrior. An incredibly intelligent man who made something of himself despite the odds. No one smoothed your way into West Point. Your record as a sniper speaks for itself. Your promotions were earned, not handed to you as acknowledgment of your family's clout. You got yourself through law school, continuing to serve the nation as reservist in the JAG Corps."

When no more was forthcoming, Richard asked, "Trying to flatter me with my own record?"

"Not flattery," swore the petty officer. "Merely an honest appraisal of the individual you are. The loyalty you show your family and friends is remarkable. Which is why I believe you should be given a chance."

"Chance for what?" asked Richard.

Glancing casually around, Sheppard said, "I'd rather not shout it up to you. We can have a reasonably private conversation even in this restaurant but not if you insist on standing."

"Please," Dante Maro once again requested.

Grabbing a chair, Richard seated himself. "You have five minutes."

"You could also have a beer," said the petty officer. "On us." At Richard's growl, the swindler inclined his head. "All right. I won't waste any more time. Major, have you ever thought of who your biological parents might be?"

"Wha—" Richard shook his head more to clear his confusion than to convey his response. "I have only one set of parents. My father and mother are the two people who raised me. No one else matters."

Sheppard raised an eyebrow. "I agree. Still, you can't tell me the question never occurred to you."

With a shrug, Richard said, "Not hard to guess. I was born back in the 'fifties. Abortion wasn't readily available at the time. Some girl got herself into trouble and found an easy way out."

"Easy!" The black man huffed. "Nothing about it would've been easy."

"Fine," said Richard. "Easier than raising me herself."

"Which would've been impossible for a sixteen-year-old to imagine," murmured Sheppard. "No home, no family to help, no job, no money. Where would she go? How would she feed you? Keep you safe? If she didn't show the sense to give you up, you might have been dead today. Not sitting in this restaurant, talking to me."

"What?" Richard shook his head again. "Spit it out. You're trying to claim you know my moth—the woman who gave birth to me."

"Yes," said Sheppard. "You know her as well—Patrice Kingsley."

For a few seconds, Richard didn't say anything. Then, he chuckled. "You do believe I'm a fool. The needy orphan looking for a family."

"No," said the con man.

"Your five minutes are up," Richard said, standing and shoving his chair aside. "I have other things to do, but thanks for the laugh."

"Ask your father," Sheppard said before Richard could walk away. "The one who raised you, not the selfish jerk who used an innocent young girl to amuse himself, then tossed her aside. The son of a bitch is dead in any case."

Heaving in an angry breath, Richard stared at the trickster.

"Ask the man who took you home," insisted Sheppard. "Ask when he met Patrice *Sheppard,* not Mrs. Peter Kingsley. Ask him where. Ask him who took him to meet her. Ask him who named you Richard. Ask him why. When you're done talking to your father, perhaps ask Patrice why she agreed to marry Peter when neither of them was ever interested in the other."

The certainty in Sheppard's tone... a violent shuddering started inside Richard. "Lies," he bit out. "All lies." Shaking his finger in the swindler's face, Richard said, "Stay away from me. Swear to God I... if I see you again... trust me, Sheppard, you're a dead man."

Pivoting on his heel, Richard marched out of the restaurant. Somehow, he held himself together until he got to the safety of the nighttime crowds on the beach. As he ran across the shore toward his apartment, there was no one to stop him. The doorman of his building might have uttered a greeting, but Richard didn't hear it as he went into the elevator.

With a soft thud, the front door shut behind him, leaving him staring into the darkness of the apartment. The Kingsley chauffeur and his wife were the ones who fed their son and clothed him. They cleaned his dirty bottom and tended to his scrapes and cuts. His ma sang him to sleep when he was ill, fussed when he did something she disapproved of.

They were his parents. Not someone who abandoned her offspring on the pretext of giving him a better life. No matter whose genes went into forming Richard, they had no rights over him.

It was all a sham anyway, a falsehood invented by Sheppard with or without the knowledge of Patrice Kingsley. Simply a ploy to trick Richard into leaving Steven.

Without bothering to turn on the lights, Richard dug through the pockets of his shorts for his cell phone. One ring, two—

"She's all right," Steven said as soon as he picked up.

"Huh?" Richard blinked. "Who?"

"Arvi," said Steven, surprise in his tone. "Your wife. Who else?" He'd said he'd contact the security firm to arrange even more guards in the hotel the two ladies were staying in.

"Yes, of course," Richard said into the phone. "Arvi."

Steven snorted. "My friend, you're a married man now. The wife's gotta think she's the most important part of your life. Not happening if you react how you did just now."

"I'll remember," Richard said. "There's something we need to discuss—"

"She said she already called your mother. Aunt Patrice was apparently around. I'm gonna bet she talked your ma into taking their side. My dear auntie is a problem. We need to get her out of the picture."

A jolt went through Richard's chest. "Get her out?" he echoed. "How?"

"I wish I knew. If Uncle Aaron gets kicked out, she would have to leave, too. But Grandfather won't fire Uncle Aaron. Forget about eviction."

Eviction. It was all Steven was talking about. With his free hand, Richard wiped the sweat from the back of his neck.

"What else did you want to discuss?" Steven asked.

"Ahh... I... I was going to say we should ignore the whole thing in Paris. Withdraw the official complaint and don't say anything else to the press. It's best we don't give more importance to your cousin's wife and grow her profile further. Could backfire if she does take the witness stand in a court battle."

"True," Steven muttered.

They hung up soon after, but Richard kept staring into the shadows in the living room, confused by his own behavior. Why the hell didn't he confide in Steven about the meeting with Sheppard? The whole story about Patrice Kingsley was a lie. As far as Richard was concerned, she was the mother of his enemies. Nothing more.

Finally turning on the lights, Richard went to the bathroom sink. Water gushed from the faucet. Splashing the coolness onto his face, he looked into the mirror. "All lies," he assured the image.

Chapter 19

Two weeks later, August 1998

Cerro Azul, Panama

The man who marched to the front of the conference hall was a veteran. Richard was sure of it.

"Hello," said the fellow. "Only some of you know me. I'm Colonel Parker from Pillar Oil Explorers."

"Mr. Armor," called Godwin Kingsley's weighty voice.

Richard knew he should respond, but his mind kept replaying the scene from ten years ago. He'd been right here in this large hall with some of the same people when the criminal named Parker raised objections to the appointment of Harry Sheppard as the chairman of the network's board of directors. Godwin later said Parker was picked as the tool because there was history between him and Harry Sheppard.

"Major," snapped Gen. Potts.

With an inward start, Richard sat up. Rolling dividers cordoned off an appropriately sized area of the same hall which held quite a crowd on the fateful evening when Parker was killed. All the thirty-plus occupants currently present were looking at Richard.

Steven was stationed at the head of the table as the CEO and chairman of the network, but he also represented Peter Kingsley Company in the eighteen-member board. The former supreme court justice and Potts, Sr. showed up for Kingsley Corp. As expected, Hector flew in to speak for Gateway, and Andrew Barrons arrived with his two sons.

Richard's own drilling company was never a part of the board. Steven would've somehow found space for his best friend, but Godwin was firmly against it. The former supreme court justice might laud the intellectual prowess of his chauffeur's son, but a servant would not be allowed to reach the same exalted heights as the master's clan. Richard was present tonight only as friend and right-hand man of the CEO.

"You're next on the agenda to speak," Potts said, reprimand clear in the old man's tone.

More out of habit, Richard mentally marked the instance as further evidence of the general's insulting behavior. Opening the folder in front, Major Armor began to list Steven's accomplishments as the ruler of the oil empire.

An hour passed before the group broke for lunch. Hector Sheppard was the first on the roster of speakers for the afternoon. The eight board members whose sympathies were with Brad— including the Barronses—would make their cases the next day.

A couple of young men in business suits moved the room dividers aside, revealing the banquet tables at the back of the hall. Dining tables and chairs were set around the space, and catering staff waited to serve the VIPs at the meeting.

Chair legs scraping the floor, Richard stood. His eyes accidentally caught those of Shawn Barrons as he glanced around the hall. Shawn's adopted brother, Daniel, followed his gaze to Richard. Andrew's face was impassive, but neither of his sons bothered to mask their hostility. Pity. Richard knew Shawn from the latter's brief time at West Point. He was decent enough for someone brought up in the lap of luxury, and Daniel Barrons was a reasonable fellow by all accounts.

"Rich," Steven muttered in a low tone as he slipped papers back into the folder in front and handed them to his secretary. "Go with me. Private lunch."

"This is a good chance to gauge what the members are thinking," Richard warned. Exquisite food, fine wine... tongues loosened.

"Someone's agreed to talk to us," said Steven, tucking a pen into the pocket of his blazer. "But not publicly. You're not going to believe who." He grinned. "Why don't we keep it a surprise?"

Amused by his friend's excitement, Richard chuckled. "All right."

#

The glass-walled lobby in the corporate building didn't help to hold back memories. Halloween night, 1988—almost exactly ten years ago, Richard realized with shock.

"Officer, this is an illegal search," said Brad's wife. She and the five idiots were at the other end of the huge lobby, arguing with the SWAT team. "We have a right to see the warrant," insisted the so-called empress of the oil sector.

"Oh, do you now?" Richard mocked from the entrance.

He took a quick visual sweep of the room, noting potential threats. There were none... except... the potted plant... the slight movement behind it... a kid? Why was a child in this building, a toddler at that? Was it Alex's son?

Walking with Steven in the direction of the CEO suite, Richard glanced to the left. Staff still manned the reception desk; employees still walked up and down. A potted plant still stood in the same spot. Was it the same one?

The boy was certainly different after his experience. Mere weeks after Alex and the rest left on their exile, his missus brought their son to visit Grandma Patrice at the Kingsley mansion. A chance encounter in the garden. The child stared unblinkingly at his family's enemy as he promised Richard's death at Alex's hands.

The toddler's words bothered Richard more than he cared to admit. Not the prediction. Something about the boy's resolve was unsettling.

Their next confrontation was in India, when fifteen-year-old Michael fired the shot which ended the battle with the Russian mafia. Richard made a few inquiries afterward. Alex's son was fully expected to follow his father's footsteps into West Point.

The single incident in India aside, Richard doubted Alex would be fool enough to endanger his only child in the war between cousins. Still, there would be nothing—no shrub—for young Michael to hide behind if Major Armor decided the boy was indeed a problem.

Nothing except the possibility he was Richard's flesh and blood.

"Rich," called Steven.

"Yeah?" Richard said automatically before realizing he'd come to a halt in the middle of the lobby.

"You all right?" Steven asked.

"I… ahh… I'm fine." The goddamned con man, Harry Sheppard, was not about to succeed. Richard was too seasoned a soldier to fall for psy ops. "Let's go," he said to Steven. "Your guest is waiting."

#

Richard had seen the older fellow at the board meeting. "Mr. Wheeler," he greeted cautiously. Brother to Peter Kingsley's mistress, uncle to Alex's half-brothers. There was nothing *half* about the way the five men stuck together, though. Patrice Kingsley accepted the twins with wide-open arms, and her sons did the same.

A jolt went through Richard's heart. Would *he* have been…

No. Gritting his teeth, Richard told himself to snap out of it.

Wheeler was one of Brad's eight supporters in the board. An enemy to Richard. Except Steven claimed Wheeler had agreed to talk.

Steven was far more exuberant than advisable, breaking out aged Scotch which surely came from Godwin's cellar. The food, as always at such Kingsley events, was prepared by the finest chefs. No business was discussed throughout, but Wheeler remained subdued, guarded in his responses to even the simplest comments.

Only when apple tart and coffee were brought around did Steven finally ask, "What did you decide?"

There was silence from Wheeler for a few moments. "I love... loved my sister. Neil and Scott are her sons. If she were alive..." He sighed. "I barely graduated from high school. Didn't go to college. The Wheelers were never poor, but the world war took my two brothers. My parents were getting old, and Maddie was not even a teenager. They needed me, and I needed a job. All I did at the interview was tell Godwin I'd be the hardest worker in the company outside of him. Even after the whole mess with Peter and his wife and Maddie... I'm aware some threats were made, but none of them materialized. Godwin allowed me to continue with Kingsley Corp until *I* was ready to move on. He even insisted I keep Maddie's twins as I wanted when Peter's wife was talking about adopting them."

Reminders of Patrice Kingsley never seemed to stop. Taking a sip of the whiskey, Richard pushed the woman's image out of his mind.

"Then, this board membership," continued Wheeler. "Mr. Kingsley... Steven... you knew damn well who I was. You could've asked my employer to appoint someone else to represent the company, but you didn't. I suppose I owe you, too."

"Think also about what happened to your nephews," urged Steven. "They lost ten years of their lives because of Brad."

"I said so to Neil," said Wheeler. "He would've been a full surgeon by now. Scott should've been working in a university lab somewhere. If either of them were interested in oil, I could've... but they're in this fight because of their half-brothers. I brought them up, but the last ten years made it clear whom they consider important. Now, I have to make my choices. No matter which side I advise my employer to pick, there will be consequences. However, chances of success will be greater if we stick with the current leadership of the network, and my personal feelings on the matter are fifty-fifty at best."

Eyes bright with anticipation, Steven leaned forward in his chair.

"Please give my regards to your grandfather," Wheeler said. "And let him know the Kingsleys will have my company's support in any board vote."

Advantage: Steven, eleven to seven.

Chapter 20

Two days later, August 1998

Upper East Side, New York City

Clutching the rolled-up newspaper in her hand, Patrice waited at the window overlooking the garden as the Lincoln Town Car nosed out of the garage. It had been decades since she visited her husband's grave, but the drive to Brooklyn would give her the privacy required for this conversation with Richard's father.

Too many people already knew about Richard's birth. Patrice herself confided in Aaron and his lady friend out of a desperate need to talk to someone. Temple, Godwin, Noah Andresen, Harry, his father, now Dante. If Peter's boys knew, they might forgive their half-brother on Patrice's say-so, but none of the five would stand up to their grandfather for Richard. Lilah, her brothers—they had no reason at all to be forgiving. Not one of them could be allowed to hear about Richard's birth until he was completely clear of potential legal trouble.

Fifteen minutes later, Patrice was in the back seat of the air-conditioned car, staring at the chauffeur's bald head. "Richard and Steven are in the Kingsley media room right now," she fretted. The two men would be bragging to the press about winning support from the enemy's own relatives.

"Richard needs time, Miss Patrice," the chauffeur said, tone stoic. "It's not easy for a man to accept such news."

"Time is a luxury we can't afford," Patrice said. "Richard caught a lucky break in the immigrant worker case."

The labor contractor used by Richard's company was sent to prison for human trafficking, including sex trafficking of minors. The FBI couldn't find any proof of Richard's involvement. He'd sworn over and over he didn't have a clue what was going on, and his adoptive mother believed him. Patrice pleaded for divine forgiveness for turning a blind eye to the episode, but she'd been a Kingsley insider long enough to know how businesses functioned. There was no way Richard didn't realize something was wrong when the amount he forked out to the contractor was so low. It was simply convenient for him to ignore the crime going on under his watch.

Richard *was* lucky, and he didn't know how lucky. Patrice was sure Harry's intention was to supply *evidence* to the feds just like Steven and Richard planted evidence which won the former SEAL a jail term.

"It's you who saved Rich, Miss Patrice," said Armor, his eyes on the highway before them. "Not luck." A motorcycle passed them on the left lane, then swinging in front with mere inches to spare.

Other drivers responded with irate honks, but the chauffeur didn't even cluck in annoyance. "Mr. Harry is holding off on paying Richard back in kind for your sake."

"Yes," agreed Patrice, sweating despite the cool air circulating in the vehicle. "The longer Richard continues to be with the Kingsleys, the further he will go. At some point, even Harry will run out of patience."

"I understand," Armor responded. "But Richard has always done his own thinking. There's nothing anyone else can do until he decides to see the truth for himself. I know my son. He'll come to me when he's ready."

#

Thirty minutes later

Green-Wood Cemetery

Brooklyn, New York

When Patrice got to her husband's resting place, she wasn't expecting to find Brad there with fresh flowers in his hand. There was mild surprise in his Kingsley blue eyes as he greeted her with a kiss on the cheek. For the chauffeur standing deferentially behind, Brad limited himself to a wary nod.

The clamor of the city didn't reach this serene place, but tourists were still present, clicking pictures and feeding the ducks in the pond. There were only a few praying at the graves.

"You look handsome," Patrice said affectionately, giving a pat to the stubble beard.

Brad flushed. "Thank you, Mother." Glancing toward the headstones, he added, "I didn't think you visited."

"I don't," she responded, seating herself on the ground and gesturing at Brad to sit next to her. "Not usually, but I've been jittery these days. I keep wondering how things might have turned out if Peter lived."

His boys didn't know the icky details of their father's death. When Patrice got the message to go to the local hospital to visit her estranged husband, she learned he'd been having chest pains and was diagnosed with an aneurysm some months before. The doctor warned him against any exertion that could raise his heart rate and blood pressure.

The warning worked for a short while—until the night he pressured his beautiful mistress into sex. The tear Peter developed in his aorta wasn't bad enough to kill him right away, but urgent intervention was needed. Even if they contacted the Kingsleys for assistance, there simply wasn't enough time to fly him to Baylor College in Texas where there was a surgeon who did such operations. After Peter's death, Maddie became sick herself, unable to even breathe properly. Some medical reason surely existed, but as far as Patrice was concerned, Maddie died of a broken heart.

"I asked Wheeler the same thing," Pushing his glasses up his nose, Brad added, "What would he have done if Father were alive?"

Patrice could imagine the turmoil on their side after the announcement by Neil and Scott's uncle. "I don't suppose you got an answer," she said. Wheeler probably did know what led to his sister's death, and some part of him likely blamed Peter. It wasn't rational to transfer the anger toward Peter's sons, but grief made most people irrational. Patrice's own first thought when she heard of Maddie's death was how the woman was at least lucky enough to make love to a man wholly in love with her. Stupid, but it was what it was.

"No answer," Brad admitted.

Neither mother nor son brought up the ongoing corporate drama after. They talked about how much the two boys—Gabriel and Michael—had grown, how different New York City was, how badly the five brothers missed Patrice over the last ten years. She promised to visit Brad's dog—Hades—sometime soon.

Only when she was ready to leave did Brad say, "Harry told me he met you a few weeks ago at the Frick House."

Patrice continued dusting off woodchips from her slacks. "And?"

"You know you could ask me for updates anytime you want," Brad said.

She noted the hint of censure in her son's refined voice. "When did you grow old enough to reprimand me?" Smiling to take away the sting of her words, she said, "Harry's hardly an outsider at this point. Besides, his opinion is likely to be more objective about the situation than what you or your brothers tell me."

Brad flushed again. "It's not as if I don't understand what needs to be done."

"I know." Reaching up, Patrice adjusted his glasses though they didn't need adjusting. "My poor child. You're worried about the consequences. For you, for the family, for everyone else. It's always been that way with you."

"Shouldn't it be?"

"Yes, but sometimes, the consequences of not doing anything can be worse."

#

Half an hour later, Patrice faced the consequences of her own inaction. Feet frozen to the spot, she stared at Richard as he sat on the only chair in the garage with a yellow folder in his hands.

His ice-blue eyes were on his adoptive father, the chauffeur. "Tell me these are fake," Richard said, immense pain in the usually impatient voice.

"Son." Armor, Sr. looked around as though making sure all four cars were present. The lights, the tools, the smell of machine oil—everything remained the same. "Your ma?"

Ignoring Patrice completely, Richard stood. "Ma's not here, or I wouldn't have…" He thrust the folder in his father's face. "This was in your safe upstairs. Pa, please tell me these adoption papers are fake. Tell me the damn con man planted them!"

Armor sighed. "No. These are the papers Miss Patrice signed the day I brought you home to your mother."

Part VIII

Chapter 21

The next day, August 1998

World Trade Center, New York City

Harry stayed quiet as multiple arguments raged around the conference table in Gateway's Manhattan office. It was not a routine board meeting this morning. The various branches of the Sheppard clan which held stock in the company had been invited to have their say before the two important votes on the agenda. Several rows of chairs were arranged in expanding circles around the main table, every one of them occupied.

Support staff scurried around, handing out documents, pens, and coffee. All appeared harried. Where the Sheppards gathered, noise and disorder were the norm. They drank heavily, talked loudly, and inevitably asked what was in a deal for themselves. Today was no exception.

Hector was seated at the head of the table as the undisputed leader of the company. Ryan and Sophia Sheppard were absent. The aging couple hadn't been to a single meeting since Harry was arrested. Besides the two brothers, the only people staying silent in their chairs were Dante, Liam, and Noah as discussion continued on the topic of what to do with the Luce stock.

Liam and Verity Luce owned the biggest chunk of shares in Gateway outside of the Sheppards, but the stock was held in trust by the board. At the onset of today's meeting, Noah Andersen announced Liam's intention to sue the board for the freedom to manage his own assets, setting off the uproar.

Noah allowed the chaos in the room to continue for a good ten minutes. As he got to his feet again, the discord quietened to soft rumblings. "May I remind you," the lawyer began, "of the excuse you gave for holding on to the Luce stock this long? All of you insisted Will Luce was killed over the embezzlement of company funds, so his adult children didn't have the right to manage their inheritance. In any case, the trust was airtight. You didn't *need* an excuse to keep the Luces from doing anything with the shares except enjoy the dividends. However, you and your acting CEO, Hector Sheppard, wouldn't allow even such a limited benefit. Your lawyers claimed Liam would use the dividend money to help Harry, and state law forbade a killer from profiting from the victim's death. Imaginative interpretation of the slayer rule, but you somehow got a judge to agree. Liam and Verity have yet to see a penny from what their father bequeathed them."

As Noah paused to let his words sink in, Harry glanced at Hector. Anger at this public reprimand was clear on the face of the elder Sheppard son, but even he wouldn't dare raise his voice against the former attorney general.

"It's been several months since Harry was exonerated," continued Noah. "The slayer rule no longer applies. William Luce, Jr. and Rhea Verity Luce are hereby demanding all dividends owed thus far, minus the amount embezzled by their father. If this board has any shame, they would also vote to release control of the stock to Liam and Verity."

Not out of shame, but because no one could find another excuse, the tally was lopsided in favor of the Luces on the matter of the dividends. Control of the stock was also returned, albeit only with two-thirds margin. Not many were willing to risk being hauled to court over what Noah said was willful misinterpretation of the law only to keep an innocent man in prison.

Liam stood. "I'm not a board member, but I did get my shares back…" He checked his watch. "…two minutes ago, and I'd like to start things on a good note. So let me first wish Harry a happy birthday."

There was sudden shifting in the chairs. A few muttered greetings came Harry's way.

With a grin, Harry inclined his head. "Thank you for remembering, my friend."

"Now," said Liam, tone changing. "I want to ask a question before Noah explains why you should be doing as he suggests regarding Harry's potential return to Gateway. Almost nine years ago, I waited outside this building as the same board gathered to kick Harry out. The court hadn't ruled on the case yet. Forget ruling, the case hadn't even *got* to a court yet. Hell, you didn't even wait for an arrest. You used my father's death as pretext to kick someone out. I'd like to know what it was Harry did to y'all that you wanted him out."

"We didn't need any pretext," argued one particular board member. "A business has the right to fire employees who do not act in the best interests of the employer."

"Not acting in the best interests according to whom?" demanded Liam. "Harry worked his butt off just as much as everyone else to build this company. He objected when Steven Kingsley took advantage of a government investigation and stole the network from his cousins. Some of you found what Steven did A-OK, but was there a vote on Gateway's official stance on the matter prior to my father's murder? A statement from the CEO? At least a memo from Hector?"

Silence reigned for close to a minute. Then, Dante said, "Let me answer the question. I am told Ryan and Sophia and their children held a discussion in their home immediately after Brad Kingsley left Panama. Those discussions were done by a family and have no bearing in a business setting. Harry still did us the courtesy of taking a leave of absence before he started working on a pardon for Brad. Even then, there was no announcement of any company policy against talking to the media about the situation. We never put Harry's involvement to a board vote until Will's unfortunate death. So yes, Liam. Your father's passing was the catalyst for Harry's ouster."

"After Harry was convicted, the board patted itself on the back for doing its bit toward justice," Noah said, remaining in his chair. "Many of you spoke against him to the press. You lot forbade him and Sabrina from selling stock because the money would be used to help the Kingsley brothers. You also withheld Harry's *dividends* with some cockamamie excuse. Sabrina's money was also mostly withheld, except for what she would need to support herself and her son. You wouldn't allow Daniel Barrons to sell his or Lilah's stock in Gateway."

"Mr. Andersen," interrupted one of the company lawyers. "Harry was accused of the murder of someone who embezzled from the company. The board wanted to do an internal review before releasing any cash. As for Sabrina... she was given shares in Gateway when she was still a child. All of it was held in trust, same as the Luce stock. Sabrina didn't ask for full control even after she got married. The stock issued to Daniel and Delilah Barrons always came with strings attached. One of the conditions on it was how Ryan Sheppard—or his agent—would control transactions as well as dividend checks. The clause was added to make sure the partner companies could never use the stock to take over. In all these cases, Gateway had the legal right to do what they did."

"What about the moral right?" asked Noah. "You made sure my client—Harry—didn't have the cash or the breathing room to fight Gateway's board as well as the flawed system which landed him in Sing Sing. Today, no thanks to any of you, he has been exonerated."

"Hindsight is twenty-twenty," someone called out. "None of us knew he was innocent. We acted on the information we had at the time."

"My client doesn't expect anyone to be clairvoyant, sir," Noah said. "However, you do have more info now. You know who the real murderer was. You know you had a hand—albeit an unwitting one—in keeping an innocent man in prison. For eight years! Yet the board hasn't taken a single step to reverse course on its unfortunate decision regarding Petty Officer First Class Harry Sheppard."

"Fact remains we don't have to give him his job back," insisted the same member who made the point before. "New York is an at-will employment state. Which would mean it's the employer's prerogative to decide who works in the business."

"Thank you for enlightening me on the law," Noah said, provoking mild laughter. "What you might want to remember is this: Harry's activities against the Kingsley family might be considered protected. He was a whistleblower. Although Dante confirmed how the Luce case was the catalyst, the board itself has insisted Harry was fired for actions considered detrimental to the network."

"Whistleblower?" asked yet another of the corporate lawyers. He chuckled. "C'mon now."

Noah smiled nastily. "We can argue about it in court. In this light, the board's act of withholding dividends takes on a new hue, doesn't it? So does the fact many of you tried to blacken Harry's reputation in the media. Both actions could be construed as malicious attempts to prevent my client from exposing Steven Kingsley's crimes... who happens to be your acting CEO's close friend, by the way."

Hector didn't respond, but his face darkened further.

"No one appropriated the dividends," the corporate lawyer said. "The cash was initially kept in trust for Petty Officer Sheppard's eventual release after his sentence, then redirected to the veteran's shelter as our COO, Dante Maro, suggested. A move endorsed by the petty officer. He signed the agreement on the matter. He also had other assets, which he allocated to the staff of his deceased wife's strip club. His lack of money to fight his case was not Gateway's doing."

"He signed the agreement about the dividends because it was a better use for the money than banking it for his old age," said Noah. "He might or might not have still decided to finance the veteran's shelter, but it should not have been done because you left him with no personal use for the cash. Bottom line is you purposefully withheld funds he could've used to prove his innocence because of the risk he posed to Steven Kingsley and the network."

"Really, Harry?" a distant cousin called from the back row. "You know that's not how it went down."

"Perspective depends on where you stand," said Harry. "From our end of things, it's exactly how it went down."

"Especially when we see how the board made no move to correct the grievous error it made years ago," Noah said. "The exoneration, the Medal of Freedom Harry was given, the support he has among the public... despite all of it, Hector Sheppard called this meeting only after I sent a legal notice. Nothing we've seen so far disproves our suspicions of the actual reason behind the termination."

"So what are you going to do now?" asked the same cousin. "Sue your own family?"

"Family." Noah clucked. "The word implies he owes you his allegiance. I have the minutes from the meeting nine years ago. One of you argued how Harry should be fired regardless of his connection to the CEO. The argument was correct at the time and is correct now. Family relationships should have no bearing on how Harry responds to the injustice perpetrated on him by this board. However, he prefers to give you one last chance to rectify your mistake. Any further action will depend on the outcome of today's meeting."

"May I?" said Hector, getting to his feet. "My name has been brought up several times as the bad guy. There are several instances I could point to where my brother was blatantly unfair to me, but I don't see the point of back-and-forth recriminations. So let me admit. Yes, I wanted Harry fired. Yes, I urged the board to withhold dividends. I believed then as I believe now how my duty is to do what's best for the organization regardless of personal feelings. None of it had anything to do with whistleblowing or other protected activity. Harry knows it, and I suspect his lawyer does, too. They're both aware it's gonna take a heckuva lot of convincing for a court to rule against Gateway on the matter. It won't be in their best interests to pursue that route."

Noah raised an eyebrow. "Allow us to decide what's in our own best interests."

Inclining his head, Hector continued, "Still, Liam mentioned how there was no official directive from the company on dealing with the change in the network's leadership. He's right. It was an oversight on my part. I assumed a verbal warning would suffice whether it was given in our home or in Gateway's corporate office. Things did come to a head mostly after Will's death. My brother has been absolved of the crime, so in the interests of justice, I'd like all of us present to vote on Harry's reinstatement. If we allow him back, he'll return to his previous position and will work under the supervision of Mr. Dante Maro. I've been carrying out my father's responsibilities as CEO, and I intend to remain in *my* position. Rest assured... Harry's return will not automatically mean a change in direction for Gateway on the network issue. There will be another discussion on the matter, and this time, there will be an official statement."

"Before you vote," Liam interjected, "remember how this business was built. All the people who worked on it and how hard."

"No one's forgotten anything," snapped yet another Sheppard cousin, "but only two factors should matter. Will Harry's return be a net positive for Gateway? Secondly, the whistleblower threat if he's not allowed to return. Will it damage the company and cause financial harm to stockholders?"

"We'll do a roll-call vote," said Dante. "Each member's name will be called, and the member may respond with yes, no, or abstain. I'll go first. Yes to the motion to reinstate Harry Sheppard to his prior position in Gateway. Hector?"

"Abstain," said Harry's brother.

"Yes," said the next member.

"No."

"No."

"Abstain."

It got to four yeses, three no, two abstain. Four yeses, four no, two abstain. Keeping his breathing even, Harry waited for the last two members.

"Yes."

Inclining his head in Harry's direction, the twelfth one said, "Yes."

Mild applause broke out. Across the conference table, Noah nodded. Liam let out an audible sigh.

Clenching and unclenching his right fist once, Harry got to his feet. "Thank you," he said. "Especially to those who spoke up for me... Liam, Dante, Noah. And Hector, thank you for allowing this vote." Glancing toward the CEO's secretary, Harry added, "I'd like my old office back. Today. Please arrange it." He grinned at Dante. "Sorry, old man, but I would also like my secretary back." After Harry's departure, Natasha had gone to work for the COO.

Chapter 22

Watching Liam and Noah file out behind the rest of the attendees, Harry waited for the inevitable conversation with his brother. He had not bothered to keep his trip to upstate New York a secret. By now, Hector would've heard chatter about the steps taken by Samba's mother to include the name of the father—Harry Sheppard—in the boy's birth certificate.

The lad certainly knew. He'd called Gateway the week before and asked to speak to Harry. Since the man in question had yet to rejoin the company, the confused receptionist redirected the kid to Dante. Samba had only one demand. He wanted to meet Harry.

It wasn't possible. The boy needed more time and attention than Harry could give at the moment. More importantly, there was simply no explaining away the discrepancies in the tale his mother weaved for him. Harry didn't have a problem lying through his teeth if it would actually help, but Samba was rapidly getting to the age where he'd pick up on the falsehoods and would hate his mother for the deception. Remaining incommunicado was Harry's only option if he didn't want to add to Jorah's problems.

Placating the boy with lies about Harry being out of town, Dante hung up. He made his displeasure clear to Harry. Dante had been an exemplary parent to his only child who now lived in California. The son—an aeronautical engineer—was a busy man, and Dante had been widowed for a long time. He was clearly lonely, which made him even more angry on behalf of the lad desperate to hear from his father. He was right, of course, but being right didn't help him come up with a solution.

Nor could Dante stop gossip from spreading. The receptionist who took Samba's call was a Sheppard, and she tattled to other members of the family who worked for Gateway. They were aware of Hector's connection to the town where Jorah lived. They also knew Harry never showed qualms admitting to his relationships before. Speculation was rampant within the clan on Samba's actual parentage, and Hector would want to make his stance clear to his younger brother.

Sure enough, Hector said, "Harry, a word while you're waiting for your press conference."

Noah had previously arranged a quick media event after the board meeting. Whether or not Harry was welcomed back into the family fold, the papers would want every dirty detail, and he could use the opportunity to hammer home the dangers of letting power-drunk businessmen control the energy sector. It would be another half an hour before the press meet started.

With a small nod, Harry stayed in his chair as Hector shut the door behind the last man to exit the conference room. Bits of gray marked Hector's blond hair, and the fine lines around his blue eyes spoke of his age, but the boxer remained as fit as always. Hector still owned the gym he opened in his twenties. The place relocated to the South Tower years ago, operating only one floor below Gateway.

"I don't have much hope of getting you to listen to me," began the elder Sheppard son, pulling a chair back to sit. "Still, got to try one more time. Steven is the man we should be supporting."

Harry blinked. "Steven? You want to talk about—"

"He's been the good guy throughout," said Hector. "When Genesis was in trouble, he offered to get Godwin involved. We were nobodies, and Steven still offered help."

Of course Hector didn't give a damn about the Amish girl and her son. With difficulty, Harry pushed aside thoughts of the disturbed young lad.

"Genesis existed at the time only thanks to the cash from Lilah's parents," Harry pointed out. "Andrew loaned us the money to start Gateway."

"Because he wanted our support in adopting Dan."

"And Lilah agreed to the adoption only because we—the Sheppards—were desperate for funds."

"She and her brother were amply repaid," bit out Hector. "Just how many times do you need this explained, Harry? We didn't *have* to give Lilah or Dan anything after losing Genesis. It's how the market functions. Investors lose money if the company goes under. But Father gave them stock in Gateway, anyway, which is now worth millions. Not to mention the billions they stand to inherit from Andrew."

"Stock they never asked for," Harry countered.

Groaning, Hector said, "Regardless, she was repaid. Andrew himself wouldn't have been with Brad and his brothers if not for Dan. They're family."

"Sabrina is our sister. She's married to Alex."

"An alliance you arranged," Hector said bitterly. "You made sure she never got a chance to meet Steven."

"No one can arrange for two people to love each other," Harry said. "I might have encouraged Alex to spend time with her, but they fell in love all by themselves. There's also Aunt Patrice. She's family, too, no matter how many times removed. The Sheppards have always considered blood as blood no matter how many generations separate us." And no matter how easily they stabbed each other in the back.

"*Aunt* Patrice." Hector visibly gritted his teeth. "She was one of the people I called when Sanders got Father and Mother arrested. Damn woman wouldn't even pick up the phone."

Because she— Harry couldn't say it out loud. Even if Patrice gave her permission, Richard wouldn't want the story to become public knowledge. Nor would the info change Hector's mind about Patrice or her sons. "All our ties are with Brad and his brothers," said Harry. "They're not perfect, but Brad is still miles better than Steven."

"So you say," retorted Hector. "Steven is a better leader in my opinion, and I value my friendship with him."

Harry inclined his head. "I value my friendship with Alex."

"Enough to give up the rest of your family? Father and Mother agree with me about leaving Steven in charge of the network."

"I cannot bail on Alex for them," said Harry. "Not for you, not for anyone else in the family. Not even for wives and children."

"Father is sick. He had a heart attack while you were in prison. Who knows how much time he has left?"

"This situation is killing him," agreed Harry. "Mother, too. No one wants to see their grown children fighting."

Hector asked, "Will you step aside? For their sake."

"Will you?"

"My position on this has always been about what's good for Gateway and the Sheppard family. Yours is about which Kingsley gets to control the network."

Harry sighed. "It was never about the Kingsleys. Believe it or not, it's not about Lilah, either. She would tell you herself. When we started this alliance, I was dumb enough to dream it would be a benevolent structure. What it ended up being is yet another empire."

Hector's eyelids flickered. "Regardless of your current thoughts on the network, it exists, and Steven is in charge. Gateway will continue to support him. I won't forget to send out an official statement about it this time. If you oppose us openly at the network's board meeting..."

"I'll be out once again," Harry acknowledged, "but I can't retreat. My conscience won't let me leave the likes of Steven in charge."

"I don't believe this." Face ruddy, Hector slammed a fist on the table, making a glass totter. "You're essentially turning your back on the company we built as a family. You're turning your back on your own blood."

"I don't have to," said Harry. "Gateway might not support Brad, but you don't have to support Steven, either."

"Stay neutral?" Hector asked incredulously. "Even if I do so for your sake, the shareholders won't let it be. They will riot."

"In which case, recuse only yourself from the board vote with the reason you have connections to both sides. Let Gateway's board decide—without your input or mine—what they want to do. Let someone else deal with the network. At least Father and Mother won't be forced to watch us fight."

"But you won't return the favor."

"I can't," said Harry.

Chapter 23

Later in the day

"What the hell is going on?" Alex asked, confused by Dante's news.

"Shh." The COO of Gateway threw a furtive glance around his office suite even though the two men were alone. Dante had already been wrinkled and gray-haired when the five brothers and Lilah left on their exile. The man couldn't be more than sixty now, but the expression of doom on his dark face made him seem like some ancient oracle. "Hector's idea," said Dante. "I'm sure of it."

As soon as Alex got word on the outcome of Gateway's board meeting, he'd grabbed a six-pack and headed to the company offices at the World Trade Center. After the Wheeler debacle, this was a turn worth celebrating. A chance to bring the numbers at least back to where they were. If Harry could get Gateway to switch sides...

There was also another matter they needed to discuss—Harry's idea of going after Kingsley Corp to stop Steven. Like Alex, his brothers had been stunned at the suggestion and didn't know what to say. It didn't take them more than a night to decide the plan was out of the question. The business wasn't merely a source of income for the clan. It was part of every Kingsley's identity. The five of them simply weren't sure how to inform Harry and the rest of their well-wishers.

Alex would sit with Harry and chalk out an alternative. What better time for it than Harry's own first day back in the family fold?

What Alex didn't expect was to be dragged straight into Dante's office. Apparently, Steven already showed up to congratulate the newly reinstated executive, in his hands a bottle of the finest wine from the Kingsley cellar.

"Steven works here now," Dante reminded Alex. "Or he was at the gym."

Alex huffed out a breath, trying to tamp down sudden anger. Hector's boxing gym was one floor below Gateway's HQ. Peter

Kingsley Company's New York offices were also in the South Tower, same as Barrons and Gateway. Kingsley Corp digs were farther up Manhattan Island along Corporate Row, but Steven ruled the oil empire from the same chambers once occupied by his cousins.

"Chances are he stashed a bottle in his desk for precisely this situation," said Dante, "and ran here as soon as Hector called with updates."

"Nah." Shaking his head, Alex set the beer on the small table by the door. "I mean yes. Steven could've anticipated this outcome, and Hector probably did call, but why?"

"Heh?" Dante blinked rapidly. "The Kingsleys are worried Harry will talk Gateway into changing votes is why."

"I get it," said Alex. "What I mean is Steven and his buddies framed Harry for murder. They know he ain't having a change of heart about..." Alex growled. "Is Natasha in the room? Harry shouldn't be left alone with Steven. I don't trust the damn sonuvabitch."

"Steven's not gonna attack anyone here." Dante's brows drew together. "Right?"

"I don't trust him," repeated Alex, turning to jerk open the door.

"I'll go with you," said Dante.

#

The door to Harry's old office suite was wide open. Alex charged in ahead of Dante, only to stumble to a halt.

There was no blood, thank God. No signs of yet another attempt on Harry's life.

Clerks were carrying files in and out of the main room. A cleaning lady was running a cloth over the furniture, and Natasha flung out directions in an imperious voice, telling the two janitors exactly how her former/current boss liked the room set up.

Along the wall to Alex's left was a love seat which hadn't been there ten years ago. Stretched out on it was Harry, apparently taking a nap in the middle of the chaos. His head was on one of the armrests, his legs flung across the other. Business suit, tie, gleaming dress shoes—everything remained unwrinkled, spotless.

Seated in a chair pulled up next to Harry's head was Steven, the bottle of wine in his hands. He was also dressed for business unlike Alex who was in jeans and a tee. The thieving sonuvabitch glowered at the new arrivals.

"What the..." Palms up, Dante turned to Natasha.

She rolled her eyes. "Harry said he was tired after the press conference and went to sleep, but Mr. Kingsley still insisted on coming up to the office. He says he'll wait until Harry wakes."

Of course Steven knew Harry was trying to dodge an unpleasant conversation.

Alex glared at his cousin. "Guess what, Tash? I don't mind waiting, either." He dragged one of the rolling chairs to the foot of the love seat. Budweiser set on the carpeted floor, Alex plonked himself into the leather chair.

A couple of seconds passed with Dante and Natasha gaping first at Alex, then at Steven, then back at Alex. Even the clerks and the cleaning staff stopped their work to watch the unfolding scene. "You two are just going to sit there and stare at Harry?" Dante finally asked. "While he sleeps?"

"I'm not going anywhere," said Steven.

"Me, neither," said Alex. It wouldn't be long before Harry was forced to open his eyes and throw the criminal out instead of simply avoiding him. *Nap, my ass.* The setup was faker than Sabrina's attempts at working out. Alex smiled at the thought of his wife. The mischief in her bright-green gaze, the love and laughter in their home, the sounds of the two boys and Hema and Tara—family gave a man a sense of belonging.

"I have to get this place ready," Natasha said severely.

An incomprehensible mutter came from the love seat. Swinging his legs out, Harry sat up and stretched as though actually waking from a snooze. He blinked sleepily at Alex. "Hey! Whatchu doing here?"

"I got here first," said Steven.

Jerking slightly, Harry turned in the other direction. "Steven! What a surprise!"

You ain't winning an Oscar anytime, mate, Alex said silently.

Holding up the bottle, Steven inclined his head. "Your secretary took down my name for an appointment before whatshisface showed up."

Alex hoped like hell his brother-in-law remembered how the Kingsley cousins weren't above a little poisoning. The damned wine would have to be flushed down the toilet.

"Put me down in the book, too, please," Alex said to Natasha.

"You don't need an appointment to talk to me," Harry pointed out.

"Merely keeping it official," said Alex.

"Oh?" Harry raised an eyebrow and stood. "I didn't plan on starting work until tomorrow, but..." Glancing at his secretary, he asked, "You think we could get a few minutes? Alex, let's—"

"I should get the first turn," insisted Steven. "I was here first."

"But I saw Alex first," Harry objected.

Steven's glare got more ferocious. "Is this how Gateway conducts business?"

"Alex is also younger than you," Harry said without missing a beat.

Wha— Alex blinked.

"What?" Steven asked. "He's not a two-year-old to get first dibs on some toy. Enough fooling around... let's talk like grown men."

With an audible huff, Harry signaled Natasha to clear the room. Everyone left except Harry, Alex, Steven, and Dante. Leaning a hip on the ebony desk, the COO kept watching.

Once the door closed, Harry sat back down. "All righty then. Steven, my brother considers you a friend, and Alex is married to my sister. To the family as a whole, I suppose the two sides are somewhat equal. So I'll give you both a hearing. If this is an attempt at getting my blessing, lemme make it clear I speak only for myself. Yes, I was allowed back into Gateway, but it doesn't mean I'm in a position to promise the company's support to anyone. There *is* a possibility Hector will let the board make the decision on their own, but I'm fairly confident they won't be following my lead. In fact, they're more likely to do the opposite of what I suggest and show me the door yet again. So there you have it. Me on one side with no billion-dollar business to give me clout or the entirety of Gateway. What do you want? Alex, you go first. Me or Gateway?"

"What a damn question," Alex exclaimed. "You were there for me and my brothers when we split from Kingsley Corp. You were with us through thick and thin. Yeah, we'd like Gateway's support, but I don't give a shit about the company if it means you're not with us."

Steven sat up in his chair and stared incredulously. At his spot next to the ebony desk, Dante straightened.

Harry didn't respond for a couple of seconds. Then, he turned to Steven. "You heard it, my man. If Gateway decides to stand by you, so be it. I'll be with Alex and his brothers."

Chapter 24

A few hours later

Of all the people Lilah expected to call her, Harry's ex-wife was not one. Verity Luce should've been the last person to send an urgent summons to the Temple residence asking Lilah to show up at Harry's apartment. Apparently, he and Alex were hammered. Too drunk to even answer the darned phone. The caller left a message on the answering machine, which Verity heard. Despite the late hour, David Kingsley's secretary was on his way to talk to Harry. Verity contacted the first person she could think of—her brother.

Liam was back home in DC and out on a date, so he directed his sister to ring Temple's residence. After the morning meeting at Gateway, Noah had gone to Albany to confer with the governor of New York and the two U.S. senators from the state. Lilah was the only one left in the household who could do something.

When she exited the car in front of the apartment building, her eyes went to the plaque on the edifice next to it. Genesis—the name of the Sheppards' old company. This five-story structure bearing the same moniker housed homeless veterans. An old fellow was seated on the stoop, staring in Lilah's direction. "You're the broad from the papers," the man stated, eyes squinting in the dark, weather-beaten face.

The guard driving the car pulled away, looking for a parking spot close by. His comrade took half a step forward as though to hustle Lilah inside.

Ignoring him, she asked the old man, "Did you need something?"

"No." He shrugged. "I 'spect you're going up to see the petty officer. Tell him thanks from me. I meant to a while ago, but he leaves us alone unless someone asks to talk."

"Thanks for..." Lilah queried.

The old fellow looked upward. "This place. What else? The petty officer and the lawyer—Andersen—got us a roof over our heads."

Noah decided how Temple Foundation allocated its funds, and Harry redirected his dividends over the last few years to the organization. Part of it went to the down payment for the building, the rest serving as seed money for a legal aid office for prisoners, social rehab for them after release, jobs training for disabled cops and correction officers and military veterans, and scholarship programs for the children of those killed protecting their fellow citizens. Businesses smelling PR soon started donating. In recent years, even parent-teacher organizations working with troubled teenagers had approached Noah for help.

There were also Harry's outside interests, the sports bar/restaurant chain operated by the former angels of Eden being the main one. Liam oversaw the enterprise.

"Some of the younger men here were in Iraq," continued the elderly veteran. "They agree with what the petty officer said on TV about the oil business." Harry had been blunt in his assessment of the current state of the energy sector. The oil network was supposed to prevent instability, but the wrong leaders could well create chaos to suit their purposes. Such chaos would include war, economic devastation, death. "If there's anything we can do to help..." offered the old man.

"I'll let him know," said Lilah.

"Also, a couple of us did the run this year with Rolling Thunder," said the fellow. Lilah's unfamiliarity with the event must have shown, and he explained, "It's a motorcycle rally in DC on Memorial Day weekend. You know, for POWs and MIAs. Since the petty officer likes to ride, we thought maybe he could go with us next year."

"I'm sure he'd love to," Lilah said. Harry didn't get many chances these days to take his Harley out on leisure runs, but he would find the time for a cause so close to his heart. Alex would probably want to go as well.

Once the two idiots sobered up, that is. Stomping up the five floors to Harry's home, Lilah ground her teeth hard enough to give herself a jaw ache. At the door, she turned to her guard. "Please wait here."

Huffing out a breath, Lilah raised her knuckles, but the door flung open before she could knock. A platinum blonde dressed in ripped jeans and a designer crop top stood with her hand clutching the knob. "Thank God," breathed Verity, her voice lilting.

That bad? was Lilah's first thought. Loud singing came from within. Not terribly off-key, but certainly high in decibel level.

"Liam said Alex would be here, so I stopped by to say hello," Verity explained, some of the former hostility returning to her tone. "And I wanted to thank Harry for what he did about the stock. They were already celebrating. Then, the Kingsley fellow called."

"You're staying until he's gone, right?" Lilah asked. The presence of the former Mrs. Harry Sheppard was needed to ward off any accusations of hanky-panky with Alex. If Verity left, there wasn't even the option of dragging Sabrina to the East Village apartment. She and a couple of friends from her hacking days were at some auto show in Kentucky. The other way for Lilah to escape charges of adultery was to have her guards inside, listening to the conversation—something she didn't want. "Please," she requested Harry's ex.

Verity didn't respond for a few seconds. Her dislike of Lilah was clear even before the exile. That Lilah never did anything to sabotage Harry's marriage was irrelevant. It didn't matter how Verity had moved on with her life. Lilah would forever be the other woman in Verity's eyes. God only knew what she thought now since neither Harry nor Lilah had made any moves to get together.

"Whatever," Verity finally said. "But only because Liam said you might need help with the Kingsley person."

Entering the apartment was like stepping through a time warp. Oh, things had changed. The television was much larger, and there was now an intercom to communicate with anyone at the main entrance of the building. The refrigerator looked too high-end to be the old one.

The men sprawled on the couch were the same old Alex and Harry. Joking, laughing, totally smashed. Beyond business meetings.

"Hell-lo, Lilah!" Alex called, waggling his eyebrows. "Did you bring a birthday present? I brought beer!"

"I can see," Lilah said dryly. Her gift—a toy version of Harry's Harley—was probably in the office. There would also be an envelope containing the IOUs from the card game she made him play at the end of the exile. He'd refused to rip them up and throw out the pieces, and he refused to return her Eiffel Tower pendant even when she mock-threatened him with the small claims court.

"Born to Be Wild," Harry belted out, holding up his glass in greeting.

Massaging her brow with a fingertip, Lilah tried to figure out a way to salvage the situation. The Kingsleys were sending yet another emissary for one single reason. Alex's refusal of Gateway's support had confused Steven and his father, and they were fishing for info.

At the moment, the duo in the apartment could not be trusted not to blurt every thought to the enemy.

Calling the emissary to reschedule was the obvious solution. After all, those who showed up after sunset—without even an appointment—ran the risk of not getting the meeting.

Thing was Lilah harbored a suspicion Alex himself showed up with a motive besides celebrating Harry's birthday. Alex was here to tell Harry that Kingsley Corp was off-limits, and Lilah was anxious to hear the outcome of the discussion. Without the emissary, she wouldn't have an excuse to stay.

Lurching to his feet, Harry inquired with all the gravitas of conveying mission-critical information, "Did you hear about Gateway? What Alex did?"

Verity groaned. "Yes, she knows what Alex did. *I* know what he did. The whole building probably knows by now."

Harry shook his head. "Great friend. Couldn't ask for better."

Hiding a hiccup with his hand, Alex called, "So're you. The best."

"I've been listening to this for the last two hours," moaned Verity.

"Lilah," called Harry. "I'm gonna tell only him... the safe house."

"Safe..." Lilah blinked. "Sorry, what?"

Holding a finger to his lips, Harry said, "Shh... it's a secret, but he can visit."

"A secret," Lilah echoed, trying to make sense of the words. Any emissary would be equally confused— "Why not?" she asked, grinning at a sudden idea.

Verity frowned. "Heh?"

"Harry, does the liquor store down the street deliver?" Lilah inquired. "I feel like some wine. Also, the guards are going to need chairs."

"Wine?" parroted Verity, gray-blue eyes rounded. "Chairs? Have *all* of you lost your minds? What about the Kingsley person?"

"He's gonna tell Grandfather..." Alex started. With a grimace of intense concentration, he corrected himself. "He's gonna tell Uncle David..." Alex waved his bottle about. "...what he sees. Friends. Nothing matters m-more. No network or nothin' comes... I don't care... damn board."

Yes, the two idiots were indeed celebrating a birthday. And mourning the final nail in the coffin of a straightforward win with a successful board vote.

Well, Lilah would make sure the Kingsleys didn't get the satisfaction of watching the enemy bleed. And no corporate spy was going to get any usable information from Harry or Alex tonight.

Two hours and a bottle of sweet Rosé later, the two men were where she wanted them.

Lilah tilted her glass one way and the other as she studied the emissary. Harry remained on the couch and didn't break his song to acknowledge the visitor, while Alex was inadvertently rude. Rising from his spot on the couch, Alex wobbled toward the one free chair in the room and pushed it with his foot all the way to the emissary.

"No, thanks," said the chap, eyeing the chair with an expression of distaste. "I'm good up here."

Shrugging, Alex mumbled something and stumbled back to the couch. Lilah and Verity stayed put in their own chairs, within reach of Alex.

"I wanna nap," announced Harry, yawning.

Alex snickered. "For real th-thish time?"

Harry fell on his side and stretched his legs down the couch. Which meant his shoes were now on Alex's lap.

Alex yawned, too. Slouching, he appeared to be trying to put his feet on the coffee table. Somehow, he ended up placing one foot on Lilah's knee and the second on Verity's thigh.

"Get your..." Verity pushed the offending foot from her lap.

Scooting the chair back, Lilah stood, and Alex landed on the floor. Consequently, Harry suffered the same fate but hoisted himself to a sitting position, back against the arm of the couch.

"Maybe I... ahh..." The emissary looked around the room as though searching for an escape route. "I should go."

"Go," Harry said. "And tell 'em *all* to have a party. Who knows what's gonna happen tom-morrow?"

"What?" asked the emissary, sounding dazed.

"Godwin 'n' David 'n'... 'n'... whatshisname?" Harry continued. "The gen'ral."

"Potts," said the emissary.

"Yup," said Harry, nodding heavily. "Look at this guy," he continued, indicating Alex who appeared to be settling on the floor. "Tell that dumbass... you know... Steven... he picked on the wrooong man. Wrong woman, too." Harry somehow clambered to his feet. "I wasn't there." His stance was dangerously unsteady, and the words were slurred. Still, the air in the room seemed to vibrate with sudden tension. "She needed me, and I wasn't there. So tell 'em to whoop it up now. Alex and I will come by. Soon. Got some scores to settle."

#

Shutting the door behind the emissary, Lilah turned. "Alex, one of my guards can drive you—"

"Nope," he said. "I want Chinese."

There was no more alcohol, but Harry and Alex went on eating and singing without showing a single sign of wanting to sleep. Each time Lilah suggested to Alex that he leave with one of her guards, he claimed he wasn't ready yet. Verity stayed, thank God, stating she was also now too drunk to drive. Close to dawn, Harry recovered enough to play on his saxophone while Alex boogied with Verity.

Collapsing into a chair after an energetic twirl, Alex said, "Phew, I'm beat. Harry, man, let's talk now. Important stuff... business."

"I s'ppose you want privacy," Verity said, getting to her feet. "But I need to crash here for a while. Dibs on the bed."

"Ain't anything you can't hear," Alex said. "The plan's not gonna work, anyway."

"What plan?" Harry asked from the couch.

Neither he nor Alex sounded as slurred as before.

"We can't attack Kingsley Corp," stated Alex. "My brothers agree."

Moving as quietly as she possibly could, Lilah adjusted herself in her chair. Verity remained standing, confusion in her eyes as she glanced from one man to the other.

Harry turned his head just enough to stare at Alex. "What do you want to do then? Steven will get all of you, especially Brad."

"I know," admitted Alex. "Neil and Scott's uncle... Gateway... the deadline... we're in deep shit. But there's gotta be some other way."

Harry sighed and brought the saxophone back to his lips.

Say it, Lilah urged. *Tell him the only other way out is an antitrust investigation. Destroy the network. No network... nothing to fight over.*

The first notes of "Stairway To Heaven" flowed. The song Harry used to play for her.

Breaking off after a couple of lines, he asked, "Trust me?"

Alex frowned. "What do you mean? Yeah, I trust you."

"I mean it's…" Heaving in a deep breath, Harry said, "We're not there yet. Gotta hold 'em for now."

Nodding, Alex said, "We do have to think about it more, but I want everything to be over soon. My wife… my son…"

"This is boring," Verity announced. "I'm going to sleep."

Message received, Lilah said in her mind. Harry wanted to hold on to his cards for now, biding his time until zero other options were left before the Kingsley brothers. She just hoped he realized Alex was right. They *were* in deep doo-doo.

On the coffee table, the phone rang. It was Verity who answered. Frowning mildly, she held it out to Lilah. "For you… it's Mr. Andersen."

Lilah glanced at the clock on the device before putting it to her ear. 4:30 AM. "Noah?" she queried. "Everything okay?"

"The officers at the house told me you were at Harry's," the old lawyer said abruptly. "I tried reaching both of you on your phones."

"Mine probably needs to be charged, but…" Lilah started, then stopped. Noah knew she wouldn't forget the threat of legal action from Brad. This call was about something else.

"The U.S. embassies in Nairobi and Dar es Salaam just got bombed," said the former attorney general. "CIA thinks it's bin Laden."

Part IX

Chapter 25

Two weeks later, late August 1998

Long Island, New York

There he went again, serenading the bloody motorbike! The voice was nice, though, with just enough depth to it to avoid being heavy. Setting the sketchbook on her bed, Tara went to the window. Michael was down in the yard, shirtless as he worked on the scratched and dented Yamaha he rolled home two months ago. The chick he was dating was probably pissed. He'd spent every free minute of summer vacation with the bike, either screwing back the rearview mirror after it fell off for the zillionth time or taking riding lessons from Maestro Alex.

Sabrina glared at the Yamaha every time she met it. Still, Maestro's wife was happy to see father and son finally talking.

Tara didn't get it at all. Maestro knew the right thing to say to her even after her mother's death. While Tara's own parents didn't think twice before sticking her with a drug lord for a guardian, it was Alex who insisted on getting her out of the mafia's line of fire. The same man couldn't seem to find the words to apologize to his only son.

"I'm sorry," muttered Tara. Sorry I didn't tell my brother to stop acting like a jealous *burro* over stupid gossip. Sorry I let him get us all into trouble. Sorry I had to leave you and your mom. Sorry I couldn't find a way to make it back to you sooner. "How is it hard to say?"

"Depends," said a voice behind Tara.

Startled, Tara spun and clapped a hand to her forehead. "Gabe!" She'd thought everyone else was downstairs, talking to their visitor—Sabrina's brother. He'd shown up to wish Hema luck as she left for college.

No matter what else was going on, they talked mostly about the network, which Tara wasn't interested in. Some stupid guy called bin Laden was another hot topic.

Gabriel stayed put at the open door, a large bowl in his hands. "Whatchu doing?" he asked, tossing popcorn into his mouth as he craned his neck toward the windows. There was no way he could spot Michael in the yard from that angle, but the loud singing gave away the object of Tara's scrutiny. Gabriel's eyebrows rose. "Ooohhh..." he said meaningfully. *"¡Mi'ja!"*

Scowling, Tara said, "Hey, don't start thinking stuff. I'm studying for my placement exam." The school wanted to test her before deciding which grade to park her in. "Mike's making too much noise," she complained. "It's distracting."

"Yeah?" Gabriel nodded, taking a step into the room. "Lemme tell him to shut the hell up—"

"No," Tara said quickly. "I was gonna close the window when you scared the shit out of me."

She didn't want him spotting the sketch pad on the bed. The stupid book was only partially hidden by the messy sheets, and it was open to the pencil rendering of Michael on his bike—*sans* a shirt. Faded jeans, a bandana. Flute hanging from one of his belt loops since he played it like a dream. A gun was tucked into his ankle boot for the way he showed up in Tara's life on a helicopter, wielding a weapon like some warrior angel.

No one would believe her claim that she was only trying to sketch designs as she did for almost everyone she met.

"A'right," said Gabriel. "Hey, when you get some time, you think you can teach me how to dance? Some proper stuff, I mean." Holding the popcorn bowl to the front like an imaginary partner, he took a few steps as though in a ballroom. "There's this chick. She's a gymnast. Her coach hates me."

"D-dance?" It took Tara a second to drag her mind to this new topic. Gesturing with her hand, she asked, "Her coach hates you because you can't dance?"

Gabriel flushed. "See... back when Mike and I were kids, I... ahh... stepped on her toes at the school dance."

"Yikes." Tara grimaced. Gabriel was more than six feet tall and played American football. He was also training to be a firefighter. "How bad was it?"

"She needed a cast," Gabriel admitted. "Damn coach wouldn't even let her talk to me afterward. Thing is she's nice, and she thinks I'm nice. Except, she won't go with me to any of the dances until I take lessons."

Snickering, Tara said, "Victor and Alex are both great dancers."

A shadow passed across Gabriel's face. "They weren't here to teach us."

"Of course," Tara muttered. "Another one with lousy daddy skills."

"You can say that again," agreed Gabriel.

#

"One... two... three... keep your chin up," Tara said to Gabriel as they waltzed along the rubber-matted floor, trying to ignore the glowering boy slouching in the chair next to the wall.

At their end of the massive basement was the mini gym with a punching bag and weights and treadmill and whatnot. Plenty of space still remained for Tara to give Gabriel his dancing lessons. The television and couch were in the middle, and past the stairs was an empty area, but the flooring there was concrete. Not a comfortable spot to twirl barefoot.

Maestro's son could damned well stop sulking and learn to share the gym. Actually, Michael looked cute in the boxing jersey and trunks, all intense and focused when he threw jabs at the bag.

He resembled his uncle—Sabrina's brother—more than Maestro., except for the translucent brown irises. Alex was more Mr. Nice Guy while Michael... the broody look was *mucho* sexy.

Tara blinked hard. "Chin *up!*" she said to Gabe, her left hand rapping him on his shoulder. They were also wearing tees and shorts—good attire to dance in—but no shoes so that she could see exactly what her student was doing wrong. "Look at my face."

"I *am* looking at your face," he insisted, "but I gotta check my feet, too."

"One... two... three... and... one... two... three..." Tara continued, keeping time with the music from the CD player. The TV was on mute with Leonardo DiCaprio on screen.

Did Michael have any Italian in him? Tara gritted her teeth, reminding herself for the hundredth time to take no notice whatsoever of the boy. She needed to remember the Barbie doll he was dating. So sweet that Tara almost puked.

A strange sound erupted from Tara's mouth, somewhere between a gag and a chortle.

"What?" Gabriel asked. "I'm doing my best, okay?"

"No," said Tara. "I mean I wasn't laughing at... *chin up!* You're a lot taller than me." The football player/aspiring firefighter was hu-mon-gous! If she looked straight, her eyes would land on the crucifix hanging between his pecs. He also wore a beaded bracelet, something to do with a Native American goddess. "It's weird when you're this big and you keep trying to see where your feet are going," Tara complained.

"I can't help being big," objected poor Gabriel. "If I don't look down, I will stomp on *your* feet."

"Dude," called Michael, tone annoyed. "Get over here."

"Don't distract me," snapped back Gabriel. "This is difficult enough already."

Suddenly, Gabriel was being shoved to one side. Maestro's son was close to six feet in height, but his cousin, the boy mountain, wouldn't have expected to be thrown to the floor by the shorter kid.

"What the hell?" Roaring, Gabe leaped up. "Prepare to go down!"

Before Tara could manage more than a small scream, the two idiots were rolling around on the rubber flooring, kicking and punching and grunting.

"Gabe," Sabrina's voice called from above. "Mike..."

A chair crashed in the basement. Hands cupping her mouth, Tara stared wildly around, not having a clue what to do.

"What's going on there?" Sabrina asked. The light tread of her sneakered feet pattered down the stairs. Following her was Alex, his heavier footfalls punctuating hers.

With lightning speed, the stupid boys separated and sat up on the mat. "Nothing," they claimed in unison.

Stopping midway along the steps, Sabrina eyed the disheveled duo on the floor, the toppled chair. "Mmmhmm." Glancing at the speechless Tara, Sabrina requested, "Let me know if you see blood."

As she turned to leave, Tara blurted, "Wait! Aren't you gonna stop them or something?"

Sabrina shrugged. "They'll stop when they get tired."

"B-but..." Tara stuttered.

Alex snorted. "Don't sweat it, champ. They're only blowing off steam."

The minute the words were out of his mouth, Maestro knew he said the wrong thing. The consternation in his eyes made it evident. Michael's face turned dark as it always did when his father addressed Tara as champ.

"How would *you* know?" Michael asked, voice abrupt. "You ain't seen me or Gabe fight before."

"Mikey..." started Sabrina.

"Please," said Alex. "Let me. Best if we take care of this soon."

Heaving himself up from the mat, Michael mocked, "You know how many times I told myself you would be home... soon? Ma would stop crying in her room... soon. People would stop asking weird questions about you and Lilah... soon. I didn't realize you were busy playing dress-up, instead."

Tara didn't know where to look. She didn't even dare breathe. Gabriel stayed put on the mat, the stony stare he directed at Maestro making it clear where his support lay.

Alex remained silent, not offering Michael the apology he was most certainly owed. Sabrina opened her mouth as though to object to Michael's words.

Turning to her, the boy said, "You don't have to say it, Ma. The papers make up all kinds of shit about Lilah. I know!" Gesturing at Alex with his thumb, Michael continued, "And nobody cares about how he dressed in India. It's not the damn point. He was supposed to be home... with... with... with *me.*"

Michael's voice broke on the last syllable. His shoulders shook.

"Oh, baby," whispered Sabrina.

Gabriel threw a glance at her and stood, sauntering casually to his cousin's side.

You better say it, Maestro, Tara urged mentally. *Say it now. I'm sorry.*

"Son," muttered Alex.

"Don't," said Michael, his light-brown eyes glistening. "I'm not your son. All this time... why would you come back? You had your own kid. Her!"

Wha—what? Tara couldn't help the small squeak which escaped her mouth. Sabrina started, then winced visibly.

"Not fair, Mike," Maestro said. "Leave Tara out of this. She didn't do anything to you."

"Yeah?" taunted Michael. "How about I leave *myself* out of it, too? Just like you got your *champ,* I got someone who would know when Gabe and I are fighting for real. Only Uncle Harry gets to tell us off. He was our dad until now." Eyes still on Alex, Michael inclined his head toward his mother. "You don't even know *Ma.* I bet she hasn't told you about the program she wrote for Lilah."

"Mike!" snapped Sabrina.

Not paying any mind, Michael demanded, "Ask her. Or you know what? Ask Lilah because Ma's not telling you a thing. Ask who saved your asses in Cuba. Here's a clue. It wasn't Uncle Shawn. Not Uncle Harry, either."

Alex's confused gaze went to his wife.

Seeing it, Michael chuckled without mirth. "Gabe, let's get out of here, man. I got enough parenting tonight from people who think DNA's all it takes."

A second passed before Alex glanced back at his son. "Go," he agreed. "Maybe the fresh air will help you think clearly. Mike, you're only fifteen, but it's old enough to understand hindsight is twenty-twenty. There wasn't a single day in the last ten years I didn't regret not listening to your mother. I wish I told my brother not to trust Steven and his uncle. But once it was done..." Alex shrugged, the movement heavy with remorse. "... there was no other option. I deserved all the punishment I got. You and your mother didn't, but you two—and Gabriel—got punished, anyway."

With a dismissive shake of his head, Michael addressed his ma. "Gabe and I will probably grab some pizza. We'll be back in a couple of hours."

Green eyes hard, Sabrina nodded. "Go and cool off. When you return, it had better be with an apology."

"Apo... no way." Tone heated, Michael said, "You gotta be kidding me. Apology for what? He's the one who left. And he needs to hear what you did for—"

"I'm not talking about your dad," said Sabrina. "Thrash out your differences with him however you please, but my boy, you do *not* get to insult Tara under my roof. She's a guest in our home, and lemme remind you... Alex is alive today for you to fight with because of her and her family. So practice saying sorry when you're at the pizza place. You savvy?"

Michael's mouth opened, then closed as though it dawned on him for the first time how *humiliating* the last five minutes were for Tara. "Sorry," he mumbled, turning toward her. "Didn't mean to... uhh... you're cool."

Drawing herself up to her full height of five-and-a-half feet, Tara snarled. "I don't care. You... you..." Here she was, taking his side against Maestro—*Maestro,* who really was a father to her—and the boy... there weren't names foul enough to call him. Marching to Michael, she announced, "I'm moving in with Lilah."

Alex ptchaaed. "Tara," he called.

Not even bothering to respond, Tara stomped up the stairs to the living room.

Chapter 26

Next day

"Until you finish high school?" Lilah asked, feeling out of her depth. Settling teenage disputes was not one of her strengths. "Two years on that little couch?"

Sitting cross-legged on said couch, Tara slurped cornflakes from a bowl. "Last night, you said I could stay as long as I wanted."

Sometime before dinner, Sabrina had called with the information Alex and Tara were headed to The Hermitage. Somehow keeping his face straight, Noah showed the girl to Lilah's room.

After a lengthy fuming session where Michael was wished all manner of illnesses which would render him... umm... unable to perform, Tara slept for a good twelve hours. She woke only toward the middle of the morning, accepting the offer of cereal and milk for a late breakfast.

"Of course you can stay," said Lilah, "but you'll also want your own space. Not live out of your luggage." Plus, there was the sewing machine Tara intended to plant in the former president's workshop. "Tara girl," Lilah cajoled, setting her notepad on the coffee table. "Mike's been downstairs since the crack of dawn." The boy was skulking around the garage as Mr. Temple worked on his models, the morose grunts drawing puzzled looks from the retired politician. "He's really sorry for what he said. Let him apologize, and both of you can move on."

"I'm not going back to his home," Tara repeated for the hundredth time. "If you don't want me here, maybe you can check me into a hostel or something."

"Not happening," Lilah said, smiling. "You're one of us now, which means you're stuck with us." But no matter what else Lilah said—pointing out how thoughtless the male of the species could be at this age, how Michael simply forgot everything else in his anger at his dad—the unhappy young lady wouldn't budge. Nuh-uh, not at all. "What's really going on?" Lilah eventually asked. "I've never seen you this upset before."

"Tell me," Tara demanded. "What would you do if a boy you liked said it to you?"

Lilah laughed. "The boy I liked back then was also an idiot, but..." She blinked.

A sound of consternation came from Tara. Her eyes rounded in panic. "I didn't say it. I mean I said it, but I didn't mean it that way. Like as in just-like, not like a boyfriend or something. Don't tell anyone. *Please?* Swear on your life you won't."

"I never heard a word." Lilah bit her lip, trying to refrain from laughing again. "He has a girlfriend."

"Yeah... the Barbie doll." Before Lilah could object, Tara said, "I know it's mean, but have you *seen* her face? And I'd kill for those boobs and the figure. Barbie personality, too." Tilting her head this way and that way, Tara batted her eyelashes. "'Hi, baby.' 'Sure, baby.' 'I love you, baby.' Hell, she's so frigging sweet *I'd* want to... uhh... I'm not gay, but you know what I mean."

Thoroughly entertained, Lilah nodded.

Tara glared. "Okay, so I'm jealous." With a mournful sigh, the girl set her bowl on the coffee table right next to Lilah's notepad. "How can anyone compete with perfection? Michael's not perfect."

"Clearly."

Tara giggled dreamily. "He's a little dumb. I mean he is smart *and* dumb. All that super-high IQ, and he's not afraid of anything. Sabrina said he rescued one of your friends when the World Trade Center thing happened. He was a kid then!"

"He also turned his gun on you when he showed up in Goa," Lilah reminded the girl, feeling positively evil. Her eyes almost teared from the effort not to howl her head off.

"To compensate for the wind," Tara reproved. "He wasn't trying to kill *me*. Maestro said so. Didn't you hear?"

"Uh-huh. So it was all physics?"

"Exactly," said Tara. "Poor Mike. So many things happened to him, and he's so... *I* love my family, too. You know all the problems my father had with the resort and Prince and everything else. But Papa will always be my papa. Same for Michael. He loves his ma and Gabriel and his uncle and everyone else. He'd do anything for them. For Alex, too, but Michael doesn't wanna admit it."

"They have issues to work through," Lilah murmured.

"Yeah, they do," the girl agreed vehemently. "*I* like to deal with stuff, put it behind me and move on. Mike's different. I'm gonna have to make arrangements for the resort when my papa's old because I don't want to run it. I don't even want to learn how. Maybe we'll hire a manager or something. Mike will probably come back from college and find a way to do the oil business *and* whatever other thing he wants to do for himself. The military, his music, computers... whatever. If he's not any good, he'll keep on working at it 'til he's good. He's intense... won't give up. He won't give *in* with Maestro, either."

Once again, Lilah merely inclined her head.

"But it's dumb to go completely overboard," Tara said. "Like yesterday. Someone needed to tell Maestro off, but Mike didn't have to... he didn't have to drag *me* into it."

"No," agreed Lilah.

"But he did anyway," the girl brooded. "Yeah, Mr. Michael Kingsley can apologize all he wants, but I have my self-respect. No boy is worth giving it up. Now you see why I can't go back?"

Lilah huffed inwardly. Teen angst made for great comedy, but peace and quiet were critical to her work. Lilah needed to clear her mind of all extraneous thoughts and prepare for the eventuality of a congressional investigation. There was also the private meeting she requested with Andrew regarding Amber. Surely, he could be trusted to give them the answer now that they were all on the same side.

None of it mattered to a certain lovelorn sixteen-year-old. Lilah smiled wistfully as she remembered herself at fifteen. Genesis was in trouble, but she and Harry still found time to—

"All right," she said to Tara. "Stay with me for now, but we should come up with a better solution for you than hiding here. Also, what do you want me to tell Mike? He won't leave without talking to you."

"I don't care," Tara said.

#

Trying to keep a straight face, Lilah eyed the two young people at the dining table. Michael had invited himself to lunch. Tara kept her gaze on the lemon-pepper chicken, studiously ignoring the boy's mumbled pleas to talk.

His sad-looking motorbike followed Lilah's car to school as she took Tara for her placement test. Michael loitered in the school premises for two whole hours, but the girl sailed out with her nose in the air and did not deign to glance at her supplicant.

When Gabe showed up at Temple's home, Tara chatted with him very animatedly about how well she did on the test. They then switched to a discussion of good luck charms. Tara's skepticism was clear in her eyes, but she nodded along as Gabe described the powers of the White Buffalo Woman bracelet he got from his former foster mother who lived in San Diego. Poor Michael was forced to listen to it all in silence, alternately making puppy-dog eyes at Tara and shooting near-murderous glares at his cousin.

Retreating to the library with some silly excuse, Lilah snickered a couple of times. Then, she clutched her belly and howled.

"What's the joke?" a rich, deep voice asked from behind.

She started with a squeak and wheeled around. "Harry!"

He was standing next to the wall where portraits of Temple's parents were displayed. Sauntering toward her, Harry said, "It's good to see you cut loose this way."

She glanced toward the door. "I should probably go."

"Nuh-huh. It would be dumb to take you to court simply for walking into a room I happen to be in. Now, I wanna hear what you're laughing about."

A couple of minutes spent chatting surely couldn't hurt. Wiping tears of mirth from her lashes, Lilah said, "Right now, I'm the audience of one to a teenage sitcom."

Harry was also chuckling by the time she finished her story.

"I shouldn't laugh," sputtered Lilah. "Poor Erika. Oh, and I swore on my life not to breathe a word about what Tara let slip."

A hand to his heart, Harry swore, "Her secret is safe with me, but my money's on Mike. Since my boy is smarter than his uncle, he won't let her go without a fight."

"Is that so?" Lilah arched an eyebrow. "What if my girl decides he doesn't deserve a second chance?"

Something glittered in the coffee-dark gaze. "Then, he'll kick himself for being dumb enough to hurt her and dream every day of what might have been."

Rolling her eyes, Lilah laughed. "Cheesy! I hope *Mike* will have better lines."

"Hey!" Harry chided, the unfazed grin setting her insides aglow. "A little cheese goes a long way when reality is this damn messy."

Youthful voices drew their attention to the yard. All three teens were on the driveway. Gabriel seemed to be attempting to mediate, but Tara was still facing away from Michael. Gabe took Tara's elbow in his hand, urging her in the direction of the side gate. He said something about pizza and signaled Michael to follow. Behind them, a croaking frog hopped across the stone-paved path.

"Do you think the two of them will figure it out at some point?" Lilah asked in hushed tones as she watched from the window with Harry by her side.

"I hope they do," he said. "I hope they live happy ever after, away from the complications created by the rest of the world."

"Ever after?" she murmured. "Fifteen and sixteen are still children. Who knows how they'll feel once they grow up?" The trio was at the gate now, waiting for the security officers to open it remotely. The frog leaped onto a lawn chair, darting its tongue at some unseen insect.

"Who knows?" Harry echoed. "Could be a summer fling. Could also be they're meant to be together. Maybe he'll even find himself thinking one lifetime with her wouldn't be enough."

Squinting at him in mock reproof, Lilah teased, "More cheese."

"Yeah," said Harry. "But it also happens to be true. Some love stories don't end even with death."

She didn't say anything for long moments. "Harry," she eventually whispered. "I'm scared."

"Me, too," he admitted.

"Reality *is* so messy." Lilah closed her eyes for a second. When she opened them, the little group was walking out. The gate slid shut. "Look at them, Harry. All three of them. How do they find happiness away from everything else that's going on? We're all consumed by the network, including the boys. Michael was there when Major Armor raided the office in Panama. Five years old, and he... Sabrina says he had nightmares about it afterward. Even now, he hasn't forgotten what happened that day. He asked to go with Alex to the meeting with Steven's lawyers. Tara's life hasn't exactly been a picnic, either, thanks in part to us."

"I know," said Harry, "but I'm still hoping." Turning, he stood with his back against the glass panes. "Lilah, there's something I—"

Outside the walled yard, a car backfired a couple of times. An engine vroomed in the street. The startled frog jumped off the chair and scurried away.

In an instant, Harry's stance changed, going from the tenderness of a lover to the alertness of a hunter. Wheeling around, he stared hard at the side gate. Lilah never even saw him reach for his gun, but it was now in his right hand.

"What's wrong—" she started.

A scream rent the air. "Tara!" shouted Michael, terror in his voice. "Help! Somebody, help!"

Part X

Chapter 27

A few hours later

Cerro Azul, Panama

"Jesus!" Steven breathed into the phone, stalking up and down the CEO suite in the corporate headquarters of Peter Kingsley Company. Richard and Phillip Potts were also present, both talking on their own mobile devices. On TV, the evening news crew speculated on the motives behind the drive-by shooting in Sands Point, Long Island. Hanging up, Steven said, "It's not JD."

Jack Drummond, a.k.a. JD, had been looking for a chance to get back at Brad and his brothers for what they did to him. JD even mentioned targeting Victor's and Alex's sons once. Charles was another possibility, but he normally wouldn't have interest in a killing which didn't give him personal pleasure. Still, JD could've instigated Charles. It had happened before. Thankfully, the movements of both miscreants were accounted for, and JD was incredulous at the suggestion he would be dumb enough to hire a hitman to open fire near a former president's home.

Besides, JD's father, a retired financier, was already plotting his son's return to Congress. According to Phillip Potts, Drummond, Sr. used to be the go-to guy for a certain Irish cartel when they wanted to launder their ill-begotten wealth. He maintained interest in a couple of the nightclubs used for the purpose. The old fellow got away with it by playing both sides and pointing governments in the right direction when his mafia bosses allowed. He also understood the value of patience and advised his son to wait for the right opportunity to strike back at the enemy.

From one of the chairs, Richard nodded as he continued listening to an old acquaintance from his lawyer days who knew a surgeon at North Shore University Hospital. Phillip stood next to the window, impatiently waiting for his contact in the Bratva to come on line.

Frowning, Steven remembered his plan to check on Richard. They talked nearly every day, either in person or on the phone, and Steven knew almost to the minute when the slight distraction started. The nasty little trick played by Cousin Brad's missus shouldn't have been enough to scare Richard. Then again, marriage did change men, made them more mindful of the women in their lives.

More puzzling was Richard's disinclination to swing by New York. According to Arvi, he regularly talked to his ma on the phone, but the visits had dwindled to zero. It had gotten to the point where even the Kingsley patriarch asked the chauffeur if anything was wrong. He also made a call to Arvi, telling her she could always contact him for help in case of trouble. Her pleased reaction made it clear Richard never warned her about the manipulative old man.

"The girl's out of surgery," announced Richard, snapping his phone shut. "She's stable. Barely. Two bullets were dug out from the lung and another close to the spine. Victor's son got grazed on the shoulder. Superficial injury. He was chasing the bike, so they took one shot at him before escaping. The cops found the bullet in a tree trunk. The other one—Michael—was trying to stop the bleeding from the girl's wounds. No injuries on him."

"Thank God," Steven said, making a mental note to force a conversation on the topic of Richard's own well-being once the latest ruckus over the network settled.

"Her being okay won't make a difference to us," Richard said grimly. "The shooting happened near Temple's house. For now, Nassau County Police Department is not ruling out the possibility he was somehow meant to be the target. The Secret Service is also investigating."

"Mr. Temple wasn't even outside according to what they're saying," Steven pointed out, gesturing at the television with his thumb.

"Not going to matter," said Richard. "He did get shot once, and the shooter was never found. The feds will investigate the current incident until they find someone plausible to pin it on."

The only remaining suspect Steven could think of was someone from the Russian mafia. Any other troublemaker with a peeve against Brad and his brothers would've targeted one of them or Lilah, not some random child who just arrived in New York. On the contrary, the Bratva had suffered a defeat at the hands of Alex, and the girl was involved in the confrontation. Still, shooting at her in the vicinity of The Hermitage? Stupid idea.

"It *was* the Bratva," said Phillip, hanging up his own device. "My contact confirmed it."

Steven groaned. "Why? I thought the mob would have more sense than to invite attention from the Secret Service."

"Not an officially sanctioned hit," explained Phillip. "Some damn fool in Goa decided his ego was worth the risk. His cousin in Brooklyn is apparently an even bigger idiot, and he brought a third one along for the motorbike ride to Long Island. They didn't bother asking any of the bosses."

"Get rid of all three," Steven ordered. "Tonight." If the American government zeroed in on the Russian mafia, the culprits could blab about the Kingsley connection in hopes of a lesser sentence.

"It was being taken care of even before I called," said Phillip. "The bosses aren't happy about what happened, either. We'll get confirmation once everything's clear."

Steven nodded. "Now, I can talk to Grandfather. Rich, why don't you go with me?"

"Another time," Richard said immediately. "I need to get back to Texas. There's a meeting with the new labor contractor. Got to make sure this one's legit."

The reason was solid, and there was absolutely nothing to suggest Richard was lying. No red face, no shifty gaze. Yet Steven couldn't shake the feeling something was wrong.

"Try to make it to New York in the next couple of weeks," he suggested. "Grandfather's getting annoyed. He said he expects you to show up at the next meeting with the legal team."

Chapter 28

Next morning

Long Island, New York

"I spoke to Tara's father," Brad said to Godwin. "His flight should get here sometime tomorrow."

Only a single family member was allowed with each critical care patient, and Sabrina had insisted on staying overnight. Lilah was supposed to arrive after breakfast. Brad didn't feel like subjecting himself yet again to her cold contempt, so he showed up shortly after daybreak to visit Tara.

Godwin's arrival was a surprise. The Kingsley patriarch wasn't planning to intrude. Only wanting to check personally with the doctors that the girl was out of danger. Besides Brad and Godwin and the Kingsley security contingent, two others were present in the

ICU waiting area, but they were sleeping in chairs at the far end of the hall. Hades, the pup, lay peacefully at Brad's feet.

Giving the mutt a last pat on his head, Godwin sat back up. It was one of the traits Brad shared with his grandfather. The patriarch refused to get another dog after the German Shepherd he loved passed on years ago.

"Wheeler was with Neil and Scott when they got the news," said Godwin. "He said all of you seemed quite fond of the girl. So where's everyone else?"

"We *are* fond of her," said Brad, sipping creamy cappuccino from the Starbucks cup. The former justice had brought coffee with him. "Alex thinks of her as a daughter. He waited here until the doctors confirmed Tara would be okay. We all did. The police said it looked like a mob hit, so Alex and Harry went to Brooklyn to talk to a few people—officers in the corrections department. They have inside sources in the Bratva. Goan cops are asking questions, too. I hope we get proof of who paid the shooters, but Harry says chances are low. The mafia knows a hundred ways to hide money."

"The child is all right, which is a better outcome than what most families face under such circumstances." Godwin cleared his throat. "But I don't believe Steven is involved. Even he's not fool enough to try something of the sort at this time. Harry and Alex are going to find the mafia was acting alone."

"I trust your judgment," Brad said. "Still, we wouldn't have been sitting here if Steven didn't send the mob after us in the first place."

"Which is why I suspect this incident will push you into taking the legal route against your cousins. If you do go to court, Charlie's bad behavior with Lilah is going to come up."

"I don't like the idea of washing dirty laundry in public," Brad assured his grandfather. "Unfortunately, we don't have many options left. Military records will be presented as evidence. Once stakeholders understand what kind of a man Steven is, the board will be forced to take action against him."

Godwin regarded his grandson in silence. After a few moments, the patriarch said, "Brad, you used to come to me for advice before. Will you take some from me now?"

"Always."

"We Kingsleys are a passionate lot. There's evidence of it dating back to the time the family name started appearing in records in England. Falling in love where we shouldn't, duels, and so on, but the ladies we tangled with were invariably noblewomen. Refined, not merely beautiful. Even in recent history, my father was married to two wives. My own mother came from Austrian aristocracy. She didn't live long enough to see me grow up, and I had little contact with her family afterward, but everyone who knew her talked about how graceful and dignified she was. Except during her illness, obviously. Poor woman. She would've been tremendously embarrassed by it in her lucid moments."

Not quite certain how he was supposed to respond, Brad took another sip of coffee.

"My point is," Godwin continued, "until her malady became public knowledge, my father was envied by his peers for having someone like her as wife. And unlike some others in our social class, she was faithful. He, on the other hand..." Godwin sighed. "Sylvia, your great-grandmother, was gorgeous. She also remained loyal to my father for as long as they were married. Do you know what happened after he died?"

Silently, Brad shook his head.

"Andrew's uncle wanted to marry her."

"Andrew?" Brad echoed. "As in Andrew Barrons?"

"The same. I was around twenty at the time... at West Point, like other Kingsleys before me. Douglas MacArthur was the superintendent when I joined. Of course, he was not *the* General MacArthur yet, but you could already see him going places. Great man. The academy didn't get accreditation until after him, but I still joined."

"Able-bodied Kingsley men must serve," recited Brad.

"You remember," Godwin said approvingly. "It was my last year there when Father passed. There would be mandatory service in the army afterward. Not to mention my plans for a legal career. My academic record was exemplary, and Father had already made sure Harvard would take me. There was also Kingsley Corp. Our senior executives were excellent, but they needed direction from the family. My brother—*half*-brother—was sixteen. Sylvia helped, of course, but she didn't have an official role in the business, so most of it fell to me. The secretary would bring papers to the campus every Friday to save me the time of travel. The leadership team met every other week at the local lodge."

"Busy," muttered Brad.

Godwin smiled. "I'd say so. News got to me about one of the Barronses hanging around Sylvia at almost every social event, but I didn't pay attention. Not in the beginning. Then, the fellow—a retired lieutenant colonel—made himself impossible to ignore. He proposed to her. Sylvia didn't say yes, but she didn't say no, either. To this day, I don't know what prompted her to ask for a week to think about it. Perhaps the idea of propriety as Father had been gone less than a year. Anyway, her staff got worried she was being taken advantage of and came to me."

A secretary, the driver, even her personal maid... anyone could've tattled to Godwin.

"It would've been quite the coup for the Barrons family," Godwin mused. "According to the agreement my father signed,

Sylvia's son would inherit the entirety of Kingsley Corp, but I would remain the president for my lifetime. Well-salaried but no stock. If she married one of the Barronses, they would have a say—albeit indirect—in how the company was run. I informed Andrew's dad—lover boy's big brother—how I would also be acting CEO until my brother turned twenty-one. The clause was part of the deal my father signed with Sylvia. It would give me enough time to do serious damage to Barrons O & G if I so chose. They were big, so the Kingsleys would suffer in equal measure, but it was a better option than simply surrendering. The Barronses quickly lost interest." Godwin laughed a little.

"Fascinating." Brad coughed.

"Quite so," Godwin murmured. "Like my own mother, Sylvia was beautiful and graceful. Self-educated but clever and clearly accomplished. Still, the men in our circle believed she would be open to offers such as the one from the Barronses. Which she was."

The suitor in question suggested marriage, nothing scandalous, but it was a different generation. Godwin was plainly insulted, not merely angry about the attempt to usurp control of Kingsley Corp.

"Too bad my father could never see her true nature," said the patriarch. "Virtue is not an easy quality to find in a man or a woman. Virtuous women should be respected and protected. On the other hand, a beautiful face and charming voice can make us forget how women's weakness is only in physical strength, not in cunning or the capacity to stab you in the back. An unethical woman can corrupt a man's soul to the point he willingly abandons other ties. Which is what happened to my father with his second wife. And perhaps to Alex with Lilah."

Brad started. He opened his mouth to speak. "I... ahh..."

"Sylvia was only my stepmother, but I was still embarrassed. Imagine if my father had been alive. Imagine how humiliating, how emasculating it would be for a man to hear his wife's name linked with someone else."

Many *someone elses*, Brad thought bitterly.

"I kept away from marriage precisely to avoid such traps," Godwin continued explaining. "There were opportunities, but I didn't want to."

From the vicinity of Brad's shoes, Hades whined. Perhaps the animal was picking up on his human companion's unease. Fingers trembling, Brad bent down to soothe Hades with a couple of pats.

Glancing toward the double doors leading to the ICU, Godwin said, "Son, I'm afraid you're going to find yourself in a similar situation. If you go to court, there will be talk about Charlie's behavior toward Lilah. Steven knows this, and he's prepared to retaliate by bringing up her history with Alex."

"How?" Brad asked. "Aren't there laws against it? I realize you can't discuss Steven's plans with me, but..."

"Correct. However, in this case, I'll be doing both sides a favor by being blunt. If Lilah testifies about what Charlie did, Steven's lawyers are going to force a retelling of the entire tale from the beginning on the pretext of explaining *your* behavior. Why you kept her out of the discussions about the Iran deal. Why you wouldn't speak up for her during the interrogation even after you heard how Charlie... ahh... dishonored her. The gossip about her and Alex will thus be brought up, and both of them will have to answer questions. Shameful enough for the culprits but more damaging for you."

Brad opened his mouth, then closed it.

"Right now, there are only rumors about them," said Godwin. "A reasonable percentage of the public understands tabloid chatter for what it is—worthless trash. They see you as a good leader who was tricked by unscrupulous relatives. The moment the stories about Lilah and Alex are confirmed, the perception will change.

You're going to be seen as a man who was driven by jealousy into a colossal gamble with the safety of Americans. No sane politician will take your word for anything. They will not take Steven's, either, but it's a different matter."

Brad set the coffee cup on the side table. Sweating, he asked, "What should I do?"

"If you do go to court," Godwin said, "don't let Lilah take the stand. Don't even bring up what happened to her. Then, Steven won't get the chance to drag all of you through the mud. The judge will not let attorneys introduce details which are not relevant to the argument, so make Lilah irrelevant. Steven wins because he doesn't have to answer uncomfortable questions, and you win by avoiding having the sordid story of your wife and your brother aired in public. As far as the case is concerned, the truth is on your side, Brad. You took Steven's involvement in the Iran deal as an olive branch from him. You thought the family would finally start functioning as a single unit, but he tricked you."

"Yes." Speaking rapidly, Brad admitted, "I even thought we could eventually merge the two companies back into Kingsley Corp."

Godwin nodded. "I know how your mind works. You're an honest man. The truth is all you need to win, not Lilah. She's not some magic weapon you can use against Steven without hurting yourself. Don't use any magic weapons, including Harry."

Brad blinked. "Harry?"

Waving a hand, Godwin said, "He's called the kingmaker... which essentially means you didn't get where you are entirely on your own. If he wins back chairmanship before *you* win your case, it will reinforce the impression."

"I don't consider it a problem," Brad objected. "Harry does what he does because he believes I'm the best candidate to lead the network. He has talked to the press about me right from the beginning."

"You *are* the best candidate," said Godwin. "However, after the Cuba incident, you'll need to convince the public, not just Harry. Ask him to put down his weapons for your sake."

Chapter 29

Two weeks later, September 1998

Long Island, New York

"Coward," Lilah spat at Alex. Not deigning to say another word, she strode out of the library in Temple's home.

Staying put on the couch, Alex waited until her back disappeared through the door. "I don't care what she—or any of you—calls me," he said to the four other occupants of the room. "She cannot testify."

Outside the windows, thunder crashed, making glass panes shudder. The Labor Day storm which descended on New York City had turned the sky gray, matching the mood inside the house. Alex held his palms up in a plea for understanding.

The looks of abject frustration on the faces of the other four men didn't change. Dan sat at the table next to the window, making notes, while Noah and Falcon Papazian remained in their chairs. Harry continued pacing the room, his stride agitated. Not one was making an effort to see things from Alex's point of view.

Everything seemed to be crashing down on him all at once. He'd been prepared for Michael's explosion. The boy deserved to have his say, to hurt his father as he was hurt. What Alex never saw coming was the wound inflicted by Sabrina's silence. All these years, and his wife never said a word about her part in the Cuba episode.

What happened to the trust between them? Sabrina's response to the question was an incredulous look.

Before Alex even processed it completely, Tara got shot. She'd just returned home from the hospital, the poor girl. An unauthorized hit by junior members of the Russian mob, said Nassau PD. The two shooters were found dead with the bike next to their corpses, all ready for Michael and Gabriel to identify. Almost at the same time, Goan police stumbled over the carcass of one of the thugs who previously faced off with the exiles. Bullet hole in the forehead, the dead body was left someplace the cops couldn't miss. The Bratva was clearly signaling its intention to move on, but security was enhanced at the Kingsley residence in Long Island regardless.

Which gave Alex the reprieve he needed to fix his marriage, but Sabrina absolutely refused to cooperate. She told him to put himself in her shoes and decide if he would trust himself ever again not to prioritize his brothers over her.

Love was not a zero-sum game, dammit! Alex would die for his wife and their son, but how could anyone expect him to give up his family?

Then, Brad called a meeting of all five brothers. Once again, Alex was deputized to talk to Harry about their concerns. To Dan, too, as their commander in chief.

Alex was prepared for their anger, but the first thing he saw when he walked into the library was a corkboard sitting on a tripod right below the portraits of Temple's parents. Red circles were drawn around pictures of Kingsleys as though on a target map. It was only terrible timing how Lilah brought it down the same morning, but Alex lost it at that point. He announced how even if he were to die destitute on the streets, he wouldn't let her hurt anyone he cared about. Lilah wouldn't be allowed to testify, he insisted over and over. Which led to her outraged exit.

"I don't like the idea of going to court to begin with," he stated to the rest. "Uncle Aaron asked us to try talking to Steven one more time. Court or negotiation, I'm not going to embarrass my family with the stories about me and Lilah. Falcon, you're our lead lawyer. Can you tell me there will be no questions about the two of us? If there's a way to stop it from happening, she can testify."

"No," acknowledged Falcon, his rounded eyes sharp and bright. "When you go to court to argue your case, it cannot be with the expectation the other side has no zingers to land. However, in this instance, all you need to do is tell the truth. There was never an affair between you and your sister-in-law."

"Which will make Brad look worse," Alex said grimly. "Because our old employees are going to be subpoenaed." The non-disclosure agreements signed by staff wouldn't prevent them from being summoned to give evidence. "They'll testify about the fights between Brad and Lilah... over an affair which happened only in his head." The court, the media, and the public would immediately conclude the eldest Kingsley brother was unfit for command. Steven might still lose his position, but Brad would never recover from the humiliation.

"What do you want to do then?" Harry asked, continuing his angry prowl. "Sweep everything the Kingsleys did to her under the carpet? Let Steven control the network?"

"Not the Kingsleys," Alex snapped back. "Only Steven and Charlie were involved. I can't embarrass Brad—not to mention my wife and child—to get back at those sons of bitches."

"Don't drag Sabrina into this," Harry warned. "Or Michael. You know damn well they wouldn't agree with you."

"Maybe," said Alex, "but I still can't do it."

"My sister gets thrown under the bus once again," said Dan, tone bitter. "Forget the part about getting justice. Everyone *expects* her to testify. What do you wanna bet Armor and Steven will leak to the press she didn't show up precisely to avoid questions about her personal life?"

"The media will decide all the rumors are true," Harry agreed. "Some sleazy bastard is also going to swear left and right how the part about her being married to all five brothers is gospel truth. The public will end up imagining Lilah as some kind of toy passed around between the men in the family. *Her* reputation is clearly not a priority for the Kingsleys."

"C'mon," Alex huffed. "Maybe we should announce she's actually married to all five of us. At least it will put a stop to the shitty gossip about how I slept with my brother's wife. She'd be my own wife."

"Wife?" Noah parroted. Clucking, he looked away. Falcon simply sighed.

Stopping mid-stride, Harry stared in incredulity.

"What the hell?" ground out Dan.

Lightning once again flashed across the dark sky. Rain continued to pour.

"Sorry," Alex said, his face heating. He stood to face Lilah's twin. "It was a stupid thing to say."

Dan stood as well. "Lemme leave before I beat the shit out of you," he said. "Harry, we'll talk later tonight. I trust you can handle this."

Watching Lilah's brother stride out, Alex grimaced. "Sorry again."

"Yeah, you *are* sorry," Harry spat. "You pathetic excuse for a man."

"Harry," Noah called, but the attempt at peace-making went unheeded.

"You jumped at the chance, didn't you?" Harry asked, pointing a finger at Alex. "The minute Brad blabbered about what might get asked, you jumped at the chance. You never wanted Lilah to say anything about the damn assault because it wouldn't stop at Steven and Charlie. Godwin and Potts would be forced to answer some tough questions. You were looking for a way out, and Godwin's conversation with Brad gave you one."

"Again... I don't care what you call me," Alex said doggedly. "How the hell am I supposed to look my grandfather in the eye and accuse him of enabling a sexual assault?"

"How the hell did you point a gun at another human and pull the trigger, Captain Kingsley?" Harry roared. "You did it because it was your duty. No one gets to play soldier without being ready, willing, and able to die for your countrymen *and* to kill for them. You'd better be ready to do your duty in court, too."

"The army didn't ask me to kill my own family."

"If the Kingsleys aided and abetted a criminal in a plot against the United States, you bet the army would've asked you to shoot," Harry said.

"Grandfather did not plot against—"

"Yes, he did." Eyes bright, Harry accused, "Even after it was clear Lilah was innocent, Godwin continued to argue to keep her imprisoned under false charges. It could suggest to the court and the media how he wanted her to go down for treason regardless of what actually happened. A reasonable judge might ask why. A reasonable judge might even conclude Godwin was not working in the interest of national security. Quite the opposite, in fact."

"Could you at least *try* to look at Cuba from another point of view?" Alex pleaded. "Lilah was not the only one who got hurt. It wasn't a picnic for the rest of us, either, including Grandfather."

"The public's going to see it my way," Harry said. "You don't want to take the risk. Brad's stupidity gave you the perfect excuse."

"Believe what you want." Alex's voice trembled, but he was beyond caring. "Bottom line is court is an option only if we leave my grandfather out of it."

"How can we leave him out when he was an active participant in the military interrogation?" asked Falcon. "Even if we ignore the assault, Justice Kingsley and General Potts will be called to testify. Or are you and your brothers planning to leave their names out of the lawsuit?"

"No." Correcting himself, Alex said, "I mean... yes."

"What do you mean yes?" Noah asked. "Do you want us to pretend Godwin was never in Cuba? The transcripts will prove otherwise. If we don't use those transcripts, we have no case."

"I don't know." Groaning, Alex collapsed back onto the couch. "I simply don't know what to do. I'm not looking for a win for win's sake. I don't need Kingsley money to support my wife and kid. If the last ten years taught me anything, it's how to survive on little. Still, my brothers and I built Peter Kingsley Company, and we want it back. Also, unless Steven dies conveniently, I don't see him stopping the attacks. Brad will have to keep looking over his shoulder for the rest of his life. Lilah deserves justice. But how are we supposed to do any of it without hurting the people who made us who we are?"

Harry muttered something under his breath.

"My father took off when I was four," Alex went on. "He abandoned his family, his wife, and his sons. Only Grandfather was around for me and my brothers afterward. I'm not going to do what my father did, Harry. I will not abandon Grandfather."

"It's not the same situation," Noah said.

"No," agreed Alex. "It would be worse. Grandfather is old now. General Potts is also getting up there in age. It would be a shitty thing to do to... I can't lose my grandfather. No way. And what if we don't win? All of it will have been for nothing!"

Burying his face in his hands, Alex willed it all to somehow stop. He simply wanted his family intact. He wanted his wife, his child, the life he threw away in a moment of stupidity. No more.

There was a sigh, a shift in the air as someone else sat on the couch.

"Alex," Harry called, tone now mild.

Alex didn't look up.

"Someone I know once told me fear of loss stopped her from speaking the truth. Sounds like you're afraid, too. You think you could lose your family, your identity, like you lost your father when you were a kid. You're afraid of losing Godwin before he actually passes."

Alex dropped his hands, but he kept his eyes on his shoes. "I know he'll go someday. Yeah, Grandfather's healthy for someone in his nineties... except for blood pressure problems according to Uncle Aaron... but time always wins. Still, what a way to end a life like his. Being ripped apart in public by his own grandsons for something he didn't have the power to stop. And *I* would be the one to do it to him. How do you think he'll feel about me afterward?"

"My father had a heart attack," Harry reminded Alex. "He's seventy-two, turning seventy-three in a few weeks. I'm scared Hector will call one day and tell me Father's gone. I know there's a good chance I won't be by his side when it happens. I also know he's not too happy with me for going against Gateway on the network issue. Regardless, I have to do my duty. So do you."

"I'm not as detached. Hell, I don't *want* to be."

"Death is inevitable," Harry said. "For all of us, not only Godwin. Religion says the essence of us goes on—the soul, the spirit, something of the sort. I believe it does, but the time between our first and last breaths is important. We need to carry out our duty as living entities, or existence becomes meaningless. A guard dog must protect, or he's no longer a guard dog. A tiger hunts, or he's reduced to a house cat. A teacher teaches; a doctor heals. If you let fear of loss stop you from doing what you must, life will become pointless and eventually end in redundant death. A soldier cannot freeze when faced with an actual war."

"I don't have a problem fighting wars," said Alex. "The outcome is what scares me."

"The outcome is what you don't have control over," Harry countered. "Worry about what you *can* control. Like your own actions. Do what you need to do and accept the end result—positive or negative—with equanimity."

"Equanimity!" Alex shook his head. "I can do nothing and be happy. Much easier."

"Making your peace with potential results is not the same as stopping trying," Harry warned. "Every minute of every day, all of us must keep trying to do the right thing. We could win or lose, but we can't stop trying."

"You keep talking about the right thing," said Alex. "What *is* the right thing here? Some situations are black and white, but this ain't one of 'em. Not to me, at least."

"Ask your own conscience the question," Harry said.

Alex heaved in a deep breath. "My conscience and my mind are telling me the same thing. Sacrificing a few of my selfish needs to keep the family intact is not a big deal. I'll be happy to live quietly someplace where I don't have to hear about the oil network ever again."

"Careful," said Harry. "You're again crossing the line from love and empathy to cowardice. Would you give Michael this advice? I bet you'd tell him running from life never works. On some level, you'll still think about the work you left unfinished. You'll be bitter about what you sacrificed. Don't base your actions purely on your personal needs, but you do have to carry out responsibilities. Then, appreciate what life offers in return. Even if you make mistakes, it's better to do something."

"C'mon, Harry," Alex scoffed. "We've both done things we regret." Like burning an entire village to the ground.

"How do you avoid regrets if you have at least a couple of morals to rub together?" Harry asked. "Yeah, there were times when I refused to understand how ends don't justify the means. I made some terrible decisions, which I will regret until the day I die. Doesn't give me the excuse to retreat from the world and refuse to do my damn job."

Heaving himself from the couch, Alex went to the window. The storm was still going at full strength, and the air inside the room was heavy with moisture. Beyond this residence and its garden was Alex's own home. His wife, their son, Victor's son... they'd waited almost a decade for justice. "I get what you're saying," Alex mumbled. "Intellectually. But making myself follow through is a different matter. I might as well try to control the weather."

"Think back to your military training," said Harry. "If the instructor told you to put mind over body, you'd do it. You'd work on it day in and out until it became second nature. This time, put your conscience in control of your consciousness."

Turning back to the room, Alex asked, "Have *you* been able to do it?"

Harry shrugged. "I try every day. Sometimes I fail; sometimes I win. But I will never stop trying."

"You talk like it's damn easy." Raking his hair with a hand, Alex said, "Most people—regular men—wouldn't agree. Are you claiming to be God or something?"

There was an indecipherable mutter from Noah.

Harry got to his feet and faced Alex. "Each of us is made of many parts. There's a little of everything in everyone. How we present to others depends on what aspects of ourselves we choose to emphasize at a given point. I'm my soul, my mind, and my body. I am my own beginning, middle, and end. There's good in me; there's bad in me. I can be Alex among the Kingsley brothers. I can be Steven, too. I am human, I am demon, and yes, I am God."

Alex blinked. "Dude!"

Laughing quietly at the collective shock in the room, Harry urged, "Look within yourself. Go home and lock yourself in a room if you have to. Focus on what your conscience says, my friend, and find God in you."

Chapter 30

Harry waited in silence, watching the former sniper making his way out of the room. Noah and Falcon were quiet, as well.

"Fascinating debate," Falcon commented the moment Alex's back vanished around the corner. "I didn't realize you were spiritual, Harry."

Taking the deck of cards from his pocket, Harry said, "Eight years in prison gives a man enough time to reevaluate the past. The spiritual stuff is what comes out when you spend day after day going over all the mistakes and the whys and the hows and what you could've done differently."

"Do you believe in God?" Noah asked.

"I believe..." Pausing, Harry shuffled. "I don't talk to the Almighty on a daily basis, but there was a time in my life when I demanded answers. Why did something evil have to happen?"

Noah chuckled. "Did He respond?"

"In my mind, yes," said Harry. "I was told to find my own answers. The purpose of my existence. I figure all of us have some sort of a job to do in this world—our individual missions. Me, you, Alex, everyone. I believe the higher power we worship gives us the freedom to decide how to carry out our missions. Or to not do anything, which itself can be a powerful form of action. His omnipresence and omnipotence are revealed as much in the collective actions of all of us as in the high-octane scenes from religious texts."

"The quiet miracles," remarked the former attorney general.

"Right," said Harry. "The journey of humanity toward the divine depends on millions upon millions of such miracles."

There was a sound at the door. Without looking up, Harry knew who. The fragrance of blue lotuses gave her away, but he would've known without the perfume. Something shifted within him when she was near. Elation, anticipation, an explosion of internal energy. Words clamored in his head to get out. It *would* take more than this lifetime to tell her everything he wanted. To love her as he wanted.

"Game?" Falcon invited her.

"Not today," Lilah said. "Dan left his notebook here."

The book was on the table by the window where Temple usually played chess. Instead of taking it and leaving, Lilah settled into a chair and started leafing through.

Harry dealt the cards.

"What do you think?" Noah asked. "Is Alex going to stick to his mission?"

"He's at least going to try," Harry said. "Alex is a good guy, Noah. The best of men under most circumstances. Don't forget what he did for Lilah when they were in India."

"High praise," observed Falcon. "'The best of men.'"

Noah shook his head. "I agree Alex is an upstanding citizen, but his attachment to his family is stronger than any sense of right and wrong."

"I don't really understand it," Falcon said. "Alex is not a child to be this afraid of losing his grandfather's approval. He's a veteran who has seen enough of the world. Good God, he's been on the run for the better part of a decade thanks to his family. Harry, you said you spoke to him about Justice Kingsley's part in the saga. The other four brothers don't know the whole story, but Alex? He should've been ready to wash his hands off the Kingsleys by now."

"I would say it's precisely because he knows what Harry thinks," countered Noah. "Alex feels more compelled to protect his family because he understands what could happen if he lets Harry loose. Moreover, I'm gonna bet Alex does recognize the truth on some level but is trying his best not to acknowledge it. Or his entire childhood will have been a lie. The safety and security he found with Godwin after Peter left..."

Falcon huffed. "Fun times ahead when we get to court."

"*If,*" corrected Noah. "Not *when*. Right now, all five of them want to give diplomacy one last try because it's what Godwin would want."

"Steven's still not going to cooperate," Harry said, "Godwin knows this. He's partly playing the role of concerned elder and partly buying time. Our deadline gives us only until December 2000 to reach a decision. About two years. The longer we go without taking steps toward an actual lawsuit, the more it cuts into the time the public gets to chew over what is said in court."

"Time!" Noah snorted. "It's ironic how Alex thinks his grandfather is at death's door while Godwin's acting as though he's going to outlive everyone around. The man's ninety-three, same as Temple. They both have blood pressure problems, and Temple's got arthritis. *I'm* ninety-two. My doctor's been talking about upping those horse pills he gives me for diabetes. How much time does any of us have left?"

"You, my friend," Harry said, gesturing with a card, "are going to live forever. What would I do without your conniving self?"

Noah laughed. "I *am* in full possession of my mental faculties. So are Temple and Godwin."

"It means Justice Kingsley could live to see his side win," Falcon muttered. "The number of days we get in court will be immaterial when our star witness cannot testify." If Lilah insisted on it, the five brothers would not cooperate with the war at all. "Even if we're talking only about scoring political points and not a favorable ruling from the judge, the idea that the other side cheated won't be enough to tilt popular opinion. Especially when a widely respected former supreme court justice is arguing for Steven. We have Andrew, but he's a businessman, not a... a..."

"Symbol to rally around," completed Noah. "In an ideal world, citizenry and leaders would come together for a righteous cause, but we don't live in an ideal world. The seven supporters we currently have..." The former attorney general listed the big names in the energy sector who were against Steven. "They're mainly looking out for themselves. Politicians who have a problem with the existence of the network also can't be trusted not to prioritize themselves over societal good."

"Both groups appreciate the power of the network," said Falcon, "but don't like playing junior partner."

Noah nodded. "The public will see through their cries about justice in a heartbeat. Trust in those who run our institutions has plummeted because the regular man and woman understand at least on some level how they're being used. They need a people's hero to follow into battle—a personification of both their anger at the system and their hope for a better tomorrow. Temple wanted..." The former attorney general threw a quick glance at the woman sitting next to the window. "Lilah, he called you Minerva once, didn't he?"

Briefly looking up from the notebook, Lilah gave a noncommittal smile.

"The goddess of knowledge?" Falcon raised his eyebrows. "Wow."

"Temple liked to write poetry," Noah explained. "So yes... some hyperbole, but he did see Lilah as his intellectual heir. A leading figure for the future." With a sigh, the former attorney general mused, "Temple had so many plans. Falcon, you read a couple of his journals."

"He was authoring Lilah's life," stated Falcon. "The mentor *and* chronicler."

"Yes," Noah said. "Unfortunately, the Kingsleys managed to do a number on her reputation. Also unfortunately, we still need our symbol. Our best bet for putting a face on our cause at this point would be you, Harry. I remember the support for General MacArthur back in the 'fifties. The public outrage when he was fired... there was quite a bit of the same anger when it became clear you, a highly decorated veteran, spent eight years in prison for nothing. *Vox populi* sees itself in you and considers you a hero."

"*Populi* only know what media tells them," Harry retorted. "*We* played up the wronged hero idea after I got out of Sing Sing... even before, during the Sanders episode. The public doesn't have a clue about what stupid stuff I did over the years. My friends and family who do know have been more forgiving of my mistakes than I deserve."

"Whatever the reason, the average man trusts you over the others involved in this debate," said Noah. "Their faith could end up being our sharpest weapon. As far as your inner circle is concerned… forgiveness is easier when we see someone fight hard for what's right. I'm sure Alex and his brothers realize you're not perfect, but they, too, have strong faith in you."

"Alex is a loyal friend," Harry acknowledged. "The rest are grateful for my help, but gratitude has limits as we saw today."

"Yup," said Falcon. "Brad wants *you* to step back, too, not just Lilah. If you return as chairman before him, he won't get the chance to redeem himself in the public eye."

"I heard the message loud and clear," Harry said. "It was a long shot, anyway, and my own family doesn't like the idea of me being front and center in this war. So I'll respect everyone's wishes and stay in the background as friend and supporter."

Studying his cards, Falcon asked, "Friend and supporter in doing what? We won't win a board vote. Negotiations won't work. Contrary to what Alex imagines, a lawsuit where we disclose bare minimum information is not getting us anywhere. Hell, we may not win even with the whole truth."

"They have also ruled out going after Kingsley Corp," added Harry. "It's good to catch a break. Finally!"

The other two men stared for a couple of seconds. The former attorney general gestured with a hand. "Go on."

"We—and I mean all of us—are going to jump off the cliff." At the sudden silence, Harry chortled. "The next round of talks will get Alex and the rest to the edge of the cliff. Climbing back down the slope will not help because surrender won't stop Steven from attacking Brad. The only remaining escape route will be along the steep side."

Harry threw a half-glance toward Lilah. Her eyes were fixed on the open journal, but she'd be listening to every word.

"Falcon," Harry called, returning his gaze to the cards in his hand. "Let's contact the Kingsleys about this peace summit Godwin so badly wants. One condition: it won't be between lawyers or emissaries this time. All of us must be in the same place, meeting face-to-face. I'll withdraw my claim to chairmanship as Brad requested, but no one said I couldn't join the negotiations. Once it's done, there will be only one way remaining to win the war without bringing Lilah or Godwin into it. Only one way to make sure Steven has no reason left to attack Brad or anyone else. It will be a purely political war fought before the United States government over a single question. Should the network continue to exist?" *Phase two begins,* he said to himself.

Part XI

Chapter 31

Two weeks later, late September 1998

Trenton, New Jersey

"You knew what he was going to say, didn't you?" Patrice whispered. Sixteen years old, pregnant, friendless.

"I had some idea," Senator Temple admitted. "I've seen enough of his kind."

Summer of 1949 was the one and only time Patrice was in this city before. The then-senator's office had been in a busy neighborhood, which was all she remembered about the location. When she left, she was taken straight to The Sacred Heart Home for Unwed Mothers in New Orleans.

"Patrice," a male voice called.

"Hmm?" With a start, she returned to the present and glanced toward the front of the car. Aaron was driving, having been invited to this last-ditch attempt at peacemaking ostensibly because this was meant to be a family reconciliation as well. All for the benefit of the media, of course. Judith—his lady friend—had come along solely out of curiosity about Harry, the former SEAL and oil broker who was constantly in the news.

"You won't be allowed in the conference hall," Aaron reminded Patrice for the hundredth time. "Promise me you'll stay in the suite."

"I'll be with her every minute," Judith soothed.

Richard's silence was what concerned them. The moment his father confirmed the truth, Richard stalked out and never returned. He still talked to his adoptive mother, but Patrice got nothing. No phone calls, no letters, no messages. The news had turned his world upside down, and her existence stood in the way of his friendship with Steven.

Patrice was beyond caring about potential danger from any quarter. She showed up here only so she could take a peek at her firstborn from a distance. She needed to make sure he was all right, at least outwardly. Staying locked in the hotel suite would not suit her plans.

"I'll do something," Aaron assured Patrice. "The talks are supposed to go on over the entire weekend. We'll find a way to get you into tomorrow night's dinner. Your sons... Peter's boys... are here, so we have an excuse."

When the car cut through downtown, Patrice caught sight of a familiar logo. Gateway, the Sheppards' company. Judith was also staring at the board, with the red, curvy arrow forming the G, followed by the remainder of the name in no-nonsense black typeface.

"The New York-New Jersey Harbor is the biggest petroleum products hub in the United States," Aaron reminded her. "Not to mention the pipelines. *Of course* the Sheppards have a presence in this state. They do brokerage and trading and retail."

In fact, Hector Sheppard, as supposed neutral party, suggested holding the talks in this particular hotel since Brad did not want to go to Cerro Azul where he'd be forced to watch his enemy ruling his former kingdom. The conference center was outside Trenton, closer to Princeton. The acres and acres of woodland surrounding the buildings would provide privacy to the bigwigs showing up. There was also a helipad for those who didn't feel like taking the road. The Kingsleys—not including Peter's sons—would stay at the former hunt club on the same property which had been converted into a luxury inn.

#

"No, I don't mind," Patrice assured Victor on the phone. "I would've liked to join you boys tonight but not for a working dinner."

Lilah's brother and the lawyers would be with the five Kingsley men. Lilah herself declined to take part in further negotiations, but she authorized her twin to speak on her behalf. As for Harry, he was invited by David and Steven Kingsley to join the family for a private banquet. Richard was expected to be present.

"Just make sure I have a spot at your table at the official dinner tomorrow," Patrice said to Victor.

In fifteen minutes, Patrice was in Aaron and Judith's suite, staring at their guest in confusion. "'Evening, Aunt Patrice," Harry greeted from the dining table.

Judith was seated on his right, a bowl of her favorite fruit—bananas—in front. She was munching on one. CNN played on the TV set against the wall to the right, and a somber news anchor announced something about impeaching President Clinton.

With a quick look at the screen, Harry turned back to Patrice. "Thanks for inviting me."

"Huh?" Patrice glanced at Aaron. "But I..."

"I didn't, either," Aaron said dryly.

"An oversight on your part, I'm sure," Harry said.

Judith tittered, her delight at this rule-breaking fellow very clear. Finishing the banana, she dropped the peel into a second bowl.

"C'mon, Aaron," Harry said. "You don't seriously expect me to break bread with Steven, do you? The last time I was invited by him, he tried to get me arrested."

With a sigh, Aaron turned off the TV and gestured Patrice toward the dining table. "This was not a wise decision, son," he said.

Raising an eyebrow, Harry asked, *"Pour quoi?* Why?"

"Steven's a fool," Aaron said, seating himself. "He looks at these lawyers—his employees—and thinks he's won already. He believes Major Armor alone is enough to win the case for him. Not to mention Father and the Pottses. So Steven doesn't see the point of negotiating. The dinner invitation was my brother's idea. David's hoping he can flatter you into switching sides. Since you declined the invitation, he—and Steven—will decide to feel insulted."

Judith waved a hand. "Let them be insulted. What are they going to do that they haven't already?" She pushed a bowl toward Harry. "Dinner won't be ready for a few more minutes. Here... have fruit."

Glancing down, Harry said, "Uhh... thanks." Squaring his shoulders as though preparing for battle, he added, "If you really want me to."

Judith frowned for a second and followed his gaze to the empty peel. "Sorry!" she squeaked. "Wrong bowl."

Fingers over his mouth, Aaron laughed. Despite her worries, Patrice also couldn't help laughing.

Afterward, no one brought up the ongoing war over the network. The talk was all about the internet and how it was changing the world. Harry was curious about an online book retailer called Amazon. He'd mentioned the company to Shawn, who proceeded to wax poetic about the future of e-commerce. Even Lilah was cautiously optimistic though both she and Shawn harbored misgivings regarding the current euphoria over dot-com stocks.

Aaron Kingsley, however, was more interested in the regulations governing cyberspace. *Very* interested, thanks to his conversations with Noah Andersen.

"Section 230," Aaron said, waving a fork around.

Apparently, some law called Communications Decency Act had been passed, and there was strong feeling at The Hermitage about it. Andersen and Lilah had gone on about how the nation kept repeating the mistakes of the past. Standard Oil, Peter Kingsley Network, online services...

"Service providers are protected from liability for content posted by users," griped Aaron. "Providers are also allowed to moderate objectionable third-party material even when such material falls under constitutionally protected speech."

"Who gets to decide what's objectionable?" completed Harry, taking a sip of white wine.

"So you've thought about it," Aaron said, sitting back in his chair.

"Some," said Harry. "Mostly, I've been listening to Lilah and Shawn argue. He's all for it. I believe he and his colleagues are worried how litigation will stifle growth. Noah and Lilah claim bestowing immunity while still permitting moderation will allow a few wealthy individuals to control our communications. They can tell us what we may discuss and not get sued for it."

Aaron nodded emphatically. "Essentially, our ability to debate as a collective might one day depend on what the rich and the powerful deem appropriate. Even the topics discussed might be up to them."

"Almost like mind control," Judith said.

"There's more," said Harry. "What if the companies collude someday the way we did with the network? And what if governments use the providers for propaganda? Voters will hear only a single, pre-approved point of view. Any dictator around the world will thus be able to create the perception of legitimacy. It could happen even here in the United States."

Patrice shuddered.

Noticing it, Judith said, "Well... we're in our sixties. Maybe we'll be dead by the time computers take over."

They then started talking about New York and the changes in the city over the years, about the looming new millennium, about George Clooney, the actor on whom Judith harbored a major crush.

"What about me?" Aaron complained after she went on and on about Mr. Clooney, setting off more laughter.

Patrice couldn't believe how happy the evening was. Like it used to be in the short time she and her sons lived in Panama, but the tensions simmering under the surface eventually shattered the illusion of happiness.

It was only when coffee was brought around that Aaron asked Harry, "Why put yourself through this when you know Steven won't cooperate? Lemme tell you something else: Steven's been in training all these years. He goes to Hector's gym almost every day when he's in New York. No one thinks anything of it, but I'm worried. Why does a businessman need to train with professional boxers?"

"Dante mentioned it to me," Harry said. "The staff at the gym say Steven makes it a point to train out of his weight class. Taller, heavier opponents. He's very good by all accounts. Still, it's unlikely he's expecting an actual fistfight over the network."

"I suppose not," acknowledged Aaron. "But it shows how far he's prepared to go. And he holds long grudges. All the fights with Victor and Alex when they were boys..."

Patrice's heart thudded in alarm.

"We can always hope everyone grew up," Harry said with a small grin. "I know... it ain't happening. Regardless, negotiations are necessary. I can't let blame fall on Brad and Alex and the rest for not doing everything in their power to avoid a corporate war."

"Corporate war for everyone else," fretted Aaron. "Family war for the Kingsleys. All thanks to Steven."

"Nuh-huh," said Harry. "The rest don't get to escape responsibility. If Godwin and David wanted, they could put a stop to Steven right now. You, too, Aaron."

"Me?" asked a surprised Aaron. "How?"

"You could contest David for leadership of Kingsley Corp," Harry suggested. "As the CEO of the parent company, you could instruct Steven to stand down. If he doesn't, you could vote with our side to kick him out."

Patrice leaned forward, putting worry aside to listen. Aaron could also instruct employees—including Godwin—to follow company policy. The Kingsley patriarch would have no excuses left for why he was with his criminal grandson.

Harry went on, "The idea of making you the CEO must have come up at some point, right? As far as I understand, the agreement between your grandparents only states Sylvia's bloodline has to inherit. You're also her grandson, same as Peter and David."

"I was born out of wedlock," pointed out Aaron. "My mother was a secretary at Kingsley Corp. Working class Jewish family from Brooklyn with no connections to the upper crust."

Harry frowned. "So?"

"So..." Dabbing his mouth with a napkin, Aaron continued, "Sylvia wasn't rich or blue-blooded, and she was called a gold digger until the day she died. Her son—my biological father—was considered worse than useless, but he married someone in his own class and produced David and Peter before spotting my mother in the secretarial pool. The extended family was fine with my brothers being CEO, but they would never accept me."

"My God, Aaron!" breathed Harry. "How can you... why are you still calling them family?"

Aaron shrugged. "It was simply the way things were back in the good old days. My father—I mean Godwin—welcomed me in when most other men wouldn't have. He made sure I was accepted as part of the household. Except for the one thing."

"The one thing?" Harry asked in obvious disbelief before turning to Patrice. "Victor never married Gabe's mother. She wasn't rich or aristocratic. Gabriel is Catholic with Lakota heritage. He's your grandson, Aunt Patrice. Would you put up with it if the Kingsleys said 'except for the one thing'?"

"No," Patrice said instantly. "But I don't make decisions for the Kingsleys."

"Which means they wouldn't accept Gabe, either," Harry said grimly.

"Son," Aaron called, tone placating. "What I'm trying to say is the family—as a whole—values two colors. First blue, then green, and I didn't bring either. Father stood up for me, but the CEO would need support from more than one man. A chief executive would find it difficult to function without acceptance from the leadership team, which I would not get. Father knew it, and he made the best decision possible under the circumstances. I don't hold it against him."

"He could've fought for you," insisted Harry.

"He could've," agreed Aaron. "But at significant cost to the unity of the family." He held up a hand. "Before you say it... no, there's no unity now, but I would never want quarrels to start on my account. Father wouldn't risk it, either, unless there were extenuating circumstances." With a sad laugh, Aaron continued,

"Right before Mr. Temple got shot, he updated me on what was going on behind the scenes. I'm not so blinded by my love for my father to refuse to believe... Peter's boys, however... well... I'm sure you know by now. My point is I get what Father is doing. I don't condone it, but I understand his reasons. He does believe there are extenuating circumstances."

"Which for him has always been the family as a whole," Harry remarked, tone hard. "Not individual members of it."

"Men in my father's position make such choices all the time," Aaron said. "Perhaps it seems unfair to people on the outside."

"Perhaps?" Harry parroted. "Aaron, you're excusing him, too, same as Alex and the rest. What the hell is it about Godwin that inspires this kind of loyalty?"

Judith groaned. "You know how many times I asked this question? In my opinion, he focuses on the most vulnerable. Gets them when they're feeling all alone in the world and makes them feel safe. Also, they've seen Godwin withhold affection from David and Steven when they didn't meet expectations. It makes the rest worried about losing parental approval."

Emotional manipulation, Patrice said to herself.

"Aaron didn't have his father to begin with," mused Judith. "Brad and the rest lost their father twice. Once when he left, then when he died. Losing Godwin would be like losing a parent yet again. That crushing sensation, the feeling of being completely unmoored..." Judith shuddered. "The younger they were, the worse it would've been. No one would want to go through it ever again."

"The idea terrifies me even at this age," Aaron admitted, shoulders slumping. "Harry, I *will* offer my opinion every chance I get. I will counsel everyone against this insanity. If I'm asked to testify in court, I promise to tell the whole truth and only the truth. But I cannot—will not—otherwise go public against my family."

For a few moments, Harry simply studied the older man. Then, he sighed. "I had to try. Time's running out."

Aaron inclined his head. "I get it."

Turning to Patrice, Harry said, "Major Armor is next on my list. He got enough of a break to think things through."

Around the handle of the coffee mug, Patrice's fingers trembled.

Chapter 32

Elsewhere in the hotel

Richard would've laughed if he were alone and not in this old-fashioned dining room with Steven and his parents. This time, there was no one the Kingsley patriarch could blame but himself for failing to foresee how his weapon could be turned against him. And what a spectacular failure.

Godwin thought he left the brothers with only one viable option: surrender, where they would perhaps agree to permanently sign away administrative rights in exchange for release of dividends on their stock. The former supreme court justice never expected the con man Harry Sheppard to come up with an alternative. Scorched-earth warfare.

Brad and his brothers believed destroying the network was a great compromise. As far as the five men were concerned, they would be sacrificing something material to avoid hurting their beloved grandfather and their former dean. Since Godwin supposedly was not in it for personal gain, there was nothing he could say to dissuade the self-righteous idiots.

"No way," Steven said, sipping wine. "It's an empty threat. Waste of time. They'll lose." From the time Brad contacted Godwin with the update, Steven kept saying the same thing.

Steven's father blinked rapidly in response, and his mother remained focused on her salad. She was the only woman present. Charles, thankfully, had kept his mouth shut all through dinner. The serving staff stood out of earshot but ready to help when needed.

"I'm not sure it's empty," David said, dabbing at his mouth with a napkin. "As of now, Brad has no hope of winning either before the board or in court. If the network is declared illegal, you won't have legal grounds to hold on to Peter Kingsley Company. Your cousins will at least get their own business back. I agree with Father. Let's take this seriously and come to a power-sharing agreement for now. Once they scrap the plan for the antitrust investigation, we'll figure something out."

Steven growled. "I already made my position clear to both you and Grandfather. Let Brad go to the Congress. Every damn clown in this country who has to sit in traffic for a while writes their congressman, anyway, and Brad's merely going to be one among the crowd."

"Steven," called David, tone high in exasperation. "You know it's not the same. If he asks for investigative hearings, the government won't have a choice. Not as things stand."

Previously, Brad wouldn't have dared make a public request for political intervention because the resultant economic chaos would've wiped out any chances of him getting the network back. Now, if the government demurred about holding hearings, the five men could retaliate by *causing* market fluctuations. Politicians were no doubt shitting their pants at the possibility. Godwin's brilliant strategy pushed Brad to the point where he was the only one with almost nothing to lose and a heckuva lot to gain.

"Do you hear me, Steven?" David asked. "If you refuse to talk, the hearings are happening. No doubt about it."

"I know how DC works," Steven said. "Yeah, the hearings are happening, but we have serious heavyweights on our side.

Politicians will listen more to a retired supreme court justice than some random antitrust attorney. We're not going to lose."

The clearing of a throat announced the presence of the head waiter. Exquisite cuts of meat were served, perfectly grilled to preserve flavors. Wine glasses were refilled.

"I see three ways it could play out," Richard said once the staff returned to their former spots. "One: Clinton administration gets an investigative committee to drag out proceedings until after the deadline. Then, they would intervene. A new chief could return Brad's company to him. Two: the network gets declared illegal, and your cousins get their business back. Three, we win, and the network remains intact. Chances are reasonable with your grandfather as the lead attorney, but we can't expect a slam dunk."

"Maintaining *status quo* will be easier on politicians," Steven contended. "Brad and the rest will apply serious media pressure to change minds, but—"

"PR will be critical," agreed Richard. "Key advantage for us is voters won't give a damn about antitrust law as long as they don't have to fork out more cash at the pump. We should remind people how good the markets have been over the last few years. Also, hint about economic chaos in the absence of the network. Then, we call for more regulation to keep the structure in check instead of doing away with it altogether. It should calm any remaining fears about anticompetitive practices."

"Fear is always a great motivator," Steven acknowledged, "but we might not need it. Grandfather's planning to request closed hearings."

"Closed hearings?" Richard sat up. "You mean... no press presence?"

Steven nodded in satisfaction. "None whatsoever. There won't be any media releases, either, until the entire proceeding is completed." If the public didn't hear what was being discussed, it wouldn't react in undesirable ways.

"Any committee would gladly sign off on the request," Richard said slowly.

"Yeah," Steven said. "The decision would then depend on the arguments from the two sides, and we would have the upper hand thanks to Grandfather. So let Sheppard do whatever. If he wants to have dinner with Uncle Aaron and Aunt Patrice, he can."

A jolt went through Richard. He just couldn't escape mentions of Patrice Kingsley.

A sixteen-year-old girl saw a chance to hide her mistake and marry rich at the same time. All these years, and Patrice didn't make a single move to claim her firstborn. Not even when her idiot sons taunted him as the chauffeur's kid. Now, when the five idiots were in trouble, she sent the con man to talk to Richard. Unfortunately for her, the infant she gave away turned out to be the one who could think for himself, and he wanted nothing to do with any of them.

#

Next morning

Richard had to give it up to the con man. If Steven ever harbored the slightest inclination to share power, Petty Officer Sheppard's performance today would've snuffed it out. Sheppard was shrewd, choosing his words carefully, infusing them with just enough insult to enrage the intended listener but not so much as to be credibly accused of sabotage.

"Imagine the strength of the Kingsley family if Brad and his brothers were to return home," said Sheppard, walking up and down the front of the classroom-style conference hall.

Behind him was the head table with a microphone set up for the speaker of the moment, but Sheppard had declined to sit.

Godwin, General Potts, David, and Aaron were all there along with Andrew Barrons as the elders trying to reach an amicable solution.

Richard could only assume the disabled former president didn't want to join the other men on stage and make himself the object of scrutiny. He and his pal, Noah Andersen, were in the audience, seated to the right of the room with Brad and crew. The woman—Lilah—wasn't around. Steven chose to stay on the left side, with Richard and Phillip and the Kingsley team.

The rest of the attendees also appeared to have split themselves between the two sides. Thanks to Hector recusing himself, members of the Sheppard clan picked whichever side they wanted to support. Dante Maro—the COO—and Liam Luce were of course with the five brothers.

"Peter Kingsley's sons built the network," continued the younger Sheppard brother. "The current stability in the markets is in part thanks to this structure. So imagine them back in charge. The same people who agreed to take the worst half of their family's holdings and built it into a powerhouse business. The same team which brought down a criminal like Jared Sanders. Who else here can make similar claims?"

"The same men wagered their company on a foolish business deal," called out one of the board members.

Sheppard inclined his head. "A fake deal brought to them by the current CEO's uncle Stanley for the sake of his nephew. The network was able to weather that particular storm because of the safeguards put in place by Brad and his brothers. So imagine how much more powerful this network would be if we could have peace between the two factions."

On and on it went. After Sheppard, Noah Andersen was on schedule to speak. For an old man, the former attorney general was certainly spry, but he opted to sit in the speaker's chair.

Sheppard had been canny enough not to take any names except poor Stanley's, but Andersen clearly didn't give a damn. He'd never missed an opportunity to rebuke Steven, Charles, and Stanley in the media, but Richard was usually left alone. Tonight, the chauffeur's son also found mention as part of a quartet of evil. The dangers of corporate war, the risks taken by prior unscrupulous businessmen—the implication was clear. The current CEO of the network would lead them all to catastrophe. With each anecdote, Steven's face grew darker.

Other board members spoke, some in support of Steven, some against.

"My understanding is the former justice is fully in favor of a diplomatic solution," Sheppard said, microphone in his hand once again. "We haven't heard specifically from General Potts, but I assume he agrees with Godwin, or he would've spoken up. Mr. David Kingsley—CEO of Kingsley Corp—has also expressed support. So has Mr. Aaron Kingsley. Let me say it again so no one in this room misses the following facts: yes, Godwin and the Kingsley elders are with Steven. Yes, General Potts will also argue for Steven. However, they all said previously how they didn't completely comprehend what Steven was up to in Cuba. Now, they're all in favor of negotiation. In the Kingsley family, Steven is alone in his refusal to compromise. He alone will be responsible for leading us to war."

There was a scraping sound to Richard's left as Steven pushed his chair back and stood. "What the hell is this?" he asked, voice trembling in rage. "Why am I getting cast as the bad guy? Brad and his brothers happily agreed to gamble with their company. When they lost, they went crying to their friends."

"They want their toys back," called out someone, causing laughter.

Not bothering to look away from Sheppard, Steven said, "The business was originally part of Kingsley Corp, and they managed to lose it. Sorry, but no. They're not getting it back. They're definitely not getting the network back. I'll face them in court or the Congress or wherever. If I lose, so be it, but I'm going to win. The law is with me. *I* am the good guy."

"The good guy?" asked Sheppard. He laughed, but there was nothing funny about the sound. "The *good* guy? You and your cronies attacked your own cousin's wife!"

Richard sat up. So did Phillip. There was collective shifting in the room as eyes turned toward Charles who was slouched in his chair, mostly asleep. The relative hired by the Kingsleys to babysit the family moron was right next to him.

"His sister-in-law," Sheppard reminded the audience.

Leaning toward Richard, Phillip muttered, "I thought they weren't supposed to mention her."

"Only in court," Richard muttered back.

Sheppard's gaze wandered over the room until he got to Richard. "What kind of a man attacks his own brother's wife?"

Staring back unblinkingly, Richard said, *No. I'm not falling for your mind games.* Although if Richard knew about his origins, he would've stayed the hell away from Brad's wife. In the end, it all boiled down to Patrice's silence.

Steven snarled. "This is enough," he said. "I am done."

Ignoring his father's repeated calls, Steven stalked away. Richard would've followed, but someone needed to keep an ear out for talk among the board members, and Steven's own family would be no help.

With an audible sigh, Aaron stood. "It's time for lunch in any case. Let's reconvene after."

\#

Peter Kingsley's bastard sons were talking to their uncle at a table to the far end of the banquet hall. Brad, Victor, and Alex conferred with Dan Barrons only a few feet from the Kingsley twins.

"Do you think Wheeler will change his vote?" Phillip asked Richard, keeping his tone low enough that the other two at the table—Charles and his minder—wouldn't hear.

"No," Richard said shortly. Wheeler had not been happy with what he saw as his nephews' disloyalty. Neil and Scott clearly valued their half-brothers more than their mother's family. Patrice's acceptance had a lot to do with it.

Scott suddenly looked up, catching Richard staring. Inclining his head slightly, Richard turned back to his food.

"Keep an eye on Charlie," he said to Phillip. "I'll go and get Steven." Lunch break was almost done.

Steven's mother and father were in his room with Grace Kingsley talking to her son on the couch. Richard would've left to give them privacy, but Steven said, "Why bother, Rich? Ain't anything you haven't heard before."

"This is not going to end well," Grace fretted, her expression hidden by the thick glasses. "Hector's brother is a smart man. Please, Steven. Listen to your grandfather. Make a deal with Brad. We'll worry about the rest later."

Holding up his index finger, Steven said. "Not happening. And Mother? I'll thank you not to bring it up again."

"We're all going to end up in trouble because of you," said David.

"Really, David?" asked Grace. "Because of him? You didn't say a word all these years and... the entire family is to blame for this. Steven, for God's sake, go back to the conference."

"Oh, I'm going," Steven said. "Only because I don't want to listen to any more of this."

#

An apology? Once again, Richard was struck by the urge to laugh. Sheppard had gall.

"Keep the network," repeated Sheppard. "Return Peter Kingsley Company to your cousins with the apology you owe them, and we'll call it done."

Steven said, "I did nothing illegal. Why should I apologize for someone else's stupidity? You talked about me attacking a sister-in-law. How about Cousin Brad selling out his own wife?"

"What happened between husband and wife is for them to settle," Sheppard said. "What you did was in the context of a power grab. Right in the presence of your family!"

Tuning out, Richard glanced to the right where Brad was. Glasses on his nose, he was staring at the head table with an apologetic look. Damned fool actually believed his grandfather wished them well.

Patrice did her idiot sons a disservice by not acknowledging the one man who would've knocked some sense into their heads. Richard could've shielded Brad from Godwin's machinations. Richard would've told his brother to be grateful for the good fortune tossed his way in life, including the wife he got handed to him on a platter.

Andrew Barrons's booming voice dragged Richard back to the conference hall. Not as if it mattered. They were simply going around in circles with accusations and counteraccusations. Sheppard made his way back to the chair next to Alex's. Before sitting, the former SEAL squinted in Richard's direction but didn't otherwise acknowledge him.

#

Richard had just stepped out to make a phone call when another loud voice caught his attention. Victor's gigantic form was stomping up and down the carpeted hallway, talking on his cell phone.

"Please, Luisa," the boxer-turned-chef said. "I know what I did was terrible, but..."

Luisa? The ex-wife, Richard recalled. No question she was unhappy with Victor. Nine years without a word would test the patience of most people. At least there were women in the picture for Victor and Alex. The other three didn't seem to have any social life. Brad, of course, needed to maintain decorum since he and his missus weren't officially divorced. The twins were probably being circumspect to avoid making the tabloids.

Reminding himself it wasn't any of his business, Richard headed toward the armchairs next to a potted plant. The labor contractor was waiting for a call from the owner of Armor Drilling Company. Richard was just about to cross Victor behind his back when the former boxer turned and spotted him.

"Honey," said Victor, "lemme call you back."

"Don't," said the voice on the phone.

The single-word response was loud, and Victor clearly realized Richard heard. His face went red. Tucking the device into his pocket, Victor barked, "What are you looking at?"

Richard held up both arms and continued toward the chairs.

"Damn chauffeur's son," Victor said from behind.

Richard wheeled around with every intention of taking a swing. Victor was in boxing stance already, his fists balled. The idiot was *looking* for a fight right outside the conference hall where his brothers were desperately trying to save their business from Kingsley clutches.

Shaking his head, Richard collapsed into one of the chairs.

"What's the matter?" taunted Victor. "Too chicken?"

"No," Richard said pleasantly. "Wondering how you escaped getting your ass whupped all these years. Learn how to behave with your elders."

"Heh?" Victor's mouth opened comically. "You're the same age as me."

"Five years older," Richard corrected.

"So?"

"Old-*er*," Richard enunciated, laughing. "Elder."

"Victor," someone called from the door to the conference hall. Scott Kingsley had arrived in search of big brother. Blinking at a laughing Richard, Scott asked, "What's going on?"

"Dunno," said Victor. "Maybe a screw came loose in his head."

At the comment, Richard laughed even harder.

"Here we are," Victor went on, "trying to prevent a goddamn corporate war and..."

Something he'd clearly forgotten when he was groveling with his ex.

"War is inevitable," stated Scott. "The only way to stop it would be to lock Harry up forever and send all the Kingsleys on exile. You... me... the rest... Steven... Charlie... the uncles... everyone."

Victor jerked back in obvious surprise. Laughter stopping abruptly, Richard stared at the youngest of the five brothers.

"Who would be in charge of the network then?" Victor asked as though what Scott suggested were actually an option.

Scott shrugged. "Don't know." Glancing toward their enemy, he added, "Maybe him."

Mockery even from the mild-mannered astrophysicist? Before Richard could respond, Scott placed a hand on Victor's shoulder and guided him back to the conference room. The scientist was merely protecting the former boxer from their adversary.

The five of them always stood back to back. It was them against the world. Suddenly, Richard was sure—very, very sure—he would've been welcomed into their tight little band. If Victor knew the truth, he would've crushed the jaw of anyone who dared taunt Richard.

This—*this*—was what Patrice Kingsley stole from him.

#

Richard's lack of focus wasn't getting any better. He couldn't stop staring at the five brothers sitting on the right in the front row, at the man sitting next to Sheppard's currently empty chair.

Alex, the brother most like Richard. In an alternate universe, Richard would've been the one showing young Alex how to hold a weapon, taking pride in his accomplishments. They would've eventually fought together, drank together, learned about life together.

Alex indeed got everything life had to offer. Starting from his birth, he triumphed where Richard failed. Alex grew up in the Kingsley mansion, safe in the warmth of his mother's love. No one called him a bastard. No one mocked him with the label of being a servant's son. Alex had his brothers looking out for him, his teachers to guide him through his training as a soldier. Friends, women... everyone saw him as the Kingsley golden boy, the one destined to be the hero-prince. Decorated veterans like General Potts and Harry Sheppard sang Alex's praises.

An accident of birth was all it was. Alex was lauded everywhere and by everyone, while Richard was left out in the cold, forced to make his own way in the world.

No one gave him a chance except Steven. If Patrice Kingsley's sons knew about their illegitimate half-brother, they might have accepted him, but not one acknowledged the chauffeur's son like Steven did.

"Five regions," Sheppard said to the audience. "Brad is not asking for the entire Peter Kingsley Company. The three original regions he and his brothers started with—Latin America, Africa, India—as well as the Caribbean Islands and Alaska."

"I don't care what they ask for," Steven insisted. "It's not going to happen."

"Why did you agree to this meeting then?" asked Andrew.

"I wanted to make sure they... all of you... understand my position," Steven said. "Cousin Brad does not have any legal claims on the network. After what he did, he has no moral claims, either. Even Peter Kingsley Company was formed by splitting Kingsley Corp, and my father was already the CEO at the time."

"Acting CEO," Sheppard interjected.

"What?" Steven snapped.

"*Acting* CEO," repeated the con man. "Mr. David Kingsley was never actually given the title of CEO, was he? Your grandfather kept hoping Peter—Brad's father—would return and reclaim the title. Sadly, Peter didn't return, but his sons did."

"Grandfather was grieving Uncle Peter," Steven said through gritted teeth. "He still is, so no one's had the heart to suggest changing my father's title. Regardless, Peter Kingsley Company was originally part of Kingsley Corp, and my cousins cannot have it back after being irresponsible enough to create national security problems. There will be no five regions. Before anyone asks, they're not getting five divisions in the company, either. I will not give them enough space even to pin a thumbtack."

Chapter 33

Later in the evening

"There's absolutely no reason I shouldn't have a friendly conversation with any of you," Harry said to Steven, keeping his tone light.

The clinking of cutlery and the hum of chatter continued in the banquet hall, but almost every eye in the room was turned toward Steven's table. Alex and his brothers had left before dessert was served, escorting their mother back to her hotel suite. Given the waste of time the weekend proved to be, they didn't plan to return. Their absence meant Harry's visit to this particular table would give rise to speculations of potential backstabbing.

Almost all of Brad's enemies were gathered here. Richard Armor and Phillip Potts were of course present, but both remained silent, letting their friend do the talking while they enjoyed rich chocolate liqueur. The piece of shit called Charles was sitting next to his brother, a moronic leer on his face as he asked a waitress for something. The other criminal—Jack Drummond—also opted to show up. One tore Lilah's clothes and dragged her bloodied form to the military court in Cuba. He slit Lupe's throat and stuffed her body in a trash bag. The second man went to Beijing in search of Lilah, planning to rape her before killing her on his brother-in-law's orders.

Soon, Harry promised them silently.

Armor wasn't much better than his cronies. Harry would never forget how the major instigated the sexual assault on Lilah. Steven and Richard then spent ten years ripping apart the reputation of the woman they assaulted. If it weren't for the promise Harry made to Patrice... but there was a second reason for him to talk to Steven's best friend and right-hand man.

"You sure didn't seem friendly when you were talking about me at the meeting," Steven mocked.

Harry grinned. "Morning was about network business. Right now, I'd like to have a private chat with Major Armor about one of the charities he contributes to. It's a veterans' benefit scheme, something we're both interested in."

"Forget it, Sheppard," Steven said. "I don't trust you."

"Why don't you let your pal speak for himself?" Harry asked pleasantly.

Steven flushed.

Before he could retort, Armor said, "Steven's looking out for me. I would do the same for him."

With a huff, Harry said, "I'll ask Dante to go with us. He'll make sure I return you safe and sound to the same chair you're sitting in." When there was no response, he added, "Thirty minutes, Major. I doubt it will take as much but definitely no more than thirty. Your friends can call the cops on me if you're not back by then."

#

The bar at the main hotel was crowded, and Harry didn't feel like drinking in any case. Nor did Dante and Armor. The weather was pleasant enough for a walk to a secluded corner of the garden, a few feet from where tall sconces lit the stone path. Only chirping crickets were present to witness the conversation.

Without beating around the bush, Harry asked, "Why are you still with Steven? No matter what he claims, he's not the good guy. Loyalty to friends is admirable but not when it gets to the point of enabling habitual criminal behavior. Especially not when the bad behavior is against your own family. You're an intelligent, self-made man. You know better than this."

"Family?" Armor asked. "DNA is not the only factor which counts. Steven's been an actual brother to me without being related by blood. Whatever I did so far was for my friend's benefit, and I did it gladly."

Including asking Charles to drag Lilah naked to the interrogation room if needed.

An exasperated huff came from Dante, but he didn't say anything. He'd already expressed his qualms about the entire attempt, accompanying Harry only because they agreed Patrice was done dirty by the Sheppards. Keeping his breaths steady, Harry told himself to remember his reasons for initiating this conversation.

"Your pal Alex and his brothers have done nothing but insult me at every turn," Armor finished bitterly.

Feminine laughter erupted some distance away, causing all three men to look toward the brightly lit hotel building. There was no one walking down, no one approaching the group standing in the shadows.

"Alex and the rest don't know about you," Harry pointed out. "Once they do—"

"What would it change?" snapped Armor. "Am I supposed to pretend the past didn't happen?"

No, Armor would not relent, let alone regret what he did. The brothers he wouldn't acknowledge were equally callous. They were happy to let the media caricature Lilah as a—

Suddenly, Harry had enough.

"Your brothers would be thrilled to forgive and forget," he mocked. "Aunt Patrice would want them to. She always wants them to stick together and share everything. Imagine! The same men who called you names in your childhood now falling all over themselves to make you part of the family. They would even make you the CEO of Peter Kingsley Company since you're the eldest. Yeah, you're technically not a Kingsley, but if Neil and Scott can accept Patrice as a second mother, why the hell can't the five of them accept you as Peter's son? Patrice herself is a Sheppard by birth, so you'd be related to me, too. The boys—Gabriel and Michael—would call you uncle. And hey... maybe you would get a turn with Lilah. You know, since she's supposed to be married to all the brothers."

Too far, Harry's conscience howled. The moment the words popped out of his mouth, Harry knew he went too damned far.

The angry look on Armor's face froze for a second. A sound of shock erupted from Dante, quickly subdued.

"As you said, I'm an intelligent, self-made man," Armor mocked right back. *"Of course* I believe you mean me well. *Of course* I take your word for it about being accepted as Brad's big brother. The rightful heir if you want to be fancy about it. Still, *Miss* Patrice got herself pregnant with some Greek fellow's brat and didn't think twice before giving me up. I do have to give a thought or two to the people who brought me up as their own son. I was the chauffeur's son when I enrolled at West Point. When I got to be a lawyer, I was their son. When I opened my business, I was their son. Hell, I even married the woman my mother introduced to me. It wouldn't be fair to any of them if I decide at this stage that I'm actually Peter Kingsley's son. It wouldn't be fair to Steven, either, when he's depending on me to fight the case for him. So no, thank you. I'm happy where I am."

"Last chance," Harry warned, calculating rapidly. Some way to limit the damage... "Aunt Patrice hasn't said anything to Brad and Victor and Alex yet, but once she—"

"She doesn't have to tell anyone," the major interjected. "I, too, said and did enough to the five of them over the years. No point now in putting a gun to their heads to accept me. Who knows? If they do put me in charge, I might feel compelled to turn around and hand everything to Steven."

"So you're prepared to go to war with your own kin," Harry stated. "Because of this dispute over a business which ain't even yours."

With a short laugh, Armor said, "You think this war's about the network? It's been a long time coming, Sheppard. I remember Alex swearing he'd kill me if we ever met in battle. Didn't Victor promise to break Steven's thigh? Pretty sure there's something dramatic planned for Charlie, too. Hell, you talked about Stanley—*Stanley*—today. He did nothing to you except for the one time he helped his nephew. Dan's made it clear in his interviews he's pissed at General Potts. For what? The man was the head of army intelligence, and he was merely doing his job. Who's left? Godwin? There's still you and Shawn to attack the old fellow, but my money's on one of the five, most likely Alex. The pain's sharper when it's your own blood stabbing you in the back. So go ahead. Go to the Congress and destroy it all."

#

Harry and Dante waited in silence as Armor marched off. When the major disappeared around a corner, Harry turned to Dante to suggest returning to New York.

A fist landed on Harry's jaw. Dante was not a particularly muscular individual, but the jab did sting.

"I deserved it," Harry acknowledged, rubbing his cheek.

Shaking a finger in Harry's face, Dante said, "You deserve helluva lot more. I should beat the crap out of you for what you said. My God! If Lilah gets to know... some friend you are."

Pivoting on his heel, Dante stomped off.

"Old man," Harry called. Loping, he closed the gap. "There's no excuse, but I lost my cool for a second, all right? You, of all people, should know I wouldn't hurt her."

Dante stopped and turned to face Harry. "Lost your cool? What would you have done if the major accepted your stupid offer?"

"If he really believed I would pick him over a friend... lemme put it this way... I made a promise to Lilah. Everyone who was in Cuba that day—every single one—will pay for what he did. Which includes Major Armor."

Not looking even slightly mollified, Dante repeated, "You offered her to a man who ordered an assault on her. I can't believe... we'd better pray the tabloids don't sniff out what happened. No one's going to care if you actually meant it."

"Armor won't talk," said Harry, hoping like hell his assessment was correct. "He doesn't want anyone to know about Patrice, but—"

Dante slashed a hand through the air. "I don't trust him. He's always bleating to the media about how tough it was for him growing up and how hard he worked to get where he was. No, not correct. He did bleat... once or twice. The press smelled ratings and ran with the story. A lot of reporter types buy his hard-luck act about growing up poor. Poor! Poor is what *I* was before your father gave me a job. Poor is what my neighbors in Harlem were back when I was a boy. Not the likes of Armor who... he grew up with every advantage in the world except his folks weren't as rich as the Kingsleys. Guess what? Very few people in the world are born with Kingsley kind of money and power. The rest of us simply want a way to provide for our families, maybe to make sure our children have it easier. We don't have the time to go around feeling bitter about those who already made it."

"Listen to me, please—"

"And what if he were actually poor?" Gritting his teeth, Dante glanced around unseeingly. "Show me a single poor man who raped someone because of his poverty. I would never have... most of the men I know from back in the neighborhood... it's the rich fellows who think they can do whatever the heck they please. Hector's not the only one even in our own circle. I could name a dozen I wouldn't want anywhere near my wife—God rest her soul—or a daughter. Bottom line is poverty doesn't make anyone a sex assaulter. Armor's background shouldn't matter even if he were poor. He's a criminal of the worst kind. Ready to attack women to feed his ego and his bank account."

"I agree, which is why I—"

"Didn't you hear what he said? Whatever he did was to make his friend happy. And you... you... why did you bring Lilah into the conversation?"

Harry growled in guilt and frustration. "Why are you insisting on taking my words literally when I told you I didn't mean it?"

Smacking his own forehead, Dante said, "Point is all his admirers—especially the women who feel sorry for him—*will* take you literally and on purpose. And Armor doesn't need to talk to the press. His wife is a writer. If she and the rest of them find out, what you meant won't matter. As Lilah's friend and main supporter of the Kingsley brothers, your words will seal her fate. She will always be seen as a woman who was shared by five men, then offered as a... a... *prostitute* to the same criminal who assaulted her."

"No one's gonna talk," insisted Harry. "Not as things stand. Armor doesn't want the story to become public any more than me." Placing a hand on Dante's shoulder, Harry added, "Listen, old man, you're going to be my insurance just in case. As long as we're alive, it will be his word against both of ours."

A couple of seconds passed in silence before Dante heaved in a breath. "There would be no need for insurance if you listened to me in the first place. Why did you bother to talk to Armor? What was even the point of telling him about Patrice? You knew he wasn't changing his mind."

"It had to be done... and not only because of Aunt Patrice."

"Another of your crazy schemes, I suppose," said Dante. "Explain."

Harry gestured with both hands. "As Armor told us, this war is not only about the network. It's a clash of many resentments, many fears, many allegiances, many ambitions. Before it ends, I can almost guarantee Armor will point his weapon at Alex. When it happens, I want the major's hands to shake. I want his vision to be blurry. I want the hatred he's carried all these years... his armor, so to speak... to be stripped away."

"You just bought enough time for Alex to shoot first," said Dante, understanding dawning in his voice.

"I will not let Alex die," declared Harry.

Chapter 34

The moment Richard returned to the dinner table, he wanted the solitude of his hotel room. Not his home, where Arvi would need at least perfunctory attention. She would also have more questions about Mrs. Brad Kingsley. Arvi's near-obsession with the woman was starting to wear on Richard.

Steven looked puzzled and slightly concerned when Richard pleaded a headache, but it was no lie. Avoiding the nosy stares directed his way, Richard marched out of the banquet hall. He didn't even glance toward the table where Godwin was seated with General Potts and a few of the Kingsley lawyers.

Moments later, Richard collapsed—fully clothed—into his bed. Unfortunately, the clamor of thoughts simply refused to die down.

Memories, the missed opportunities, everything that might have been…

The shrill ring from the side table jerked him back to the present. The clock next to the phone said two hours had passed since the banquet was set to end. "Hello?" Richard said into the device, making himself sound groggy.

"Rich?" came Steven's grim voice. "Sorry to bother you, man, but we need to talk. Grandfather's not happy."

Forcing a chuckle, Richard asked, "What else is new?"

"No… seriously… he's pissed about how you went with Sheppard. Once you left dinner, Grandfather sent a message about a meeting in his suite. My father was also there. They were going on about the times you missed meetings in New York. You know… recently. Grandfather thinks you're not reliable. He doesn't want you making leadership decisions for our team anymore."

"Not reliable?" Richard snapped. "So what's he planning to do? Fire me?"

"No," said Steven. Slight awkwardness in his tone, he explained, "He wants to assign you to work with someone. I don't know… help one of the other lawyers so someone can keep an eye on you."

"Not happening." Swinging his legs out, Richard sat up on the edge of the bed. "I've come too far in life to play some S.O.B.'s flunky now. Don't ask me to, my friend."

"What the hell am I going to do?" brooded Steven. "Grandfather absolutely refuses to… he won't give you another chance. If I force the issue… what if *he* backs out?"

"Lemme make it easier for everyone," said Richard. "I quit. You can tell Godwin it was no picnic working for him, either."

"Rich!" exclaimed Steven, sounding frantic. "Don't do this to me. I need both of you, or Cousin Brad's gonna win."

"You will always have me," Richard said. "Maybe not as official part of the team, but you can still talk to me, can't you? Whatever advice I would've given as your attorney, I will give as your friend. Trust me... I will be with you all the way to the end no matter what Godwin has to say about it."

Or what anyone else in the world had to say.

#

"Great," Richard muttered, staring at the duo who showed up at the door five minutes after the conversation with Steven. Peace was clearly not in the cards tonight. "I suppose you've heard the whole story," he said to Aaron Kingsley.

Too many damned people were in the know, except Richard himself until recently and the five idiots who still believed he was their servant's son.

Peering up and down the carpeted hallway, Aaron said, "Let's talk inside before someone sees."

The five brothers had already left town, and the rest of the Kingsleys—including Aaron and Patrice—were staying at the luxury inn located on the same property. Still, the Sheppards, the Barronses, and other businessmen were around and would definitely wonder why the mother of Brad, Victor, and Alex was visiting their sworn enemy.

"Please, son," Aaron added.

Richard stepped to the side to allow them in. "Major," he corrected, closing the door. "Or Armor. I'm the son of the chauffeur as you're aware. What can I do for you, Miss Patrice?"

"No," she said, shaking her head. For as long as Richard could remember, Patrice had been small and skinny, and she'd clearly lost more weight. There was plenty of gray in her brown hair now, and her face appeared pale under the bright lights in the room. "You know who I am."

"Yes," Richard bit out. "I also know how old I am. You had a few years to acknowledge me but didn't."

"Circumstances..." she started.

"What circumstances?" he asked. "The fact you married a rich man and had three kids with him? Nothing's changed there. So why are you here now?"

"Richard," Aaron called.

Holding up a finger, Richard said, "I'm not an idiot, sir. Sheppard must have told both of you what I said, and the *only* reason Miss Patrice still came to me is she realizes the situation is going to escalate. She wants to make sure her sons don't get any boo-boos."

"You happen to be one of her sons," Aaron said.

Richard huffed in irritation. "Once again... no. I'm Richard Armor, adopted son of the Kingsley chauffeur. My birth mother was callous enough to give me up. What kind of an evil woman gives up her newborn?"

"The kind who didn't have another way to feed and protect you," Aaron said. "And Patrice didn't simply give you away. You were adopted into a loving home, where she was able to keep an eye on you."

"She was about to marry into the Kingsley family," Richard said. "From what I understand, her husband knew about her little problem. She could've found a way to keep me, but she didn't because it might have interfered with her plans for the future. She could've given me all the advantages her other children got, but she didn't. So she has no more claims on me."

"Be angry," Patrice said, voice trembling. "You have every right. But if you continue with Steven, you're going to end up fighting your own brothers. I don't want my sons hurting each other."

On a mirthless chuckle, Richard said, "That ship has already sailed."

"Nobody can change the past," Patrice said, tears flowing down her cheeks. "But we can move on, can't we?"

"Move on?" Richard asked. "How? Withdraw from the case? Steven's depending on me."

"If you can't withdraw," Patrice said, "at least don't do anything besides advising Steven. He will ask. You know he will."

"So?" asked Richard. "People have been expecting Alex and me to come to blows for years. He has Sheppard helping him now. If they create problems for us, Steven will expect me to take care of them. There are only two ways out for me. Either tell the truth and dump Steven or have everyone believe I left because I was afraid of coming face-to-face with the golden boy. Not happening. I'd rather put a bullet to my own head."

Sobbing openly, Patrice said, "I'm going to lose a son one way or the other."

"How about this?" Richard asked. "As far as the world is concerned, you have five sons, including the two from your husband's mistress. I won't do anything to Brad, Victor, Neil, or Scott. Alex is a different matter. If I die, you'll still have Alex. If he dies, I'll call a presser and announce I'm your son. Your number will remain a nice, round five."

"Richard!" exclaimed Aaron.

"What?" mocked Richard. "Are you going to call the cops and say I threatened your family? Go right ahead. They've threatened me plenty of times. In front of witnesses, too, including her."

"What I want is for you and everyone else to stop trying to kill each other," Aaron said. "Yes, you've had problems in the past, but you've given as good as you got, Major. More, in fact. I was there, remember? I saw all of you in action. And if you can forgive the other four, why not Alex? What the hell did he do that's unforgivable?"

Nothing at all. Except Alex was everything Richard could've been if he got the chance. The chauffeur's son would not find peace as long as the Kingsley golden boy remained alive.

Part XII

Chapter 35

Two weeks later, October 1998

Long Island, New York

"I forgot, okay?" Michael said, hoping it would put an end to the damned interrogation.

"How could you forget?" Tara asked, tone grumpy. "I don't believe you. First, you say there was no reason. Next, you claim you got mad at us for taking up too much space. In this giant basement! Now, you have amnesia."

At least they were talking. As soon as he was allowed to see her after the surgery, Michael again apologized for being a shithead during the argument with his father. He also apologized to his ma for divulging her secret without her permission. Ma looked startled, then gratified. Maybe the blood loss made Tara less angry, but she finally muttered, "Cool." Nor did she object when Sabrina told her she was returning home with them. There would be no more discussions of hostels or crashing at Lilah's.

The hospital okayed Tara to start school only the week before. Everyone at Schreiber High—including Michael's dumb friends— was curious about the girl who was in the news. She sat in the cafeteria and told the story as though she were actually conscious at the time. Juicier details/crazier lies appeared with each recounting, which Michael and Gabriel dutifully corroborated.

Unfortunately, relentless rain and doctor's orders confined Tara to the house in the evenings. They couldn't even walk the half a mile to the beach.

Most times, Tara rested on the couch in the basement and sped through homework, then bugged Michael and Gabriel to entertain her. The chick seemed to enjoy hearing Michael on the flute, although she looked about ready to pass out when he played "Barbie Girl." Tonight, they decided to watch TV in said basement. Somehow, it made Tara remember the fight which led to her walkout, and she wanted to know what caused it.

Michael tried every excuse he could think of, but his adversary was relentless. Gabriel was no help. The schmuck simply went on smirking.

It's a guy thing, Michael tried out in his mind. No, it would only lead to more questions about what guy thing. Michael wasn't about to admit he thought stupid Gabe was dancing with her on purpose to make fun of his cousin for liking her.

"There must have been a reason," Michael finally said, "but I don't remember now. I *may* have been irritated because you guys were loud. How does it matter, anyway?"

"I just want to know," Tara said. "Why can't I know?"

"*I* want to watch football," interjected Gabriel. The Vikings were playing, and he was a big fan. "The game's about to start, so can you both shut up?"

"Don't say shut up," Tara reproved. "It's rude."

Gabriel turned in place to stare at her. "You curse all the time."

"But I'm not rude," Tara insisted, looking mutinous. "Cursing is different."

Gabriel groaned. "Bro, can you take her for a walk around the yard or something? Girl's cranky."

With a growl, Tara sat up, then winced. The surgical wounds, obviously, which she seemed to forget about every other minute.

Michael snorted, turning it into a cough when she glared. "I gotta finish my history homework," he said, "and the damn textbook's in the kitchen. Do you wanna stay down here or go up with me? I'm making popcorn."

The kitchen was quiet, Michael's history book open on the small dining table in the center. The Nokia 9110 Communicator his mom recently bought was also there. The device actually had a QWERTY keyboard and not just a T9 keypad.

"Your mom's a huge feminist," Tara said suddenly.

"Big time," said Michael, grabbing a bag of popcorn and tossing it into the microwave. "She says everyone's a feminist if they believe in equal rights."

Tara settled into a chair and tapped on the mobile phone with a delicate finger. "I heard her and Lilah talking. Sabrina was so pissed at Maestro and everyone else for stopping Lilah from testifying. And they went to *Harry* to discuss it. Sabrina said if Lilah were a man, these guys would've given her a medal."

"Sounds like Ma," Michael agreed.

All the adults were currently in Mr. Temple's home, talking to the lawyers. Politicians from both major parties were already contacted about an antitrust investigation. Loose ends had to be tied off to avoid charges of opportunistic ethics regarding the problematic nature of the network. Media writeups had to be sent. Even the businesses on their side raised several questions about the process and the desired endpoints. Yeah, they were all busy.

Uncle Dan was again in Spain, meeting with refinery owners. Michael's ma used the excuse of school not to allow him and Gabe to accompany Dan. As though they couldn't fly there for a weekend to scout out the town. The bull run wasn't even on at this time!

What happened to Tara made Sabrina even more obsessed with the safety of the kids in her care.

Guards patrolled their yard and monitored access points from the electronic surveillance room. The alarms and stuff on the windows and doors were also updated. Michael still couldn't believe it. With all the other people around—people directly involved with the network—Tara was attacked.

Michael's heart sped unpleasantly at the memory. As long as he lived, he wouldn't forget the sight of Tara's blood spilling between his fingers as he tried to put pressure on her wounds. The secret service officers had sprinted out in seconds, replacing Michael. Still, the smell of warm iron, the wheezing sounds from the unconscious girl—

"What's the matter?" Tara asked as Michael waited next to the microwave. "You look funny."

Michael shrugged. "Nothing. I mean... I was remembering... I'm glad you didn't die."

Rolling her eyes, she said, "I'm glad I didn't die, too. Tell me why you were fighting with Gabriel."

"Uhh... I was..."

The microwave pinged, and the buttery smell of popcorn spread through the kitchen. Hurriedly ripping the bag open, Michael stuffed a handful into his mouth. Heat exploded on his tongue. He spat, spewing popcorn everywhere.

Tara giggled. The familiar glint in her dark eyes intensified. As always, her curls bounced around like they were playing background dancers to her body. And what a bod! The tee looked weird with the bandages underneath, but the rest of her was trim and athletic. The legs... Lordy, the legs.

Michael ran to grab a broom and started to sweep the spilled popcorn. He needed to keep his back turned to Tara before she noticed something different. "Do you have a boyfriend?" he blurted. The moment the words were out of his mouth, he wished he could take them back. *He* had a girlfriend. "I thought he might be worried or something after what happened."

"I don't..." she started. "There was one, but I dumped him."

"Why?" Cleanup done, Michael plonked himself into a chair and dragged the history text closer.

Munching on what remained in the bag, she said, "He got too handsy."

"Oh." Suddenly, Michael got a mental image of some schmuck trying to force a kiss on an unwilling Tara. Dude was lucky he wasn't in the room, or Michael would've broken his dumb jaw.

"Why are you looking like that?" Tara asked.

Michael cleared his throat. "Like what?"

"You have a girlfriend, so why shouldn't I have a boyfriend?"

"No... I mean... yes..." Michael shook his head. "I wasn't thinking anything about your stupid boyfriend."

"So you won't mind if I get a new one?"

"No," Michael said shortly. She sounded peculiar, like... like... since Tara woke from surgery, she'd stopped ignoring him, but it didn't mean... did it? She even smiled at him once or twice. "Do you want me to mind?"

Her face went all funny and red. "No! You're an idiot. Why would I want you to mind?"

Michael stared hard for a couple of seconds. She looked like she was waiting for him to say something further. Taking a deep lungful of air, he asked, "Would you mind if I minded?"

Her breathing seemed faster than before, and she appeared a bit unsure for the first time since they met. Words running together,

Tara countered, "Would you mind if I told you I wouldn't mind if you minded?"

Michael could feel the widest grin he ever had coming on. "I don't mind..." He frowned. "Could you say it again? Just to make sure we're thinking the same thing."

"All right, brother and sister!" boomed Gabriel as he danced his way into the kitchen and made straight for the refrigerator.

Quickly flipping through the pages of the textbook, Michael rearranged himself into a nonchalant slouch. Tara sat straight and picked a single kernel of corn to nibble on.

Turning, Gabriel took a swig from his can of Coke and scrutinized the other two. Brows drawing together, he asked Tara, "You all right?"

"I'm fine," she said. "Why?"

Gesturing with the can, he said, "You're sitting kinda stiff. I thought maybe the pain's back."

"No," Tara said.

"Cool." Gabriel added, "Bro, my girl wants to watch some chick flick this weekend. Go with me, please. Bring Erika."

Erika... shit! Michael darted a glance at Tara's face. Her expression was frozen as though she, too, forgot about Erika's existence for a brief time. "Nah," he said. "Love you, man, but no."

As soon as Gabriel returned to the basement, Tara pushed her chair back and stood.

"Don't go," Michael said urgently. "I mean don't take it back. Please? Gimme a couple of days to talk to Erika."

"I'm tired," Tara announced, scurrying toward the stairs without a backward glance.

Shit, Michael muttered again in his mind. *Shit-shit-shit-shit-shit.*

She probably thought he was a cheating jerk. Or she was uncomfortable because all the horny thoughts Michael entertained about her were suddenly obvious.

No, he said to himself. Michael would simply have to learn how to act normally around Tara. The last thing he wanted was to provoke her to walk out a second time and get shot by who knew which villain.

Chapter 36

A day later

On the CD player in Temple's workshop, Frank and Nancy Sinatra hummed the last few notes of "Somethin' Stupid." Massaging her brow with a fingertip, Lilah reminded herself for the hundredth time there was no need for Tara to avoid the one window in the workshop. The Hermitage was fitted with top-of-the-line security features, including bulletproof glass.

The girl was here with the silk ties she made for the former president's security officers. She wanted to thank them for helping save her life. Temple and Noah also got one each. All giftees appeared quite tickled.

Michael had escorted Tara across the yard, but he was staring at Temple's current project—a replica of the Eiffel Tower—as though he never saw it before. The young lady was also working hard at avoiding Michael's eyes. Lilah bit back a smile. The angst of puppy love would always trump any political drama.

Their other visitor looked slightly impatient. For Andrew Barrons, few things outside his business were worth the time. At least he showed up here at Noah's request.

Please let there be something, Lilah murmured in her mind. It was imperative to find ways to take out one or more of the leaders of the Kingsley army.

Another five minutes passed before Noah and Lilah escorted the oilman to the library. Andrew was a couple of decades younger than the former attorney general, but the driller was huffing and puffing by the time they got to their destination.

Noah took his position next to the corkboard with the Kingsley family tree. One picture had been removed from the board—Amber's. Lilah took it out before bringing the board down to the library, or the Kingsley brothers would've tattled to their grandfather.

Flicking only a brief glance at the images, Andrew slumped onto the couch. With a cough, he dug into his pocket.

Watching him put a pill under his tongue, Noah asked, "Are you all right, Andrew? You took some medicine when we met at your house, and Neil thought it could be nitroglycerine."

Andrew waved a dismissive hand. "Getting older like everyone else. The cardiologist wants to do a procedure next week. Forget about it for now and get to the point of this meeting."

Lilah rolled aside the section of the bookshelf behind which was the steel-doored locker. Retrieving a snapshot from the locker, she seated herself in one of the chairs. "I'm sure you know her," she said, sliding the photograph across the coffee table.

A teenager dressed in a two-piece polka dot swimsuit laughed at the camera. Short, blonde curls framed the oval face, and beads circled her neck. Barefooted, Amber was leaning back against the railing of a ship, clicked in the act of blowing a kiss to the photographer. At the lower right corner of the image, flamboyant cursive said, "Love you always. Amber Barrons."

The change in expression on Andrew's face from mild interest to dismay was so swift that it was comical.

Lilah held herself still, not saying a word. In the other chair, Noah also stayed silent, waiting for Andrew to slip up, to say something.

"How..." the oil driller croaked. "Temple?"

"He'd planned to talk to Godwin about her," Noah said, tone steady.

"To Godwin?" Andrew frowned. "But why? He already knows."

Already? It didn't make sense.

Like Lilah, Noah didn't respond out loud.

It took Andrew under ten seconds to lean back on the couch. "You don't have a clue," he mused. "You were hoping to catch me off-guard."

Noah sighed. "Look, Andrew. I didn't call you here with a trap in mind. What we do know is Amber's story was what Temple planned to use against Godwin for Brad's pardon. Then, the assassination attempt. Until now, I couldn't ask you for more info about the girl because there was a chance you would go straight to Godwin with it. Since things changed, please tell us what it is about Amber that would spook Godwin."

"Why would..." Shaking his head, Andrew asked, "Did Temple actually tell you this, or did you add two and two and come up with five? Because I don't understand why he would think this old story would work on Godwin."

"It shocked *you,*" Noah pointed out.

Face flushed, Andrew coughed again. "The whole episode was unpleasant for all concerned. Not something I wanted to remember. There's nothing else."

"Are you sure?" asked Noah. "I shouldn't have to tell you... Dan's right now in Muskiz with Saeed al-Obeidi, talking to the refinery owners. In about two weeks, they'll make the first official complaint against the network. Once they do, other unaffiliated companies will follow."

A jolt went through Lilah's chest as it did each time the town in Northern Spain was mentioned. The Kingsleys had strong connection to the area through their relative, Jack Drummond. His father was part-owner of one of the nightclubs in nearby Pamplona, through which an Irish cartel moved black money. Nightclub meant performers, and underground gossip among strippers in the Schengen travel zone got to Eden in Berlin, the club once owned by Lupe Valdez.

Their side was able to keep tabs on Drummond through Eden. The criminals in the region would also use the same network to keep a list of everyone who helped Peter Kingsley's sons. Dan put himself in danger each time he traveled to Spain.

"I expect Congress to start investigative hearings in three to four months," continued Noah.

The former attorney general was talking to every politician he could think of to make it happen. So was Andrew.

"What the committee hears from both sides will decide whether they refer the case to the Justice Department." If the lawyers at Justice also agreed the network's existence violated antitrust laws, the government would go to court to get an order for dissolution. "If there is any way at all to stop Godwin from testifying... the word of a former supreme court justice will carry considerable weight."

"Should've thought about it before you started down this road," retorted Andrew. "I didn't want to get involved, but y'all forced me to, anyway. Then, Alex came up with this dumb idea of not using any 'magic weapons.' What kind of la-la land does he live in? Too bad Dan won't let Barrons withdraw, or the minute I heard..."

Huffing, Noah said, "I agree with you on the sheer stupidity of what Alex and his brothers said, but they're not going to change their minds. Which makes it critical for us to find some other way to weaken the enemy. If there's anything in the Amber story we can use against Godwin…"

"There isn't," said Andrew, getting to his feet. "Now, lemme tell you something else, Andersen. I don't appreciate being ambushed like this. The same goes for you, Delilah."

Watching him march out, Lilah said, "He's lying. There *is* something."

"I agree," said Noah. "Problem is he would've blabbed if he believed it would help us take out Godwin. Barrons O & G stands to lose if we go down."

"So either we're totally off-track," Lilah muttered, "or he's not talking for some other reason." Some reason more important to Andrew than his business.

Chapter 37

Next week, October 1998

Upper East Side, New York City

The monitor beeped at a steady rate, reassuring the patient on the bed he was still alive. Although from the words of the doctor who showed up to get consent, Andrew could have a heart attack, a stroke, kidney failure, could end up getting his leg amputated, and might even die during the procedure. But—the medic-in-training hurried to add—a coronary stent was a routine event. Not a big deal, really.

"Yeah, yeah, whatever," grumbled Andrew. "Let's get this over with." The corner suite in the VIP section of the hospital was bright and airy and boasted of large windows with stunning views of

Manhattan Island. There was none of the clamor usually associated with healthcare facilities, and the brochure promised world-class cuisine. Andrew would've preferred to trudge through the dirtiest of the oilfields he owned.

The junior doctor announced that Andrew was the next patient in line for the cath lab. The young fellow left with the signed forms, pulling shut the door to the VIP room.

"Behave yourself in there," Daniel said, tone light. "Don't give the staff a hard time and don't push them to release you before you're ready."

Shenanigans over the network aside, no one could ask for a better son and heir than Daniel. Andrew disagreed with the idea of a sister's needs trumping the investments of hundreds of Barrons shareholders, but the bond with his twin was probably part of what made Daniel the caring son he was. He was in a business suit and would return to work as soon as he heard the procedure went without a hitch. Andrew insisted on it. Work was worship as his own father had been fond of saying.

Caroline was also present. Even as a seventeen-year-old, she'd been elegant, stylish, and used to dealing with the moneyed class thanks to her father's career as a high-ranking diplomat. Besides, she inherited the ambassador's knack for getting ruffled egos back to the negotiating table. Perfect wife material for a wealthy businessman. Caroline wanted escape from the household which included her papa's much younger second wife, and the pre-nup Andrew offered was quite generous. She agreed to remain physically loyal and keep her lips zipped about the war injury he sustained in Okinawa. They'd been stuck together long enough to develop friendship of a sort.

The other one—Shawn—had called in the morning to check on Andrew. Which was unexpected given how the young man continued to hold a grudge over what happened decades ago. Shawn still refused to understand how going public forced Andrew's hand. The news about the then-heir would've caused shareholders to revolt. Other businessmen could potentially have refused to work with Barrons. Disinheriting Shawn was essentially a business decision.

In any case, oil and gas didn't really interest him, and he made a success of himself in a field which was more tolerant of his odd preferences. Shawn also had an active love life—*very* active, given the number of men featured with him in gossip magazines.

"Are we all set, Mr. Barrons?" an overly cheery voice asked. A smiling face peered in through the open door.

"Could you give me a minute?" Andrew asked his wife and adopted son. "I need to make a phone call."

Daniel huffed. "I thought we agreed not to—"

"It's not work," Andrew said. "I... ahh... want to talk to Shawn."

The surprise on the faces of the other two was obvious, but Daniel inclined his head and guided his sister—his half-sister—out. His stance with her was nearly as protective as it was with Delilah.

One of the transport personnel asked if he and his colleagues could stick around and unhook hospital equipment. Responding with a wave of his hand, Andrew made the call.

Shawn picked up within a couple of rings. The familiar sounds of an office could be heard in the background. "Everything went well?" Shawn asked.

"They're just moving me to the lab," said Andrew, keeping an eye on the staff bustling around. They weren't likely to understand most of what was being said, but he kept his voice low regardless. "I'm calling about something else. I met Andersen last week. And Delilah. They wanted to know about Ambrosia."

"Amb... Amber?" Shawn's surprise came through clearly. "Why?"

"So you didn't tell them," Andrew brooded.

"No. I promised you I wouldn't, and I kept my word. Although... Lilah did ask me about Amber once. She said she was just curious."

"And?"

"I said I'd heard about her but didn't know anything more than everyone else. Oh, and the beads were simply in the house, and I found them. She said there's a photograph."

"I saw," Andrew said impatiently. "I don't get why Delilah thinks it's important for the network."

"Really?" asked Shawn. "As in important *now?* Not just back when Amber was supposed to marry the Kingsley guy?"

"Correct."

"Doesn't make sense."

"Yeah," said Andrew. "Something's not adding up."

"We have to go now, sir," said the female transporter.

Holding up a finger, Andrew requested some more time. "Listen, Shawn. These people gave me a spiel about... er... the chances of dying."

There was a cluck at the other end of the line. "C'mon, Andrew, you're not going to—"

"I'm serious," Andrew said. "If something does happen to me, I want you to know your obligation to me will be over. Talk to Delilah about your... about Ambrosia. If there's any way the info can help with the network issue, we should use it."

"But wait until after you're not around to hear people say embarrassing things," Shawn stated, tone exasperated. "Thirty years later, you're still the same self-centered asshole." He growled. "Andrew, if Amber's death does have something to do with the network, Lilah needs to know. Now!"

"But what could it be?" Andrew mused. "Andersen insinuated it's why Temple got shot."

Shawn hissed. "My God! I did think he got shot to keep him from helping Brad, but if Noah's right, *you* could be in danger."

The man who hired the assassin could've thus far believed Andrew knew nothing incriminating. Or the Barrons chief executive could've been kept under surveillance to make sure he made no alarming moves. The act of aligning himself with the returned exiles would definitely be cause for alarm for the enemy.

"I would've agreed with you," Andrew said, motioning to the hospital staff he was finally ready to get on the gurney. "Except the markets will react if anything happens to me. Foolish move to make right when the government is breathing down everyone's necks. Anyway, I simply don't see how the story could embarrass anyone other than me."

"I'm flying to New York tonight," Shawn announced. "As soon as you're out of the hospital, we're going to call Lilah. Before it's too late."

Chapter 38

Forty-six years ago, November 1952

Upper East Side, New York City

"Too late now," said the woman in the sickbed, her tired voice still carrying a thread of the spirit Temple remembered.

The cancer which spread through her body had eaten up much of the beauty, reducing her to almost skin and bones. She'd refused an actual hospital, though, preferring to spend her final days in her magnificent suite in the Gilded Age mansion. Sylvia Kingsley, *née* Fontaine, wanted her last sight to be of the opulence of silk-lined walls and glittering chandeliers and velvet sheets, of uniformed servants waiting to cater to her every whim. No one else was present at the moment except her firstborn. No one else could be allowed to hear the last of the secrets she would leave with her son.

Chuckling, Sylvia repeated, "Too late. For her and for me."

Temple didn't ask how she could laugh about her impending death. Sylvia would exit life the same way she lived it. Mocking the world for imagining she could be crushed. What he couldn't figure out was if she actually realized what she was saying. The amount of morphine pumped into her veins to keep her from feeling pain had surely loosened her tongue.

"You don't believe me?" she asked, drawing her head back on the pillow to peer at him.

"I do," Temple muttered. He wasn't even shocked any longer. That came when he first heard the story a day before. He spent the entire night thinking, going over Amber's every encounter with the Kingsleys. He still didn't understand why Sylvia was revealing the entire sordid saga to him when she'd been a full participant in Godwin's campaign to rid himself of the problem created by Amber.

"It had to be done," croaked Sylvia. "So many years of planning. One silly girl could've destroyed it all. She could not be allowed to marry Godwin."

Like the rest of New York, all Temple heard initially was how the Kingsley drunk refused to marry Amber because she was playing him against a former lover. Godwin declared he would not pressure his half-brother, so Amber stormed into the Kingsley mansion and demanded *he* marry her instead. After all, it was his idea to drag her into a marital alliance with the Kingsleys. When she was thrown out, she showed up at his office and threatened a breach-of-promise lawsuit. Her spiritual adviser, a priest named Axeman, cornered Godwin at a social event.

Godwin Kingsley was too enamored of his own reputation and too attached to the family honor to marry a woman intended for his half-brother no matter what the lady wished. Nor would he ever allow a woman to hold any kind of power over him. On Sylvia's part, an alliance between the son of the first Mrs. Kingsley and the Barronses was not to be tolerated. Godwin and Sylvia got Rev. Axeman out of the way by having him transferred to a war-torn country in South America where he was promptly killed by some malcontents. The Kingsleys then pushed and pushed a young woman in desperate circumstances. They maligned her character and painted her crazy from a need for revenge. Amber wouldn't have dared say a word about the child she carried until there was a father she could point to. She stood to lose more if he publicly denied paternity.

If Andrew Barrons didn't agree to take her in...

Luckily for an innocent child, the oilman saw something in the situation for himself. A chance for an heir. Only a few knew Shawn wasn't Andrew's son. Temple was aware of the oil driller's war injury, but he'd actually believed the kid belonged to the boyfriend Godwin claimed to have existed. So did Andrew.

Temple thought Godwin and Sylvia were doing Amber a kindness by keeping their mouths shut about the child. Now... Sylvia had always been ruthless, but Godwin...

"He made a mistake," Temple said. "But he could've..."

Sylvia laughed again. "You're a politician. How can you be this naïve?"

He wasn't. Reputation *was* important for supreme court justices. Not to mention the family's standing in society. Those in the same social strata as the Kingsleys were no strangers to such behavior from men, but actually acknowledging what happened would lead to a major scandal. Especially when the woman involved hailed from another old-money clan.

Godwin would've seen no choice but to completely discredit Amber. He knew what she could end up doing, but he went ahead with the plan, anyway.

"God," Temple whispered. One mistake, a single mistake on the part of an otherwise exceptional man—it *was* too late now.

Amber had agreed to leave her baby with Andrew and return home to rebuild her life. However, her traumatized mind slipped over the edge after the birth of the child. She'd been gone for more than two years, and the boy was known to New York society as Andrew's son. Amber's parents—the lad's maternal grandparents— were given a tidy sum by Godwin and weren't inclined to pursue the matter further when doing so would only malign the reputation of their departed child. They were not aware of the boy's actual paternity, either.

If the truth came out, the Kingsleys still wouldn't acknowledge the child, and humanity was unkind to those it perceived as orphans.

"Too late," Temple agreed.

Of the five people who knew the whole story, two were dead already and the third dying. Once Sylvia passed, only Temple and Godwin would remain, and they would also carry the secret to their graves.

#

Back in the present, October 1998

Upper East Side, New York City

Temple hadn't been back to a hospital since the time he got shot. It was not a memory he cherished, but this one—at least this section—looked more like a five-star hotel. Art on the walls, potted plants and flowers, sunlight and cheery warmth everywhere. Noah surely had a reason for being this bright-eyed about visiting a medical facility, but the décor couldn't be it. The former attorney general appeared almost giddy with excitement as he marched alongside Temple.

A woman in blue scrubs sprinted past the secret service officers, making Temple miss a step. As the closest officer steadied the former politician with a hand on the elbow, the woman ran in through a door at the far end of the hallway. Three people—two male and one female—remained outside the room. A patient's family, perhaps. Yeah, fancy furnishings aside, this was still a place for the sick and the dying.

Pace suddenly slowing, Noah called out something, and one of the men turned toward the approaching group. Daniel Barrons. His sister—Andrew's wife—was next to him. They appeared to be in intense discussion with the third person. A hospital official from the badge on the lapel.

The former president frowned. Who were they visiting? Surely, not Andrew. The man was a good couple of decades younger than Temple and Noah. Which of course didn't mean much when it came to illnesses.

"What's going on?" Temple muttered to Noah, but as always, his brain failed him at exactly the wrong moment.

Noah didn't appear to have understood the words. He surely couldn't have forgotten how the Barrons men were not on the list of visitors allowed in Temple's home. When Temple ran into any of the Barronses in a public place, he made sure to stay where everyone could see there was no *tête-à-tête* happening. Being seen talking with the former politician would be dangerous to Shawn's health.

Despite it, Andrew showed up in Long Island recently. Now, this.

As Temple got closer to the room, he noted the pallor on the faces of the brother-sister duo. Noah, too, was frowning, having picked up on the tension.

Daniel was clearly unhappy about something. "I left..." he said to the hospital official, "...why did you..."

Palms upturned, the official launched into an explanation. "...can't stop... patient allowed the visitor..."

"Everything okay?" Noah asked Daniel.

Tapping his mouth with the back of his knuckles, Daniel said, "No. Andrew went into... we didn't realize... the front desk..."

Another man joined the group, this one wearing a security guard's uniform. Whatever he said only served to make Dan angrier. Lilah's twin was not the sort to raise his voice, but he stabbed at the air with his index finger, saying to the hospital official, "Call the police. If you don't, I will."

The police? Was there an accident? An attack? So why was Andrew here in a private room instead of the ICU?

"Hey," Dan shouted down the hallway, raising his arm.

When Temple stumbled around, he saw yet another familiar face. General Potts was exiting what appeared to be a conference room. There were two hospital guards with him.

"Stop the..." said Dan, striding down.

The security guard with the hospital official said something and sprinted around to block Dan's way. The Barrons heir seemed ready to knock the guard to the floor and tackle Potts who stood watching the scene with an impassive expression. Noah and one of the secret service officers went to Dan, clearly urging him not to escalate.

Temple frowned again. Why was Potts here? There was history between him and the Barronses. Potts certainly didn't show up to visit Andrew when he was ill.

"Dan," a trembling voice called from behind. Caroline Barrons was still at the door where they left her. If she'd been pale before, she appeared paper white now. There were no tears on her cheeks, but her shoulders were heaving. A fellow in a lab coat stood next to her, looking somber.

"No," said Dan, back at his sister's side in seconds. "God, no."

As he drew her against his shoulder, Temple caught sight of the room through the cracked open doorway. A few hospital personnel were moving around, one of them writing in a chart. No one was checking on the man who lay motionless in the middle of the bed. A flat green line sped across the monitor on the wall.

"Andrew?" whispered Temple.

Part XIII

Chapter 39

Six months later, April 1999

Trinity Church Cemetery and Mausoleum

Washington Heights, New York City

Sitting next to Shawn on the gray stone retaining wall, Lilah watched while Daniel and Caroline offered respects at the newest granite memorial amid the clutter of previously departed Barronses. It was Andrew's birthday, and Caroline wanted to visit. He would've been seventy-four if he lived.

Strange how time abruptly ended for the dead while it continued to move forward for the rest of the world. When Andrew passed in early autumn, the thick-trunked old trees overlooking the grassy knolls would've been shedding leaves. Green was now sprouting back on the same branches. Past the low mounds, the blue-gray waters of the Hudson went on flowing. Even in the tranquility of the burial grounds, sounds of continuing life intruded—human voices from not too far away, the rumble of traffic, an occasional honk.

The survivors might grieve, but they would also eventually move on. Caroline wasn't ready to let go yet, but—

"I don't understand it," Lilah murmured, pulling off her fleece and tossing it to the side. It had been chilly in the Adirondack Mountains where she spent the last two days rappelling in an attempt to bring order to her thoughts. The air was much warmer in the city. "Shawn, my mama was only a few years older than Caroline, so it was never a mother-child equation. Plus, Caroline made it crystal clear she wanted nothing to do with Mama or me. But Papa loved all three of us—Dan, me, and Caroline. So why did she... to simply waste her whole life like this!"

Shawn shrugged. "Caroline was only seventeen when she married Andrew. More sheltered than you were at the same age. My guess would be she didn't think things through, and Andrew was not above taking advantage of her naiveté. Then, she was stuck." Divorce would've been scandalous back in the day, and her family was not rich enough to see her through it unscathed. "Andrew and Caroline got along well enough in any case. Although I didn't anticipate her being this crushed at his passing."

"Still," whispered Lilah. "We could've supported each other. If only she said something to me..." Even now, Caroline wouldn't talk to Lilah if she could possibly help it.

Faraway expression on his face, Shawn said, "Life seems full of if onlys."

"If only Amber never died?" Lilah asked gently.

"Yes," said Shawn. "If only her parents didn't take money from the Kingsleys. If only they decided to take me, instead." By the time Shawn realized he was Amber's son, his maternal grandparents had passed. He added, "And if only you trusted me enough to tell me her death was important."

Cheeks heating up, Lilah said, "I didn't want to make you choose between me and Andrew. I didn't know that he..."

"...wasn't actually my father," Shawn completed. "If only Andrew hadn't been this selfish. But he genuinely believed there was nothing in the story to embarrass anyone other than himself. What I can't believe is the arrogance of letting Potts into his room."

Security camera footage from the hospital and staff testimony agreed how General Potts merely showed up at the front desk and asked to visit his old acquaintance. Andrew himself allowed the general up.

"Arrogance is the right word," Lilah said. "Andrew wouldn't have believed the Kingsleys would dare attack him."

The oilman went into cardiac arrest during Potts's visit. According to the nursing staff, the general immediately called for help. CPR was started in under a minute, but the patient didn't make it. Hospital management contended how Andrew was merely one among the small number of patients who arrested during coronary stents. On Dan's insistence, an autopsy was performed, but there was nothing to suggest foul play. High-dose intravenous potassium—the method suggested by the forensic expert Dan hired—wouldn't show up in post-mortem blood tests.

Brad and his brothers refused to consider the possibility of Andrew's death being murder for political purposes. They laughed at the suggestion of their former dean's involvement. The five men weren't told about the Amber episode because, of course, they wouldn't believe it. Other than the Barronses, only Noah and Harry were in the know.

"It was about Amber's boyfriend," Lilah insisted. "Your biological father. Sending Potts on a mission to kill was risky, and Godwin wouldn't have done it without a solid reason. The two men who could've told us what's going on—Andrew's gone, and Temple's not talking any time soon."

"I doubt Andrew knew anything," Shawn said. "The Kingsleys clearly thought he did... or that he knew enough to help us puzzle it out... but nah. And Noah did put the question to Temple." Direct questions, photographs... there was no coherent response from the former president. "There's nothing to point to Godwin being the pops. Plus, why would the existence of an illegitimate child be a reason to kill in this day and age? All of us agreed it couldn't be the case."

All of us? Lilah asked in her head.

When the Barronses argued over the possibility, Shawn nearly had a meltdown. He did *not* want any connection to Godwin. There was no actual proof, Shawn said over and over.

The Barronses had gone through every bit of paper, every nook and cranny in Andrew's various offices and properties. Caroline even reviewed the floor plans with an architect, paying good money to check for possible hidden safes. Nope, there was nothing.

Worse, Amber and her parents had been cremated. Shawn couldn't use DNA to prove he was *her* son, let alone his paternity.

"I suppose daddy dearest could be some outsider with a claim on Kingsley Corp," Shawn acknowledged, "but Noah said he studied the succession arrangement. The entirety of the stock was willed to the children of Old Man Kingsley with his second missus—Mr. Temple's mother. No loopholes." Godwin was to get a fat paycheck as president, and extended family would get cash payments from their trust. Shawn was not a threat to anyone's pocketbook.

"Let's look at it from a different angle," Caroline said, walking up with Dan. "Does the why matter? Fact is Godwin's worried about something related to the story. Fact is the only part we don't know yet is the boyfriend's name."

"If the problem were the boyfriend, *I* would've been the primary target," Shawn argued. "I carry the man's DNA."

Dan made a sound indicating disagreement. "The law won't let you get a DNA test merely on the basis of a hunch, so why would Godwin take the risk of killing you? Secondly, you're a healthy man in your forties. It wouldn't be easy to pass off cause of death as natural. Potts can't simply walk up to you and inject potassium."

Caroline paled before visibly collecting herself. "Also, everyone thinks you made the computer virus which helped..." She inclined her head toward Lilah, the glance dismissive. "...her in Cuba. After Temple got shot and the thing with Harry happened, it wouldn't be easy to arrange an accident or such for you. The police would immediately suspect homicide."

Telling herself not to let Caroline's disdain get to her, Lilah called, "Shawn, Godwin might have decided it was unnecessary risk at the moment, but he would've kept an eye on you."

Shawn stared unblinkingly at the rest of them for a couple of seconds, appearing to mull the possibility. "Let's say you three are correct," he said eventually. "Godwin's under twenty-four/seven protection now. Getting close enough for a DNA sample to do an unauthorized test is almost impossible, but let's say we somehow prove I'm his spawn. Again, why would Godwin kill over it? He didn't succeed with Temple, but an assassination attempt on a former president is no joke. Then, Andrew. What's the motive to go to such lengths to keep my existence a secret?"

No one had an answer.

Heaving herself up from the retaining wall, Lilah dusted off the seat of her jeans. "I have to get to a doctor's appointment in a couple of hours." Tara wanted to see a GYN. The shooting apparently caused her menstrual cycle to go haywire, and she was anxious about it. "Afterward, there's my meeting with Falcon and Noah. Lemme see what Noah suggests."

Yeah, Congress approved their request to move the hearings to May on account of Andrew's death. On Memorial Day, 1999, Brad and his brothers would face off with their cousins on the banks of the Potomac River.

The proceedings would be closed to the public. There would be a gag order on both sides once the hearings started, making a media campaign against the network impossible. Outnumbered and outgunned, they would face the Kingsley army led by the former supreme court justice.

"Getting Godwin on *some*thing is critical," Lilah said grimly, "or we'll lose."

#

"How's that working out for ya?" shouted the journalist waiting at the gates of The Hermitage. The photographer with her continued snapping pictures.

Inside the car, Lilah kept her eyes straight ahead and willed the security detail to let them in faster.

The guard in the driver's seat peered out. *"The Texas Social Register,"* he murmured, presumably reading off the badges worn by the yellow press duo. "They're far from home."

The journo's question had been about Lilah supposedly picking Alex over the Lone Star State's resident hero/philanthropist, Major Richard Armor. The latest slur on her character was how she humiliated Armor by calling him the son of a chauffeur when turning down his offer of marriage. That, too, in full view of the guests at the Barrons garden party so long ago.

There had also been a strange story in the same sleaze rag about Lilah laughing at Steven when he fell into a pool at the mansion in Cerro Azul. For the life of her, she couldn't remember any incident even remotely similar.

Both Noah and Lilah harbored suspicion that the new round of fairytales was instigated by Mrs. Arvi Armor.

The gates slid open. The car nosed its way in.

"Do you ever think of what life would've been like if you made a different choice?" the reporter hollered after them as the tall, solid panels closed. "What would you be doing right now?"

I'd probably be dead, Lilah muttered in her mind. She might not have many nice thoughts about the Kingsley brothers, but at least they weren't murderous sex offenders like Armor and crew.

There was some time remaining before the meeting with Noah and Falcon. Walking up the stairs to the studio apartment, Lilah promised herself two days when this was all over. She would jot down the bullet points of her own biography—her actual parents, her childhood, her brothers, the half-sister who still pretended she didn't exist, the man she loved, the dreams she lost. Then, she would burn the papers. Some stories were too close to her heart to be shared.

And some stories were clearly dangerous. There was no question in Lilah's mind that Godwin was Shawn's father, but a piece was missing somewhere, perhaps something connecting the Kingsleys to Amber's death.

Shutting the door to the apartment, Lilah shuddered. To think Shawn might be Godwin's blood.

The folder on Amber was on top of the desk where Lilah left it. Leafing through the same documents she spent years staring at, Lilah mulled what she knew. After Amber's death, Andrew insisted on an autopsy since he didn't want to risk more rumors. Statements from the staff who discovered the body, the police report, newspaper clippings… all led to a single conclusion. Dogged by whispers of insanity and poor moral character, Amber committed suicide. There was no evidence of foul play.

"She was merely hounded to her death," Lilah muttered, exchanging her contact lenses for glasses in the bathroom. Amber's spiritual adviser, Rev. Axeman, had claimed something of the sort.

Lilah straightened. Whirling around, she ran back to the folder on her desk. Where was the page she needed? There—the story about Rev. Axeman. Conveniently for the Kingsleys, he was transferred to Colombia in the middle of a civil war and was killed soon after his arrival. The one man who might have known about the pregnant girl's mental health. He might have known if the

Kingsleys spread gossip on purpose, fully expecting Amber to slip over the edge.

Still, being emotionally abusive was not illegal even if it led the victim to harm herself. The reverend did not actually die at Godwin's hands. The then-supreme court justice wouldn't go to prison for either demise, but his entire life would be torn to shreds if the story came out. If he hadn't chosen to retire, he could've been impeached. Even this long after Godwin left the court, the judgments he handed out would be called into question. The Kingsley name would be tarred because of *him*. He would've been seen as a morally weak man—much, much worse than the stepmother derided by the family as a gold digger. The egotistical patriarch would've been terrified of the possibility.

Terrified enough to hire an assassin for a former president and to kill Andrew. Now, Godwin could actually face legal trouble.

#

"Lilah," a familiar voice called as she sat on the stool next to Temple's worktable.

Turning in place, she saw Noah at the door leading to the garage.

"What are you doing here?" asked the former attorney general, looking around. Temple himself was not present. No secret service officers, none of Lilah's own guards. "I thought you were going to join the meeting."

Lilah shrugged. "I came to talk to Mr. Temple, but he'd left to visit Wilma." Temple's former secretary was in poor health.

Noah remained at the doorway, raising an eyebrow when Lilah didn't finish her explanation.

"Tell me," she said conversationally, throwing a quick glance at the worktable. "How long has Temple been communicating with you through his models?"

For a few seconds, Noah stayed still. Then, he sighed and walked in. "Only a couple of months," he admitted. "I think he was trying before, but I just didn't pick up on it. We... ahh... talked about something you and I couldn't discuss, or I would've updated you already on what was happening."

Lilah picked up one of the little blocks of wood lined up at the foot of the table. The crude markings done in black ink suggested a human face. "A row of people," she mused. "*Little* people. The average man?" When the elderly lawyer didn't respond, she reached to the other side of the table and plucked a slightly larger block. "The Kingsleys, I presume. Maybe Godwin, General Potts, the rest."

"I can't tell you," Noah insisted. "We can't take the risk of you getting kicked out of the hearings for violating the gag order." At her sudden movement of objection, he said, "Yeah, yeah. I know. You're not supposed to testify, but the committee needs to see you every single day. When they finally vote, they should remember you."

Lilah studied the former attorney general for a moment or two, then inclined her head.

"Before you ask," Noah said, "I did try talking to Temple this way about Amber."

Holding up a hand, she said, "I know you would have. He wouldn't cooperate because he didn't dare."

No matter what Temple communicated about Godwin's role in the two deaths, without actual testimony from the former president, the charges would be dismissed by the media and the public. Shawn might still have confronted the Kingsleys. Knowing what they did to Amber, Temple would've seen the possibility of her son being hurt by his psychopath of a father.

The Amber mystery was finally solved. If only there were a way to use it.

Chapter 40

A day later

Long Island, New York

Pregnancy test! Tara snorted mentally. The stupid doctor had insisted on it no matter how many times the seventeen-year-old patient swore she had yet to do the deed. The rest of the hormone tests were still not ready, but the woman already concluded it was stress. *Duh!* Tara didn't need a medical degree to make that diagnosis. What she asked for were pills to fix the problem, but the doc was quite firm on how they needed to give the body a chance to heal itself. She told Tara to forget her menstrual cycle for a while and focus on other things.

It wasn't as if Tara didn't have plenty of stuff to occupy her mind. Her future as the best fashion designer the world ever saw, for instance.

Draping the brown leather jacket around the shoulders of the headless mannequin, Tara stepped back to admire her creation. "There," she announced to her audience. Well, to the four people seated on chairs in this particular corner of the basement. The two adults at the other end of the vast space were busy with their own discussion and hardly paid attention to the very first Tara Mathur sale. A princess minidress in golden tulle with built-in shorts, fitted lambskin jacket decorated with patches from the buyer's various wins at her sport. "Classic, but with an edge."

"Beautiful," Hema said, clapping. She was home from college for a weekend.

"It looks…" started Gabriel, tilting his head to the side. "Dunno… short?"

Gabe's gymnast girlfriend swatted him on his shoulder. *"You* are not wearing it; I am." She was getting ready to go away for Olympic training, and the dress was a gift from Gabriel. It was nice of both of them to give Tara a chance.

"I didn't mean I don't like it," Gabe complained. "I like short. Short is good."

"Is it all you have to say?" Tara asked, glaring.

Holding up both hands, he said, "Fashion ain't something I get, okay?" Turning to the boy sitting next to him, Gabe added, "Bro, help me out here."

"Looks cool," Michael stated. "Her stuff is always cool."

Tara's heart skipped a beat as she mumbled her thanks. He looked hot, especially with the light stubble which appeared on his cheeks in the evenings. Plus, Michael had caught up to Maestro in height, with muscles to match.

"Cool's a good word," Gabriel announced. Chair legs scraped the concrete floor as he stood with a digital camera in his hands. Posing the designer and the customer next to the outfit, Gabriel snapped a picture. "Short *and* cool is what I meant to say."

Hema rolled her eyes and groaned. "Mike, maybe you should ask Erika if she wants a Tara Mathur original."

Returning to his seat, Gabriel echoed, "Erika? They broke up months ago."

Hema made a yikes face. "Sorry! I didn't know."

"We're good," said Michael.

With a nod, Hema soothed, "It happens. She's in college now. New interests, new people."

He didn't correct her and managed to turn the conversation to Hema's own college life. It wasn't the first time Tara noticed Michael avoiding speculation on the topic of dumper versus dumpee.

Both he and Erika let everyone assume she dumped him, not the other way around. The only reason Tara knew what actually happened was Gabe's girlfriend who marveled at Michael's stupidity in letting go of a girl like Erika. Confusion didn't begin to describe Tara's feelings when she heard.

As far as she could figure out, the breakup happened two days after she was stupid enough to drop hints about her crush. Six bloody months, and not a word to Tara about it. God, she felt so dumb now!

There was a clatter from across the basement as Sabrina's brother stood from his chair. So did Maestro Alex. "You said it yourself, Alex," Harry was saying.

The decibel level lowered, and Tara couldn't hear anymore. The men were closer to the gym, which was the length of a large hall from where she was.

Michael totally looked like his uncle. Except, Harry grinned and laughed and cracked jokes even when he talked about serious stuff, and Michael looked deliciously broody even when he joked around.

Tara didn't mean for her next breath to be a sigh, but it startled Gabriel and caused his right eyebrow to shoot up. Giving a weak smile in response, she said something about packing up the outfit for his girlfriend.

The other four continued B.S.ing about some mail-based video rental service called Netflix. Apparently, Michael had started watching dance tutorials on DVD in preparation for junior prom. *Of course* he had. The boy probably thought Tara would get the wrong idea if he asked her for lessons like his cousin.

Carefully removing the jacket and the dress from the mannequin, Tara returned them to garment bags. A couple of other items were on the clothing rack, including a dress for herself for the upcoming dance. Yeah, where she could watch Michael leap around with every girl except her.

Eyes on the heavily sequined dark-green frock on the rack, Tara was mulling options when she heard Harry and Alex approaching. They said something to the boys, but she tuned them out as she usually did. It wasn't as if Tara didn't want the good guys to win, but she simply couldn't work up any interest in corporate stuff.

"Yeah!" Gabriel boomed. "We're gonna beat them."

Tone flippant, Tara said, "Beat them good, Maestro. They tried to kill me. We should kill them all off and get their clothes afterward. I could use some scrap fabric."

It took a few seconds for the shocked silence to register. When Tara turned to the rest of the group, Alex was staring at her with a deathly pale face. Everyone else looked extremely uncomfortable. Harry appeared watchful.

"Sorry," Tara said instantly. "Stupid joke."

"'S'all right," said Gabriel. "You weren't listening."

"We were talking about Dad's grandfather and the old dean," Michael explained, getting to his feet. "Mr. Papazian sent confirmation about them arguing for the network on the first day of the hearings. Uncle Aaron and Uncle David will be with them, but we don't know yet if they're going to say anything."

As though Michael never spoke, Alex said, "Grandfather gets his suits tailored by the same shop his father used. I don't suppose the fabric's anything fancy. Same for Uncle Aaron and Uncle David. I doubt General Potts knows anything about fashion. He probably gets clothes from veteran-friendly stores. You wouldn't like the material even as scrap."

Cupping her hands to her mouth, Tara mumbled, "I'm so sorry, Maestro. I'm so, so, so sorry." God! How could she have been so dumb, so horrible to a man who'd been nothing but kind to her?

"You didn't mean it," Michael said quickly. She didn't know when he moved to her side, but his fingers were at her elbow. The feather-light touch somehow steadied her. "Everyone understands," he insisted.

"Of course I didn't mean it," Tara said, dropping her hands. "But it was still stupid and horrible... and... and stupid. Totally uncool no matter who we were talking about. I won't do it again."

Visibly gathering himself, Alex said, "Right. *I'm* sorry, too, champ. It shook me for a bit, and I didn't know what I was saying."

Heaving a sigh of relief, Tara watched as the two men marched up the stairs and disappeared.

"Thank God," Hema muttered. When everyone turned to look, she explained, "I meant Michael and Tara. I guess you two made up, huh? Sabrina was worried you were back to not talking."

Michael withdrew his hand from Tara's elbow so fast that he nearly lost his balance and fell.

One, two, three, she counted in her mind, resisting the impulse to kick him in the nuts.

#

A month later, mid May 1999

Neon lights flashed as kids gyrated to "...Baby One More Time" in the darkened gym. Skin hot and flushed, Michael tossed the empty plastic cup in a trash can before heading toward the boys' restroom.

Passing the couple making out in the brightly lit hallway, he muttered, "Jeez." The restroom was crowded, and at the far end of the sinks were a trio of sophomores snorting coke. The whole damned building didn't seem to have any unoccupied space for Michael to sit and think quietly.

He tried the yard, but it was also plenty busy with students and chaperones walking around. A police vehicle was stationed along the driveway, lights flashing. The cops weren't there to bust kids for smoking weed or doing lines. The school probably asked Nassau County PD to make its presence felt to deter any incident like what happened in Columbine the month before. Two losers had shot and killed their classmates. Michael still couldn't believe it. What a shitty thing to happen to the families.

Shaking himself mentally, Michael returned inside. The moment he actually found an empty classroom, a familiar voice called, "Mike! Wait up." Tara, the source of his current dark mood, marched down the hallway, skirting yet another couple with their hands all over each other.

Tara cleaned up well. *Really* well, with black curls held up in a ponytail and her sparkly green dress and the chunky black heels which made her legs seem a mile long. Thanks to tonight's crowd, Michael also got close enough once to smell her perfume. Something lemony and herby. He went hard as a rock in five seconds flat.

Michael made sure to stay ten feet away afterward, but he needn't have bothered. Every other boy had been sticking around Tara the entire night like ants on Jell-O. All the while, she didn't even glance in Michael's direction.

Until now. Except her eyes were narrowed, and her hands were balled into fists as though preparing to inflict serious damage.

Stomping to the door where Michael waited, Tara snapped, "I've been calling since you left the gym."

"I didn't hear," Michael said honestly. Sounds of the party barely dulled even this far down the building. "What's up?"

"I wanted to ask you the same—"

A roar went up from the gym, and Michael lost the rest of what she said. Shaking his head, he signaled incomprehension.

"I want to know—" Tara started again, but "Ski-Ba-Bop-Ba-Dop-Bop" thundered down the hallway.

Stepping inside the brightly lit classroom, Michael signaled her to follow. While he shrugged off the black blazer and tossed it onto a desk, Tara swept a quick glance over the rows of empty chairs as though making sure they were indeed alone. At the windows, one of the blinds was partly up, revealing a half-moon in the dark sky. The student parking lot was visible, but those walking to their vehicles were too far to see or hear what was happening inside. The cop car was still stationed in the driveway.

Tara shut the door. Almost immediately, there was relative quiet—at least enough to speak. "What is *wrong* with you?" she asked heatedly.

They were standing close enough for Michael to get a sniff of the lemony, herby scent again. Hurriedly sliding into a chair, he mumbled, "Me?" The black dress pants were relaxed in fit, but he wasn't taking any chances.

"Yeah, you. One of your stupid friends asked me if I have cooties or something. Or why did you keep running away? I didn't even know what 'cooties' were!"

"It's this..." Michael gestured with his hand.

"The jerk already told me," Tara said through gritted teeth, all five-and-a-half feet of her—plus the heels—looming over Michael as he sat at the desk. "For your information, I do not have body lice!"

"I didn't say you..." He shook his head slightly to clear the confusion. "I never said... *you* are the one running away. Not me. In the gym... like you don't know me."

"*Really?*" she asked, her thick, dark eyebrows drawing even closer. "Was I the one who talked about boyfriends and minding and all that after I got back home from the hospital?"

"Huh? Yes, you were."

The reminder seemed to throw her a little. "Well, you said it, too."

"Yeah," acknowledged Michael. "Then, you ran away. See? You ran first."

"Because you were dating Erika!"

"I said I would talk to her, and you still ran."

Tara took a couple of deep breaths, but her eyes remained narrowed. "But you broke up with her, anyway."

"How am I supposed to keep dating her when I'm thinking of you all the time?" Michael blurted.

There. He'd said it. Now, he could only hope the admission didn't make her uncomfortable enough to actually run away from home.

"Thinking of me?" With an incredulous snort, Tara asked, "So why were you acting all weird after? Like I wasn't even around sometimes. Then, you'd be all nice to me. Running away, coming back, running away, coming back, running—"

"Stop, please." Michael sighed in exasperation. "I told you I was gonna talk to Erika, and you still left. Which means you didn't care. So if I kept saying stuff, you would've thought I was a stalker. And we live in the same house. You already pulled a dumb stunt like going to live with Lilah, and I didn't want you getting shot again. Get it?"

"I was embarrassed, you... you stupid boy! You already had a girlfriend."

"I told you I would talk to..." Michael groaned. "Why are we fighting about the same thing over and over? I just didn't want to make things weird." A thought occurred. "Did you *want* me to say something after I broke up with Erika?"

Tara's expression changed from angry disbelief to slightly guarded, and she took a couple of steps to the rear. "Did you want me to want you to say something?"

"Oh, no." Scooting the chair back, Michael stood. "We're not doing this again. I think you're amazing. You always make up your own mind, and you're funny and not scared of anything... usually. I like you. Really like you." With his index finger, he poked at his left chest. "I like you up here. Not just... er... the other stuff." Hurriedly, he clarified, "I like the other stuff, too. Like kissing... maybe more. So what do you say?"

Tara looked dazed now. There was something else in her dark eyes, something Michael was pretty sure was on his face as well.

Skirting the desk, he reached for her hand. He could feel her tremble, but she didn't move away. "Will you kiss me?" he asked, tone low. "I don't have cooties, either."

All of a sudden, her fingers were in his hair. "Yes," she said, tugging him close.

The softness of her lips, the warmth, the taste of fruit punch... they got only a moment or two to savor the kiss. Michael couldn't tell who went crazy first, but it was like they were trying to devour each other. His foot skidded, colliding with something before he found his balance. She moved in tandem as though they were dancing together. A chair crashed, but Tara's shuddering breaths in his ear drowned everything else out. Her perfume... the feel of her hands on his shoulders and back... Michael couldn't make himself slow down.

"What are you *doing?*" another familiar voice boomed from the door.

It took Michael a couple of seconds to stop sucking face with Tara and look up. She stayed put where she was, her forehead resting on his shoulder.

Gabriel stood right outside the classroom, his mouth opening and closing as he stared first at his cousin, then at Tara, then back at Michael. The Scatman song was playing again in the gym.

"Since when?" Gabe finally asked.

"Since five minutes ago," said Michael, sounding hoarse.

"I thought she was gonna kill you or something," Gabriel explained his presence. "For the cooties thing. But..." He blinked rapidly as though still unable to believe what he saw.

"Go away, Gabe," Tara instructed. She didn't sound quite normal, either.

"Rude," Gabriel reproved.

"Shut the door, man," said Michael. "And don't tell anyone."

There was no predicting how his parents would react if they knew. Would they even let Michael and Tara live under the same roof as boyfriend and girlfriend? It was the last thing any of them needed on their minds at the moment.

Part XIV

Chapter 41

Two weeks later, May 30, 1999

(the afternoon before Memorial Day)

Washington, DC

The obelisk-shaped Washington Monument loomed against bright-blue summer sky, its likeness glinting in the waters of the rectangular reflecting pool. At the other end of the pool was the Lincoln Memorial. This afternoon, veterans and Gold Star families would rally here to demand action on POWs and those who were missing in action. Even now, motorbikes decorated with flags were thundering past.

Spotting the riders he was waiting for, Harry waved. The veterans who lived in the building next door to him waved back. "Maybe you and I will go next year," Harry hollered over the roar of several thousand bikes.

"Maybe," Alex agreed, the grimness of the last few months failing to dissipate from his face. "I wish there were no need for rallies like this. All these unnecessary wars."

"Yeah," said Harry, tugging at his collar for relief from the scorching heat. "Men sign up to serve but many a time end up serving as cannon fodder to protect the interests of the rich. Still, there are causes worth fighting for—the lives of the people you love, your fellow men and women, their freedoms, *your* freedom."

"I would kill to protect my wife and son," Alex said. "But it doesn't stop me from hoping for a magic solution. A miracle."

Harry was hoping for a miracle, too. Digging into the pocket of his pants, he tugged out the burner phone. Only one man had the number. No calls, but that would happen only in emergencies. Less traceable didn't mean untraceable, after all. "My old colleague is waiting for me," Harry said out loud.

He remained in the same spot until Alex was on his way to The Hay-Adams—the historic hotel—before turning toward the bikers still rolling post. The veteran from New York, halted on the pretext of drinking water, held up a thumb.

Nodding, Harry jogged toward the main road. No vehicles which could be traced back to him waited at the sidewalk. Not his Harley, not his car, not even a cab. Catching the keys tossed at him by the veteran, Harry straddled the Kawasaki Ninja. "Thanks, my friend," he said.

Twenty minutes later, he was at his destination. Walking into the part-spice market, part-bakery, Harry was hit with zesty and sugary aromas. "Baklava," he requested the teenager at the counter.

When he sat at the long table, there was a fellow on the second chair to the right, a tall, skinny man with his nose buried in a newspaper. "It's confirmed," the skinny fellow said without looking up. "Steven's doing his own presser tonight."

Harry bowed his head in acknowledgment. He'd expected as much. Neither party could forgo a last chance at shaping the narrative.

"The same time as you as a matter of fact," continued the skinny man. "Also, Godwin is the lead lawyer." Once again, a known detail.

"Anything on the note?" Harry asked, keeping his tone low.

There was a sigh from the right. "I tried."

"Shit," muttered Harry.

The note Temple sent to Godwin in Cuba was still missing. Or maybe it was destroyed already by David Kingsley. The missive would've been proof enough of Godwin's perfidy even if the former president could no longer testify against his stepbrother. The last hope of defeating Godwin without involving his five devoted grandsons was gone.

"You'd better get back to your post before they start wondering," instructed Harry. "And Yuri? Be careful."

#

Five minutes later

Elsewhere in the city

Snapping the phone shut, Lilah returned to the table and shook her head very slightly. Expectation faded from Noah's face, expression turning stoic. Dan ran a finger over his eyebrow and acknowledged the news. The rest continued their chatter.

"You can't run off in the middle of a debate," complained Shawn.

Mustering a smile, Lilah sat back down. He didn't know Harry was still looking for the note. Shawn simply didn't want to confront the possibility of Godwin being the papa.

"Can we discuss something else?" Sabrina asked, sounding disgruntled. "I can't believe *I* want to stop talking about computers and the internet, but you two have gone on about it long enough already."

Temple was also present at the restaurant. So was Grayson. Lilah's guards and the secret service officers were seated at strategically placed tables, shielding the group from other diners. The kids—Michael and Gabriel and Tara—were out, waiting for the concert at the bike rally to begin. Only a short walk away from where the restaurant was, there would be another concert tonight, the one by the National Symphony Orchestra. It was scheduled to start the same time as the press conference.

"The internet's an important topic," Lilah insisted, taking a sip of iced tea. "Constant vigilance is the price we must pay for a functioning democracy."

Groaning, Shawn said, "Who's disagreeing with democracy? The internet's in fact going to make the world more democratic. No more gatekeepers to decide what news is fit for the public to hear. Information is power, and power will return where it rightfully belongs—to the voters."

"Online service providers are businesses," said Lilah. "Not the same as the web-using public. Let's not conflate the two. Giving these tech companies immunity from being sued for content while still permitting moderation will essentially allow them to control communication. The bigger they grow, the tighter the control is likely to get. This power you're talking about? It will be in the hands of rich businessmen, not voters. Imagine them colluding. Imagine the government taking over a media network like they threatened with Peter Kingsley Network."

"These are not the kind of businessmen you're used to," Shawn objected. "They're not in it for themselves."

Lilah sighed. "Which would make it worse. We, too, believed we were going to save mankind from itself. Imagine someone else who wants to re-engineer the world after his own vision of an orderly utopia. Imagine him—or her—monopolizing communication channels. All you'll be allowed to hear will be his vision. Anyone who disagrees will be silenced. Oil is bad enough. We can live without it—not easily, but we can. Without open communication, a free society will not continue to exist. People need to pay attention to this problem *now*."

"You're too cynical," Shawn complained. "It might not matter, anyway. Technology sector is a disaster waiting to happen thanks to all the damn amateurs throwing money around. Crazy!"

"Enough," Sabrina snapped, holding up a finger. "You're both on timeout as of now. Give the rest of us a chance to talk. Dan, what's happening with you and Amy?"

"Heh?" Shaking his head as though in bemusement, Dan sat up. "We're fine. Why do you ask?"

"No reason," Sabrina admitted. "I want happy news. That's all."

Dan laughed. "Well, we *are* happy, which is good. She would've liked to be here, but someone needs to keep the business going." Amy would be Dan's agent at the Barrons corporate office until he returned. "I plan to be with you guys however long it takes," he added, tone determined. "Even if it means commuting between New York and DC every other day."

Dan didn't need to say it out loud for his twin to understand. His job would've been reasonably quick if Lilah's interest in this fight were only about payback for what the Kingsleys did. She could've filed a civil suit against the clan and their cronies even without cooperation from Brad and his brothers. Which, unfortunately, wouldn't destroy the oil empire.

"Fight the good fight," Lilah murmured. "Life's more about the fight itself than the win. Right, Danny?"

Her use of his childhood nickname made him smile. "Right, but the Kingsleys *will* pay for what they did. So will General Potts."

"Well," said Noah, setting his napkin aside. "We'll know tonight if we even have a prayer of winning."

Chapter 42

A few hours later, 7:50 PM

The Hay-Adams Hotel

The long, hot days of summer were upon them again, and the sun had yet to set. Nevertheless, the manmade lamps circling the wraparound terrace at the rooftop event venue were brightly lit. Lights also glinted in the park which stood between the historic hotel and the building across the street—the White House.

Hands on the metal railing protecting the terrace, Temple ignored the muted chatter going on in the rooms behind and stared at the edifice he resided in for eight years. Back then, there were times when he longed for solitude. These days, he cherished every moment he got with those he considered family—Noah, Lilah, Sabrina, the two boys, Harry. Temple's son, the Harvard professor, hadn't visited in close to a year. The lack of warmth would not surprise anyone who knew what a lousy father Temple was. Didn't matter. The silence still hurt.

Tonight, however, Temple needed a moment to himself. A moment to relish the beginning of this final chess match with the one other person who was no longer family. He remembered the events leading up to his first meeting with Godwin at their half-brother's birthday party.

Temple, Sr. had been honest with his only son about his beginnings. The politician was the last in a long line of men rumored to have started with a non-fighting member of the Knights Templar. Their original name was something else, and the fellow who made the move to the new continent adopted a different moniker as homage to his heritage. The old fellow—Temple, Sr., not the immigrant from the sixteen-hundreds—got to his forties before remembering he needed a child if the family's legacy of service to humanity was to continue after his death.

Oh, he admitted it didn't hurt that Sylvia was a beautiful woman, but the union was mainly intended for him to get an heir without having to find a wife and for her to gain entry into the movies. There was also their common goal, something their son wouldn't learn of until adulthood. Anyway, within weeks of giving birth, Sylvia handed her baby boy to his father and walked out of their lives.

Temple, Sr. paid close attention to his heir's upbringing and taught him not to be bitter about his mother's absence. She was who she was, and there was no point in expecting any differently. Besides, Temple was meant for bigger things than petty peeves about uncaring relatives. Like his forebearers, his life was to be dedicated to the service of mankind.

Still, Temple managed to watch every movie Sylvia ever featured in. The arrival of an invitation to a birthday party was when he first realized his mother got married. He was around thirteen—close to fourteen—and birthday boy was turning ten.

After introducing Temple to his brothers—one half and one step—Sylvia called her firstborn into her suite. Private conversation between mother and son, everyone assumed.

Which it was. She asked a few questions about school and his plans for the future, but what Sylvia Kingsley, *née* Fontaine, mainly wanted was a favor. She didn't trust the son of her husband's late first wife. There had been arguments over Sylvia's demands on how the family company would eventually be divided. In the weeks since then, one of the maids saw Godwin beat Sylvia's son with a cane. When confronted by his father, Godwin claimed the younger lad was slacking off, and big brother was only trying to instill discipline. Sylvia wanted to make sure everyone was aware of Temple's existence so the deposed Kingsley heir would think twice before attacking his half-brother again.

The teenaged Temple was confused about how to feel. Sylvia was a stranger he knew only from motion pictures, and ten minutes in her company turned out to be exhausting. She'd merely been looking out for her own blood with her demand for the entirety of the family business. Still, her stepson was fourteen—around the same age as Temple—and couldn't be expected to simply forgive and forget. But beating up a ten-year-old? Even if Godwin had been genuine about correcting his little brother's behavior, the situation didn't seem quite normal. Also, Temple supposed he owed Sylvia something for the act of giving birth.

He sought out Godwin and challenged him to a chess game, which they fought to a draw. Godwin was impressed. So was Temple.

Many games had been played between them since then. There were no more reports of beatings meted out to the half-brother, but Temple doubted his presence had anything to do with it. He saw no signs at all of psychopathy. Not until much, much later would he realize how deep Godwin's loathing of his stepmother went.

"Mr. Temple," a woman called, startling him back to the present. The tone was low and slightly raspy.

His true heir, the one who would carry on the legacy.

Lilah was not a child born of his blood. She was forged in the blaze which engulfed the Egypt-Libya border crossing so long ago. The flames left their outward mark on her voice, and the girl was smelted into the kind of hero Temple once envisioned. A fire princess whose values determined her nobility. A warrior whose spine turned to steel in the crucible of life. A leader who would put her people's needs above all else. The daughter of Temple's heart.

When Temple turned, Lilah said something he didn't understand. Behind the French windows, the rest of the team was talking to the press. No one paid any mind to the duo on the terrace, not even the damned tabloid fellow Eugene Bishop. He was waddling around Harry and Alex with his camera, no doubt concocting yet another outlandish story in his mind.

At the podium, Noah tapped on the microphone for attention. Temple joined Lilah as she stepped back inside and shut the glass door behind them.

The venue was L-shaped, and the media was allowed only on the long side. In fact, all who were expected to testify before the senate committee were limited to the long side. The short arm of the L was cordoned off from the rest, with temporary screens blocking the glass walls looking out to the terrace. No one would see the occupants of the chamber before Noah was ready for them to be seen. Timing would be critical.

"Ladies and gentlemen," called the former attorney general. "Thank you for joining us."

Chapter 43

8:00 PM

"Thank you for joining us," said the master of ceremonies, an actor and WWII veteran himself.

The crowd of half a million gathered on the West Lawn of the United States Capitol erupted into massive applause. The host started with how they were there to honor all those who died in service of the republic since the American Revolution.

The orchestra director strode onto the stage with his baton, shaking hands with someone before taking his position. The United States Armed Forces Color Guard stood to one side, holding flags.

"Please rise for the national anthem," the director requested.

To those gathered in the rooftop hall at The Hay-Adams, Noah said, "Stand if you can with your hands on your hearts and stand for those who no longer can."

On the large-screen television in one corner, the musicians of the National Symphony Orchestra started "The Star-Spangled Banner" as the color guard dipped all standards except the U.S. flag.

"O say, can you see..." sang a duo of familiar young voices inside the room, startling Harry.

Interested eyes swung toward the right corner of the stage where Michael and Gabriel stood. The lads had not been photographed often, but at least some in the media knew who they were. Cameras flashed.

Next to Harry, Alex sang along, but his puzzlement was obvious. Harry glanced toward the center of the stage where Noah was, but the former attorney general kept his gaze straight ahead.

"O'er the land of the free and the home of the brave!" the boys finished triumphantly.

As the audience broke into a smattering of claps, Noah said, "Thank you."

At a signal from the former attorney general, Gabriel pointed the remote toward the TV and lowered the volume. The two young men leaped off the stage and swaggered into the crowd to stand next to Shawn.

"This weekend," Noah continued, "America will take the time to remember our fallen. The best tribute we can offer them will be to teach our future generations—the millions of Michaels and Gabriels watching the concert from home—that freedom is not free. It takes awareness of the inalienability of the rights promised to us by the Creator and not bestowed by any manmade authority. A divine truth, if you will. It takes constant watchfulness to maintain. It takes courage. It takes sacrifice." Mouth quirking a little, Noah added, "Truth without valor is useless; valor without sacrifice is meaningless."

Returning Noah's smile with a slight one of his own, Harry asked silently, *What are you up to, you canny old man?*

Standing at the back of the crowd with Temple, Lilah willed herself to relax. The secret service officers would already have checked out the venue, and everyone on their team was safely inside the room. The Kingsley brothers, the Barronses, Harry, Dante, Sabrina, Tara, Hema, Grayson, Falcon and a couple of his legal assistants, Liam and Verity, Saeed al-Obeidi... representatives of the seven supporting board members had also shown up. *Six* companies, since Dan would speak for Barrons.

Alex and Harry were toward the front of the room. Neil and Scott stood with Liam, only a few feet to the left of Lilah. Victor was by the door, and Brad... she did a quick visual scan of the crowd. On the television, the orchestra continued to play in muted tones, and on the dais, Noah gave a brief summary of the events which brought them to this point.

Leaning slightly to the side, Lilah muttered to one of Temple's security officers, "Have you seen Brad?"

He nodded. "Yes, ma'am. I saw him earlier. He walked in with Mr. Andersen."

So where was the eldest Kingsley brother now? Lilah's own guards were right behind. Turning, she was about to ask them to check when Noah announced over the microphone, "Daniel Barrons."

"Thank you, Noah," said Dan. He swept a glance over the audience. "And thank *you* for showing up on a long weekend to hear us talk. Rest assured, no one's rehashing the same legal arguments. What I want to do tonight is reflect on what we—as civilians—are willing to sacrifice to safeguard our freedoms. I'd like to introduce you to a few men and women who *are* prepared to stand up and make their voices heard even if it costs them."

Alex wished he picked someplace else in the room. This close to the stage and surrounded by journalists, it wasn't easy to have a private conversation. Keeping his decibel level as low as possible, Alex muttered to Harry, "Who's Dan talking about?"

"No idea," said Harry.

"But first, our team," said Dan. "You just met Michael and Gabriel. They're young and won't be allowed to actually testify, but make no mistake, they have a stake in this as much as anyone else." Dan moved on to Alex, Victor, and Harry, listing their heroics in the military. "There are many, many Iraqis who still remember Captain Victor Kingsley with gratitude for getting them out of Saddam's clutches."

Daniel rapidly went through the names of everyone else expected to speak at the investigative hearing. Not quite listening, Lilah eyed Victor. If she took the long route along the periphery of the room, she could probably reach him without attracting attention and starting speculation on what they were talking about. The journos could not be allowed to realize Brad was missing.

She was about to take a step when a feather-light touch landed on her elbow.

"Brad," croaked Temple. With obvious difficulty, he articulated, "Okay."

Shaking her head, Lilah said, "But..."

"Okay," repeated Temple.

Lilah huffed out a breath. So the former president and his pal had stashed Brad somewhere. She couldn't imagine why they would risk press commentary on the absence of the deposed CEO, but there was surely a reason.

"And now," said Noah, "we want you to meet the man at the center of it all. A man who was cheated by his own blood, wrongly accused of betraying his nation, and driven out of his home along with his wife and brothers. A man who survived almost a decade in exile. A peace-loving man who was ready to give up everything only to make sure the empire he created was functioning honorably. My friends, Mr. Brad Kingsley."

Accompanied by two guards, Brad walked in through the main door. A few claps started, then faltered to a stop as someone else followed.

Harry blinked as he recognized the bear-like form of Arthur Berra, the warden of Sing Sing. He was in a brown suit as usual. Marching two steps behind was Officer Regina Berra, once the bane of Harry's existence, then friend. Not in uniform, but her posture and attitude were a dead giveaway. Passing Harry on her way to the stage, the officer gave a brusque half-nod.

Then came a man in a wheelchair, pushed along by one of the veterans who lived in the shelter next door to Harry. More veterans followed, one with an empty sleeve pinned to his shoulder, one still in the motorcycle gear from the afternoon. He sketched Harry and Alex a salute.

"Hi, handsome," cooed a high-pitched voice. Nikki, former strip club dancer, fluttered her eyelashes at Alex. Her hair was again pink and sleek. "It's been a while."

"Who..." Alex started but gulped as Nikki leaned sideways and planted an elbow on his chest.

"Hold that pose," came the voice of Eugene Bishop, the proprietor of *The Big Apple Reporter.*

"Stop," Alex said, trying to swat the camera away. "My wife's here."

Harry snorted.

"Cut it out," hissed Regina Berra. She'd doubled back to haul Nikki's ass to the stage. "You!" Regina shook a finger at Bishop. "I'll meet you outside when this is over."

Staring at the scene with bemused expressions were two other women—Jorah and her aunt, the Amish ladies. With them were a couple who looked like they could be Jorah's parents.

"What the hell is going on?" Alex mumbled to Harry, inclining his head at the group. "Why are all these people here?"

"Not a clue," admitted Harry.

They just kept coming. Dan introduced one as Suthanu, a Nepali girl who'd been rescued from sex trafficking along with Hema. Suthanu flew in especially to express solidarity with the man who saved her from near-certain death. Her hug nearly knocked Harry off his feet before she scampered away to talk to Hema and Lilah.

Following Suthanu were unemployed oil workers helped financially by Harry and Alex and Victor with the money they made from the Sanders episode. Some who were once part of Peter Kingsley Company showed up. Current oil workers, with strong representation from a certain neighborhood in San Diego, California. Firefighters from Nassau County, Long Island. Latino immigrants. Teachers who'd been part of Temple Foundation's outreach to troubled young people. Recovered drug addicts, former prisoners, disabled cops, active-duty cops. Union members. Pencil-thin boys with barely any hair on their faces proudly proclaimed they were computer geeks. Elbow-patched professors in their thirties and forties admitted to hacking when it was new and exciting. Volunteers from a charity organization which helped the AIDS-afflicted in gay and trans communities announced their intention to support whomever their director—Shawn—supported.

Some of the older black men clearly knew Dante. Natasha, Harry's secretary, brought in two women who waved at a shocked Lilah—her old friends from school.

The stage was nowhere big enough to hold everyone. The partitions between the two sides of the L-shaped venue were removed, and the supposed core team was pushed back. Stumbling, Alex and Harry retreated to where Lilah stood with the former president, protected by her guards and the secret service officers. Holding bottles of water, Falcon and his two assistants also joined the group.

In front of the press was Brad, surrounded by the unexpected arrivals. On the television, the orchestra continued to play.

"Harry, what—" started Lilah.

"Don't ask," advised Alex. "He doesn't know. I don't, either."

Falcon, too, shook his head in ignorance before guzzling water from the disposable bottle. He seemed to be enjoying the chaos.

"Good afternoon," Warden Berra said into the microphone. "I'm—"

"The Bear," called out a reporter, eliciting laughter.

Patting a hairy ear, the warden grinned. "Goddamn right. I suppose you do the prison beat, young lady. Well then... you probably know Harry was a guest at our facility for a few years. He saved my daughter's life once. He also saved the state quite a bit of trouble during a prison riot. I owe him, but it's not the reason we showed up tonight. My daughter Regina and I got to know Harry rather well during his time with us. We reached the conclusion he was innocent long before the court agreed. We also got the opportunity to learn more about the oil business than we ever imagined. Harry's right. What's going on now is a subversion of our democracy. An extra-constitutional ruling system is being built, and it affects all of us whether we realize it or not. I'm here to give our elected leaders my opinion. Andersen was clear I could get into trouble with the state for speaking out, but I must. The Berras do guard duty for America, not for its politicians. My loyalty is to the people of New York and of the U.S. by extension, and it compels me to ask our representatives in Congress to put a stop to this nonsense. Tear the damn network down!"

A roar went up from the crowd. Cameras continued to flash, and tape went on rolling.

Someone handed the microphone to Jorah. She stared at the thing as though not quite sure what to do. At a nod from her aunt, Jorah started speaking. "I... umm... *I'm* here for Mr. Sheppard... Harry. I think... I *know*... he wouldn't be with Mr. Brad Kingsley if he didn't think it was right. Wherever right is, Harry will be there, and wherever Harry is, they will win. I'm sure."

"Yay!" shouted the veteran in the wheelchair.

The room exploded into more cheers. On screen, the master of ceremonies announced the "Armed Forces Medley," to be performed by the orchestra and the military choruses.

Above the tumult, Lilah managed to say, "You've become a god to these people."

"Great," Harry muttered uncomfortably. "Exactly what I wanted."

Falcon grinned at the rest and raised his bottle in salute. *"Our* quartet is complete." At Harry's questioning look, Falcon explained, "Noah called Steven and his friends the quartet of evil." He seemed about to elaborate, but a flash came from somewhere, making him blink and step back.

"Hold it right there," said Eugene Bishop. He snapped a picture of Harry, Alex, Lilah, and Temple standing together. "Good shot," Bishop said in satisfaction.

Laughing, Temple pointed toward the stage. "Better," he said. Noah had executed the plan brilliantly.

Brad Kingsley, the ousted emperor, didn't have a former supreme court justice beside him. There was no former dean of

West Point. No board members, no lawyers, no former president or attorney general, no Harry, not even brothers.

Steven would be at The Willard InterContinental right now, being photographed amid his family and friends, his wealthy supporters, his high-priced lawyers.

Tomorrow's papers would carry the two images juxtaposed. The money and the privilege and the power on one side would be glaringly obvious. On the other would be the ordinary men and women of the United States. The working stiffs, the entrepreneurs, the activists, the disabled. The old, the young, the in-between. The ambitious, the talented, the brave. The forgotten, the ignored, the marginalized, the mocked.

The voters.

"As the Army keeps rolling along," the military chorus ended.

Chapter 44

Next morning

The hearing room in the Hart Building wasn't anything special. In Temple's time in the Senate, he'd spent countless hours in chambers similar to this one. Most were a couple of floors in height, windowless but with glass panels set along the two side walls through which the media and spectators could observe proceedings. There were, of course, no observers today.

The rest remained more or less the same. The same garishly bright but television-friendly lighting, carpeted floor, backdrop of the marble slab carrying the seal of the U.S. Senate, the American flag. Tables were arranged in a wide U for committee members, behind which was a second row of chairs for staffers. In the other half of the room was classroom seating for those waiting their turns to testify.

Two tables—each seating four—were set in the large gap between the politicians and the audience. Those currently being questioned would take their places there. Microphones were provided at each witness chair and for every senator. A camera was set up in the center of the chamber to tape the proceedings for government archives. There was also a big-screen contraption mounted on a rolling table which would show what was being recorded. The public wouldn't get to see any of it.

The two warring sides were already settled into their respective chairs, the five brothers and their supporters on the right and the Kingsley clan on the left. With a slight shuffle, the last attendee walked into the room, causing almost everyone to twist around to check. Temple had seen the young fellow before, hanging around Charles. The straggler swept a quick glance over the room. His gaze faltered for a fraction of a second when he got to Harry, but both men turned away without making any signs of recognition.

Another sound drew Temple's attention back to the front. The seven committee members—including the chairman—and their staffers filed in. All the senators took a minute to walk into the audience to greet the former chief executive of the nation. They also stopped by Godwin to pay respects.

When the senators finally took their seats, they would each find a folder with a list of the witnesses for the day and printouts of important records. Each member would also have copies of a couple of newspapers from the morning.

The former president stared at the witness table where the Kingsley patriarch sat with General Potts and two other men, presumably junior lawyers.

Your move, brother, Temple said to Godwin.

Part XV

Chapter 45

"Have you heard the story of sour grapes?" Godwin asked pleasantly.

Sitting in the audience behind his grandfather, Steven grinned in relief. His worries after seeing the papers were for nothing.

Yeah, yeah, public support, but the votes which counted would be cast in this room, and those would depend on the arguments presented to the committee. And with the first sentence of the opening statement, the former supreme court justice reduced Brad's case to pettiness.

Godwin went on to summarize the formation of the network, the transition of control, every compromise the five brothers offered only to return to power. "Finally, when it began to sink in that Brad Kingsley would never return as CEO," continued the family patriarch, "he and his brothers discovered how the very idea of a network was anticompetitive. Members of the committee, I hope you see this sudden awareness of market ethics for what it is."

The television on the rolling table to the right showed the audience what would be on government records. Steven had been warned how every expression of every witness would be captured, every instance of anger, of dismay, of elation. He was told to maintain decorum when it was his turn to speak, but he couldn't help curling his hand into a triumphant fist.

Next to Steven, Richard stayed silent. Steven was thankful his friend consented to show up given how humiliating it had to be for him to simply watch from the sidelines. All the main players were here, including Charles. Only JD—Jack Drummond—was missing. Unlike Charles, the former congressman got caught in his crimes, and his presence was likely to annoy the committee.

"There is, of course, interconnected ownership between member companies," Godwin conceded. "However, no one... not a single entity... has gone beyond the boundaries set by United States law and legal precedence. Also to be noted: the network has operated magnificently over the last decade, maintaining stability in the markets. Senators, you do not need me to remind you about the prosperity enjoyed by the nation—indeed, by the world—today. You also do not need reminders about what could—and would—happen in the absence of economic and political stability. To summarize, the network has broken no laws and has been a force for the good. It will continue to be so... but only if our elected representatives wish for lasting peace within our borders and outside of it. That is all from me at this time."

"Mr. Papazian," called the chairman of the committee—the senator from Colorado. "Your turn."

The lawyer cleared his throat. Next to him were two men Steven didn't recognize, likely junior attorneys. Cousin Brad was also at the witness table for this inaugural session.

"Excuse me, Mr. Chairman," called Brad, raising a hand. "May I say something? I feel it's important."

Brad's lawyer turned sharply to glance at his client. In the audience, the four younger brothers shifted in their chairs. So did most others on their side. Next to Alex, Sheppard was leaning forward, chin resting on interlinked fingers.

The committee members glanced at each other. "Of course," the chairman eventually said.

"Thank you, sir," Brad said. "This is a hearing, but the men I'm facing are my own family. Mr. Godwin Kingsley, General Potts, Mr.

Aaron Kingsley, Mr. David Kingsley... these are the four men who taught me the values I hold dear. Anytime I found myself at crossroads, I turned to them for counsel. If they weren't available, I asked myself what they would do. A revered former supreme court justice and the former dean of the nation's most elite military academy. The elders of one of the oldest American families, members of which have contributed blood and sweat to our nation. My brothers and I were blessed to have their support."

The television showed Cousin Brad's pious smile, his hand on his heart as he bowed slightly toward the Kingsley table. Steven gritted his teeth.

"Today," continued Brad, "I find myself at crossroads yet again. Today, I'm on my own without the family I always turned to for guidance. Grandfather, I realize I can't call you to ask what to do. Still, I can and will request your permission to proceed, and I hope your goodwill remains with us. General Potts, you've always told your students to do the right thing. Well, we *are* doing what we firmly believe to be right, and I hope some part of you recognizes this as your own success as a teacher."

"Shit," muttered Richard.

Shit was about right. Politicians greatly appreciated tradition and deference to rank, and the expressions on the mugs of the committee members made it clear the whiny idiot managed to parry the blow from Godwin's sharp words. The patriarch and the general had no choice except to nod in appreciation or appear ungracious.

Face perfectly straight as only a man hiding a grin could make it, Falcon Papazian said, "If the committee agrees, we would like to leave Mr. Brad Kingsley's words as part of our opening statement."

"A bit unusual," said the chairman, "but I don't see a problem."

"Thank you, sir," said Papazian. "Now, ladies and gentlemen of the committee, I would also like to start with a story. It's customary for writers to offer a dedication first, I believe. So let me do the same." Pausing, the lawyer smiled. "To the One They Called God; To the Best of Men; To That Goddess of Knowledge; To the Chronicler."

Papazian then recited a summary he somehow made seem epic even in the space of five minutes. He narrated the tale of a man who was once the leader of the free world, of his dream of building a just society. Of his quest to find his intellectual heir and his first sight of her at the Egypt-Libya border as she emerged—nay, was born—from fire. Of his encounter with the seventeen-year-old SEAL candidate and sax player who shared his vision and was willing to sacrifice everything, including his life, to see justice done. Of the entry of the hero-prince into the lives of the other two young people. Of the marriage between the fire-borne princess and the scion of the president's own clan.

Of the enemy they faced, the empire they built. Of the emperor's blind faith in the goodness of his family in particular and mankind in general, of the dice game he was conned into playing with his brothers' and wife's lives as stake. Of the exile, their return, and the war they intended to win on behalf of humanity.

"Leaders of the American people," called Papazian. "Heirs to the great democratic experiment called the United States. Over the coming months, you will hear the specifics of our complaint. Someday perhaps, you and the rest of the world will hear the human part of this tale as well in further detail. In this saga, you will find men and women seeking the purpose of their existence. You will hear about their actions, both honorable and dishonorable. You will marvel at their passion. At the end of it all, you will hope for their redemption. *Our* redemption, because their history is the history of every era from the beginning of mankind. The challenges they confronted were faced by generations before and will be encountered by generations to come. What you don't find in their story, you won't find elsewhere."

The committee chairman took off his glasses and scribbled something on a notepad.

"Ornate language... wouldn't you say?" Papazian smiled again, and several of the senators responded in kind. "There is, of course, a point to my pomposity. For one, the decisions reached by this committee will carry global implications. In effect, this is a world court and deserves ceremony. For another, I wanted you to understand the men and women involved in this war, to see the events through their eyes. Going forward, I hope you, too, come to the realization that an empire is only as benevolent, as just as its rulers. It is only as mindful of the rights of the ordinary citizen as its leaders."

There were nods from committee members, and the junior senator from Texas leaned forward in obvious interest.

"When Steven Kingsley took over," said Papazian, "the empire became the very evil it was designed to combat. The network did break several laws, which we will prove in the coming sessions. The peace and stability Justice Kingsley spoke of? It is merely the silence of slaves who're yet to be aware of their enslavement. The prosperity we see today is what we got by bartering the freedom of the man on the street, in the factories, on the battlefield."

An uncomfortable mutter went around the room.

"The term 'sour grapes' was used by the former justice." Papazian acknowledged, "Yes, Mr. Brad Kingsley initially tried to negotiate. During the process, we heard from the small businesses harmed by Steven Kingsley's business tactics. We also saw how his approach to governing had supporters within the network and outside. Mr. Brad Kingsley and his team realized how the risk of tyranny would continue no matter who ruled the network. The wealth and the power promised by the empire will continue to attract corruption. Ladies and gentlemen of the committee, the network must go."

Chapter 46

Week 1 of the hearings

"I realize Mr. Mathur has nothing to do with the oil sector," said Godwin Kingsley. "Nor is he American."

In the audience section, Harry didn't say a word. This was a move he didn't see coming but should have, given how canny the former supreme court justice—Steven's lead lawyer—was.

"But the U.S. government is looking into antitrust complaints brought by non-American businesses," reminded Godwin. "So non-citizen witnesses should be allowed. Mr. Mathur's testimony will demonstrate the collective thought process of the Kingsley brothers."

"Prince's brother-in-law," Noah muttered from the chair next to Harry's. "Of all people."

At the witness table, Falcon maintained his noncommittal expression and continued making notes. By his side was Brad, the television screen showing the shock on his face. His mouth opened slightly, but the eldest Kingsley brother fell silent before uttering a syllable. No excuse. There was no goddamned excuse for all of them forgetting the Indian hotelier.

One of the junior lawyers on Steven's team read out loud from a document. Prince's initial attempts to launder money through Peter Kingsley Company which supposedly triggered suspicions in the government about the five brothers, the interrogation in Cuba, Lilah's mockery in the military court of the idea of them making a deal with the drug lord...

"Brad Kingsley and his brothers knew you were married to this... this Mr. Prince's relative," said a committee member, the senator from Illinois. "Correct?"

"Yes," mumbled Mathur, his gray head hanging down. The skinny fellow refused to meet the eyes of the former exiles.

"And who among the five of them approached you for help?" asked the Illinois senator.

"Mr. Alex Kingsley did, through a mutual acquaintance," Mathur said.

"The transgender woman," the chairman stated.

Mathur nodded. "I owed money to my wife's family... to Prince. Mr. Brad Kingsley promised to pay off the loan once he got back to the States. Prince never knew the Kingsley brothers were hiding at the resort."

"Big risk you took there," commented the chairman, disbelief clear in his tone. "Sheltering fugitives wanted by a drug lord."

Of course Mathur knew he wouldn't be believed without coming clean about the deal he made with the Kingsley brothers to kill Prince. The former exiles had decided against divulging the info to the feds even with the immunity offer because the agreement didn't include Mathur.

Even if it did, American promises carried no legal weight in India. Mathur could get into trouble with law enforcement at home for being an accessory to murder. There were also Prince's former associates in the country who could decide to make an example out of Mathur.

Lack of immunity for the episode meant the Kingsley brothers had no way now of throwing Mathur under the bus and revealing the actual bargain they made. Moreover, without incentive to keep his mouth shut, the hotelier could divulge Brad's disgusting instruction to Lilah to cooperate with Prince. Which would further support Godwin's contention how Peter Kingsley's sons were in this war only for themselves. *Of course* the five brothers had narrated the entire tale to their grandfather, and he knew exactly how to use it.

"I would've asked about Prince's reaction once he realized what you did," remarked the Illinois senator. "But the last he was heard from was a couple of years ago according to our investigative agencies. Off the coast of Goa, where the Kingsley brothers were hiding."

Mathur stuck to saying he wasn't aware of where Prince went after his yacht was spotted in the Arabian Sea.

"Mr. Brad Kingsley," called the California senator. "Your explanation on why Mr. Prince offered his assistance?"

"Respectfully, ma'am, he didn't," said Brad. "Mr. *Mathur* offered assistance in return for help with loan repayment. He made it clear."

The silent stare from the questioner made her skepticism also clear.

"Mr. Kingsley," the chairman called. "The committee will need time to review this new information. Then, we'll have more questions for you."

#

Week 2

"Is there any evidence for your claims Mr. Steven Kingsley contracted Prince to kill you?" a committee member asked.

"No proof except what Prince said to us," Alex admitted reluctantly. "There is no question, however, that they were abducted by him. The American government has enough documentation on it."

"Mr. Steven Kingsley said to the FBI he had no clue what Prince wanted out of it," the same committee member—the Texas senator—pointed out.

"I'm giving you his reason," said Alex. "Our cousins attempted to make a deal with Prince and got caught in his trap, instead. Prince tried to blackmail us about killing our cousins, for which we would of course be blamed. As ransom, he wanted our signatures on a contract to set up a money laundering operation when we returned home. Which was why Brad decided on a rescue mission."

"The FBI believes the escape was merely the lucky outcome of an encounter between Prince and a rival gang," said the chairman. "Do you have any proof of *you* rescuing Mr. Steven Kingsley from Prince's custody? Photographs, copies of port records... anything?"

"We didn't have the opportunity to take pictures," Alex stated. "Honestly, we didn't even think about needing evidence. At the time, our primary aim was to get Steven and Charlie—Charles—off Prince's boat. Victor and I put them on the ramp, where port authorities found them."

"You also claim you got help from one of the Chinese gangs," the chairman said reprovingly. "I must say the things I'm hearing about your adventures don't seem very positive."

"We didn't get help from any gang," corrected Alex. "We simply informed one of the groups in Macau how their rivals would be at a certain place. The resulting confusion allowed us to finish the job and make our escape."

"You then met Prince in India," said another member.

"We were trying to *hide* from him," Alex corrected yet again. "And from his local associates. Through Rekha, the transgender woman who was referred to earlier, I already knew Prince had family in Goa who wanted out. We contacted Mathur."

"And my colleagues and I are to simply take your word for it how the promise of cash was enough for Mr. Mathur to offer you sanctuary," remarked the same member. "At the risk of his drug lord relative finding out."

There was nothing Alex could add in the absence of immunity. Nothing to correct the impression how he and his brothers would go to any length to get what they wanted, whether it be working with a drug lord or destroying the network.

#

Twenty minutes later, it was Dan's turn to face an incredulous committee.

Tone ominous, the chairman asked, "You accused a decorated soldier, the former dean of West Point *and* former head of army intelligence, your former *teacher*, of murdering your father? Without an iota of proof?"

In the audience, Lilah gritted her teeth. *Brad or one of his brothers, of course.* The leak came from them. Dan wouldn't dare turn around to the five men and ask them what the actual hell.

Shifting in the chair next to Lilah's, Shawn cursed under his breath.

"No, sir," said Dan. "I did not accuse General Potts or anyone else of murder. Our side had a couple of unfortunate events occur within a short span of time, and Andrew's death happened during the general's visit with him. The *statement* you referred to was made during a discussion with my sister's husband and his brothers. Nothing else."

"You also saw in military records how General Potts was instrumental in detaining you while the investigation on your sister and her family was going on," a committee member remarked.

While she was being *assaulted* by the Kingsleys, Lilah noted grimly, but Dan couldn't make the correction without contributing to the idea he was after revenge. He simply nodded.

The Barronses' role in this investigation was being discredited as had been that of the Kingsley brothers. Two sessions in, and out of the main players in the game, Harry was the only one whose credibility remained intact.

"May I request this committee to hear from Mr. Victor Kingsley on this matter?" Falcon asked, looking up from a note.

"Yes, sir," Victor confirmed five minutes later. "I asked to be called to speak because I created this situation and wanted to explain. Yes, Dan—Mr. Daniel Barrons—was angry in the hospital about the general being allowed in, but he never made any outright accusations. Later, he mentioned the possibility of homicide only to us—to his own family, to me and my brothers, to his friends. No one else was around for the conversation. My brothers and I took it as grief talking, which was truly all it was. Moreover, our plans for the network were made much before. Barrons O & G voted in favor of dismantling the network months before Andrew died. The decision was not made out of any need for revenge."

"So how did Justice Kingsley get to hear of it?" asked a committee member.

Victor flushed. "I was the one who went to our grandfather—Justice Godwin Kingsley—with the information. I shouldn't have, but at the time, I believed it was also a personal conversation."

Lilah threw a glance at Godwin's face. The former justice of course realized his reputation for fair play just took a hit.

"But Mr. Daniel Barrons did ask for an autopsy," the chairman pointed out.

"Yes," acknowledged Victor. "I would've done the same in his place. It's best to know for sure. Closure and so on. Once the cause of death was ascertained as cardiac arrest—perhaps a result of heart disease, perhaps a complication of the procedure—Dan dropped the matter. He never talked to the media, never even went to the police, which he would have if he actually believed what he said before. I'm sorry, sir... Mr. Chairman... but a man is allowed to grieve his father in the company of those he trusts. It was not an accusation. There was never any question of revenge. Only of justice and rule of law."

Chapter 47

Two weeks later, June 1999

Long Island, New York

Harry stopped pacing the garage—there wasn't enough space—and sat on top of stacked tires near the right wall. With the exception of Lilah, the rest of the team was present, occupying folding chairs set wherever space could be found around three cars.

Falcon and Alex went on with their argument. In the adjoining workshop, Temple continued his labors, Frank Sinatra playing "That's Life" on the CD player. Despite air-conditioning, a faint smell of gasoline and warm rubber lingered.

Groaning, Falcon asked Alex, "Why didn't you bring it up?" There was no way in hell Steven and Charles and Major Armor went to meet the drug lord without informing the Kingsley patriarch. "It was a missed opportunity."

"There's no proof," the former sniper stated, his tone stoic, "and I'm not going to lie."

Falcon groaned again. Everyone else present—besides the five brothers—also made various sounds of frustration.

"I'm not asking you to lie," said Falcon. "I would *never* ask you to lie. At the same time, we're not doing a criminal trial. We don't need to prove anything beyond reasonable doubt. As others pointed out, there's a good chance your grandfather did know about the proposed meeting between Steven and Prince. If you merely suggested it, you could've done some damage. Not in legal terms. There's no press around even for media trouble. All we needed was to create doubt in the minds of the committee members about Justice Kingsley's reliability."

Therein lies your problem, bud, Harry muttered mentally. Lilah might be gagged by her husband's insecurities, but committee members would eventually review the events in Gitmo with or without her. The Kingsley patriarch was counting on his reputation as a scrupulously honest arbitrator of justice to get him unscathed through the investigation. If Alex even hinted how his grandfather might be less than perfect, albeit involving a separate incident, a pattern would start to emerge.

"I will not condemn Grandfather for things he didn't do," Alex insisted.

"He is condemning *you* for things you didn't do," Harry said. "My friend, if you won't acknowledge what's going on, lemme do the honors."

Sudden wariness popped into Alex's eyes.

"Let's be generous to Godwin and say he was completely unaware of Steven's plans," said Harry. "Well... the moment you opened your big mouths on your return, he did hear what actually happened. The entire Prince saga from start to finish. Yet Godwin chose to imply to the committee how you and your brothers were making illegal deals with a drug smuggler. Either he doesn't believe your story, or he doesn't care what's true. You can't correct him without bringing up the unfavorable parts, which is again something he knows. End result is the five of you are taking a beating at his hands. Say something at least to defend yourself. One word suggesting his involvement in the Macau episode would make him back off."

"Bro, maybe we should..." started Victor.

"No," said Alex.

"You heard what Falcon said," Victor tried again. "Grandfather wouldn't actually get into trouble with the law for it since there's no proof."

"No," Alex said a second time. "It wouldn't be fair. I don't want anyone else talking about it, either." It wasn't possible in any case. Only the five Kingsley men and Lilah could bring it up to the committee since only they were present in Macau.

"Actually, there's no evidence *we* colluded with Prince," Scott said. "Simply the suggestion of it from Grandfather. So we, too, won't get into legal trouble."

"Okay," Brad said, blinking, "but can the committee stop us from getting our business back because of Prince? There was a statement made about how executives who partner with international criminals shouldn't be in charge of even a standalone business in a critical sector."

"I'm glad you asked, because the comment is something we should discuss," said Falcon. "Energy sector means national security implications. The committee might not wait for hard evidence for actions other than criminal charges. They could well bar the five of you and Lilah from ever working in the sector again merely on the basis of suspicion. The government could even get a court to agree. Which means you could lose Peter Kingsley Company completely even if we get the committee to dismantle the network."

"Same for Steven and Kingsley Corp," mused Brad. "Because the committee heard about his attempt to have Prince kill us."

"Yes," said Falcon. "The decision will come down to which side the members believe. As things stand, they're more likely to take the word of a former supreme court justice. Which was why it was important to implicate your grandfather in it."

"One more thing to think about, Brad," said Noah. "Godwin knows the possible consequences, and he knows Falcon would tell you. It would be his duty as your lawyer. Godwin's putting pressure on you to withdraw from the antitrust investigation altogether to avoid the possibility of a complete loss. If you're not there to be asked questions about Prince, the committee might not pursue the matter."

The Kingsley brothers would retain at least a small chance of keeping their own business, but their allies would be left to fend for themselves. Odds of the network being declared anticompetitive would go drastically down.

"What a damn mess," Shawn muttered. Dan continued to stay silent as did Liam. Standing, Shawn announced, "Well... since we don't seem to be getting anywhere, I'm heading home for the night."

"Me, too," said Neil. "At least we have three months until the next session."

The hearings would not happen in consecutive weeks. The senators would want to study the material they were already presented. They would even conduct their own investigations, then summon the warring groups back for more questions.

Tired and irritated, everyone started to leave.

Glancing at the clock on the workshop wall, Harry debated whether to linger until the rest of the team left to update Lilah. She no longer showed up to talk strategy with the Kingsley brothers. As she put it to Noah, there was no point trying to wake those who were faking sleep. Oh, Lilah would continue to attend the hearings to force the committee to see her face.

Maybe on the phone, Harry decided. What they could say over a telephone line would be limited, but the chat would be lengthier.

"Harry," a refined voice called from behind. Brad, pushing his glasses up his nose.

"What's up?" Harry asked.

Brad waited until his brothers straggled out. Besides him and Harry, only Noah and Temple and a secret service officer remained in the garage.

"What's your gut feeling about where we stand at the moment?" Brad asked.

"We almost fought to a draw," Harry said, "which is a miracle all things considered, but Victor, especially, did some damage when he spoke up for Dan. The senators now know Godwin is ruthless enough to use a private conversation about a very personal matter. Like Falcon reminded us, the committee ain't a court of law, and perception sometimes matters more than legality. So yeah... at least some members will hold it against Godwin. And even if Alex didn't aim directly at Godwin, questions were raised about Steven. However, Steven continues to hold the advantage."

Hands in his pockets, Brad nodded. "It *is* a huge advantage to have a former supreme court justice argue for you. Do we even have a prayer of winning?"

"Not when we're actively trying to lose." Harry sighed. "Brad, if you and your brothers are serious about the network, we'd better start thinking about how to inflict damage on your grandfather first, then General Potts, then Major Armor."

"War was an abstract idea until now," Brad admitted. "I lost sleep over the possibility of hurting my family but never stopped to think about them hurting us. More to the point, all those people who turned up to support us... I was humbled, Harry. It was just... just incredible. So how can we look them in the eye if we—as you said—actively try to lose?"

"Ask Alex the same question," Harry suggested shortly. "Tell him to either wake up now or wait for Armor to shoot him in the head."

Part XVI

Chapter 48

A day later

"Papa didn't tell even me," Tara brooded, swinging a bare foot back and forth from her perch atop a tree branch. Her slip-ons lay discarded on gnarled roots.

Michael continued doing pushups on the lawn. "Fifty-six..." He grunt-counted, his thin gray tee stained with sweat and grass. "Your father... fifty-seven... is an adult. Fifty-eight... what he did... his problem, not yours. Tell her, Gabe."

Gabriel was stretched out on the ground, not bothering with calisthenics or even with speaking. Like him, Tara didn't feel like doing anything fun. Michael, too, had to be pissed about the situation no matter how objective he acted in front of Tara.

"Uh-huh." Frowning heavily, Tara asked, "So how come you're doing this stupid stuff instead of practicing music like you were supposed to?" The flute case lay unopened on the lawn because Michael was not in the mood to play.

"Ain't stupid," Michael said. "Sixty-two... it's called training. College... West Point... fitness assessment next week."

"Get fit *when* you go to military college," Tara muttered. "What's the point of doing it before?"

Michael glanced up for a second. "I'm signing up to defend my country. Sixty-eight... gotta be prepared. Right, Gabe?"

Gabriel was all set to go to the Barrons refinery near San Diego for summer training with their firefighting crew. He'd also signed up for classes on management of oil disasters. Yeah, he would agree with his cousin on the importance of preparation.

Other than mumbling something indecipherable, Gabe didn't respond.

"What's stupid is..." Michael went on. "...seventy-one... blaming yourself for what your father did."

"Don't patronize me," Tara snapped.

"Patronize..." Stopping midway, Michael flipped to his back. "I wasn't."

Ignoring him, she fretted, "I should've called the girls at the resort every week like I promised." Even if her papa had been too afraid of Kingsley clout to inform his former allies, someone would've known he wasn't going to be in Goa for a few days.

"Maybe you could've warned Uncle Harry if you knew," said Michael, heaving himself up to sit next to her on the tree limb. It was low enough and he was tall enough for his feet to touch grass. "Thing is you *didn't* know, and you didn't have any reason to ask." Mock-preening, Michael added, "Trust me on this. I got years of therapy after my dad and uncles got arrested. I used to think I should've done something to stop it."

"Heh?" Tara's mouth fell open. "Wasn't it like ten years ago? How old were you?"

"Eleven years now... almost." Michael calculated. "I was five."

"Jeez," said Tara.

"See?" asked Michael. "You understand when it's someone else. Gabe, tell her I'm right."

Once again, Gabriel didn't respond.

"I kinda know it already." Tara tapped her temple with a finger. "Up here. And I know Maestro's not blaming me for it, either. But it's so... so... I have no idea how to put it in words."

Her papa had hurt people she'd come to think of as family.

"We get it," said Michael. "Gabe. C'mon, dude, wake up! Tell her."

"Uh-huh," Gabriel grunted again. He wasn't sleeping. Eyes wide open, Gabe stared at the sky.

"Gabe," Michael called for the umpteenth time. "You listening?"

"She dumped me," Gabriel said abruptly.

"What?" Michael asked, shaking his head in incomprehension.

"Dumped..." Tara started before what Gabe said sank in. "Oh."

"Yeah," Gabriel said, his tone bitter.

Apparently, the gymnast with Olympic hopes told her now-former boyfriend how she wasn't going to regular school, anymore. Like many other young athletes in training for the biggest sporting event in the world, she would be homeschooled and didn't want to think about anything external. Not even Gabriel. The gymnast added how it wouldn't be fair to him if they didn't break it off now.

Slipping off the tree branch, Michael sat cross-legged on the ground. "Damn," he said. "You okay, man?"

Gabriel sat up and shrugged a giant shoulder. Then, a strange sound came from him. A couple of tears rolled down his cheeks.

Tara leaped down and was about to offer a hug when Michael started contorting his mug into weird shapes.

"What?" she mouthed.

Michael tilted his head meaningfully in his cousin's direction. Gabe had twisted himself to face away from Tara.

Got it, she mimed to Michael. Gabe didn't want any girls seeing his manly tears.

As Tara trudged back toward the house, she spotted one of the guards in the yard, watching to make sure she made it safely inside. Besides the alarms at the doors and windows and bulletproof glass, motion detectors and security cameras surveilled the yard, and there was always someone staying awake in the electronic monitoring room. Two men patrolled the exterior day and night. The entire security team had surely learned what happened at the hearings. They would all be wondering what Tara was still doing in a Kingsley home.

God, Papa, she thought despairingly. *Why?*

When she got to her room, blinds were up at the window overlooking the garden. Michael and Gabriel remained under the tree, talking.

Michael was like Maestro Alex in some ways and in some ways not. Maestro loved his family, and so did Michael, but father could see no fault in the people he cared about while son refused to put blame in the wrong place. Michael was also not as forgiving as Maestro. Still, the son planned to follow his father to military college.

Tara frowned. Maestro had apparently been sent to the Pakistan-Afghanistan area. Would Michael also have to go to dangerous places? Tara didn't like the sound of that.

As though aware of being under scrutiny, Michael looked up and grinned. Making a silly face at him, Tara whirled away.

The boy was perfect. Well... not really... but Michael was the right kind of not-perfect for her.

She really, really liked him, Tara thought dreamily, plonking nose first into bed. And he really, really liked her.

Chapter 49

The four-vehicle garage attached to the Kingsley residence was designed for utility, not comfort. The AC was nearly useless, and the single source of light was barely functional.

The glowing wall sconce was next to the door to the main house, which left the far side of said garage in the shadows—where Michael's motorbike and his mother's blue Subaru Outback were parked. Unfortunately, the swing-arm floor lamp he'd lugged from the basement wobbled whenever he tried to prop it at the right angle to check his progress with the bike.

Stay there, Michael warned the damned lamp for the dozenth time, pointing a finger. Keeping a death stare on it, he managed to crouch next to his bike. The moment his head was near the ground, the lamp teetered and tumbled again, clattering when it hit the concrete floor. The bulb hissed and shot sparks, barely missing Michael's face. He rolled out of the way, losing a Birkenstock in the process, and swore long and loud.

Hopping to slide the sandal back on, Michael studied his electrical adversary. The metal stand seemed to keep its balance only with the swing arm pointing at an obtuse angle of about one-thirty-five degrees. Michael would have to work with whatever light he got thusly or postpone the repair job until the sun came up. Nah, he needed to finish it tonight.

In half an hour, Michael hauled himself to his feet, using a rough rag to scour acrid grease from his hands. His old tee and tatty jeans were also stained with machine oil. No matter. The Yamaha was an elderly beauty and required TLC if he wanted her in working condition. Michael got his junior license in February, the week he turned sixteen, and could ride unsupervised during the day. Okay, so the beach was within walking distance, but Michael still wanted to ride his bike to the shore.

If only he could come up with some excuse to take Tara out without the ever-present guards. Gabriel, too, would go with them, obviously. He needed to do something besides sit around and mope until he left for California for his summer job. *All* of them needed to forget the stupid war with the Kingsleys for at least a day.

Not as if Michael planned to do anything dumb. Not with Tara in tow. But it had been a whole effing month since they came clean about what they really thought, and Michael wanted to kiss, dammit! Gabe wouldn't mind taking off for a couple of minutes at the beach. Michael drifted for a moment, imagining him and Tara on the Yamaha, riding alongside the waves.

He opened his eyes in a hurry. Dinner had been torture enough with her freshly showered scent drifting to him each time she shifted.

Grabbing the wrench from the floor, Michael once again knelt by the Yamaha. "My girl," he said out loud and rolled his eyes. Cheesy shit. Gabe used it for his girlfriend. *Ex*-girlfriend now. Michael needed to come up with something less barfy.

"Are you talking to the bike?" an amused voice came from the direction of the door.

Startled, he straightened quickly and bumped his head on the handlebar. Michael bit back the pithier curses springing to his tongue.

Tara, wearing a long, whitish tee which reached just above her knees, stood in fuzzy slippers. Holding a magazine, she made her way to the window overlooking the yard and sat on the wide sill. It was shut, of course, and the glass was bulletproof, but the blinds were up, revealing the cloudless sky with its half-moon and the stars.

"I thought you went to bed," Michael said.

She sat with her legs crisscrossed, settling the magazine on her lap. "*Vogue* last month had an article on swimsuits. I never designed bathing suits before, so I thought... but I left the magazine in the living room. When I got downstairs, I saw the light in here and..." Tara grinned. "...heard you smooth-talking your bike."

Tossing the wrench aside, Michael sauntered to the window and leaned his shoulder against the wall. Was it Snoopy on her nightdress? For a chick who constantly thought about fashion, comfy clothing seemed to be her go-to in the privacy of her own space. *Probably better for my peace of mind,* he acknowledged. Hard to get turned on with Snoopy staring him in the face.

The AC which was about ten feet away gave one old college try to generate air current before dying back down to its low rumble. The pages of the magazine on Tara's lap fluttered. The breeze could barely be classified as cool, but Tara shuddered and crossed her arms over her brea— *Chest,* Michael corrected himself. *Don't even think the other word.* Not with his parents upstairs and likely to check on noises coming from the garage.

"Are you taking it to West Point?" Tara asked. "The bike, I mean."

"Yup," Michael said enthusiastically. "I can't wait."

Tilting her head, Tara studied him. "What's the deal with you and the army? You have *so* many options. I mean... you're planning to do computer science, anyway, so why not at an engineering school? Shawn would hire you afterward. Hell, he'd hire you even without a degree if you asked. There's also oil, and Mr. Andersen says you're good enough for music school."

"Yeah, but..." Michael hesitated. "Uncle Harry asked me the same thing before, but it's hard to explain. Bad stuff happens all the time like it did with my family when I was a kid. I didn't know how to make it right, but I wanted to."

"You said you stopped blaming—"

"It's not about guilt," Michael said. "I wanted to set things right and make sure no one got a chance to hurt my family ever again— my dad and mom, my uncles, Lilah, Uncle Harry. We were the good guys, and I wanted us to win. Dunno if anyone told you about the World Trade Center thing back in 'ninety-three. The bombing?"

Tara nodded, adjusting herself more comfortably on the windowsill.

"I think it was when I first realized there was evil everywhere," Michael went on contemplatively. "Not just in my field of vision. Uncle Liam and I saw the van, you know... when we drove into the garage. The two of us made it out, but a couple of people didn't. Then, we heard the van was rigged to explode. I started thinking about what might have happened if we realized there was something wrong *before* the bomb went off."

"Dumb boy," Tara said severely. "What would you have done?"

Staying put in his spot against the wall, Michael shrugged. "Point is I wanted to be in a position where I could stop the next sonuvabitch who tried to attack the U.S... like I wanted to with my family. Uncle Harry says defending the nation is not only about defending the land and the people. It's also about defending the ideals of the U.S. Constitution."

"You listen to your uncle a lot," Tara commented.

"Yeah," said Michael. Then, he sighed. "Look, I know you think I'm being unfair to my dad. Maybe I am... but he... I kinda get it. He made one bad decision, and everything went to hell. Just gimme time, okay?"

"Did I *say* you're unfair?" Tara asked. "I'd be mad, too, in your place. I still wish things were different for you and Maestro. He's not like Victor. I guess Victor loves Gabe, too, but Maestro would've actually been a dad."

"I suppose," Michael said, "but he wasn't around, and we both gotta play the cards we got." Grinning, Michael added, "Uncle Harry would say so."

Tara snorted.

"Dad was my hero when I was a kid," Michael went on. "Then, Cuba happened, and there was Uncle Harry. Don't get me wrong... Ma brought up Gabe and me. She's amazing—like *really* amazing— and Uncle Harry was our father. We used to talk to him about our plans. I think I picked West Point because of my dad, and Uncle Harry tried to make sure I knew what I was getting into. Yeah, stupid politicians do stupid things and start stupid wars, but our fellow citizens are still worth fighting for. The human ideal is still worth dying for. You know what I'm saying?"

"More or less, but don't use that word," Tara said.

"Heh?" Michael frowned. "Which word?"

"Dying." Tara shuddered.

Michael laughed a little. "It's a risk you take when you sign up to serve."

"Yeah. Doesn't mean I have to think about it."

"There's active-duty commitment for five years after West Point," Michael blurted before he could catch himself. As though she ever agreed to anything that long!

Not objecting to the presumption, Tara stared for a few seconds. "Shit," she eventually said. "I was afraid of that. Like five years of fighting? Dangerous business?"

"Some, probably," Michael admitted.

She cursed again, continuing to stare. "I'm blaming Maestro and your uncle for this. You could've been an IT guy who's not into ideals and stuff. Puny biceps and no pecs."

Chortling, Michael flexed an arm, showing off said bicep.

Mimicking his movements, she did the same. Perhaps because she was sitting cross-legged on the sill, the thin fabric of her tee stretched across her chest. She wasn't wearing anything underneath.

Thoughts of West Point vanished in a nanosecond.

Military service? It was in the distant horizon.

America would surely understand.

Damn, Michael thought.

The two adults in the house would show zero understanding. Even kissing was a distant dream with his parents sleeping upstairs. Not to mention Tara hadn't shown any indication of being ready.

Keeping his eyes on Tara's face, Michael tried his best to ignore the curve in the periphery of his vision. "You wanna arm wrestle?" he suggested out loud. *Crap.* Too sexual?

Mouth opening slightly, Tara asked, "What? I came here to... uhh... read my magazine." Her gaze went to the periodical on her lap.

Way to go, Kingsley, Michael jeered. She probably thought he was a creep.

As though just remembering something, she looked up quickly. "And why would I want to arm wrestle when I *know* I'm gonna lose?" she asked. "You get more muscles every day!" Her gaze lingered on his chest and shoulders.

Every drop of blood within his skull shot to his groin. *Be cool,* he ordered himself, casually angling his body to the side. *Something else to focus on... school... boxing... Mike Tyson!* That did it. The boxing legend's fighting face was enough to quell any tender emotion.

Her tongue darted out to flick the corner of her mouth.

Tyson, Tyson, Tys—

Raising both arms, Tara raked her fingers through her curly hair. When she tilted her chin up, moonlight drenched the small patch of skin below her ear.

Voice choking, Michael asked, "How's..." Who could he ask about? Her father? No. The salon girls, her friends back in India? "Hema?" Michael blurted. "She called you before dinner. Right?"

Seconds passed as Tara subjected him to a glare. Her breath whooshed out in a rueful half-sigh. "She's fine. I'm fine. We're all fine."

Okay, what ticked her off now? Surely, Tara couldn't have meant to... had she been doing it on purpose? Nah. Tara had only been downstairs to get the—

Swooping down to steal the magazine, he took a glance at the cover. It was in fact *Vogue* as she claimed.

"What are you doing?" Tara asked, clambering to her feet. "Give it back!"

Narrowing his eyes, Michael asked, "Did you really leave it in the living room?"

"What do you mean?" Tara snapped. "Give it *back!*" She tried to snatch it from him, and Michael—almost instinctively—lurched a couple of feet to the rear.

She lunged toward him, swatting at the magazine. Her annoyance gave way to sputters of mirth, and a rosy hue bloomed on her cheeks.

Guffawing, Michael whirled and dashed between his bike and the SUV toward the far wall of the garage, all the while waving the periodical in the air. Tara gave chase, threatening murder and mayhem through helpless laughter.

There was a small table in his way, which he vaulted across. "I don't think so," he called out in a sing-song voice. "You came here to talk to me. Admit it."

"I admit nothing," she said loftily. Kicking off her slippers, Tara lifted her arms high in the air to do a couple of pirouettes.

"You wanna dance?" he asked, still gurgling. "Wait 'til I get my instrument." Hastily, he clarified, "I mean for music... *musical* instrument. My flute."

Confusion at his correction, recognition of his train of thought, more hilarity exploding... Tara didn't bother hiding any of it. "Get your 'instrument.'" Waggling her eyebrows, she added, "I'll be ready for whatever you want... to play, I mean."

Tone strangled, Michael laughed again and looked toward the door. "Shit. We can't. Everyone's upstairs. They'll wake up."

Tara's sputtering stopped, and she made a face. "Everyone's always gonna be upstairs until we go away to college. Then, we'll be in two different places."

They clearly weren't talking about music and dancing, anymore. "Yeah," he brooded.

"Do you get to go home from military school?" she asked. "On weekends and holidays?"

"Not much," Michael admitted.

"So..."

"So... God, Tara, what are we going to do?"

"At least there won't be dozens of girls," she grumbled, "hanging all over you."

There *would* be a few female cadets at the academy. Only not as many as at regular universities. Would there be dozens of boys at the fashion institute? Michael found himself taking an intense dislike to the idea. It was weird, this possessiveness.

"You'd tell me first if you found another girl," she acknowledged, shaking a finger at him. "But I don't want you to find someone else. Trust me, I'd be super mad."

Michael grinned in relief. All righty, so they were on the same wavelength. "I won't even look at other chicks," he swore.

She grinned back, her teeth peeking out to bite a corner of her lip.

Michael's heart stopped, then raced. *"I* wanna do that," he said.

He didn't remember skirting the table and getting to her side. He sure as hell didn't remember what he did with the magazine.

Tara was in his arms, and they were kissing as though their lives depended on it. The minty taste of her mouth, the soft smell of whatever she put on her skin at night... somehow, they ended up with Tara sitting on the table near the back wall, her hands trembling as she fumbled with the two buttons on his tee.

"Hold on," he said, lifting his head. In less than five seconds, the shirt lay on the floor.

Slim fingers convulsed around his deltoids. Crescent-shaped nails left pinpoints of pain on his upper back. She gasped when he gathered her close in one sudden move. Her legs wrapped around his hips, and her lips grazed the skin over his collarbone, leaving them both quaking.

"Tara," he whispered.

Mutely, she looked up at him.

"Tell me to stop," he begged, dreading she would, indeed, send him away.

Shaking her head, she said, "Don't wanna." Then, she tugged him down for more kissing.

"Okay," he murmured when he came up for air. "Okay," he repeated. Putting a couple of inches between them, Michael glanced around the garage. "Not here, though. Listen… go upstairs for now. Gimme five minutes. We gotta make sure…"

He needed to grab the condom he kept in his wallet. Also, stealth was required to make sure no one else in the house, including the security officers, saw him sneak into Tara's room. Dammit, the blinds at the garage window had been up the entire time. He could only hope neither of the two outside guards had walked by and witnessed what was going on.

#

Next morning

"Could you pass me the syrup?" Michael asked Tara. "Please."

"Of course," she said, tone lofty enough for breakfast with the British queen.

Taking the bottle, he said equally formally, "Thank you."

Across the kitchen table, Sabrina broke off from whatever discussion she was having with Alex. Pinning the three teens with a glare, she asked, "Did you fight again?"

"No," Michael and Tara responded almost at the same moment.

It took Gabe a few seconds to look up from the stack of pancakes and sausages on his plate. Clearly, the breakup had not affected his appetite. "Nope," he added to what his cousin and Tara claimed.

Eyes narrowing, Sabrina studied each of the three in turn. *"Something's* up."

"What?" Alex asked, laughing. "They're just sitting quietly."

"Which is how I know something's up," Sabrina said.

"We're okay," Michael assured his ma.

Out of the corner of his eye, he caught Tara's grin, which she concealed around a forkful of pancake. Grabbing the glass of OJ, Michael hid his own smug smirk. Oh, yeah! They were more than okay.

Part XVII

Chapter 50

Nearly three months later, September 1999

Week 3 of the hearings

Washington, DC

Steven couldn't quite get a read on how the morning was going. A few small companies from Europe and Africa bellyached about their peeves with the network. Falcon Papazian and Dan Barrons sat with company representatives while they testified. Not commenting much, committee members listened to everything. As always, Godwin and Gen. Potts were present at the Kingsley witness table with two junior lawyers. They weren't saying anything at all.

A couple of hours passed, and Dan got another turn in the hotseat along with Cousin Brad. The duo seemed to have ready answers to every damned question.

"Peter Kingsley Network was structured so it owned large percentages of pipeline operators," stated a committee member. "Would you say it's an accurate characterization?"

"Not direct ownership," said Brad. "The network did purchase stock in strategic companies, but we were scrupulous about keeping it within the boundaries set by U.S. law. Those businesses in turn owned chunks of various oil-related businesses... and so on."

"A true network, a web of connections." Looking over the rim of his glasses, the member smiled. "With the chairman's permission, I'm going to clarify something for myself and my colleagues. We'd like to step farther back in time to when you and your brothers—

and Petty Officer Sheppard—launched your campaign against Jared Sanders. One of your complaints was how he owned chunks of various pipeline operators. So how did you propose your organization to be different?"

"If I may, sir," requested Dan Barrons. "The major difference was in how Brad and his brothers operated. How the member companies were expected to operate. To use your example, Mr. Sanders's holding company bought up large percentages of several pipeline operators. He would then increase transport charges but assign huge discounts to his own refineries and drilling companies. The small businesses which couldn't afford the fees would go under, and he'd gobble them up. The network under Brad set fair and flat fees as a whole, and it was reviewed annually to adjust for market forces. The charges were never so low or high as to destroy those who opted to stay outside. Any discounts applied—such as in cases of humanitarian crises where we supplied fuel at cost—had to be approved by the leadership. Such approvals happened fairly quickly, I might add."

"Seems like a good system," remarked the committee member. "On paper. What would happen if one of those small outside companies made an important discovery? Let's assume someone invented a cheaper way to extract oil or transport it. Or there was breakthrough in renewable energy research. Wouldn't such new technology negatively impact the bottom line of the member companies of the network?"

"It would," acknowledged Brad, "but the agreement all of us signed accounted for such potentialities. We were to negotiate for use of such discoveries even within the network, including renewable energy research. Let's say one of us—perhaps Barrons O & G—discovered a method to harness solar winds. Obviously, the network would benefit from getting a percentage of new Barrons earnings, but the other companies would like to use the technology. The network would negotiate."

"And if the inventor didn't agree?" asked the politician.

"As in any other sector, the rest of us would have to adapt, innovate, and compete," said Brad. "Or we'd go under. Strong-arming was not allowed under any circumstances."

"Then, Mr. Steven Kingsley took over," said the committee member.

"Correct," said Dan. "Brad made the biggest mistake of his professional life in trusting his cousin Steven and was forced into exile. Harry—Petty Officer Sheppard—was imprisoned on false charges of murder. Under Steven Kingsley, what was meant to be a support structure for the energy sector turned into an evil empire. Coercion became standard operating procedure."

Allegedly, Steven muttered in his mind. Godwin should've corrected the claim, but the supposed legal eagle continued to be silent.

If Richard were around, he would've insisted on clarification being entered into government records. The hearing would not have proceeded until the correction was made. Thanks to Godwin, Richard had nothing to contribute in DC and had returned to Texas to his own business.

Next to Steven, Phillip Potts shifted in his seat. He would also have noted Godwin's lack of response. Charles was on Phillip's other side but was worse than useless. Thank God for the minder, or Steven would've had to check on his brother's whereabouts every couple of minutes.

"This seems like a good point for a break," announced the chairman. "We'll talk more about what happened after the change in leadership when we return."

#

The afternoon didn't go much better for Steven. If Brad and his brother-in-law led from the front in the morning, Alex and Victor attacked from the flanks in the second half of the day with support from others. Papazian called the Kingsley duo by their ranks, sneaking in a couple of lines about their heroism.

"My brothers and I didn't know what Steven was doing during our exile," Alex said. "We didn't have any contact whatsoever with the oil sector during the time."

Apparently, toward the end of Sheppard's prison term—more precisely, after his second medal from the United States government—certain oil companies started contacting Saeed al-Obeidi and Dan Barrons. Both men were closely associated with Sheppard and the prior leadership of the network.

Policies pursued by Steven and his associates were rubbing businesses outside the network the wrong way. They were initially wary of making noise because of the clout of the Kingsleys, but once there was hope of Sheppard being freed, outside companies saw a chance to push back.

al-Obeidi took up, "There's a refinery in Muskiz—the northern part of Spain. You will remember how they filed the first official complaint against the network. The CEO traveled to Oslo, where I live, only to talk to me about his concerns. I'm a small businessman, but I happen to know Dan quite well, and Barrons O & G is a heavyweight in our sector."

"And you asked Mr. Barrons to investigate?" prompted the chairman.

Dan nodded. "The Spanish company did not feel comfortable approaching me directly. Not in the beginning. While I, as an individual, remained fully supportive of my sister and her family and Harry, Barrons O & G maintained neutrality. Andrew, like everyone else in the network, did not want to put personal relationships ahead of what was good for the nation and the world as a whole. Secondly, the CEO of the Spanish refinery was not quite sure Barrons and others in the network were not already aware of Steven Kingsley's approach to competition."

"In which case," a member mused, "the Spaniards could've found themselves in more trouble."

"Correct," said Dan. "They have nearly a thousand employees to think of."

Saeed and Dan contacted other small businesses. Noah Andersen got involved. The former attorney general and Harry Sheppard advised the companies to give them time. Once Brad returned—

"We already anticipated a fight over the network," said Dan. If Brad and his brothers got complete control, it would've been relatively easy to return to the policies of the network's infancy. Even with only partial control, they could try to undo the damage caused by Steven's policies. "However, we realized there was a strong possibility Steven would refuse to cooperate. So Harry and Mr. Andersen zeroed in on an antitrust lawyer to represent us— Falcon. I mean, Mr. Vahagn Papazian."

Most committee members, including the chairman, leaned forward. "Interesting," commented one of the senators.

"Quite prescient," agreed his colleague. "Mr. Andersen," she called. "You and Petty Officer Sheppard foresaw the two groups ending up before a congressional committee a few years before it actually happened."

Steven almost cursed out loud at the brown-nosing. Sheppard wasn't supposed to speak, but there was no ignoring him when he was constantly around Alex, and the number of times the committee members referred to "Petty Officer Sheppard" was getting ludicrous. The PR stunt pulled by their side with the random people they dragged in was clearly paying dividends. Sheppard was a hero to the masses, and politicians had taken note.

"When my brothers and I returned home," Alex said, "our first inclination was to preserve the network. I mean... considerable effort went into building it." He detailed their attempts to sway the board, then negotiate.

"Yes, ma'am," said Victor. "We did consider legal action as a third possible option. It wasn't something we looked forward to, given how anything we said in court would be dissected by the media." He paused to take a deep breath, slitted eyes going briefly toward the Kingsley table. "It would've caused distress not only to us but also to others who were horrified by much of what happened yet were unable to stop it. However, given Cousin Steven's attitude, court appeared to be the only way forward. By then, it had been seven, maybe eight months since we returned, and we'd heard from multiple small businesses about what Steven was up to."

"More alarming was the support Steven found within the network," said Alex. "And outside of it."

"Even if we won in court," Victor said somberly, "we'd be looking over our shoulders constantly. It could be Steven. It could be someone else with an eye on the prize. There's no way to account for every trick a greedy basta... a greedy executive might pull. Almost a year ago now, the five of us agreed to approach the government to consider dissolution of the network. None of this—absolutely no part of what we're doing here—can be characterized as sour grapes. Not if you're a fair man."

Bullshit! Steven muttered to himself. Harry Sheppard cooked up a reason to destroy the whole damned network so the five idiots would get at least their business back. The selfish sons of bitches were now positioning themselves as holy warriors fighting a just war.

And Godwin had yet to raise a single objection.

#

"You're a fool, Steven," Godwin stated. The man was ninety-five. He took pills for blood pressure but was still steady on his feet and sharp in eyesight. "The hearings are not a television show. Nor are we in a regular courtroom. I can't leap from my chair and yell, 'Objection!'"

Pacing the carpet, Steven let out a bark of laughter and looked around. Other than Richard, everyone on their side had gathered in Godwin Kingsley's suite. No one would speak up in support of Steven, but all of them knew he was right.

"Mock me all you want," Steven said, "but you could've intervened some other way. You could've sent a note to the chairman."

"And?" asked Godwin. "Do you think it would stop the questions? Steven, it's an *investigative* hearing before a congressional committee. Not a courtroom. Politicians set the rules, but within those constraints, the two sides may present their cases however they please. Moreover, the senators are entitled to ask whatever questions they deem appropriate on whatever topic even if we never bring it up. Yes, it could include what you and Armor and Charlie did to Lilah. Fortunately for you, Brad listens to me. Or he would have brought it up as a way to show your character. *She* won't dare put in her two cents because her husband and his brothers would stop cooperating. Believe me... the committee is wondering why no one's talking about it. They're going to assume the silence is deliberate—an attempt to spare Lilah the trauma of reliving the dishonor. They will also do their best to avoid calling her with the rationalization that the argument is over the legality of the network, and the disrespect you showed her does not directly relate."

Still, if the senators decided they needed to hear from Lilah, it could happen. As was happening now with Brad and his insinuations about what a villain Steven was.

"So what is your suggestion?" Steven asked, not bothering to hide his frustration. "Let Cousin Brad say whatever he wants about me?"

"Yes," said Godwin. "Until it's our turn to speak. Then, I'll present your take on matters."

"But it won't..." Steven started, his voice raised. "You know what I think, Grandfather? You're playing both sides. You're leaving yourself an out... if Brad wins."

"If Brad..." Godwin smiled, sending an icy shiver up Steven's spine. "You're not accusing me of forgetting my responsibilities as a lawyer. Are you, son?"

"Are *you?*" Steven asked, maintaining eye contact. They'd come too far in this fight for him to back down out of fear.

"Father," called David, heaving himself up from his chair. "Steven didn't mean—"

"I believe he did," Godwin said.

Muttering something about idiots, Aaron shook his head and stayed put on the couch. Charles and the minder were at the small dining table with the Pottses. Steven's maternal uncle, Stanley Gander, was also present.

"Steven," called General Potts. "You're not a lawyer. You've never been in politics. Let your grandfather decide how best to convince the committee, or you *will* end up losing. Now, apologize to him, please. You got where you did only because of Justice Kingsley's hard work."

"With all due respect, sir," said Steven, getting angrier by the minute, "you weren't around when my cousins and I lived in the family home. You didn't see how differently our grandfather treated us. I was always—*always*—mocked as the bad one. Even when Victor beat the crap out of Charlie, my brother and I were blamed.

The fair and impartial supreme court justice was anything but fair within his own household!"

"Enough, Steven," said Aaron. "General Potts might not have been there, but *I* was. I saw everything you did."

Steven ptchaaed. "Yeah, Charlie and I retaliated. What else did you expect? The grownups who were supposed to protect us didn't do shit. And we were again punished. Alex was the prince, and Cousin Brad was the favored heir. They got away with everything. Even now, Grandfather doesn't want to fight them. Hell, he probably wants them to win. Then, he'll switch sides."

Aaron opened his mouth to respond, but Godwin held up a hand. "I did what I believed to be right as a father and grandfather and as the president of Kingsley Corp," said the patriarch. "You believe I was unfair. Children often do. We're talking about something else at the moment. I'm here as your attorney today. I spent my lifetime learning law, upholding it. Find me a single judge, a single lawyer, a single politician who will say I was unethical, unfair, or even misguided in my judicial opinions. You cannot. It's a lawyer's duty to represent his client as best as possible, and I've always done my duty."

"Again," Steven said through gritted teeth, "if you're looking out for me, why aren't you telling the committee how Brad and the rest of the losers are lying through their teeth? Justice, my ass! They want power. Nothing else."

"Listen to me carefully, Steven," said Godwin. "We got to this day because of your stubbornness. You refused to negotiate. Now, when you see how your cousins are putting up a better fight than expected..." The patriarch heaved in an audibly angry breath. "We'll have our chance over the next few sessions. I promise there will be no reason for you to berate me again. Brad and his brothers will not win against me. Not unless I die."

Chapter 51

Fall 1999

Weeks 4 to 10 of the hearings

Harry pinched the bridge of his nose with thumb and index finger, sitting silently by Alex's side as the Kingsley patriarch faced off with his grandson. No, there would be no actual cross examination, but whenever it was Godwin's turn to speak, he cut down every damned contention made by the five brothers. The other four at least tried to return fire, but Alex couldn't bring himself to do even as much.

"The refinery in Muskiz," Godwin said at the end of the morning session, "was reported multiple times for violation of the safety protocols the network insists on. Nearly a thousand employees as Mr. Daniel Barrons said. About six thousand people live in the area. *They* would be the ones to suffer in the event of a disaster. Men and women and children would die. Those who survived could face lifelong illnesses. All Steven Kingsley did was to warn the executives of the refinery how he could not let anyone in the network continue to do business with them under the circumstances."

"Thank you, sir," the committee chairman said, nodding deferentially. "Mr. Alex Kingsley, we'll have more questions for you and your brothers and Mr. Daniel Barrons when we reconvene. I believe Mr. Barrons went on site to meet the refinery's CEO. I want to know what kind of inspections he did. What actions were taken... and so on."

#

One loose wire, Harry muttered in his mind.

The citation was the first of such complaints mentioned by Godwin. Steven tried using the minor problem noticed during a routine inspection as leverage against the refinery. He bluntly told the executives there would be a penalty to pay. The leadership of the outfit laughed in his face but soon found the network's member companies indeed refused to purchase oil from Muskiz.

Then came other problems, all seemingly minor as well, all possibly attributable to a combination of incompetence and bad luck. A small leak, which took days to get fixed thanks to the uncooperative attitude of a couple of engineers. A supervisor who ended a lunch break two minutes earlier than expected, leading to a union walkout. A complaint about a gas odor, which shut down operations for a few days and turned out to be nothing. The refinery started taking heavy losses. One of the network's members put out hints about buying the outfit.

Thankfully for the refinery's owner and CEO, it was when Saeed and Dan came into the picture. The duo had been keeping an ear out for murmurs against Steven, anyway, and they found dirt fairly early in the game for once.

Dan waited until he was certain the Spaniards weren't in fact in the wrong, and Saeed made sure they cleaned up the remaining operational concerns. Then, Dan called a presser and all but announced Steven was a greedy idiot. Which encouraged a couple of European companies also outside the network to resume normal relations with the refinery. They were back in business and soon filed an antitrust complaint.

"Mr. Kingsley," the committee chairman called, nodding toward Alex. "Justice Kingsley has stated how the safety concerns were significant. Mr. Daniel Barrons claimed they were trivial. My colleagues and I need this disagreement explained."

C'mon, Alex, Harry prompted. *If not Lilah,* you *need to explain everything.*

Falcon Papazian had pleaded with the five brothers to let Lilah testify. As a chemical engineer who understood the technical *and* financial aspects of the oil sector, she would've been the ideal witness to answer the question. It wasn't happening. Nor could Harry say a word thanks to Brad's other worry about the perception of him as a puppet leader. The committee was also unlikely to ask Harry to talk when he was not directly involved in any of the incidents.

Falcon still asked Harry to join Alex at the witness table because the middle Kingsley brother wilted each time he was forced to contradict his grandfather. Harry's presence was an effort to remind Alex of what was at stake, but it wasn't working.

Say it, Alex, Harry urged. *In your considered opinion, supported by your early experience working for Kingsley Corp under the same Godwin Kingsley, such concerns popped up from time to time and were quickly dealt with. After all, machinery could malfunction despite diligent upkeep. Ask the committee to arrange an independent assessment.*

An honest evaluation by an engineering team would not deem the findings cause for even a citation such as the one originally received. Simply a matter of routine maintenance as Dan said.

"I suppose it's a matter of what different people find acceptable in different work environments," Alex finally muttered.

There was a small sound from Alex's other side, quickly smothered. One of Falcon's assistants, frustrated as hell at the clients. Falcon himself sat straight-faced. Back in the audience, Dan would be wanting to beat Alex to a pulp.

#

"I didn't know," maintained the hapless Nigerian who managed the pipeline company. Criminals had built a diversion to steal crude which was already purchased. "The buyer informed us how the delivery fell short, and we immediately investigated. We also purchased more crude with our own cash to make up for the buyer's loss."

"Still, sir," said the senator from Utah. "It's hard to believe no one noticed an extra pipe being built to steal the product."

"It is exactly what happened," the Nigerian repeated. "Unfortunately, such occurrences are not unheard of when there are thousands of miles of pipelines. The police tried to find the missing workers, who we believe were responsible. However, temporary workers come and go, and we don't necessarily know enough details about them to track them down."

The chairman inclined his head. "Thank you, sir, for traveling to the U.S. to answer our questions. Now, unless my colleagues have other—"

"I mean," continued the witness. "Mr. Steven Kingsley's own friend got into trouble with the FBI because of some contractor. Wasn't Mr. Armor investigated for child trafficking? Steven Kingsley himself shot someone in front of a room full of witnesses."

"Yes," the Texas senator agreed. "Both concerns were investigated. Major Armor was cleared, and the Las Vegas incident was determined to be self-defense."

"If I'm not mistaken, the exact terminology used in Mr. Armor's case was 'no evidence of the owner's involvement,'" the Nigerian pointed out. "Mr. Armor simply said he didn't know what was going on, and the government couldn't prove otherwise. The network took his word for it without a second thought given to the ladies and the children who were trafficked. In our case, no one suffered except us, because we felt ethically obligated to reimburse the buyer for the loss. Yet Mr. Steven Kingsley protected his friend, sending out a memo at the same time about my company's unreliability."

#

An oil spill, tankers which didn't pass inspection, overtime work, even a less than acceptable number of security guards at a drilling site... week by week, session by session, Godwin and his team dismantled every argument made about the network's anticompetitive tactics.

Outside the senate office building, trees changed colors. The days got shorter, nights longer. The air cooled, blowing crackling leaves off the branches and down the streets.

A political drama called *The West Wing* debuted on NBC to great critical reviews. Viacom and CBS merged. So did Exxon and Mobil, forming the world's largest corporation. Cross-network text messaging became a reality.

Global population hit six billion. The Russian president appointed the country's spy chief as the new prime minister, a fellow called Vladimir Putin. Like his predecessors, Putin wasn't expected to last long in the position.

"The Nigerian gentleman who spoke to us a couple of months ago was correct, of course," conceded Godwin. "His business is owed recompense for the losses they suffered as a result of the network's actions. However, the issue with the particular company was one—exactly *one*—mistake the committee found amid the thousands of such decisions made by the network's leadership over the last decade. The CEO of any organization gets paid to make hard choices. Some of those choices may be controversial and some tremendously unpopular, but the job's got to get done. Very occasionally, there's an error. Nothing anticompetitive about it."

"Mr. Brad Kingsley," called the chairman. "Would you concur?"

"With the general idea, yes," said Brad, "but—"

"And your brothers? You were the executives of the same collective prior to Mr. Steven Kingsley taking over."

Alex was in the chair next to Brad's. "Yes," he said, tone subdued.

#

"What the hell are you doing?" Harry asked through gritted teeth as his brother-in-law washed his hands at the sink.

The men's room in the senate office building was empty except for the two of them. It was still not the right place for this conversation, but Alex was supposed to testify again in the afternoon. It would be the final session before politicians returned home for Christmas break, and the words they heard from the former sniper would remain on their minds until the government reopened in the new millennium. If he dithered again...

"I'm doing all I can," Alex said.

"All you're willing to, you mean."

Alex turned to face Harry, guilt and unhappiness clear on his face. "I get it, man. Everyone on our side has his or her own reason not to want the network to continue, but you also said ends don't justify the means. So how can you rationalize going after my grandfather for something he had no power to stop? Which is what it will come down to if we claim he's laying it on about the problems with the small companies."

"Or if we talk about him letting Steven go to Prince," agreed Harry. "The committee will make the connection to Cuba and Godwin's role there. An *m.o.* will emerge. Captain Kingsley, you're a damn traitor!"

"Traitor?" echoed Alex. He shook his head tiredly. "Even the military hears out conscientious objectors. Well... my conscience objects to what you're asking."

"What does your conscience say about keeping faith with the people who trusted you?" Harry asked. "You're lucky Dan hasn't... you basically told the committee he doesn't hold the same safety standards as the Kingsleys. I'm sure you know the kind of trouble Barrons O & G is in for thanks to the one statement. The only reason Dan and Shawn are still with you is Lilah, but forget them.

Barrons is big enough to survive a little tough love from the government. They're also going to survive a tussle within the network. Even the other six board members who back us can hold their own. What about the small businessmen? Regular people came out to support us, Captain, only because they felt strongly about what the Kingsleys did. A government official like Warden Berra could find himself in deep shit if the committee rules in favor of the network. Steven would make sure of it. What about the people who already died because of Steven? Remember Lupe? How about Will Luce? You claim Liam is your friend."

"Most of what you listed relates to business," said Alex, "and politics. If our side loses, it's going to be a matter of losing money and power. Maybe someone will lose a job. Yes, Liam's father died, and so did Lupe, but attacking my grandfather is not going to bring them back. It's not going to undo what Charlie did to Lilah. If I do what you want... my God! Grandfather could actually get accused of... I don't know... some crime against the nation only because he couldn't stop what happened in Cuba. It would actually kill him. I want to win but not on those terms."

"Do you hear yourself?" Harry asked incredulously. "Money may not be important to you, but working people need their paychecks."

"We can take care of—"

"What about justice?" Snarling, Harry went on, "Why am I bothering? Lilah's right. You're faking sleep. If you tell yourself Godwin didn't intend any of it, you can pretend it would be dishonorable to attack. You can pretend your attitude ain't about self-interest alone."

"It isn't—"

"You stopped Lilah from testifying about Cuba or about anything else," said Harry. If she tried to do it, anyway, Godwin's reputation would take a hit, but it wouldn't be enough to declare the network illegal. Not if the Kingsley brothers quit the war in a huff.

"This again." Alex groaned.

"Your brother got me to promise *I* wouldn't put myself front and center, either." Harry nodded. "My family, too, was against it, so I held back. But enough is enough. If you won't put a stop to Godwin, I will. Let Falcon call me to testify. I'll tell the committee exactly what Godwin did through this entire saga."

"Harry, you weren't around in Cuba or Macau. You don't have the standing to testify."

With an unpleasant smile, Harry said, "True, but I was with you in Argentina. I remember quite well who sent us there."

"Argentina?" Alex's jaw dropped open. "Have you lost your goddamn mind? You're going to tell the committee my grandfather planned a genocide that we executed. Not to mention Mr. Temple."

"It would be better than surrendering without even making a pretense of fighting," said Harry. "Temple would agree. What's the government going to do to him? The man's almost ninety-five. By the time the case gets through all the courts in the country, he'll be gone. As for me, I'm prepared to return to prison if it puts an end to your grandfather's games. And yeah... there's your former dean. His presence in Brussels is a matter of record while Phillip Potts and his assassins were trying to dispatch me in New York."

Harry hadn't said anything to the cops at the time because the Pottses would've fallen on the sword to protect Godwin, and it would be a wasted card. Perhaps now was the moment to play it.

"Dude," started Alex. "Will you stop with the threats... where are you going?"

Harry had turned toward the door, opening it. Outside in the sky-lit atrium would be the two groups, getting some air before the hearings resumed. Tourists, staffers, the senators themselves, the ever-present media... quite a few witnesses to what he was about to say to the lawyer, but it couldn't be helped.

Ignoring Alex's repeated calls to stop, Harry jogged toward the atrium. In under two minutes, he spotted Falcon amid the crowd near the east wall where the sculpture was, chatting with Noah and Dante. Above the five tall, metal mountains hung black metal clouds. A brightly lit Christmas tree stood next to the sculpture, with a piano below and someone playing "Jingle Bell Rock" on it.

Not far from Noah, Falcon, and Dante were Godwin and his guards. Brad was also present, talking to his grandfather.

"Harry!" Alex called for the umpteenth time, the urgency in his tone clear even over the music and the hum of dozens of conversations.

Raising a hand toward Falcon and the two men with him, Harry took one step into the atrium. A weight landed on his back. Hands grabbed his arms at the elbows. Harry stumbled forward a foot or two and shook off the hold.

Curious stares, a couple of surprised laughs, a camera flash... ignoring everything, he skirted a potted plant against which a large tire was propped up for whatever reason. A young man with a badge pinned to his lapel stood next to the tire, saying something on his phone about some senator's troubles with his SUV.

"Wait, Harry," said Alex. "Please!"

Another whoosh in the air, Alex tackling a second time. The weight slamming into Harry slipped down his back, and he found himself caught by the leg.

"Let go," Harry ground out, barely keeping his balance.

"Not until you calm down," Alex said from the vicinity of Harry's knee.

There were more camera flashes, people stopping to gape. The staffer talking on the phone about his boss's car problem also turned to stare. Harry was close enough to Falcon and Noah and Dante to see the surprise in their demeanor. Godwin and Brad, too, were peering in the direction of the scene.

Grunting, Harry tried to keep moving. He managed to take one step, dragging Alex along. "Let go," Harry said again, but Alex simply refused to release his hold.

Roaring, Harry grabbed the tire propped up against the potted plant and heaved it high. Someone—a woman—screamed. A male voice shouted for security. Those who were in proximity to the battling duo ran for the doors.

"Harry!" shouted Falcon, bounding toward the chaos. With him were Brad and one of the secret service officers, Noah and Dante following as fast as they could. Godwin was also approaching Harry and the errant Kingsley grandson. The piano music from the east wall came to an abrupt halt.

"Stop!" yelled someone. "Put it down, sir!" A female cop came into view, her hand on the butt of the gun on her belt. A couple of colleagues accompanied her, one of them in a Santa hat.

"Ma'am," said the secret service officer, flashing his badge. "I know him... both of them. They're not dangerous."

"Yeah?" she snapped. "Tell him to put the fucking tire down."

"Harry," called Dante. "Listen to her."

"Please," added Falcon. The antitrust lawyer held up both hands in a soothing gesture. Noah and Godwin had caught up as well, the former justice's guards with him.

Taking a deep breath, Harry said, "We're good." He set the tire back near the potted plant and nodded at the open-mouthed staffer. "Sorry."

Alex, too, let go of Harry's leg and clambered up. "Sorry," he echoed. "We were talking about... ahh... hockey... ice hockey. Got a little out of hand."

"Hockey?" The cop stared hard at the two men. "Are you kidding me? Take your dumb fuckery outside. This is government property."

"We know," said Noah. *"They* know. Officer, they're with..."

Briefly, he explained the two miscreants were with a former president of the United States. It took only a minute or so to convince the cops, but they warned Harry and Alex of consequences if either as much as tossed a used napkin into the wrong bin.

When the officers left, Brad asked, "What?" Eyebrows drawn, he flung his hands in the air. *"What?"* It seemed he could manage only the one word.

Godwin inclined his head in the direction of the tire. "Was it meant for me?" he asked Harry.

Wiping the sweat off his top lip with the back of his hand, Harry stayed silent. Thankfully, Alex, too, kept his mouth shut.

"I'm flattered," Godwin went on, a hand held to his heart. "Tabloids claim you've become a god to the common man. The Almighty forced to take up weapons against me. What better compliment can I expect?"

No one laughed. The secret service officer and the high-priced Kingsley guards would've been trained not to, and there was nobody from Godwin's side to appreciate the old man's sarcasm, not even his grandsons. The crowds were slowly gathering back, with many still gawking at the scene.

With a small chuckle, Godwin added, "I'll see you inside."

Noah waited until the former justice was out of earshot. "I'm not going to ask why," he said to the two culprits. "I'm not even going to remind you of the repercussions if either of you gets thrown out of the hearings. Just get your rear ends back where they belong and try to stay out of jail."

Dante nodded once as though in agreement, but he didn't say anything.

"Noah," called Alex. "It was my fault. I... ahh... we were talking about..."

"Understood," said Noah. "Do I need to tell anyone here open brawling is not the way to solve our problem?"

Harry sighed. "No," he agreed. "And right now, there seems to be no solution."

If he went to the committee about the massacre in Argentina, Godwin would be down for the count. However, it would still leave Steven in charge, with both Temple and Harry out of commission. The Kingsley brothers would also stop cooperating.

"I was trying to tell you," Alex said, "before you ran out here. Dude, there's a way to avoid implicating Grandfather in Steven's schemes and still win. I mean... Steven's the one in charge of the network and made all the decisions. Grandfather's the president of Kingsley Corp, one single business in the network. He would only know what Steven told him, which would include the inspection findings from Muskiz. Right, Falcon?"

"Instead of arguing Justice Kingsley is... er... massaging the truth, argue he was given wrong information?" Falcon asked. "Long shot, but no harm in trying."

Very long. If the former supreme court justice said he studied the documents and concluded the network was correct in its approach, he'd be believed.

"Maybe we should ask Grandfather what to do," Brad muttered. When everyone turned to stare, he flushed. "Stupid thing to say, but we're running out of ideas."

Harry held up a finger. "Wait a second. You may be on to something."

A thought... taking shape, gathering speed...

Lip curling in anticipation, Harry said, "As Brad suggested, let's ask Godwin the question. Let's get *him* to deny knowing any more than what Steven said."

"Heh?" Falcon frowned. "Force him into an own-goal? How?"

"The Barronses," said Harry. He threw a quick glance at Noah. The former attorney general would request Falcon to play along no matter how insane Harry's scheme seemed on the surface. "Same as Kingsley Corp, Barrons O & G is also part of the network's board. How does Godwin have information about the network's activities that Dan doesn't? The Barronses have grounds to demand details. One of them has even more legit reason to confront the Kingsleys—Shawn Barrons."

Chapter 52

An hour later

Steven didn't understand why the old man was getting himself sidetracked right when they were on the verge of victory. Only half a day's worth of testimony remained, and Brad and his idiot brothers were unlikely to produce a strategy to counter the family patriarch in the limited time.

Then, Papazian declared Shawn was going to take Dan's place by Alex's side, and Godwin lost his ever-loving mind.

He started objecting. And yeah, what the former supreme court justice previously said about investigative hearings turned out to be true. Normal courtroom rules didn't have a place here. The committee got the final word, but within reason, both sides could decide on their own how to make their cases. The senators were looking thoroughly bewildered by Godwin's demands to have Shawn removed. So were General Potts and the two junior lawyers at the Kingsley witness table.

"Perhaps the former justice objects to my presence because I'm gay," Shawn said into the microphone, motioning with his hand in an effeminate manner he never exhibited before. He didn't even bother hiding the mocking smirk.

Their two lawyers—Papazian and an assistant—maintained stoic expressions, but Alex appeared as confused as everyone else in the room. The charge of homophobia clearly wasn't part of some master strategy from the five idiots.

Steven craned his neck to peer at Lilah. No obvious signs of calculation there, either. She was sitting next to Dan, both of them staring anxiously at Shawn. Mr. Temple looked grim. Andersen and Harry sat to the right of the former president, guarded expression on their mugs. Dante, Gateway's COO, was also with Harry.

"Mr. Barrons," reproved the Illinois senator. He adjusted his glasses. "I studied Justice Kingsley's work in law school, and I imagine many of my colleagues did as well. He's always been fair in his dealings, regardless of class, race, gender, or politics. I'm sure your personal life has no bearing on his current concerns."

The words were supportive, but Steven didn't like the hint of a question he heard in the senator's tone.

"Certainly not," Godwin assured the committee. There was an unhealthy flush on his face. "As I said before, someone unconnected with the energy sector should not get a say in what happens to the network. Mr. Shawn Barrons has not been a part of his family business for a long time. He has no financial interest in oil and gas. I respectfully submit to the committee that his presence is intended as a red herring."

"Mathur—the Indian gentleman—had no connection to oil sector," Shawn pointed out. "He got a say."

"He was a character witness," General Potts snapped before Godwin could speak.

"So am I," Shawn retorted. "And I disagree with the statement that I'm unconnected to the energy sector. Hell..." He did a quick nod at the senators. "...pardon my French, ma'ams and sirs, but my entire existence, starting with my birth, has to do with oil and gas. In fact, you might say I'm a petroleum byproduct."

A snort of surprise came from the audience, quickly smothered. Dan Barrons. At his side, Lilah, too, looked like she badly wanted to laugh. From their left, Victor and Liam were staring at the brother-sister duo in puzzlement, but Andersen was clearly hiding a smile. Harry kept his unblinking gaze on the Kingsley patriarch.

"Would you like to hear how?" Shawn asked the committee.

"No one's interested in your life story," said Godwin, the red slashes on his cheeks turning alarmingly bright.

Shawn sneered. "Aren't they now?"

The Kingsley patriarch made a noise which could only be described as frustrated rage. Steven didn't understand it. The old fellow was too seasoned a businessman to fall for such schoolyard tactics.

The chairman tapped on his microphone. "Let me remind everyone this is a senate committee hearing. We expect a level of decorum from those invited to speak. Mr. Barrons, please remain respectful toward others. And Mr. Kingsley—Mr. *Godwin* Kingsley—your opponents do have the right to clarify why they requested Mr. Shawn Barrons to testify. There will be no more debate on it." The chairman gestured at Shawn. "You may go ahead."

"I apologize, sir," said Shawn, demeanor turning brisk and business-like in a matter of seconds. "I should've been mindful of the traditions of this institution. As for my reason for being here... you would've already seen the transcripts from the military interrogation in Cuba. I imagine you also reviewed notes from various intelligence agencies on those events. The timeline will make it clear how my sister—Delilah Kingsley—was savvy enough to protect her computer systems from malicious intrusions *before* the home invasion—sorry, sting operation—happened. Thanks to the foresight, the Kingsleys couldn't plant evidence to implicate her in the fake Iran deal cooked up by Steven and his buddies. Since I run an IT consulting company, the feds believe I wrote the program for Lilah. I've spent the last ten or so years with them breathing down my neck, trying to produce proof. My team found traces of snooping. Trust me, we kept meticulous records of every funny finding we ran across in the last decade. Our engineers can usually tell when it's a government agency behind the hacking."

"They would've had a warrant," interjected the California senator. "I will personally check to make sure."

"Thank you, ma'am," said Shawn. "Let's give the FBI... the CIA... whomever... the benefit of the doubt and assume there was a warrant. However, a few incidents stood out. My team and I recognized the handiwork of a couple of well-known hackers. You could call them the problem children of our business. I suspect they were hired by a third party who wanted me punished for helping my sister. No prizes for guessing who. Mr. Chairman and other committee members, my rights as a private citizen were infringed upon by the shadow empire which calls itself the network. Therefore, I request the chance to speak with you, my representatives, about it."

"Damn," Steven muttered under his breath.

Next to him, Phillip shifted in his seat. "Is this going to be a problem?" he asked, voice low.

"Not sure," Steven said. "If Richard were here..."

He would know. So would Godwin, but the former justice wasn't explaining anything to anyone. Steven frowned. Godwin's hand was visibly shaking as he reached for his glass of water.

The committee members were silent for a few moments as they mulled the new info. "If what you said is true," one of them eventually offered, "there would be no explaining it away as part of a CEO's job."

"No," agreed Shawn. "It was an illegal act."

"In which a former supreme court justice would've had no part," said Alex, speaking for the first time in the afternoon.

Godwin stared hard at Alex for a few seconds. "I didn't," the patriarch assured the committee.

Liar, Steven murmured in his mind. From the time of the Cuba episode, Godwin was insistent they keep an eye on Lilah's family, especially Shawn.

"I take Justice Kingsley at his word that he was unaware of the hacking," Shawn said. "If he knew... or even suspected... a crime was committed, he would've been obligated to report it. Very likely, Steven Kingsley didn't inform his grandfather about what was going on. Steven will still insist he wasn't involved. If I understand legal proceedings correctly, Mr. Godwin Kingsley would be duty-bound to object on behalf of his client."

"Just as he was duty-bound to object on behalf of Steven with everything else," said Alex. "The refinery in Spain, the pipeline problem in Nigeria, the oil spill in the Timor Sea... all incidents which were rebranded as the network's solemn responsibility toward mankind."

"What the..." Steven muttered, trying to keep his tone low. "I don't like this."

"Me, neither," said Phillip. "Steven, let me step out for a minute. I'm calling Rich."

Steven nodded and kept an eye on the senators. They were glancing uncomfortably at one witness table, then the other.

"But..." said the senator from Texas, then halted.

"This is the problem our side faces," Alex stated. "*We* know the importance Justice Kingsley places on his responsibilities as a lawyer, but in this chamber, he's also seen as a participant in Steven's actions by virtue of family and business ties. This is not the case as my grandfather himself made clear just now. Still, it's how the situation has been perceived until this afternoon. Unfortunately, this has led to his reputation as a judge lending credibility to Steven's claims. I submit to this committee that Mr. Godwin Kingsley's statements about the network's actions were those of a lawyer representing his client to the best of his ability. He was not someone with direct knowledge of the occurrences. Therefore, the incidents should be independently investigated. I respectfully request this committee to appoint an inspector to look into the competing claims."

Multiple hushed whispers set up a hum in the chamber. General Potts was peering into the audience as though hoping to find help. Everyone was glancing at each other, at Godwin, at Alex and Shawn.

Someone tapped Steven on his shoulder. Shrugging off the touch, he mentally prompted, *Say it, Grandfather.* All he needed to say was how the hacking was a separate incident, done by some unknown party, and he was convinced about the ethicality of the rest of it. If not... an independent inspection! Steven's head swam.

None of the men involved would've been stupid enough to leave evidence, but even a neutral conclusion could prove devastating to the network. They could be found guilty of anticompetitive activity even if not with malicious intent.

Say it! Steven silently urged.

"My apologies, Justice Kingsley," Shawn said gravely. "All I wanted was a chance to demonstrate how you could not possibly be speaking from direct experience. I did not intend to be disrespectful to you in the beginning. After all, you were a close associate of my father. The Kingsleys and the Barronses have known each other way before my sister married Brad. If I remember Barrons lore correctly, there were close calls with matrimony between the two families a couple of generations ago." Shawn paused to smile. "In Andrew's absence, I suppose I could consider you my father."

Godwin clambered to his feet. Eyes wide and staring, he opened his mouth as though to speak.

Steven saw his grandfather swaying, tilting. The lawyers next to him jerked away in reflex reaction. So did General Potts. In the audience, Aaron leaped up. So did Brad.

"Grandfather," shouted Alex, bounding to the other table.

Chairs clattering, the senators stood. "Call nine-one-one," yelled the Texan lady.

Noise exploded in the chamber. Screams, bellows for help, an alarm going off. Someone blocked Steven's view. Pushing the fellow aside, he ran to the Kingsley table.

Godwin was on the floor, head cradled in Alex's lap. All the Kingsley grandsons surrounded him, including Charles. Aaron and David also stumbled to the patriarch's side. Godwin's gaze wandered through the crowd until it reached the man who didn't belong—the pale-faced intruder standing in the periphery.

Pointing a trembling finger at Shawn, Godwin said, "It wasn't you. Do you hear me? Alex, my boy..." The patriarch looked up at the grandson holding him. "Only you could bring me down. No one else. I'm proud of you."

Then, Godwin's eyes rolled back, and his body slumped into itself.

Chapter 53

A few hours later

New Castle, New York

The eighteen-passenger Gulfstream V offered no privacy for Lilah and Dan to talk to poor Shawn. The legal team was also traveling back to New York in the Barrons jet, and they were surely speculating on Godwin's disproportionate reaction to Shawn's appearance.

The Kingsley brothers, of course, remained in DC. They would not leave the hospital until they knew their grandfather was okay, and all five were grateful to Harry and Sabrina for staying to extend support.

The Barrons plane landed at MacArthur Airport in Long Island early Saturday morning. On their way down the jet bridge, Dan informed Lilah's guards she would be joining him in his vehicle since they had private matters to discuss. The guards could follow in her car and wait in the Barrons residence until their client chose to return.

From the back of the sedan, Lilah wrapped her arms around the shoulders of the blond man in the front passenger seat. She couldn't see Shawn's face, but his ice-cold hands came up to hold hers. Christmas music played on the radio.

The sky was still dark this early in the day, and Cross Island Parkway was nearly empty of traffic. Briefly glancing at the van which whizzed past, Dan returned his eyes to the front. "We're going to make a doctor's appointment for you."

Shawn turned to face his adopted brother. "Why?"

"Didn't you hear the neurosurgeon?" Dan asked. "Godwin had an aneurysm."

The medics at George Washington University Hospital had spoken to Neil in detail. The preliminary report on the MRI showed a congenital abnormality in the blood supply to the brain. One artery was supplying both thalami, whatever that was. Apparently, Godwin developed an aneurysm in said artery, which he never knew about. He didn't have any symptoms until an acute rise in blood pressure caused a rupture.

Aaron then mentioned how his brother Peter—Brad's father—died from an aneurysm as well, this one in the chest. The surgeon immediately advised all Kingsleys to get tested. Apparently, such vascular problems could run in families.

"Shawn, you could have it, too," Dan said.

Lilah sat back in her seat. "Are we sure it's Godwin?" she asked more for vocalizing the certainty in her mind.

Daniel shrugged. "There's a strong possibility—"

"It's him," said Shawn, only a slight tremor in his voice. "I saw it in his eyes yesterday. He hates me. He hates the fact I exist."

"Shawn..." started Lilah.

"It's all right," he said.

"It's not," said Dan. "Bud, there's no one around but the three of us. You want to scream... shout... I don't care. Lilah won't, either."

Instead, Shawn laughed a little. "Thanks. I'm glad I have you two. Thing is I don't know how to feel right now. I was seventeen when Andrew told me about Amber. It was like the whole world crashed around me. Andrew was never a warm person to grow up with. He was a father, not a dad, but he was still a father. Then, he wasn't. Because I was gay."

Heart breaking, Lilah murmured, "I wish we knew you then." They did but only as a remote figure, the stepson of their much older half-sister.

"I cried," Shawn continued. "I was embarrassed about it, but I couldn't stop crying. I wanted my old life back. The sense of belonging. Then, I started thinking about her... Amber. I created an alternate reality in my mind where she didn't die. A whole imaginary universe to escape to when things got tough. General Potts telling me to take her beads off was the push I needed. My father—Andrew—didn't love who I actually was, and I was being asked to give up the one person who accepted me. Stupid fantasy. Amber didn't care enough even to live."

His words ended in a small sob. Turning to the window, he stared at the lightening sky for long moments.

"I get it," Shawn eventually continued. "Mental health problems... maybe postpartum depression... not to mention Godwin telling everyone she was crazy... but it was still hard to accept. I was a newborn. *Her* child. How could she... my grandparents didn't want me, either, and they were also dead by the time I found out. At least one more person knew I existed unless he was dead, too. There was no reason she wouldn't have told the boyfriend about the pregnancy. Maybe he was already married. Maybe he was a garden-variety jerk who left his pregnant girlfriend. I didn't have any delusions of a father-son reunion. Seriously, I didn't know what the hell I was expecting from the sonuvabitch, but I wanted to find him."

"Hope," said Lilah. When both men glanced toward her reflection in the rearview mirror, she clarified, "It's hard to live without some kind of hope."

"Dunno," said Shawn. "Maybe I *was* hoping for acceptance. Maybe it's why I feel... shit... like there's nothing."

"Nothing?" Dan parroted, throwing a sharp glance at Shawn. "What do you mean by... listen to me..."

"I'm not suicidal," Shawn assured the other two. "I spent all this time looking for family and found it with you two. And Caroline. The Godwin news was a shock, but it's not going to kill me. Still, the search took up so much of my mental energy for so long, and now, it's done. My actual father never wanted me, either. Hell, he didn't want me even before I came out. The way Godwin was staring at me yesterday... what he said before he passed out... he's always hated me. Now, he's going to die hating me."

#

Harry's phone was going straight to voicemail. So was Sabrina's. Snapping the clamshell device shut, Lilah returned to the breakfast table where the rest of the family was tucking into a fragrant breakfast of bacon and eggs.

Caroline and Amy had been anxious for updates, and they informed the butler that no staff would be required for the meal. Open conversation was possible only when they were truly alone.

"Never thought I'd say this," Amy mused. "Shawn, maybe you got the better deal with Andrew. Imagine growing up with Godwin Kingsley as your dad."

"His grandsons love him," Lilah remarked, biting into buttery toast.

"Exactly my point," said Amy. "He made sure they did, then turned around and used them. He's still doing it."

"My take on Godwin is he doesn't see it as wrong," Caroline said. "Call it the big-picture mentality. Universal truths... small injustices in the pursuit of a larger justice... that sort of ideology. The larger justice for him would be the Kingsley family as a whole. There are business and political leaders who do the same, but they admit to qualms at least in private. Godwin wouldn't. He would in fact pat himself on the back for being morally superior to us lesser beings."

"Narcissism," Amy murmured.

"Precisely," said Caroline.

"Noah says the same," Lilah mentioned. "More or less."

Caroline glanced her half-sister's way for a second before turning back to Shawn. "However," Caroline continued, "My money is on the stepmother problem in the Amber episode. Godwin had *pretty* good reason to despise Sylvia. He never seemed to think much of his own father, either. Remember... Justice Godwin Kingsley was a well-known figure in legal and business circles by the time Amber showed up. Everyone around respected him, and part of the reason was surely the dignity he showed in dealing with the messy situation at home. Then, he made a mistake with Amber. Maybe timing was such that the baby couldn't be passed off as the half-brother's. Maybe Godwin's integrity—he does have his own version of it—wouldn't let him do it. If he acknowledged Amber, he would lose face with his stepmom, *and* the rest of New York would realize he was just as weak as the father he sneered at."

Lilah got it to some extent. Even the journos who argued in favor of her reduced her existence to the assault in Gitmo and her alleged romantic missteps. Her actual parents were long forgotten by society. Rarely did anyone mention her work as CFO of the network. Lilah's identity had shrunk to that of Andrew Barrons's adopted daughter, of the Kingsley wife, of a lover scorned, of a woman wronged.

It would be much, much worse for Godwin. Every good thing he ever did as a supreme court justice and as president of Kingsley Corp would be erased out of existence. His name would evoke only the memory of his affair with his brother's intended.

"He sees me as a symbol of his weakness," Shawn agreed, his tone bitter. "I didn't spot any guilt or remorse over Amber."

"Oh, there's probably guilt," contended Caroline. "We've all heard Godwin speak multiple times, at different venues. He prides himself on having a clean conscience and a spotless career. Amber's death is one episode he can't lie to himself about. In my opinion, it's why he didn't go after you. Or he could've finished you off long ago."

"Especially after Andrew disowned you," said Dan. "You were pretty much on your own at the time. Yeah, I know we said Godwin had no practical reason to go after you. Still, he could've opted not to leave loose ends."

"An accident, a fake suicide," pointed out Lilah. "Shawn, I know what it's like to be in Godwin's crosshairs. You never were. Not seriously."

"Are y'all telling me I should be grateful to him?" Shawn asked. "Because I'm not. If you're trying to make me feel better, thank you, but it's not needed. To Godwin, I'm mainly a reminder of what a pathetic man he actually is. Gay... straight... he would've hated the sight of me no matter what."

"I would even say your homosexuality helped him," said Caroline. "He now has a plausible explanation for hating you."

Shaking his head, Shawn brooded, "He'd rather be called a bigot than acknowledge me? I'm not sure how to take it."

"Take it as evidence." Dan nodded in satisfaction. "You can demand a DNA test."

"On what basis?" Shawn asked. "If Godwin lives... let's say a court allows testing. Let's also say it shows I'm Godwin's son. What's next? He didn't do anything criminal to Amber. Not legally."

"It's the cover-up," said Amy. "Mr. Temple and Andrew."

Which would've been what the former president thought. Temple would've feared Shawn was next on the list. Caroline was right. It could only have been guilt over the dead girl holding Godwin back from attacking her son.

"Problem is we have no proof he was behind either of those incidents," Shawn said. "So he's not going to jail."

"We don't need to send him to jail," said Dan. "We don't even need to get to a court. Since we have some certainty he's the daddy, you can threaten to take the legal route. The whole sordid saga will be all over the tabloids. Godwin won't be able to stand the idea. He will agree to step back from the hearings to avoid the possibility. I'm sure of it."

"Maybe the aneurysm will kill him in the next couple of days," said Shawn. "In which case, mission already accomplished. Unless the committee members decided which way to vote before my testimony yesterday."

It *was* the general expectation before Harry asked Shawn to join Alex at the witness table. "Let's hope you changed a few minds," Dan said.

He hesitated, glancing at Lilah for a fraction of a second. She knew what he was thinking. The question was awkward but needed to be asked.

"Listen, man," Dan continued. "Assuming Godwin recovers, do you want to talk to him? You know... without bringing up DNA testing or the network or anything else."

"No," Shawn said immediately. "Like I told you before... I feel nothing." He held up a finger. "I *am* feeling a little sorry for myself, but Godwin's still the same S.O.B. he was yesterday morning. Worse if anything. Now, it's not only about Lilah and Andrew. Amber needs justice, too."

As if on cue, a shrill ring interrupted the conversation—Lilah's cell phone.

A couple of minutes later, she hung up and announced, "That was Noah. Godwin's out of surgery, but the hospital's still hedging bets on the possibility of survival. The committee chairman came by to visit, and he talked to Noah and General Potts. The senators would like to postpone the next session for a few weeks... maybe even a few months... out of respect for Godwin. Also, to allow for the possibility he might recover and rejoin the proceedings." Lilah took a deep breath. "In the meantime, the committee will do their own investigation into what happened in Muskiz."

"The war's back on?" asked Caroline.

"Not only on," Dan said slowly. "Once the committee sees for itself what the deal was in Spain, there's no way in hell the vote won't go against Steven. Shawn, we might get justice, after all."

The same look of bemusement was on everyone's faces. Were they actually going to win? Finally?

Part XVIII

Chapter 54

Two weeks later, December 31, 1999

Out on the Hudson

"He said he was proud of me," Alex murmured, only vaguely aware of the view through the windows lining the gallery level of the boat. Glittering against black night sky was Brooklyn Bridge, leading to the magnificent Manhattan skyline.

Fabulous venue to ring in the new millennium, and it should've been a great party. There was no audible huff from Sabrina, but Alex heard it just the same, even over the music played by the DJ and the hum of many conversations.

He turned to face his wife, intending to apologize for being inattentive. The short, sleeveless dress in dark-blue chiffon made the gold in her hair glint even brighter. Thanks to six-inch heels, her head actually reached his shoulder. A thin string of gems sparkled around her neck, her only other jewelry the wedding ring.

"Damn, you're gorgeous," Alex said, bending to steal a quick kiss. Her lips were warm, offering a taste of fruity, nutty champagne. Sabrina's perfume usually made him think of fresh-cut grass and sunny afternoons, but tonight, she smelled of sultry summer nights. "Let's go home and celebrate on our own. What do you say we sneak out? There's got to be a lifeboat around somewhere."

Sabrina laughed and poked at his chest with her index finger, drawing a heart on the shirt visible below the blazer. "You're not too bad yourself, my sexy husband. Navy blue and beige are totally your colors." The event was semiformal, so he was tieless. "But I think our absence will be noticed."

Nearly everyone in their circle was on the three-level cruise ship, the guest list running to three hundred-plus. The main level held dinner tables, the buffet section, the bar, and the dance floor. Christmas greenery and lights were everywhere, including the giant tree near the DJ. The wide wraparound gallery where Alex and Sabrina stood formed the second level. A small number of tables were scattered here, too, and there was a second bar, but mostly, guests wandered up for the view through the windows.

A few feet down from Alex and Sabrina was Harry, standing under a holiday wreath with his phone held to his ear. Lilah and Regina Berra—the correction officer from Sing Sing—were with him. Dante was also present, looking more worried than he usually did.

The DJ switched records. In the very slight hush which followed, Alex heard Harry say on the phone, "Tell him the truth, Jorah. The longer we let it go on—"

Stopping abruptly, Harry grinned and nodded his greeting at a couple as they joined the crowd making their way to the third level—the heated deck. Alex recognized the man, a Barrons executive. More of his colleagues followed him, holding wine glasses though there was a third bar on the deck.

Barrons O & G had rented the boat a couple of years in advance for its senior leadership to make merry on New Year's Eve, 1999, and Dan expanded the gathering to include the players on their side of the corporate war. The Kingsley brothers were in no mood to party and showed up only for the sake of team morale. The announcement of the independent investigation was a relief to everyone, and this was a needed celebration.

Poor Brad was the most torn, alternating between guilt and hope. He wanted to assure everyone who supported him that the end was finally within sight. Victory... but at what cost?

"Bailamos," Enrique Iglesias invited over the music system, and a cheer went up from the guests.

Harry resumed his conversation on the phone, Dante and the two women with him plainly anxious to hear the outcome.

"When do you think we can get out?" Alex asked his wife, stealing one more kiss. The grief over the old man in his Upper East Side mansion was Alex's alone to bear. He didn't need to add to his wife's misconceptions about her place in his heart *vis-à-vis* his brothers and his grandfather.

"You know we would have to take the kids with us if we went home," Sabrina teased. They got to the marina in a single car. "Imagine the explanations we'd have to come up with."

She glanced toward the lower level where the DJ was. The three teenagers were not difficult to spot thanks to Tara's yellow dress and metallic gold jacket. Hema and her new boyfriend—a doctoral candidate—were also with the teens. "Who's the girl talking to Gabe?" Sabrina asked suddenly.

"The waitress?" Alex peered. The lady in question was holding a wine bottle in one hand, playing with her hair with the other hand. "No clue. Why?"

"Gabe's seventeen," Sabrina said, frowning. "Don't you have to be twenty-one to work on cruise ships? She's flirting with a child!"

"Heh?" Unexpectedly diverted, Alex laughed. "I'm sure Gabe can handle it. Sabrina, he's a young man now, not a boy. You did a good job raising him and Mike. Time to cut the strings. Let Gabe flirt back if he wants. Mike, too."

"They're still my sons," Sabrina said fiercely, then hmphed. "I hate it when you're the reasonable one. At least Mike's not..." She trailed off as Michael and Tara started moving to the music. They seemed to be putting on a show for the rest, waitress included. "What's he doing?" Sabrina asked, tone turning puzzled.

Watching Mike, Alex guffawed. "Boxing footwork." While occasionally twirling Tara as she danced the salsa around him.

Sabrina sputtered. "Poor Mikey. All those DVD tutorials, and this is what he got to show for it."

"Actually," Alex said, still grinning at the scene, "he's not bad. Tara's a trained dancer, and he's... Sabrina, is she teaching him, too? It looks too nicely done to be impromptu."

"Yeah, it does," Sabrina mused, brows drawing back together as she studied the duo on the dance floor.

"Let them have fun," Alex suggested. "*We* should talk about something more important—you and me."

"You and me," Sabrina agreed, shaking her head slightly as though dismissing the small worries she harbored about her boys. Turning back to Alex, she said, "Yeah, we should talk. Even Mike learned to dance... kind of... but *you're* still terrible."

"Me? What do you mean?"

"At understanding what I want." Sighing, she put both hands on his chest. "Alex, you don't have to pretend not to be worried about your family. What I'd like is honesty about where I stand in your life."

It wasn't as if Alex wanted to avoid the topic of their marriage, but they'd gone back and forth over it several times already. Clearly, it wasn't enough to tell her she was the most important part of his existence. More important than his brothers, more important than all the Kingsleys combined.

"How do I convince you?" Alex brooded, his hands at her waist.

He led her into a slower version of the salsa on the dance floor. A twirl, then a second one, and she was back in his embrace.

"I remember the first time I saw you," Alex went on, swaying in place with his wife wrapped in his arms. "Two seconds later, Harry told me to stop staring at his sister. Yeah, I got the feeling he wouldn't object if I asked you out. Yeah, he was—and is—important to me and my brothers. Still, there could've been problems if things didn't work out between us. Didn't matter. I couldn't help myself. The more time you and I spent together, the more I wanted. When you told me you were pregnant, I wanted forever. I wasn't thinking of your brother or my brothers when I asked you to marry me."

"I would've believed you," Sabrina said. "Except your brothers always came first. You and I should've taken decisions as a team, but it was always you and your family."

The song continued, and they kept swaying in the same spot. Alex opened his mouth to respond, then snapped it shut.

Seeing it, she said, "I get it. You do consider us a team, but you love your brothers and your grandfather and your uncles. It's okay to love them. It's okay for you and your brothers to make decisions together, but the *you* in that crew had to be you and me as a single unit. Instead, your choices invariably revolved around what was good for Brad and your trust in your family. Which was why I couldn't tell you what I was doing with Lilah's computer. I didn't dare because you would've tried to put a stop to it just to please Brad. You simply didn't think there could be anything wrong with a deal endorsed by your grandfather. If you'd considered the possibility for a moment like I was asking... but my word meant less. *I* meant less."

"Not true," Alex insisted. "I screwed up, but can I explain what I was thinking?" At her nod, he continued, "I didn't talk to you about the Iran deal only because Lilah would get to know, and I thought she was wrong. And..." His shoulders slumped. "...I thought you would prioritize her over my brothers. You probably *would* have, but we should've discussed it and come up with a plan to account for the possibility *I* was wrong. But I really believed it would all turn out well in the end."

"You believed it because you trusted Godwin." Sabrina took a deep breath, pushing away gently until his arms dropped to his sides. "You still do."

"Yes, but it doesn't mean I trust you less," Alex objected. Before she could retort, he added, "Trust includes acknowledging you have your own thoughts and ideas and concerns. And as a team, we should've talked things over."

It took her a couple of seconds, but Sabrina smiled. "See? It wasn't so difficult, was it? Now, if I could be sure you'll remember it the next time there's a conflict... which doesn't mean you can't tell me when you're worried about your family."

Alex puffed out a breath. "Grandfather's stable, so... dammit, there's finally light at the end of the tunnel. And it's the new millennium. I *want* to stop thinking about what else could go wrong and focus on us."

"What could go—" Sabrina started.

"Technically," a familiar voice intruded, startling Alex. "The third millennium will only start next New Year's Day," Scott pointed out. "You can wait until 2001 to... umm... focus on you."

With him were a group of women, including Nikki, the stripper-turned-occasional spy who worked for Harry. "You're so smart," she cooed at the astrophysicist. Her friends agreed loudly.

Without another word to his brother or sister-in-law, Scott and his female admirers walked on toward the deck stairs.

"Oh, dear Lord," Sabrina said faintly. *"Five* women?"

Alex chortled. "Hey, he's a Kingsley."

"Don't brag," Sabrina said in mock reproof.

"If you've got it..." Alex waggled his eyebrows.

"At least he and the kids made you laugh for real a couple of times," said Sabrina. "Now, tell me what you mean by something going wrong."

"More like what already went wrong. I talked to Uncle Aaron today."

"And?"

"He says he doesn't understand, either. What the hell did I do that made Grandfather think I was attacking him?"

"You didn't attack anyone," said Sabrina. "Shawn might have been a little mean in the beginning, but he apologized. Alex, Godwin's ninety-five. When the aneurysm ruptured, he surely felt something. A headache... dizziness... something. When he fell, he probably thought it was the end. His last memory would've been of losing the most important case of his life. At least it would've been to you, his beloved grandson, and not to a Barrons. There's always been rivalry between the families, right? I'm sure that's why he said it."

Smiling, Alex tucked a golden curl behind her ear. *"I'm* sure you love me. How else could you come up with an explanation with more twists than a pretzel just to make me feel better?"

"I do love you," she said. "And I hate Godwin for making you feel this way." Grimacing, she admitted, "All right. That was unnecessary given the circumstances. Karma's taking care of his punishment, I suppose."

Godwin woke from surgery, fully aware of surroundings but somehow numb throughout his body. Within hours, the numbness turned to pain. Terrible piercing sensation all over as though he were lying on a bed of arrows. Thalamic pain, the doctors called it.

The patriarch was stable enough to be moved to his own home and had a neurologist working with him, but everything Alex heard suggested the pain would be permanent. The strong, solid paternal figure he remembered would spend his last days in agony. Godwin was in no shape to talk for Steven.

"The law firm called Brad last night," Alex said. Not the corporate attorneys. The centuries-old group retained by the Kingsleys for generations for their personal needs. "Grandfather still doesn't want to see any of us." Including Steven and Charles, but they could at least go to the house to visit their parents. The domestic staff could give the duo whatever information Godwin chose to share.

Alex and his brothers no longer had free run of the Kingsley mansion. The law firm suggested approaching the courts. Something about the way Old Man Kingsley bequeathed his properties between the offspring of his two wives. Godwin was supposed to hold the ancestral home until his passing, then it would go to his half-brother's progeny. They'd all imagined Peter Kingsley's sons were entitled to none of it since they split from the parent company. However, Godwin's stroke caused the lawyers to review the old will. Apparently, there was a clause which put the CEO of the company in physical possession of the family residence after Godwin's time. All of Sylvia's descendants would be entitled to money from a potential sale, but the CEO would be in charge of the mansion during his lifetime.

Well, the last actual CEO of Kingsley Corp had been Peter Kingsley. David was only acting CEO even after all these years. Which set up all sorts of possibilities, but none of the five brothers was interested in yet another legal battle. Godwin was still alive, dammit.

"You know I'm not his biggest fan," Sabrina said, "but the man has the right to decide who he wants by his side at the end of his life." At the moment, only Aaron and David were allowed. "Give your grandfather the space he's asking for, Alex." Suddenly, Sabrina cupped his face with her hands, green eyes boring into his. "You know what I realized? You'll love Godwin no matter how horrible he is not to take back what he said before he dies. The man I married gives a hundred percent to everyone he loves no matter what they do to him. If I make you change, you won't be the same man."

"You could protect me from myself," he suggested, his hands on her hips. "You always had my back whether I wanted it or not. Thanks to what you did for Lilah in Cuba, she was able to argue the rest of us out of trouble. I swear, Sabrina... from here on out, I'm going to have *your* back no matter who else is involved."

"Always," Sabrina insisted, then sighed. "At least try."

"Always," he echoed, bending to kiss her again.

"Ladies and gentlemen," called the DJ. "Fifteen minutes, people, and it will be time for the *biiig* countdown. So let's bid farewell to the twentieth century with *"Auld Lang Syne."*

\#

Half an hour earlier

There it was, the signature about a third of the page down in the visitor's log—Lilah Kingsley. So her brothers had not been wrong. She did show up. Harry didn't imagine the little glimpses of her since the ship left the marina. The glint of the blue-black hair which vanished the moment he got close... the strange feeling in his chest when he heard a familiar husky voice... no one had disembarked, so Lilah was still on board.

"Thank you," Harry said to the host.

"Any time, sir," said the bald man, his back erect and manner fit for the military. "I hope you're able to locate the guest."

Yeah, and locate her before midnight. Phone connection was at best patchy, or he would've called her cell. Why *was* she leading him on this chase?

Returning to the banquet hall, Harry turned a three-sixty and scanned the crowd. The music, the snatches of conversations, the laughter, the clinking of cutlery... the air smelled of pine trees and spiced wine.

Dan and Amy were on the dance floor, as were Shawn and his latest boyfriend. Caroline was chatting with Neil and his date. Brad and Lilah usually gave each other a wide berth, but Harry checked the location of the eldest Kingsley brother just in case. There he was at one of the tables, talking to Temple and Noah. Victor was still nursing his whiskey at the next table, looking morose. Brad was forced to maintain appearances, same as his estranged wife, but Victor, despite the divorce, also chose to go stag. Alex and Sabrina were enjoying the view from the gallery. No Lilah with any of them.

Michael was of course with his cousin and Tara, all of them hovering over a platter of *hors d'oeuvres* while the server waited patiently. Something about the way Michael was leaning toward Tara... something about the way she was looking back...

Gabriel finally shook his head and took the entire tray from the server, settling it on the high-top table next to them. Laughing, Hema and her PhD candidate joined the kids. Michael looked up, straightening as he caught his uncle's eye.

Yup. All was right in young Michael's world. Raising an imaginary glass in salute, Harry turned away. He would have to tell Lilah the teenage romance appeared to be going like gangbusters. If he ever found her.

Harry knew they weren't getting any alone time. It would've been enough to simply stand side by side while the city counted down. But where was she?

Her friends, Dante...

Harry was about to check the deck when a familiar voice called, "Hey, Sheppard."

He turned to find Regina Berra standing behind, Dante and Lilah with her.

It was as though someone took a fist to Harry's chest. Vaguely, he noted the shimmery dress was not red for once. The deep-black collar left her shoulders bare, the color fading first to gray, then to silver at the knees. She wasn't wearing any jewelry except the tiny stones on her earlobes, and a large fabric flower was tucked into the loose bun. The heels put her nearly eye to eye with him. Lilah looked... he was sure she looked stunning. Probably.

All his life... he could never tell... everyone kept saying Lilah was beautiful. Objectively, Harry got it, but he could never remember it even when he was a horny young S.O.B. making love to her in his dreams. She was his Lilah, the other half of him. Nothing else mattered.

"Why the hell were you running?" snapped Officer Berra. "We've been chasing you for the last half an hour. Each time we got within ten feet, you'd be off again."

"Huh?" Coughing to clear his throat, Harry asked, *"I* was running? Never mind... what's up?"

"My dad called," said the officer. "We have a problem."

A few minutes later, Harry exclaimed, *"What the actual—"*

"Shh!" said Dante, eyes darting around although they'd picked a relatively empty spot next to a fire extinguisher to chat. "The tabloid guy is here. I don't understand why Dan invited him."

"He doesn't have his camera," Harry said almost automatically.

Confiscating recording paraphernalia was not merely about preventing bad press. Everyone on their side conveniently gathered on one ship? Yeah, security was tight. The vessel itself and the crew and all guests were thoroughly scanned before they set sail. Still, Eugene Bishop's eyes and ears remained attached to the rest of him. If he heard what Regina Berra had to say...

"Tell me the rest," Harry said to Regina in a quieter voice. "From A to Z. We'll find a way to extricate him from it. He's only twelve. The age has to count for—"

"He's out already," said Regina. She snorted. "Your brother made sure of it."

"My brother?" Harry parroted. "Hector?"

Yeah, Hector, said Regina. Thanks to him, young Samuel would suffer no life-changing consequences for the stupid stunt he pulled.

Apparently, Samba had been following the Kingsley-Barrons-Sheppard saga, at least the part known to the public through the media. It was his only source of information about the man he believed was his father.

Samba decided the one way to get Harry's attention would be to do something to help in the ongoing war. He and a couple of older—but no less idiotic—friends sneaked out of their small town in upstate New York, leaving a note claiming they would return after a night of merrymaking in the city. The families were of course upset at their disappearance, but they hoped the boys would reject the sinful world of Manhattan once they saw it for themselves. Jorah decided not to inform Harry as she'd already sensed his frustration at her unwillingness to tell her son the truth. None of them imagined the extent to which the boys would go.

The young threesome skulked around the Kingsley mansion, going unspotted in the holiday crowds thronging the streets despite their Amish garb. Why would they think of changing clothes when there was no actual plan? Only a vague idea of waiting for a chance to strike. Which came soon enough.

The Kingsley nanny took her charge—Steven's four-year-old daughter—on an evening walk to Central Park to see Christmas lights. The moment the nanny looked away, Samba snatched the baby and ran farther into the trees with his friends. What they were planning to do then was anybody's guess. Perhaps they would've called Gateway to announce the feat to Harry.

The three wannabe kidnappers didn't realize the nanny and the child weren't alone. Two guards chased the boys and found the four-year-old laughing her head off on Samba's shoulders as though it was all a big game. Despite her vocal protests about wanting to stay with her new "friends," the child was returned to her nanny. All three lads got a thrashing, only their attire saving them from being delivered straight to the cops.

The signature Amish clothing caused one of the guards to remember the stories about Harry's supposed son. Samba and his idiot pals were dragged to the Kingsley residence where the family was spending a quiet evening out of respect to the ailing patriarch.

Steven attempted to interrogate the boys in the vast basement of the mansion. Either out of fear or from sheer stubbornness, none of them would talk. Fortunately for the three, rumors about Samba's actual parentage had gotten to Steven. The elder Sheppard brother was not someone Steven wanted to piss off by getting his son—however conceived—arrested.

Well, Hector was no fool to show up at the Kingsley home under the circumstances and provide blackmail material to even those he considered friends. He made a call to Warden Berra, the one man in law enforcement who could be relied on to protect Harry's interests. Luckily for everyone concerned, Arthur Berra preferred solid land under his feet and had stayed home to celebrate. The warden tried a few times to contact Harry, but by then, the boat had left the port, and phone connection was not the best out on the water. Nor did the office staff of the cruise company seem to be at their desks for them to radio the ship. So Arthur Berra dug up the cell numbers of a couple of trusted cops in NYPD.

When he and Hector knocked on the door of the Kingsley mansion, they were accompanied by police officers who were there to check on a counter-complaint of kidnapping. After all, there was only the nanny's word to prove any wrongdoing on the part of the Amish boys. The baby was completely unharmed while the lads sported bruises, and Samba could barely walk. Harry's son was brutally beaten by Kingsley guards, claimed Hector, the boy's only crime his attempt to play with the Kingsley princess. A shocked Steven saw no choice except to let his prisoners go if he didn't want charges. Hector also warned the Kingsleys about leaking any of it to the press.

Warden Berra then took the three culprits for a quick medical exam at the Sing Sing emergency room. From the prison, Berra called Jorah to update her on what happened and told her the kids could crash at his house for the night. Arthur Berra also managed to catch his own daughter when she was in some phone service sweet spot on the ship. Regina Berra found Dante first, then Lilah, the three of them chasing Harry around the ship.

"Shit," Harry muttered.

Dante nodded. "We're lucky Steven decided to call Hector and not go straight to the cops."

"Did my brother say anything to Samba?" Harry asked Regina. Something resembling the truth behind the boy's birth.

"Nope," said the officer. "He left as soon as the kids were out."

"I need to call Jorah," Harry said. "This can't go on. Samba's escalating. A four-year-old... my God! And he's only twelve himself."

"At least she wasn't hurt," Lilah said, her hazel eyes disturbed. "Or afraid. She won't remember what happened in a bad way. Thank God."

Or it would've meant a lifetime of nightmares for the baby. Who knew what Samba would do next, who else he would be willing to harm?

"Upstairs," said Regina. "The gallery or whatever. It's the only place you get decent reception. My father said Jorah's waiting in the church overnight. In case there's more news." The church was the one building in the technology-averse community which had a phone line.

Dante and Regina pivoted toward the stairs immediately. Lilah turned away as though to return to the dining area.

"Don't go," Harry requested, holding out a hand. His fingers brushed against her elbow. His heart skipped a beat. Tucking his hand into the pocket of his pants, Harry repeated, "Don't go. I was looking for you for the last couple of hours, and it's almost midnight. We'll get to the deck right after talking to Jorah."

Lilah glanced toward one of the tables. Two blondes immediately raised their hands to wave, one of them sporting short, spiky hair. Her old friends from school.

"I was going to mingle until it was close to twelve," Lilah said, turning back to Harry. "Then, Ginger was supposed to bring you to the bridge. I should let her know there's been a change of plans."

"The bridge?" Pushing the troubles with Samba to the back of his mind, Harry grinned. "Trying to get me alone, huh?"

The heightened color on Lilah's cheeks belied the cool tilt of her chin. "You and my friends and the captain and whoever else would've been on the bridge."

"Yeah, yeah," said Harry. "Admit it, Princess. You were trying to get me alone."

"No, I wasn't, and don't call me that."

"Yes, you were, and you're *still* easy to bait."

"Sheppard!" Regina Berra called from the foot of the stairs, gesturing impatiently. Dante was already climbing up.

On his way to the gallery with Lilah, Harry grumbled, "I wish we could've had a single evening without having to put out some fire."

The expectation was the war would resume after the senate committee completed its planned inspection come summer. Godwin was in no physical shape to lead Steven's army, but the old judge's brain was still in good working condition as per reports. Neither Harry nor Noah trusted the Kingsley patriarch not to pull new tricks from behind the scenes.

Then, there was the rest of the Kingsley crew, including Major Armor. Harry had also been on the lookout for own-goals from Alex and his brothers.

No one expected trouble from this new direction.

"You're here," said Lilah, her heels going clickety-clack on the floor. "I'm here. We can deal with everything else."

Harry smiled. "A Jug of Wine, A Loaf of Bread—and Thou Beside me singing in the Wilderness—O, Wilderness were Paradise enow!"

"Khayyam," murmured Lilah. *"Rubaiyat.* From snakes to cheesy lines to quoting romantic poetry. What's next?"

"Glass lizard," Harry corrected, grinning again at the old argument from their childhood. "Not snake. And next is your turn, *habibti.* You come up with something."

They reached the phone service sweet spot promised by Regina. The call did go through, and Jorah was in the church to answer. Tearfully, she apologized for bringing more trouble into Harry's life, but she couldn't—simply couldn't—tell her son the truth about his birth.

The music stopped for a few seconds, and Harry waited until it resumed to give him cover for the conversation. A few feet up were Alex and Sabrina, swaying in place while they talked. From where Harry stood, he could see the dance floor on the main level, where Gabriel was enjoying the attentions of a female server. Michael and Tara were attempting a strange combination of boxing and salsa. Scott Kingsley walked past with a group of women.

Finally hanging up, Harry shook his head at the other three although they would've already guessed what Jorah said.

"She's making a big mistake," Dante said.

"Would it help if a woman talked to her?" Lilah asked. She could understand Jorah in a way no one else around her could.

"Dunno if it will work," Harry said, "but no harm in trying. Give it a day or two, and we can—"

"Should old acquaintance be..." a chorus crooned over the audio system, the crowd singing along. Except for the elderly former president and his entourage, everyone was getting to their feet and making their way to the heated deck with champagne flutes in hand.

Harry glanced at his watch. "Fifteen minutes," he said. "Just enough time to head up and get our drinks."

The Statue of Liberty glowed an iridescent green as she held the torch aloft before dozens of ships. On *The Shooting Star*, the deck was brightly lit. Most guests were at the railing already, facing the symbol of freedom. They were all chatting, laughing, singing, asking when the fireworks would begin. Long, black heaters set at regular intervals blasted warmth, but the temperature was anyway in the thirties, the breeze mild. The large-screen television behind the bar showed the scene from Times Square where the ball drop would happen.

Flute glass in hand, Dante turned from the bar. "Lilah, where are your brothers?"

"C'mon," shouted Liam, swigging champagne as he urged Dante by the shoulder. Verity and her date were with Liam. "Dan and Shawn are over there."

Alex and Sabrina were also with the Barronses. So were the other Kingsley men. Lilah's two school friends were sauntering up, as well. The kids—Michael and Gabriel and Tara—headed to a different spot, along with Hema and her new boyfriend. The teens were also holding flute glasses, presumably something non-alcoholic.

Lilah waited until she snagged one of the soft woolen wraps piled on a table. Walking with her a few steps behind Dante and Liam, Harry said, "My blazer would be warmer."

She gave him a *really?* look. The intimate gesture would've caused comment, so the black wrap would have to suffice. Tucking an errant lock behind the ear, Lilah's knuckles brushed against the large fabric flower pinned to her hair—a blue lotus.

"No red tonight?" Harry queried. Turning one-eighty to face her, he walked backward and patted his pocket square with his free hand. "I got this to coordinate." A holiday creation, with prancing reindeer and tumbling Santas and pinecones. In the cab on the way to the marina, Dante had declared the hanky looked ridiculous with the charcoal-colored jacket and black silk shirt.

"Who says I'm not wearing red?" Lilah asked.

It took a second to sink in. Harry missed a step and nearly stumbled to his knees. "Damn, habibti," he mumbled, returning to her side. "You planned it. You *knew* I would ask at some point, and you planned it."

Lilah snickered. "Didn't you say it was my turn?" Fingers brushing the shimmery black band around her neck, she added,

"Tara made the dress. Love at first sight for me, and she thought it would get her noticed. You and I do match, by the way. I've got gray and black."

"So you're not actually..."

Glee in her eyes, she asked, "Wearing red? I told you the truth, the whole truth, and nothing but the truth. Feel free to imagine the details."

Part-groaning, part-laughing, Harry inquired, "Are you trying to kill me? And I, too, meant what I said before. All the cheese... the poem..."

"I know," Lilah said softly. "I don't want you to stop."

"Maybe it won't be long now..." He paused, almost afraid to dream of what the future might bring. "Damn it... I *am* going to believe we're close to the end... at least for tonight."

"Me, too," she agreed.

Then, they were at the railing, sandwiched between Caroline on one side and Alex and Sabrina on the other. Couples were already kissing, wanting to bring in the new year in the midst of an embrace. Champagne flute held between his fingers, Harry leaned forward with his elbows on the railing. So did Lilah.

The backs of their hands were nearly touching, but not quite. The whisper of her breath was in his ears. The salty air carried her lotus oil fragrance to his nostrils. If he focused hard, perhaps he could feel their hearts beating in tandem.

"Ten... nine... eight..." the crowd started chanting.

There was a sudden scuffle to the rear. When Harry took a quick glance, Michael and Tara were standing close together a few feet behind the crowd, not paying any mind to anyone else.

"...seven... six..."

Lilah turned as well, her lips curving into a sweet smile as she spotted the young lovers.

"...five... four... three..."

"Forever," Michael swore loud enough for those around to hear. Flute glasses and all, he tugged Tara into his arms.

"...two... one..."

Laughing wildly, they kissed.

"Happy New Year!" roared the crowd. Fireworks exploded behind the Statue of Liberty, every color known to man shimmering in the night sky.

Touching the rim of Lilah's flute with his, Harry whispered, *Forever.*

Forever, her eyes whispered back before both turned away to wish others.

Chapter 55

An hour later

Upper East Side, New York City

The sounds of celebration from David Kingsley's wing could not be heard in this section of the mansion. Not as if there was a wild party in any case. Even before the kidnapping scare earlier in the evening, Steven had planned a limited affair with only his family in attendance. Richard and his wife joined the Kingsleys shortly after toasting the birth of the new year with his parents. Steven barely waited until the first round of champagne was poured before pulling his friend aside for a chat. In a few more minutes, Richard found himself making an unscheduled visit to Godwin's residence.

Standing outside the carved wooden door which wasn't quite closed, Richard hesitated. Inside the Kingsley patriarch's bedroom, the family had set up a sophisticated monitoring system, allowing home nurses to keep an eye on the patient every minute of the day. Still, the door could no longer be shut completely as easy accessibility would be required in a potential emergency.

The doctors couldn't tell how long the former supreme court justice would linger. Technically, Godwin could walk, talk, and do everything he did before. The only residual neurological defect from the brain bleed appeared to be pain, but it was debilitating to the point he needed medications even to wear clothes. How long could a human form suffer thusly before it gave up?

Huffing out a breath, Richard knocked. The conversation was unavoidable. What Steven said had boggled Richard's mind, and they needed to figure out how much of it was usable without the risk of backfiring.

A woman in a scrub shirt and white pants came to the door—the night nurse. Her colleague would be napping in the break room to the left.

"Major Armor," Richard introduced himself. "I thought I'd check if the justice was still awake. If not, I could return another time."

When Richard entered the room, it was to Godwin motioning from the massive bed to turn off the monitoring system. Flipping the switch, Richard took a quick glance around at the silk-lined walls, the velvet drapery, and the grand chandelier. A basket of pinecones sat on the writing desk next to the window, the pleasant fragrance permeating the room. The temperature was perfectly balanced—not too cold, not too warm.

"Hello, sir," Richard said finally.

"Close the door, my boy," instructed the figure on the bed, the voice frail. Godwin's head was still bandaged after the surgery. The deep-purple pajamas left the old man's face and neck even more pale. A silk sheet covered Godwin's lower half.

Turning to comply, Richard tried to remember if he'd been called "my boy" by the Kingsley patriarch ever before. There was a gilded chair with floral upholstery by the bedside, but Richard waited until Godwin inclined his head in an invitation to sit.

"Not going to ask how I am?" Godwin inquired, a touch of dark humor in his tone. When Richard remained silent, the patriarch said, "All right. If you won't, let me do my part. How are you, Richard? I hope you bothered to greet your mother before coming to see me. Lord knows Patrice could use a little positivity in her life."

Shock. Richard stayed put in his chair, unable to utter a single word.

Seeing it, Godwin laughed softly. "Of course I know. I've known from the moment you were born. Did you imagine Temple and Andersen wouldn't inform me before going to Armor—your father—about adoption? I didn't realize *you* knew until Harry staged the little drama of talking to you about... what was it? Veterans' programs. I'm surprised Patrice didn't fill you in on details as in who was aware of what and when."

She might have, except Patrice barely got a few minutes to talk directly with Richard. He didn't allow her the opportunity.

"Is it why you hated me?" he asked eventually. The bastard firstborn of the mother of the Kingsley heirs.

Godwin lifted an arm as though to offer a hug, then winced. The medical staff had told the family how the patriarch's entire body was like an open nerve ending. It was as though he was pierced all over by arrows, each small movement causing the darts to twist in the flesh.

"I didn't hate you," said the former supreme court justice, carefully placing his arm back on the mattress. "True... harsh words were used on occasion but because *you* hated Brad, Victor, and Alex without reason. Even Neil and Scott, and you hardly knew them. It doesn't mean I was unaware of your intelligence, your skill with a gun, your work as a soldier. You made your way in law on your own merit. The people who helped you... like General Axeman... did so because they saw your talent and ambition and perseverance. I appreciate your generosity, how you give back to the community. And I do know you've held your tongue a few times out of respect for me. When you didn't, it was to say... well... what you saw as the truth, anyway."

There was a part of Richard which wanted the old man to mean what he said. Former U.S. Supreme Court Justice Godwin Kingsley, president of Kingsley Corp, widely respected elder statesman was talking appreciatively about Richard, the boy who grew up in the apartment over the garage.

"What are your plans, Richard?" Godwin asked. "You know the truth about your lineage now. If you wanted to confide in Steven, you would've done so already. Will you go to your brothers? Perhaps it's time. Maybe all the enmities will end with my death."

"Brothers," Richard said bitterly. "Thanks to *Miss* Patrice, I was raised by a servant while her other children... Steven's been an actual brother to me. Thank you for being appreciative of my successes, but I'm well aware my friendship with Steven might have influenced some of my business partners to make positive decisions. Which is to say I owe him in more than one way. And you know what, sir? I would give up everything for him. I cannot—will not—ditch him right when he needs me the most."

"You're willing to fight your own blood for your friend?" Godwin asked. "Alex and the rest clearly don't know who you are, or I'd have heard about it. So why would they have any qualms about fighting back? Richard, Alex has Harry with him. Believe me... he will make sure the five of them do what it takes to win, and they're closer to victory than ever before. This war is not going to end well for either Steven or you. I said this multiple times before. Negotiate, then figure out what next. If you switch sides, Steven will have to agree to negotiate. He doesn't have it in him to continue on his own with only Potts for support."

"It's not only for Steven," Richard admitted. "All my life, I... wherever I went... it didn't matter how hard I worked. Someone would bring up the Kingsleys. Alex was always supposed to be the better man. Better with a gun, better with women, better everywhere. Only because of the Kingsley name. This is my chance to put an end to the mockery. Steven wants me to take the lead at the hearings. If our side pulls off a win, there won't be a single person who can claim Alex is in any way superior to me."

General Potts would've heard by now how Major Armor would be the team leader. The old man would not like working under his former student, but it wasn't Richard's problem.

Godwin uttered a sound somewhere between a sigh and a groan. "Why are you here if you won't take my advice?"

"I do want your advice. Obviously, I don't have the same stature or experience as you, and your guidance on how to proceed will be invaluable. And..." Richard hesitated for a second. "...I... ahh... need your blessing."

Godwin stared unblinkingly for a few moments. "I believe I mentioned this before," the patriarch eventually said. "It's a pity you weren't born a Kingsley. Well... if you're determined to fight, go ahead. You have my blessing. As for my guidance... for you specifically, it would be to leave your ego behind. Focus your strengths on the matter at hand. When you return to Steven, think about how best he can tackle the enemy, not what would be convenient for you."

#

Only when walking out did Richard realize he never brought up the issue of the tribe in Argentina which Jared Sanders was previously accused of slaughtering. The patriarch's earlier conversation with Steven had been muddled to say the least. The gist of it was how Godwin and Temple sent a Kingsley oil scout to Alex and his friend/mentor, Harry Sheppard. What was supposed to be preliminary negotiation prior to purchasing drilling rights turned into a chemical fire which nearly wiped out the tribe.

The best of men and God himself committing genocide! Problem was there *was* proof of involvement of one of Sanders's henchmen, an Argentine general, which didn't make sense if Alex and Sheppard were behind the crime. Also, if Godwin were to be taken at his word, he and Temple initiated the mission. Bringing it up before the senate committee could backfire on Steven in multiple ways. He could be believed, but he could also get laughed out of the hearing room. The senators could call him a heartless opportunist for maligning two men who were currently unable to defend themselves. There was also the concern of not knowing how much of what Godwin said was influenced by the narcotics pumped into him.

More importantly, the senate committee would see the legality of the network's actions as a separate issue. Even if Alex and his best buddy were thrown into prison for mass murder, the inspection in Spain would go ahead as planned.

Richard glanced at his watch. Too late to rouse Steven and drag him out for a discussion.

When Richard reached the guest room assigned to him, his wife was sitting up in bed, scribbling away in her notebook. Arvi did this frequently—staying awake at night to record her observations. He'd started jotting down information, too. The journals were kept in the strongbox at his apartment, to be opened only in the event of his untimely death. If Richard were to meet his maker before reaching advanced age, he'd want the world to know the truth about the men who thought themselves better than him.

"Are you all right?" Arvi asked, her tone carrying a hint of censure. She set the notebook and pen on the side table. "You just disappeared from dinner. Steven had to tell me you would be back shortly."

First time for everything, Richard said to himself. Arvi was younger than he would've preferred in a wife but generally low maintenance. Leaving her on new year's night was apparently the line. "Sorry," Richard said out loud, tugging his tie loose. "I went to visit Godwin for a few."

Arvi's face softened. "You should've told me. I would've gone with you. Poor man... what an end to such a big life."

Richard nodded. "From what I hear, his favorite grandsons are partying it up on a cruise ship. Celebration time for them... and for the Barronses, Sheppard, and Mrs. Kingsley."

Expression turning guarded, Arvi remarked, "You always call her Mrs. Kingsley. That woman, Lilah."

"What do you expect me to call her?" Richard asked before biting back a sigh. It wasn't as if he hadn't picked up on his wife's insecurities. "Internalized classism, I suppose," he said by way of explanation. "My parents... and other Kingsley employees... call the family by their titles. Miss Patrice because she visited before she married Peter, Mr. Brad, Mrs. Brad, and so on. I don't give a shit about titles but still got into the habit of using them."

Richard didn't do so with his contemporaries in the clan. Arvi knew it, but she didn't object to the lie.

They made love. It was a special night, after all, and Richard made sure his wife had a good time. Throughout, a part of his mind remained on the plan to deal with the enemy. Later, watching Arvi sleep, Richard wondered how she would react if she realized it was Alex occupying her husband's thoughts, not Mrs. Brad Kingsley.

#

"Sanders would know what actually happened," Richard said to Steven. "He's the one we should be talking to. I'm sure your grandfather realized why I was visiting, but he managed to sidetrack me by... ahh... bringing up negotiation. He's not planning to tell us anything more."

Turning the frosty glass of orange juice around, Steven grunted. Thanks to the late night, no one else was at the breakfast table, and the sounds of domestic staff moving about the house were distant enough to be ignored. "I don't get why Grandfather said anything to begin with," Steven brooded.

"Maybe it *was* morphine," said Richard, sipping black coffee. "Maybe it was the realization the end is near. The possibility of death does funny things to people. He might have wanted you to have the info and figure out what to do with it. Sanders might talk to us since we didn't have any part in the plot against him. Enemy of my enemy... *et cetera.*"

"Where is Sanders now?" Steven asked. "Any idea?"

It took them two weeks to locate Sanders through non-traditional channels. In one more week, they traveled to Tucson, Arizona to visit the high-security facility—the United States Penitentiary. The trip to the city wouldn't appear on records, either government or private.

#

Temperatures in Tucson hovered in the sixties, but the sun was still damned bright. Blinking rapidly, Richard waited outside the prison administrative complex until his vision returned to normal. Everything was sandy. The buildings, the earth, the rocks. A strange smell of burning lingered in the air.

"Hard to imagine getting to the point you don't want to leave prison even to die," Steven remarked, slipping on his Ray-Bans.

"Depends," said Richard. "Sanders was a powerful guy."

Steven laughed shortly. "The most powerful man in the world, I would say. Until Harry happened to him. I suppose I can see it. If Old Jared got parole, he would walk out to a very different world." No cash, no clout. No one around who cared what he did except his two girls. Both were doctors, married to colleagues, and both visited their father frequently.

"Also, the press," Richard pointed out. Sanders was yesterday's news, but some journo could still take it into his head to hound the cancer-stricken prisoner. His current state would be splashed all over newspapers, pictures included. "Well... if he wants, all he has to do is ask his family to contact you or me. We'll arrange a parole hearing and put him up in comfort afterward." Release on medical grounds wouldn't be difficult to get when he was terminally ill.

"We owe him at this point," agreed Steven.

No, bringing up the Argentina incident wouldn't stop the inspections planned for the summer. Also, unless the government in Buenos Aires decided to cooperate, it would still be Sanders's word against that of Harry Sheppard and Alex Kingsley.

The one positive outcome of Richard and Steven's visit to Tucson was the name they coaxed out of Sanders. What remained of the tribe had been bribed into not talking, but there was one person who possibly would.

Back in Steven's hotel suite, Richard made the first phone call. Major Richard Armor would fly to Buenos Aires within a week.

"Yes, General," Steven said into the phone a few minutes later, "Rich agrees with me how you are best positioned to lead us going forward." Potts was likely to act pissy for a while about being second choice, but it couldn't be helped.

Not looking up from his laptop, Richard continued to read the info on the Puelche spit out by Google. Godwin's advice to set ego aside and think of how to win the war was spot on. Neither Steven nor Richard needed to defeat the Kingsley brothers. They just needed to be defeated, and Potts had the best chance of making it happen. There would be time enough after to tell the world about the victory.

Besides, the general's son—Major Phillip Potts—was an important ally. Potts, Sr. would lead the team while Phillip would make sure the senate committee saw what they were meant to see when they went to the refinery in Muskiz.

Then, there was the unexpected weapon thrown into their laps. The son of a girl who died in the chemical fire in Argentina, who didn't care how he was financially supported by cash transfers from the bank account of a certain Lilah Kingsley. The seventeen-year-old great-grandson of the machi, the chief of the Puelche tribe, who was born mere months before the son of his mother's killer.

Chapter 56

A day later, mid January 2000

Hamburg, Germany

Phillip had enjoyed his time in the city. Some of his colleagues grumbled about being away from their families over holidays. Christmas, New Year—all manmade constructs Phillip Potts didn't believe in. The rich promoted religion and holidays and magical beings to keep the lower classes under control, hoping when there was nothing to hope for, celebrating when there was no reason to.

Phillip's father had tried his best to give his only offspring a comfortable childhood, but the decorated army general lost his savings in caring for his ailing wife. When she passed, the general was in debt to the point Phillip didn't have enough coins to pay the cafeteria lady at school for the small carton of milk. Decades went by, and he could still hear the jeering laughter of his classmates.

Just as the general remembered every word of Andrew Barrons's taunt even now. *"Friendship is possible only between equals,"* the oil magnate once said to his former roommate from West Point who showed the audacity to request a loan.

The same night, Phillip watched from under the bedclothes as his father sobbed silently in the living room. When the phone rang toward dawn, the general answered with no hint of tears left in his voice. Temple—then the senator from New Jersey—advised Potts, Sr. to approach Godwin Kingsley for help. After all, Phillip's mother had been a Kingsley charity case. She grew up in the foundling home started by Godwin's father.

Godwin Kingsley stated how the late Mrs. Potts was a sister to him in principle since the same man funded their upbringing. Potts Sr.'s loans were settled. It took him years, but he managed to pay off the monetary debt to Godwin. The moral debt? It was never going away according to the general.

Phillip didn't agree, but he wasn't making his old man cry ever again. Therefore, Phillip would obey the general's orders.

Besides, there was Steven. He possessed wealth most people couldn't begin to imagine but never acted as though it made him superior. Unlike his cousins. The entitled bastards looked down on Richard for being a servant's child. So Phillip would do what Steven wanted. Watching the Barrons heiress suffer would've brought added satisfaction.

Except Petty Officer First Class Harry Sheppard invariably got in the way. It was insane how Sheppard escaped every trap thus far. The assassination attempt while the Cuba arrest was going down, the bomb on the boat, the hired killer in Sing Sing, the prison riot...

Steven had relied on his friends and never uttered a word in reprimand when they failed him. Oh, yeah. Phillip was beginning to understand what his father meant by moral debt. Still, Major Potts was not going to take undue risk with himself or his father. They would always have each other's back.

Smiling to himself, Phillip shut the copy of *Das Kapital.* The breakfast café in the hotel had just opened for the day, and guests were already trickling in. Worker bees buzzed around, delivering croissants and fragrant eggs and freshly squeezed orange juice to diners tired from the night's revelry.

Phillip was now one of those privileged enough to be waited on. At least he had no problems admitting his own hypocrisy unlike Richard who couldn't even see it. Here was Major Phillip Potts, reading Marx while enjoying the benefits of living under the American capitalist umbrella. Of course, military budget didn't usually allow for luxury accommodations for their intelligence officers. Also, location was critical when traveling on clandestine business. Nothing fancy enough to draw attention and no mom-and-pop stores where the owners might remember you. This hotel in Neuer Markt fit his requirements and was within walking distance of many of the city's tourist attractions. Which would give cover to the meeting with his source in German intelligence.

The gent was currently at the door to the café. Without even having to look around, the bearded fellow plodded his way toward Phillip.

Chair legs scraping the wooden floor, the newcomer took the seat across the table. *"Kaffee,"* he said to the waitress who showed up within seconds.

As soon as the woman left with the order, Phillip said, "You're late."

"By two minutes," retorted the bearded German. "And you're going to wait another couple of minutes before we talk. I need my coffee."

"I'm paying you," Phillip reminded the fellow.

"Yeah, *you*," the source said. "Not the American military this time, but I have news for both your masters—Steven Kingsley *and* the U.S. government. So be patient."

"Hier ist dein Kaffee, mein Freund," said the waitress, reappearing with the coffee. *"Viel Spaß!"*

The German went through an elaborate ritual of adding cream and sugar. Taking a healthy sip, he sat back. "My girl in Eden will take the deal," he said. "She could use the money. However, we may not get much info through her. The navy fellow—Petty Officer Sheppard—tells the ladies only what they need to know at the time."

Phillip nodded. "Got it."

"But she does have connections to the nightclub scene in Spain," the German added. "Any intel she passes along to her Berlin colleagues will be seen as credible."

The intel would come from a club in Pamplona, a mere two hours by car from Muskiz where the oil refinery was located. Total Eclipse—the preferred hotspot of the spoiled young progeny of European nobility when they attempted to run with bulls.

The establishment was supposedly owned by a local, and the retired American financier called Drummond maintained only a small stake. In reality, Drummond was neither retired nor a minority partner. Oh, he'd scaled back his activities from his heyday. This particular club, however, remained a hundred percent in his ownership, and he continued to use it to launder dark money for the Irish mafia.

Many of those in charge did know what Drummond was up to, but they looked the other way because he worked as a government rat when his bosses allowed. Drummond, Sr. was also the reason his son—JD—had agreed to lie low without creating more headaches for Steven. Daddy Drummond advised JD to wait for the right opportunity to strike back at the enemy. Well... it was here for all of them. For JD, for the Pottses, for Steven, for Richard.

"Minimize casualties," warned the German. "I'm doing this only because you and Drummond have been useful to me before, and I expect our association to continue. Conscience aside, a large-scale event will bring unnecessary attention."

"Neither of us can afford attention," Phillip agreed. "What else?" The German didn't ask to meet at the café on the morning Phillip was supposed to fly back to New York only to deliver news which could've been conveyed over a secure phone line.

"How was your meeting with BND?" the bearded man asked in the way of response.

BND—Federal Intelligence Service of Germany. Narrowing his eyes, Phillip studied his source for a few seconds. "It was about the Nairobi explosion, but you obviously have something to add."

"bin Laden," said the German. "He's getting new recruits day by day. I assume BND told you about this fellow we have under surveillance." Authorities in Berlin were keeping an eye on a Yemeni student suspected of having ties to al-Qaeda.

Phillip stayed silent, not wanting to commit to anything even if the bearded man was part of the same intelligence agency.

"His roommate worries me more," said the German, tone frustrated. "Egyptian by the name of Mohammed Atta. He came here to study urban planning, then disappeared from the university in 1997. He returned last year. Apparently, turned very religious in the time. Get this... Atta reported his passport stolen."

Computing rapidly, Phillip sat back and crossed a casual leg. "You think he didn't want anyone seeing it."

The German inclined his head.

"Because the authorities would not be happy if they knew where he went on vacation," Phillip mused.

"Before you ask," the German continued, "I already tried talking to my colleagues... and my superiors. They're fixated on the wrong chap. I'm sure he's also involved, but Atta's behavior is more alarming. Frankly, my friends' lack of concern is concerning me, which makes me uncomfortable about communicating such information over the phone. It's come to the point I'm not sure my secure lines are in fact secure."

Phillip raised an eyebrow.

Seeing it, the German sighed. "Yes, I'm worried someone from my own government is spying on me. It's been known to happen. Perhaps there's a plant sympathetic to bin Laden and his cause. Talk to your chief about what I said, Major. bin Laden is escalating, and we cannot afford to ignore any potential troublemaker."

Especially not after the terrorist leader declared his *fatwa*—ruling. He considered it the sacred duty of the faithful to kill Americans, both civilian and military.

"Anything else?" Phillip asked.

"I'll send word if I hear more," the German said.

After a couple of seconds' thought, Phillip filed away the problem of the Egyptian called Atta. Oh, the appropriate agencies would be informed, but Egypt—unlike Yemen where the other suspect hailed from—was not considered a problem country. Also, passport thefts did happen and were not necessarily a sign of ill intent. The German sitting across the table looked sane enough, but paranoia was a job requirement for his chosen profession, and it could well have gotten worse over the years. Federal agents would still keep an eye out for Mr. Atta, but there were more critical matters to be dealt with.

Just like there were other issues demanding Phillip's attention. The details of the Muskiz operation were only beginning to be sketched out, and he was waiting to see the outcome of Richard's trip to Argentina. The Puelche boy's hatred for the two men who killed his mother certainly seemed promising. El Peuchen or the flying snake—the name young Nataniel's tribe bestowed on him said a lot.

"I'll talk to my father," Phillip said out loud. "He'll mention your Egyptian suspect to the defense secretary. About your Berlin girl... we anticipate it will take a few weeks for the senate committee to set up interviews in Spain. There will obviously be an on-site inspection. We expect it to happen in June... July at the latest. The inspection is supposed to be pre-arranged in order to minimize work interruptions, but we can't rule out the possibility of surprise checks. This girl should remain ready to go at a moment's notice until everything's finished. Meaning, no time off for any reason whatsoever until the committee announces its decision."

"She'll stay on the job until it's done," promised the German. "Once again... keep your plan as low-profile as possible. And no targeting civilians. If my part in it ever comes out, I want to be able to argue it was justifiable. Within acceptable limits of collateral damage."

"Intentional targeting of civilians would make us terrorists," concurred Phillip. "Neither Steven nor the men working for him— including me—has any intention of going to prison for terrorism. Trust me... we do not want any loss of life, collateral or otherwise."

"Trust you?" echoed the German. "Since when was trust a part of our game? I got you what you wanted. Now, you do something about what I said, and let's hope neither of us regrets this conversation come the summer."

Part XIX

Chapter 57

Five months later, early May 2000

Long Island, New York

"Whoaaa…" screamed Tara, sliding down the firehouse pole.

"Will you keep it down?" Gabriel demanded frantically the moment the tips of her sneakers touched the floor.

"Fire department allows visitors," Michael argued, his face as flushed and shiny with sweat as Tara's. They'd spent the last fifteen minutes taking turns down the pole. A couple of bright-red trucks stood idle not far from where they were. Dressed in dark-blue tees and shorts, other firefighters walked around, chatting, checking equipment, one swigging Coke from a giant bottle.

"Yeah, but you two are loud," said Gabriel. "I don't want to get fired for creating disturbance."

Getting kicked out of a volunteer position would *not* look good on his résumé. Gabe's current plan was to finish school, then work for Barrons O & G as part of the safety crew in the San Diego refinery. The Kingsley name would invite funny looks, but Gabriel was resigned to it.

"Did you ask about—" Michael started.

A deep alarm blared. Tara jumped a few inches into the air.

"Gotta go," Gabriel said, loping toward the uniform rack with other firefighters.

It couldn't have taken them more than a minute to don the bulky pants and coats and boots and helmets and... was that an oxygen tank on Gabriel's back? Tara peered, blinking to clear her vision.

Gabe made the sign of the cross and kissed the crucifix hanging around his neck, then patted the Buffalo Woman bracelet gifted by his foster mother. In a few more moments, the trucks vroomed out, lights flashing.

"Wow," said Michael, voice echoing a little in the empty bay.

Tara meant to ask about the nature of the emergency, but her mind went fuzzy all of a sudden. Shaking her head, she called, "Mike, I need to sit."

Two minutes later, she was in the firehouse kitchen, guzzling ice-cold water from a bottle. "Feeling better?" asked the firefighter who escorted her and Michael inside.

"Yeah," said Tara. "A lot. Thanks."

"It's important to stay hydrated," he admonished. "Rest here for a few before you go home."

As soon as the fireman returned to the front of the station, Michael crouched before Tara's chair. "Did you make the appointment with the doctor? You keep talking about it."

"It really was the heat, Mike." She wasn't wearing anything heavy, but the temperature was in the nineties.

She did need to call the GYN, though. At least she'd turned eighteen, and there was no way the doctor could contact Lilah or Sabrina without Tara's permission. It would be so bloody cringey if the ladies learned how Tara wanted birth control pills. The adults in her life had decided that moving her someplace else to live wouldn't be practical with only months left in the school year. Didn't mean they were clueless about what she and Michael got up to after lights-out. Still, hitting Sabrina with proof of her son and his girlfriend doing it under her roof? Awwwkward!

Although Tara was fast getting to the point she didn't care who found out. Her stupid hormones were driving her crazy. Sometimes, her period reappeared in three weeks. The late cycles made her anxiety shoot through the roof. Last month, there was barely any bleeding before it stopped. It didn't matter how many times Michael quoted statistics on the efficacy of condoms. The two-percent failure rate was under *ideal* conditions, and her conditions were not ideal. Tara wanted the added guarantee of contraceptive pills.

"You wanna go home or wait for Gabe?" Michael asked.

Tara screwed the cap back onto the bottle. "Don't you have to see if Gabe can get time off for Spain?"

After a lot of whining from Michael and Gabriel—and cajoling from Alex—Sabrina had agreed to let the boys go on the bull run in July. One last celebration before Michael started at West Point and Gabriel moved to California for his job. Some of Gabe's old friends from San Diego would be going along.

The inspection of the Muskiz refinery was supposed to happen around the same time, so the boys would travel with Dan in the Barrons jet. Maestro Alex, his brothers, and Harry would also be in Spain for a few weeks. Neither of the two warring sides would be allowed into the refinery while the inspection was going on. Still, being present within easy reach was important according to everyone involved, which worked out well for Michael and Gabriel's plans.

Only, Gabe didn't know if he would get enough days off from his volunteer position. He was going to ask the chief today, but of course, the alarm intervened.

"Dude's out saving lives." Heaving to his feet, Michael grinned. "Asking about vacation can wait. He'll let us know when he comes home."

"Aren't you scared?" Tara asked curiously. "I mean... we're talking about fire."

"And accidents and gas leaks and building collapse," concurred Michael, wandering around the kitchenette. "Lots of things. But it's got to be done, and why not Gabe?"

"Kinda like what you said about the army," Tara brooded. "Well, I hope America appreciates you." Giggling a little, she added, "I totally do."

He leered. "Yeah?"

"As in I'm proud of you," Tara said, batting her lashes as though the double entendre never crossed her mind. Then, she sighed. "I am, you know."

"Thanks," he said, looking adorably embarrassed.

#

When Tara and Michael got back home, Maestro Alex and his brothers were filing out the front door. Their lawyer was at The Hermitage for yet another meeting.

At least they weren't doing death watch for their grandfather any longer. To everyone's surprise, the old fellow was hanging on. The five brothers had finally been allowed to visit, and Brad—the poor chap—was so obviously thankful. Relief at seeing light at the end of the tunnel to guilt over the cost to his family... relief, guilt... relief, guilt... Tara couldn't imagine the mental whiplash.

She made straight for the kitchen. God, it was so bloody hot that her skin felt like it was on fire! A pitcher of lemonade was on the kitchen table, droplets of water beading the surface. Tara poured two glasses and handed one to Michael before plonking herself into a chair. Sabrina's voice could be heard from somewhere in the front of the house, talking about the dot-com bubble. Lilah's husky tone responded, saying something about shady accounting practices in some of the businesses which went kaput. Neither woman was going to Spain.

Tara never bothered asking Michael if she were invited on his trip. It was a boys-only deal, and they'd already found a youth hostel to crash in. If there was even a tiny part of her that wanted to go, the news about the shared bathroom smothered the desire. A bunch of drunk boys doing their business everywhere—

Gagging, Tara clapped a hand over her mouth. "Ugh," she mumbled. "I wish you didn't tell me about the hostel."

Michael snickered. "I swear... no shared bathrooms when you and I go on vacation."

Taking a deep breath to bring her disgust reflex under control, she said, "As if the parents are going to let us go off together." Her father would have a stroke, and Michael's family... actually, they would have strokes, too.

"What are they going to say?" Michael asked, waggling his eyebrows. "You're already eighteen. I'll get there in February." Both adults, officially. "Nothing's Gonna Stop Us Now," Michael belted out.

#

More than a month later, it was yet another blisteringly hot day under a misty-blue sky. Every folding chair on the lawn was occupied. Listening to the speeches at the graduation ceremony, adulthood still sounded distant to Tara.

Names started being called out in quick succession, diplomas handed out. A cheer went up as Gabriel's name was announced. He danced his way to the stage, bright-blue gown flapping all around. In the family section, Sabrina whooped, pumping a fist in the air.

Parents were the only ones who got tickets to the event, including Tara's father who'd flown in. Maestro and Sabrina remained polite perhaps for Tara's sake. Harry was in attendance as Victor's plus-one. Mr. Temple and Mr. Andersen were also present but as the school's special guests.

It wasn't until pictures were being taken next to the sign announcing the school's name that Tara felt the first cramp in her lower belly. Not hugely painful but strong enough to be noticed. She couldn't help the little wobble.

Before she could clutch something for balance, a firm hand gripped her elbow. "Steady there," said Victor. Frowning, he glanced down. "Those heels are not made for walking on grass."

"You're such a man," Tara said crossly. "My shoes are perfectly fine, thank you."

Laughing, Victor held both hands up. "Just make sure the rest of you is all right, too. Don't fall."

The rest of her was not all right.

The girls' restroom was crowded and noisy. Inside the stall, Tara stared at the unexpected blood stains on her clothes and asked the universe, *What the hell?*

#

"I'm going shopping," Tara said brightly, sitting cross-legged on top of her messy bed. Stuff did need to be bought for the dorms even though Fashion Institute of Technology was right in downtown.

From the door to her room, Michael frowned a little. "Okay," he said. "I'll call you when I get to Spain." He turned as though to leave, then turned back. "We're not breaking up, are we?"

"What?" Softening her tone, Tara repeated, "What?"

"You've been acting weird lately," Michael said. He didn't elaborate, but she knew what was going through his mind. He kept making plans to evade his mother's eagle eye, and Tara kept coming up with lame excuses.

Damn the nurse and her "if it's not an emergency, the doctor will see you in three weeks." Tara's appointment was almost exactly at the same time the Barrons jet was supposed to take off from JFK International. Which was why she came up with yet another stupid excuse instead of driving Michael and Gabriel to the airport.

"Don't be dumb," Tara said out loud. "It's just... I'm so nervous, Mike. What if I suck in FIT?"

What if she had cancer or something and didn't even live to get to FIT?

For a second, Michael simply stared. Then, he looked up and down the hallway really quickly before coming in. "Seriously?" he asked. "I never met anyone more confident than you."

"So? I don't have to be confident every single minute. We all get nervous sometimes."

Slowly, Michael nodded. "Yeah, but you don't need to be." He held out a hand.

Tara yelped as she was heaved off the bed. In another second, they were swaying together.

"Didn't Lilah's friend say you have potential?" Michael asked. "The cosmetics lady... what's her name?"

"Ginger Rose," Tara responded.

"Yeah, her. Makeup business has the same customer demographic, right? When I'm done with West Point and you're done with your degree, maybe we can have a show. You know... where you get models to wear your stuff and—"

Tara laughed. "I know what a fashion show is. But who's going to buy tickets to a show by a total nobody? I have to work my way up the ladder."

"You'll get there," Michael said with certainty.

If she didn't die before then. God, what was the doctor going to say? Maybe it *was* a thyroid problem as Google claimed. Weight gain, irregular menstruation, tiredness...

"I swear I'll attend every show," Michael continued. "If you feel nervous again, just look into the crowd. I'll be there. Maybe at the back because all the tickets are going to be sold. I'll wave to you."

And Tara fell a little deeper in love.

#

Three hours later, Tara stayed frozen in the chair in the doctor's office. She saw the numbers on the report in front, heard the chatter of voices outside the closed door. Behind the medic across the desk was the window looking out to the parking lot. A plane was zooming across the sky.

Was it Michael's? Tara wondered dumbly.

"Did you hear me, Tara?" the doctor asked, tone compassionate. "You're pregnant. Somewhere between two and three months along, I'd say."

Chapter 58

A day later, July 4, 2000

Barcelona, Spain

"Wow," Michael said under his breath. Flashing lights, ear-splitting music, booze, and girls. *Lots* of girls gyrating on the small dance floor.

Michael was merely standing on the sidelines, watching the fun with a bottle of San Miguel. Gabriel, on the other hand, was having a great time, showing off his moves to "Tic, Tic Tac."

"Your dad and uncles are cool, man," one of Gabe's buddies shouted to Michael over the din.

Harry, Alex, and Victor had promised the boys one evening before heading northwest to the refinery. The three adults were currently slouched against the bar counter, drinking beer from mugs. A chick wearing crazy high heels teetered next to Harry, grabbing his shoulder to avoid falling. He somehow managed to plonk her onto a stool before she toppled.

"You want one?" a red-haired kid drew Michael's attention, offering a small packet of pills.

High as a kite, Michael thought, noting the bloodshot eyes. Dude also brought with him a heavy smell of tobacco. Coughing, Michael held up a hand. "Thanks, mate, but I'm good." Even drinking beer felt kinda weird with his family around no matter how legal it was in this town.

"Ladies and gentlemen," called the DJ. "Someone told me we have Americans here tonight, on their way to San Fermin. Let's wish them a happy Fourth of July!"

A cheer went up, and the crowd broke into a loud rendition of "Yankee Doodle." Gabriel and a couple of his friends started showing the girls around how to square dance. The high-heel chick next to Harry gaped at Gabe while the three adults slammed beer mugs in air, marching in place to the song.

Yeah, everyone except Michael was already celebrating their impending victory. He was too damned worried about Tara to think of anything else. She didn't respond to his cheesy "i <3 u" text from JFK Airport. It would've been almost midnight in New York when the Barrons jet—a Gulfstream V with Mach 0.885 speed and range of 6500 nautical miles—touched down in Spain. As promised, he rang both his mother and Tara right away. Sabrina said Tara returned from her shopping trip with no new stuff and didn't look at a single magazine all evening. Apparently, she also went to bed early because of a headache.

An hour later, Michael slouched on the plush red sofa set against the wall, watching his cousin chat up the high-heel chick next to Harry. Pointing to the Buffalo Woman bracelet on Gabe's wrist, the girl asked something.

"My mom's family is part Lakota," Gabriel said, his voice loud enough to reach the sofa ten feet away. "Native American. I like to read about native tribes."

"Cool backstory," the chick yelled over the music.

Gabriel beamed, then looked awkward. "Are you here with friends?" he asked.

It was the last of him anyone saw until the next morning. When Gabriel finally showed up in the parking lot of Hotel Majestic, his travel backpack was on his shoulder, a blissful smile nearly splitting his face in two. The adults had already left on their trip to Muskiz—at dawn, in fact—since it was the first day of the inspection. Only the seven boys were around.

Grinning, Michael asked his cousin, "So what happened? You talk some more about the Lakota last night?"

"Not telling," Gabe said pompously. The others booed. Ignoring them, he eyed the seven motorbikes lined up with camping equipment attached. "Which one's mine?"

The distance between the cities was only three hundred miles, but they planned to see the sights along the way and enjoy one night under the stars. Once they got to their destination, the festival—San Fermin—would occupy every minute. Oh, yeah. They were going to paaarty! Or Michael could've... if Tara actually picked up the phone.

"Let's go," whooped the oldest of the crew, a rookie cop in San Diego.

"Wait a second," Michael said, bringing out the folded piece of paper from his pocket. "Checklist, everyone. Passport?"

"Check," yelled back the rest.

"U.S. driver's license?" asked Michael.

"Check," responded the same six voices.

"International driver's permit?" he asked.

Amid the *checks*, someone groaned. "Is he usually like this?" grumbled one of Gabe's friends.

"All the time," agreed Gabriel.

Flipping off the traitor, Michael called, "Helmets?"

A toilet paper roll hit him in the face.

Michael was about to reciprocate in kind when the phone rang in his pocket. "Gimme a minute," he said to the rest. "It's Tara." Finally!

Under a barrage of hoots and whistles, he stepped to the side. *"Hola!"* Michael said. "I tried to call you so many times. You all right, girl?"

"Yeah." Her normally clear voice was subdued. "Mike, I went to the doctor. She said... uhh... I'm not sick."

Michael blinked. "Good," he said. "I mean... it's good, right?" She sounded like she was still worried.

"Hey, Little Kingsley," someone called.

Pivoting, Michael glared. He was six-foot-four, dammit! But Gabriel was Big Kingsley, so naturally...

Words rushed, Tara continued, "Mike, we need to—"

"Kingsley," someone called again. "Talk to your *morra* later, yo. We gotta get going before traffic gets bad."

From the phone came a Portuguese curse, followed by, "Tell those *burros* to..." Stopping, she sighed. "It's all right. Go with them. I'm going to need your help with something, but it can wait until you're back home."

"Like with moving to your dorm?" asked Michael. "I'll have two weeks in New York before going to West Point. Plenty of time to get you set up."

"Well, it does have to be done before college," Tara said, a touch of humor returning to her voice. "Go now. We'll talk when you're back."

When Michael rejoined the group, Gabriel asked, "Everything cool with her?"

"Yeah, I think she was nervous about moving out," said Michael. "Seems okay now."

Then, they were off. Laughing uproariously, throwing taunts at each other, howling for no reason, they wound and veered through busy streets. Wind billowed their shirts, dried their sweat. Michael couldn't wait to get beyond city limits. One week of pure adventure awaited.

Part XX

Chapter 59

The next afternoon, July 6, 2000, 2 PM

Day 2 of the inspection

Bilbao, Spain

"Communist?" Harry asked incredulously. Stalking up and down the living room of the hotel suite, he instructed the caller on the speakerphone, "We need to verify this intel. Hard to believe Steven would try something this sloppy."

News had gotten to the ladies of Berlin Eden. Apparently, someone in the German government planned a raid on the club to coincide with the inspection in Muskiz. The excuse was that the establishment was functioning as a front for the now-defunct East German Communist Party to funnel money to their pals in Russia.

"Makes no sense," Scott said from one of the chairs. The Imperial Suite at Hotel Carlton was booked for the two lawyers— Falcon Papazian and an assistant—but the entire team was present for the emergency huddle.

Over the speakerphone on the coffee table, Liam said, "It's exactly what the manager heard. One of the girls here has connections to the club scene in Pamplona. She used to be a hostess at Total Eclipse—the sonuvabitch JD's place. His daddy's place, rather. Well, Daddy decided it would be the perfect chance to get back at the five of you for Beijing. He helped Steven arrange the raid."

"The plan doesn't have to make sense to us," Alex said, shoving off from the pillar next to the French doors to the terrace.

"Remember Cuba? This is the same *m.o.*—with a twist. I'm gonna bet there's something implicating us in the deal."

"But communist?" Harry asked again. "No one in their right mind will believe any of us is a closet Marxist. It's an excuse to conduct a search. Got to be. I'm betting they're going to unexpectedly find something to suggest that the results of the inspection cannot be trusted." It would be the easiest and least risky way for Steven to avoid defeat.

Collapsing into the couch, Brad groaned. "If Steven planted something in the club, we'll be in for more rounds before the hearing committee. Is this ever going to end?"

"I'm calling Noah," stated Falcon. "Pretty sure he knows people in Berlin who can look into it. Unfortunately, the way these things work..."

"We're going to run into bureaucracy," Harry agreed grimly, halting his pacing. "Today is Thursday. The raid's supposed to be tomorrow—Friday. By the time we get anyone to review the warrant, it will be past the weekend. Too late."

The inspection was to be spread out over a period of two weeks, more if needed. But the moment something incriminating was found—even as far as in Berlin—the team would turn hostile to the cause of the Kingsley brothers.

Daniel snapped his notebook shut and tossed it onto the coffee table. "The raid cannot be allowed to happen. After the fact, it will take a lot of work to convince the committee we're innocent of whatever fake charges the Kingsleys cooked up. It took Harry nearly ten years to get a pardon for Brad."

"I'll go to Berlin," Alex said. "If we can't stop the raid, Liam and I can at least make sure the place is clean before the cops show up. Right now, the damn bastards think they're going to find a bunch of women who're not used to handling situations like this.

Steven and Armor always go for the women to get to us. They tried it with Lilah. Lupe died because of them. We can't allow anything to happen to the women in the club."

"What about the warrant?" Brad asked. "What if you get arrested when you get there?"

"Why would the warrant include any of our names?" Alex asked. "Steven thinks we're in Spain."

"True," Falcon said. "However, *Liam* might be included. If he somehow gets arrested... so yes, someone else should be there."

"I agree," Harry said slowly. Something about it, though— "Liam," called Harry. "About this girl you mentioned... who's her source in Total Eclipse?"

"Baby daddy," Liam said. "Not a nice fellow from what I understand. But he let something slip during an argument about child support."

"It still doesn't make sense," Scott insisted, pushing his glasses up the bridge of his nose.

"In what way?" Harry asked. The youngest Kingsley brother might go along with the four older ones in their collective decisions, but he always had his unique perspective.

"Because it *is* the same *m.o.* as Cuba," Scott said.

Harry studied the former astrophysicist for a few moments. "People do have patterns," Huffing out a breath, Harry acknowledged, "But they could also be luring us. The warrant could well have one or more of our names by the time we get there. Or they could have something planned for the refinery, and they're trying to get us out of the way."

"We secured the refinery," Victor brooded, "but there's no way of being completely certain. I mean... workers come and go, and there are so many of them."

Every access point to the refinery was guarded, and specially hired former cops made regular patrols. All employees underwent security checks before entering or exiting the facility. All items were scanned before being allowed in or out. Personnel always carried the potential to be the weak link in any war plan, so over the last six months, management did background investigations on the staff. Still, with nearly a thousand employees, there was always the risk of one or two slipping through the cracks. Especially in an industry where contract workers were common.

"God," Brad muttered. "If it's about the refinery... is Steven gone far enough to do something like this on purpose? Not only could we lose, we could end up with deaths on our conscience."

"What would be the point of luring us if the idea is to attack the refinery?" Neil asked, tone doubtful. "Neither side is supposed to go to the place during the inspection. If Steven has something planned, we're not going to be there to stop it in any case."

"So what do we do?" asked Shawn.

"First step would be to not make things easy for the enemy," Harry said. "We split up. There's no way we can leave the ladies in Eden to deal with the authorities on their own, but I should be the one going there. After Liam, they trust me more than anyone else in this group. Alex, I do think it would be a good idea for you to go along. If this is a lure, Steven knows I'll be the one flying to Berlin. Which means he might have something planned for me in Germany and/or for the five of you here. You being in the club instead of here in Muskiz might throw him off and buy us time."

Brad nodded. "True."

"Shawn and I will drive to Saint-Jean-de-Luz," said Dan. The town was farther north on the Basque coast, just across the French border. Less than two hours from the refinery by car. "Let's see if Steven's managed to get warrants in three different countries. I will alert Barrons lawyers in any case."

"The rest of us will stay here with Falcon, and I'll contact the refinery manager to watch for problems," said Victor. The manager would be on guard, anyway. "Falcon, is there a way to preempt the S.O.B.s? You know... a warning to the Spanish government so they think twice before arresting us on some fake charge?"

"I'll contact Gray to arrange it," Falcon said. "He and Noah can in fact alert the senate committee, too, about what we heard."

"Also, let Lilah know what's happening," Harry instructed Victor. "Ask Sabrina and Tara to go to The Hermitage right away. All three of them should stay with Temple until this is over." Whoever tried to get at the women would first have to get past United States Secret Service.

"Sabrina will remember to shut down the computers," Shawn said. "We need digital barricades, too."

"The boys?" Neil inquired.

After an hour, Alex snapped his phone shut and turned to the rest. "Nope," he said. "Sabrina had all their numbers, not just Mike's and Gabe's. No one's picking up."

"They probably turned the phones off," suggested Falcon.

"Not on purpose," said Alex. "Mike and Gabe know better. My guess would be they forgot to recharge." After an entire twenty-four hours on the road, there would be no power left in the devices when the lads got to Pamplona.

"Victor," called Harry. "Alex and I need to get going. You keep trying. Tell them to get their asses to Bilbao the minute they pick up."

The Barrons jet was in Barcelona, which would be five hours by road, but renting a helicopter was easy enough. Harry still had his license, and the Robinson R44 got him and Alex to the international airport in little more than an hour.

By the end of the day, they were in Berlin Eden, sitting around a table with Liam as the hostess announced the sports bar had to close on account of an unexpected emergency. Protesting patrons were escorted out. All employees, except the manager, were asked to leave. Television screens were turned off, and every light in the place turned on.

Starting from the front door, Harry, Alex, and Liam videotaped and photographed their way through the entire club. Behind the bottles in the glass-doored cupboards, furniture crevices, inside toilet tanks... not an inch of the building was spared. Hard copies of records were always maintained, so erasing the computers was not a big deal, especially as Shawn stayed on the phone to guide them. Landlines were checked for bugs.

Any additional *evidence* discovered by cops could now be proven as fabricated.

Finally, Shawn said over the phone, "Do a master reset on all the cellular devices in the club. Get the cocktail shakers out. Make sure they're stainless steel and put the devices in them. The shakers will function as Faraday cages. No EM signals in or out. Any communication will have to be done via landlines. They could still be bugged, but there's less chance of anyone accusing us of things we didn't do."

Harry hesitated for a second before adding his burner phone to the pile. His mole in the Kingsley clan knew the number to the hotel in Bilbao. The Kingsley brothers could tell him how to reach Harry.

"The jet has been refueled," Dan informed Harry. "Ready to fly back with minutes' notice if needed."

It was well into Friday morning by then, and there was nothing more to do but wait.

#

July 7, 2000, 4:15 PM

Day 3 of the inspection

Pamplona, Spain

"What the hell is going on?" brooded Michael.

Nearly hopping around the small lobby in frustration, Gabriel cursed. "We should've checked the phones right away. I *knew* we should've."

After getting to the youth hostel the afternoon before, the entire group left their devices charging and headed out. The town was awash in white and red—white tees and pants with red sashes and red neckerchiefs. The temperature was nearly touching a hundred, but Michael and Gabriel and the rest danced like crazy to songs blasting in the streets before proceeding to the stadium for the opening fight. Three men on horseback, fighting six bulls! The crowds roared like they were insane. Fireworks, more music, more dancing...

Sweaty and stinky, the boys crashed into their beds near dawn. After less than four hours of sleep, they had just enough time to shower and change into another set of San Fermin clothes before racing to the streets to witness the famous bull run.

Michael and Gabriel didn't check for messages even when they returned to the hostel for a nap. The receptionist—a gray-haired lady—waited until the group was on its way to Plaza de Toros in the afternoon to see matadors in action. Beckoning Gabriel from the desk, she handed him a slip of paper. The note said to call Victor back ASAP. Two minutes later, the boys saw the missed calls on their phones.

Except no one was picking up when they called. Not Michael or Gabriel's dads, not their uncles, not Harry. The hotel in Bilbao said they weren't picking up in any of the rooms. Sabrina, Tara, Lilah, Mr. Andersen... no one. Michael even tried the landline at home although it was used mostly for internet connection now.

"Let's get a newspaper," he said. "Maybe one of the bigger hotels has *The New York Times* or something. If they've all been arrested... gotta be big news back home."

"Hold on," Gabriel said. "I *think*..." Scrolling through his phone, he announced, "Yup, here it is." A secret service officer's personal number.

In fifteen minutes, they were outside the hostel, straddling their bikes. Neither even waited to change from festival clothes.

"Not cool, man," complained one of Gabe's friends. "Why do you have to go if no one got arrested?"

Gabriel snorted. "We *want* to go. The Kingsleys put all of us through hell for ten years. No more. They ain't winning today." Not if he and Michael could help it.

#

Same time

Muskiz, Spain

The villa was midway up the small, green-covered hill overlooking the refinery. Standing by the open window, Richard studied the view through military-issue binoculars.

A tarred road separated the hill from the facility spread across two hundred or so hectares—more than half the size of Central Park. Oil workers clad in fluorescent-green coveralls and white hardhats walked between large crude oil tanks, pipelines, the heater, the distillation tower, and tanks holding finished products. The engineers in the inspection team had disappeared into the manager's office about fifteen minutes ago but would leave soon. Their chopper stood waiting on the heliport on the other side of the compound.

Enough light would remain after the team's departure, Richard told himself. The day had been cloudy throughout, and visibility remained moderate at best. Still, sunset wouldn't arrive until close to ten at night.

The distance from the villa to the crude tanks was about a thousand meters in a straight line. The Savage 10FP bolt-action sniper rifle procured by Potts, Sr. would work, provided Richard didn't have to battle nature. He did have a thermal riflescope for unexpected delays stretching the operation into the dark hours, but magnification would only be three to four times. Not enough for effective long-range sniping. Four hundred meters was the most he could hope for at night.

Five hours of daylight should be plenty, Richard again reminded himself.

Besides, no one in their right mind would've built a house any closer. Even at this distance and even after working decades in the oil sector, Richard could smell the sourness in the air. The humming of machinery was still audible, albeit subdued. Probably the reason the rent on the decent-sized villa was low. The smell and the constant noise would also be good excuses why the Kingsley team leased two houses—if the authorities discovered the subterfuge. This one for proximity, the waterfront residence near the Bilbao Guggenheim for comfort.

Most of Steven's team was present in the villa—Richard, Phillip, Steven himself, Charles and his minder, and General Potts. JD's job was in Bilbao, which he was eager to complete. There was one more member, one with good reason to hate Peter Kingsley's sons.

Nataniel "El Peuchen" Bronco—contract employee from a certain Puelche village in Argentina—would stay where he'd been the last few months. At his job in the refinery, where he had easy access to chemicals such as hydrogen peroxide and hydrochloric acid as well as cleaning fluids containing acetone. Immigration authorities in Spain never spotted anything alarming in the employment application of Nataniel Bronco, the son of a deceased

Argentine soldier of uncertain heritage. The name wouldn't connect the boy to his actual sire. El Peuchen's only inheritance from the son of a bitch who abused his pregnant wife was the occasional wheeze which was partly responsible for his street name.

Richard's own biological father had to be strong-armed into making financial arrangements for the child he carelessly spawned. At some point, Richard would have to decide what to do with the cash. Probably put it all in the bank for his parents. Fitting, since they'd once invested in the Athens-based shipping company on Godwin's recommendation. The enterprise was later driven under by Peter Kingsley, Patrice's late husband. Of course it was payback for what the Greek fellow did to Patrice. The Kingsleys never let any insult pass, even the ones who married into the clan.

Shaking his head, Richard set the binoculars on the console next to the window and turned.

Steven remained on the living room couch, admonishing Charles to behave himself at least until they were back in the States. The minder—Yuri—sat on Charles's other side and kept staring at his phone. The fellow had said something about a friend he wanted to meet while in Spain, but Steven was firm on this not being the time for side trips. Clearly, the message didn't sink in. Phillip was sprawled in a chair, seemingly asleep.

General Potts marched out from the kitchen, coffee mug in hand, and got to the window. "Are all the pieces where they need to be?" the general asked for the dozenth time.

Inclining his head, Richard said, "Yes, sir."

El Peuchen had insisted the enemy didn't know what he looked like, but Richard refused to take the chance. Mrs. Brad Kingsley financially supported the boy. No, the machi—the boy's great-grandmother—never sent updates, but it wasn't beyond possibility that the arrogant Barrons princess checked on his upbringing through other means. No one who could potentially ID El Peuchen could be allowed anywhere near the refinery. Besides, Harry Sheppard had escaped multiple traps which he shouldn't have been able to. Allowing him to remain in town while the operation was going down was too damned risky.

Sheppard was already in Germany. He would've considered the possibility of yet another trap but would've gone, anyway, thanks to the guilt over Lupe Valdez's death. The Barrons men were not stupid. They knew they were the only ones in this war solely for their sister's sake, and they needed to remain free to continue fighting for her. Dan and Shawn avoided a potential ambush by taking themselves off to France. Mrs. Kingsley and Noah Andersen barricaded themselves in The Hermitage.

The only ones left to keep an eye on the refinery were the Kingsley brothers. The five of them imagined themselves safe, with guards and high-powered lawyers ready to make sure there was no repeat of the Cuba episode. Unfortunately for them, the enemy needed only a few hours. JD would buy them those critical hours once the inspection team left.

With a shuffling sound, Phillip stood from his chair and exchanged a quiet word with his father. Nodding, the general joined the rest around the coffee table.

Sauntering to Richard's side, Phillip said, "I can tell when you're worried. What's going on?"

Richard rolled his shoulders. "Not sure." As the general said, every piece was in its place, including weapons. "Everything's looking perfect. All there's left to do now is wait."

"But?" prompted Phillip.

"We missed something," Richard said, feeling restless. "I know we did."

What the hell was it?

Map with markings later made by Harry and Alex.

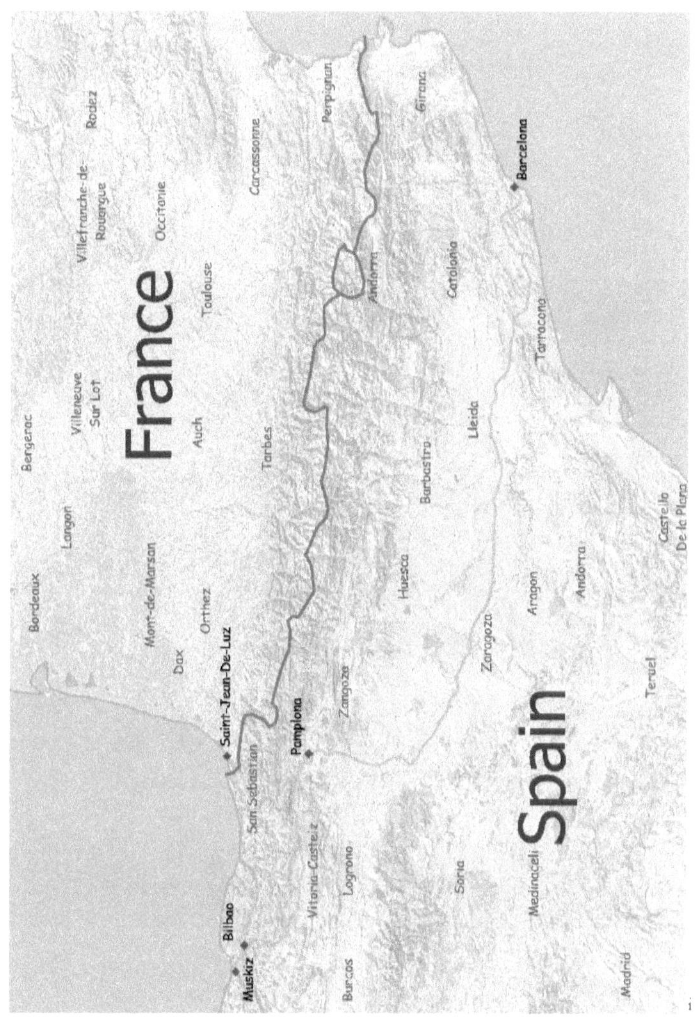

Satellite image with markings later made by Harry and Alex.

Chapter 60

Two hours later, 6:45 PM

(3 hours to sunset)

Bilbao, Spain

Travel backpack on his shoulders, Michael pivoted at the steps leading to the hotel and peered in the direction of the roundabout. Vehicles entered the traffic circle from multiple streets and streamed through. In the center of the circle was a fountain, flowerbeds and walkways surrounding it. Dozens of people strolling, kids roller-skating, someone munching on a sandwich... no, Michael didn't see any familiar faces.

There was plenty of noise, too—the cars and buses, random conversations—but no voices known to Michael.

"Let's go, bro," Gabe said from the top of the short stoop, his luggage resting at his feet. Two uniformed doormen stood ready to assist. "Mr. Andersen said we need to stick close to Mr. Papazian."

"Yeah, but..." Michael rubbed the back of his neck. "I swear I heard someone call my name."

He studied the scene for a good fifteen seconds before shrugging.

"Nothing?" Gabe asked.

Muttering irritably, Michael turned toward the hotel.

Almost immediately, there was a distant shout. "Michael!"

"I hear it," Gabriel said, leaving his luggage where it was and jogging back to the street.

A tall man wearing shorts and a tee broke through the crowd around the fountain, sprinting across the road toward the boys.

Tires screeching, a car honked irately. A *couple* of cars, but the man paid no mind.

When he got close enough, Michael frowned. The Kingsley coloring of brown hair and gray/blue eyes wasn't uncommon, but something in the man's features suggested he was one of them. Not Steven or Charles. Michael hadn't met his father's cousins in a long while, but he knew what they looked like all right. Next to Michael, Gabriel's stance coiled.

Huffing out breaths, the new fellow came to a stop. Temperature had dropped overnight to the seventies, and nor was the dude hefty, but he was still sweating like a pig. "Yuri..." he said. "Yuri Kingsley. I work for your uncle. I mean Harry. I need to talk to him. Right now!"

"What?" Gabriel asked, tone confused and hostile at the same time.

"No time to explain," the man—Yuri—said urgently. "I tried to call Harry, but his cell phone's not ringing. The hotel's not letting me talk to any of them."

"What do you mean?" Michael asked. "You don't need the hotel's permission. If you work for Uncle Harry, why didn't you just go in? Everyone's inside."

"I can't," the man said, tone frantic. "The staff won't let me, and JD went in just now. Michael—" A doorman rolled a trolley out, helping a tourist couple load their boxes into a cab. Yuri beckoned the boys a few feet down to talk. "You're Gabriel, right?" Harry's supposed employee asked. "Both of you, listen to me. All I need from you is some way to contact Harry. Steven's planning something at the refinery. Not sure exactly what. What I do know is Harry was sent to Germany on purpose. Everyone knew Dan would keep out of the way. JD—Drummond—is inside the hotel as we speak. I don't know what the hell he's got planned for your father and uncles, but it's not the end game. It can't be. Steven rented a villa near the refinery. My best guess would be whatever is going down, it's there. Harry needs to know!"

Michael and Gabriel glanced at each other. They had the phone number to the club in Berlin, but who knew if this Yuri fellow was on the up-and-up? "I'll go in and check what's happening," Michael said to his cousin. "You call Uncle Harry but don't go anywhere with this dude. Ten minutes, and I'll be back down. If I'm not..."

Gabriel nodded. "I'll take Yuri on a trip to the local precinct."

#

A few minutes later, 6:55 PM

Berlin, Germany

"Sonuvabitch," Alex ground out, listening to the update Gabe and Yuri were giving over the speakerphone. The news that Charles's babysitter worked for Harry was a surprise to Alex, but they didn't have the time to discuss details.

Harry was on the other side of the desk in the cramped office. Liam and the club manager were on one of their rounds through the building to make sure nothing was missed.

"Yuri," Harry called, pushing the unplugged monitor to one side to make room for a notepad. None of the digital devices in the sports bar were currently functioning. The cocktail shakers which functioned as Faraday cages for the cell phones were lined up along the left wall. "Anything else you remember?" Harry asked. "Some way to ID their inside man... if we were lured out, it means the bastard's someone we know."

"Sorry," said Yuri. "I wish I could've waited to find out more, but there just wasn't enough time."

His entire job involved keeping Charles out of trouble. Since Steven and Armor took care not to let the moron overhear their discussions, Yuri rarely picked up anything useful. Until this afternoon, that is. Charles was brought along so his brother didn't have to worry about him while a big operation was going down. Even then, no details were mentioned, but yeah... something big.

Yuri tried every possible way to contact Harry—calling from the bathroom at the villa, leaving cryptic messages at the hotel reception to be called back. No response.

The refinery manager was an option, but he didn't know Yuri, and Yuri couldn't be sure the manager was not the inside guy. Calling the police would be pointless. What the hell was Yuri supposed to say? Something *might* happen? Without at least some detail, he wouldn't be taken seriously. Afterward, Yuri could even be made the fall guy for his pains.

Eventually, Phillip said he was going to the refinery to talk to the inside man one last time. Charles and Yuri were supposed to tag along, then return to the official Kingsley base near the Guggenheim Museum. The idiot would be safe enough for a few minutes during the car ride to Bilbao.

The road into the refinery was restricted to public access, and Phillip had arranged the meeting near a kebab shop outside the complex. Charles and Yuri were to wait inside the restaurant while Phillip met his contact in the car. Under the pretext of using the latrine, Yuri slipped out through the back door and kept walking. Whatever the plan was, it was happening not long after the inspection team left the refinery. There was simply no time to see who the inside man might be. Not to mention Phillip's reaction if he caught Charles's minder spying.

When Yuri got to the hotel in Bilbao, the staff wouldn't let him go up to the rooms rented by the team. They wouldn't even connect him by phone. Then, he saw JD prance in, accompanied by men who looked like cops. Yuri was about to take his chances with the refinery manager when Michael and Gabriel showed up. Harry had made sure his mole could recognize all the players in the corporate war, including the kids.

"By now, Major Potts has informed Armor and Steven about your disappearance," Harry said, continuing to scribble. "They won't know for sure, but they're going to assume you came to us."

"You think they could stop the plan?" Yuri asked. "Since you know..."

"No," Alex said immediately. "Their best bet is to go ahead before we get the chance to contact authorities. Once the cops are placed on alert, the window of opportunity will close for them. Yeah, it's now or never for Steven. Armor will make sure anyone who might connect the incident to them keeps out of sight. If we later claim it was sabotage, they'll say we're trying to cover up the problems at the refinery. At the very least, they'll fight this round to a draw."

Gabriel's curse was clearly audible over the line. "This insider is the key," he said. "If we knew who he was, we'd have the whole gang."

"Armor and Potts called the inside man a boy a few times," Yuri said as Harry continued scribbling. "So someone relatively young. Also, Major Armor said something about a flying snake. Not sure what he meant."

Alex sat forward in the rolling chair. "Snake? Who do we know with a connection to snakes?"

"*Flying* snake," Gabe corrected Alex. "The only flying snake I've heard of is in Mapuche stories—El Peuchen."

"Mapuche?" Harry set his pen down. "As in Native American?" Thanks to Gabriel's mother and foster mother—both of Lakota descent—he harbored a great deal of interest in indigenous mythologies.

"Yeah," said the young man. "It's a weird snake-dragon thing. A shapeshifter. It whistles and sucks blood from sheep. From people, too. Only the machi can control it—the shaman."

Harry coughed once. "Gabe, tell me. What's the general geographical location of the Mapuche?"

"Chile, I think," said Gabriel.

Alex knew what Harry was going to ask before the words came out. "And Argentina? The Patagonia region?"

"The Puelche," Alex breathed.

"Dunno much about the Puelches," said Gabriel, "but I guess tribes in Argentina could have similar stories."

Pushing his chair back, Harry stood. "Yuri... Gabe... listen to me carefully. There's going to be a terrorist strike—a fire, possibly chemical. I'll tip off Madrid about an impending attack from Basque nationalists; it will get us faster response. Alex, call the refinery manager and have him start evacuating."

"On it," Alex said, rolling his chair to the stainless-steel shakers lined up along the wall.

"Fire?" parroted Gabriel.

"I'll explain later," said Harry. "To you *and* the authorities. Gabe, you need to stay out of the hotel. Drummond's in there. For now, we must assume he has your dad and uncles. Maybe Mike, too. Give him the ten minutes he asked for, then leave with Yuri. Unfortunately, you can't go to the local cops. We don't know who in town is in Drummond's pay. Just stay someplace where he can't get to you."

"Uncle Harry," Gabriel called. "Forget Drummond for a second. I'm a *fireman*. I should be at the refinery if there's going to be a fire."

Willing the cell phone to turn on faster, Alex ptchaaed. "The refinery has its own emergency response team. Also, town authorities will send help once Madrid gets involved."

"Barrons refinery in California is five times the size, and they have only thirty-six first responders per shift," Gabriel argued. "So a dozen men in the Muskiz facility to cover two hundred hectares. Do we even have a clue where the fire is going to start? How long will it take to convince the government to send help? Didn't you say there are almost a thousand employees? People are going to die, Uncle Alex!"

"You're eighteen," Harry said, grabbing his own phone.

"Yes," said Gabriel. "You were seventeen when you enlisted in the navy. Legally, I'm already an adult, *and* I have the training required for this precise situation. There are men and women inside the damn place who went on their shifts only to do their jobs. *My job is to make sure they go back home to their families.*"

Ring... ring... ring... Alex bit back a curse. Why the hell wasn't anyone picking up the phone in the refinery office? When he glanced up for a second, he caught Harry's eyes. The same fear was on his face as he waited for his contact in Madrid to answer. Every wasted minute could mean more lives lost.

"Uncle Harry, give me the same order you would give a subordinate," Gabriel pleaded.

"Go, Fireman Kingsley," Harry commanded, voice tense. "Yuri, go with him. Legal adult or not, the manager will want to hear from someone older than eighteen. Tell him Alex and I will be there soon. Gabe, do what you can, then get the hell out."

"Yes, sir!" said Gabriel. "Armor and his flying snake are not gonna win."

#

Ten minutes ago

Inside Hotel Carlton

Michael didn't bother asking the receptionist for permission to go up only to be refused like Yuri. Grabbing Gabriel's backpack from where he discarded it, Michael walked through the huge lobby with its pillars and paintings and red-and-gold furniture until he spotted a woman with a badge on her lapel.

"Men's room?" Michael requested. "I'm waiting to check in, but..."

"Not a problem, sir," said the lady, smiling. "Over there."

A couple of men were at the row of urinals. There was an empty stall, thank God. Inside, Michael dropped both backpacks on the floor and grabbed the documents he and Gabe couldn't afford to lose—passports, driving permits, credit cards. Michael's phone was already clipped to his pants.

There was no time to change completely. Michael grabbed a cotton hoodie and pulled it over his festival clothes. He waited until he heard the other two occupants leave before ambling out.

A hotel employee was by the elevator doors, talking to guests waiting to go to their rooms. There was a clipboard in his hands, and he appeared to be verifying identities.

A few guests were walking up the wide, carpeted stairway. Sauntering casually, Michael joined them. One flight... two... three...

Shit, he muttered in his mind. Two men in suits waited at the top of the steps, both with their backs to Michael. Not the guards hired by Uncle Brad. Michael had met them before, and they didn't have black hair. *This* duo was surely in the pay of Steven Kingsley.

Michael could see beyond the two thugs. A potted plant in the hallway, next to which were Victor, Scott, Brad, Mr. Papazian, a few other men. They were all arguing. Noise... there was so much noise...

The potted plant right outside the ant-y room was large enough to conceal Michael. From his hiding place, he could see both the office suite and the lobby with its glass walls on three sides. Michael watched as large shadows marched up and down, their heavy boots echoing frighteningly. Some of them went inside Lilah's suite, ripping open desk drawers. Someone was coiling the wires to the computers.

"You're not supposed to touch them," Michael offered timidly. No one heard.

There was noise, so much noise.

Michael blinked. This was not Panama. He was no longer a five-year-old.

"Excuse me," he called. One of the men blocking his way turned.

"Michael Kingsley," he said. "I'm with them."

The duo looked confused, then the dude on the left said, *"Uno de los hijos."* One of the sons.

"Mike," called Neil.

Everyone in the small crowd turned to check. Not bothering to offer more explanation, Michael joined his family. Four of the five Kingsley brothers, Falcon Papazian and his assistant, the two guards. They appeared unharmed if somewhat flushed and sweaty. There were at least six unfamiliar men besides the two guarding the stairs, all of them in suits. More men were inside the suite proper, going through things.

"You," snapped one of the outsiders.

Light-brown hair, blue eyes, lean build—Jack Drummond, Michael's mind computed. The criminal who beat up Lilah and tried to rape her. He also had a hand in the death of Uncle Harry's second wife.

"This is Alex Kingsley's son," Drummond said to another man, someone who appeared to be in charge. A senior cop? "Ask him... boy, you'd better tell us where your dad is."

"Alex Kingsley," one of the policemen shouted as his friend checked off something on a list. The former sniper was dragged from his office.

"No," Michael said.

A second passed. "What do you mean no?" Drummond demanded.

"No, I'm not telling you," Michael stated. "Get a subpoena if you want."

He saw the swing coming, invited it even.

"Mike!" shouted Brad.

The fist never landed. Side-stepping, Michael gripped Drummond's arm and shoved him away. "I'm not a woman," Michael warned the stumbling politician. *Ex*-politician. "Try it again, and I will break your fucking jaw."

The four uncles looked ready to pounce, but they were held at bay by the guns in the cops' hands. The lawyers appeared shocked. Lurching around, Drummond snarled.

"Mike's seventeen," Victor said to the main cop, speaking rapidly. "A minor. Anything anyone here does to him will be blamed on you."

"Señor," called Mr. Papazian, regaining his power of speech. "You said you're here on a tip about black money. The Spanish government has the authority to check it out, but physically assaulting citizens of another country—especially children—will cause international uproar. Victor's right; you're the man in charge, and you will be held responsible. I suggest you ask Mr. Drummond to refrain from starting unnecessary trouble."

Without responding to Victor or the lawyer, the main cop gestured at Michael to get closer to his uncles. "No one will get hurt if they cooperate. And no one leaves this place until we're done searching."

"Is Michael's name on the warrant?" Brad asked, pushing his glasses up his nose. "Or Gabriel's?"

"Precisely my question," said Papazian. "If not, you don't have the authority to detain him. Let him go."

"No chance," scoffed Drummond. "Anyone can be detained in an ongoing investigation."

"Not unless there is reasonable suspicion of the person's involvement in the crime." Papazian turned to the cop. "Eventually, we'll be allowed to leave. You won't have a choice because you're not going to find anything. Rest assured I will then contact the U.S. embassy. As of this moment, you're only acting on the laws of your country. Involve minors on Mr. Drummond's say-so—without any legal justification whatsoever—and you'll be crossing the line. You will be forced to answer for it in court and in the media."

The cop suddenly looked undecided. "I can't justify holding the boy," he muttered after a couple of seconds.

"Your bosses will hear of this," Drummond warned the cop.

"They won't like it, either, if the media decides to fuss about the child angle," the officer said.

"Mike," called Brad. Speaking with the extreme clarity of a man pushed beyond limits, he said, "Remember when you and Gabe tried to call us from Pamplona? We were fooled into blocking our own cell phones. The hotel said we weren't picking up in the rooms until you got the Secret Service involved. I believe our friends here fed the hotel management false info about what was going on. As good citizens, they cooperated and kept us secluded until the police showed up. We haven't been allowed to contact anyone afterward."

It explained what Yuri encountered when he tried to reach Harry. Michael nodded.

"Harry and the Barronses were lured away," Brad continued.

"Shut the hell up," Drummond said, glaring at all of them.

The main cop shook his head. "Let them talk. I don't have a choice but to let the kid go, but the rest of it... the police will do our job no matter how inconvenient some tourist finds it."

"We know there's no black money," Brad went on. "Between the six of us, we photographed every inch of this place overnight, and the pictures have been stored on a couple of laptops. The camera was mailed to New York. Anyone planting evidence is going to be in heckuva lot of trouble. Anything planted in our phones or computers will also have a time stamp proving it happened after these gentlemen showed up. I suspect the chief here understands all this. I suspect he and Drummond are merely delaying us. From what, I don't know, but I can take a guess."

"The refinery!" said Victor, both hands clutching his head. "Something's going on there."

"By the time they let us leave," said Scott, "it will be too late."

"I'll sue you for slander," Drummond threatened. "Maybe you already know something's going to happen at the refinery, and you're making shit up to cover your asses."

As though no one spoke, Brad continued, "Michael, listen to me carefully. Any potential accident arranged by Steven and crew will be big enough to catch the senate committee's attention. The only reason I can imagine he waited until after today's inspection is he wants to avoid danger to the team. Anything happens to them, suspicion could fall on Steven. Otherwise, he could well get away with saying 'I told you so' about the refinery's safety practices."

"Which means *we* lose," said Neil.

"Right," said Brad. "Regardless of who takes the blame, there's risk to anyone within the facility. They employ nearly a thousand men and women. Depending on how many work in a single shift, the number of casualties could run to the hundreds, and there *will* be casualties."

"My God," moaned Victor. "All those people... oh, my God."

"You need to call Harry," Neil said urgently. "Let him know what's going on."

"Gabe would've done so already," said Michael.

"He's outside, I presume," Brad said, inclining his head. "But Harry won't get here on time to stop the attack. He'll try to call the manager, but we don't know if their phone lines have been jammed somehow. Even if he manages to connect with the refinery, they're going to need help. We don't know if help will get there on time. We don't know if help will get there at all. Who can tell how many..." Brad threw a glance at Drummond. "...officials were bought off?"

"I *am* suing you," said Drummond.

"Michael," Brad called again. "You and Gabe need to go to the refinery."

"To the..." Victor echoed. "What the hell, Brad?!"

Falcon Papazian emitted a sound of alarm. Even the cop appeared shocked.

"There's no other option," Brad insisted. "The refinery got into this war because they trusted us. They're relying on us to help them. Well, Gabe and Mike are the only ones who can at the moment. Hundreds of men and women... are we going to let them die?"

For a couple of moments, Victor said nothing, simply staring unblinkingly at his older brother. *"Shit!"* the former boxer then roared, startling the rest. Hopping around, Victor went on helplessly, "Shit, shit, *shit!"*

"Son," Brad said, turning his attention back to Michael. "Once you warn the manager, get yourself outside the gates. Even if you merely guide people out, it will free up the refinery's crew to deal with the dangerous part. Two extra pairs of hands could make life-or-death difference to someone."

"No unnecessary risks," cautioned Neil.

Looking Michael in the eye, the eldest Kingsley brother nodded once. "You have your orders, Cadet Kingsley. The rest of us will be right behind you... as soon as these gentlemen admit they have nothing."

"Yes, sir," said Michael. "Gabe and I will do what it takes."

#

Same time, 7 PM

The villa near the refinery

"We don't have a choice," Richard called out, taking one last look at the Savage.

The bolt-action chambered in .338 Lapua Magnum featured a heavy barrel, built-in bipod, ten-power scope, and sling for transport as well as steadier prone position. A noise suppressor would decrease accuracy from his hiding place, but it couldn't be helped. Richard wasn't about to draw attention by making unnecessary sounds while providing cover for El Peuchen. The potential need for the thermal riflescope worried him more. The range of four hundred meters allowed by night-operation technology could prove inadequate for his role in the mission.

Shaking his head, Richard again reminded himself how they were on the northern hemisphere at the height of summer. The sun would linger in the sky long after he and the rest left the neighborhood.

Zipping up the drag bag disguised as a travel backpack, Richard slung it over his shoulder. "Getting the boy out has to be our top priority," he stated, exiting the bedroom. The general and Steven were seated on the living room couch, discussing the unexpected complication.

El Peuchen had already tucked the chemical mix where it would cause the most damage, but he couldn't leave before the end of his shift without causing suspicion. With every exit guarded, even slipping out to meet Phillip during his break was a risk. The boy never met anyone in the team other than Richard, who wouldn't be the one escorting him out of the country, and El Peuchen insisted on seeing the face of his intended guide before pressing the trigger. On Phillip's part, he didn't believe in distributing his imagery. The man, the time, the pickup spot—everything was re-confirmed in the brief meeting in the car parked by the kebab shop.

El Peuchen also made it clear to Phillip—as he previously did with Richard—how any attempts to do away with an ally after the fact would not be looked upon kindly by his tribe. If Nataniel Bronco didn't land in the Buenos Aires airport on time, the treachery of the Kingsleys would be announced to the world no matter what repercussions awaited his family for their role in the attack.

Phillip stayed in the car until the boy returned to the refinery grounds. The plan was to take Charles and Yuri to the house near the museum before Phillip made his way to the designated spot where he would wait for El Peuchen. Except, Charles was alone in the kebab shop.

"We can't let Charles go to the house by himself," acknowledged Steven. Who knew what the idiot would get up to?

"Especially if something goes wrong on Drummond's end," General Potts said. "Alex and Victor and the rest could well show up at the house. Or they could send cops. We cannot let Charles deal with the police on his own."

"If Phillip brings Charlie back here..." Steven suggested for the hundredth time.

The moment the evacuation started, Steven and General Potts were supposed to exit, leaving Richard to provide cover for El Peuchen until the boy made it safely to where Phillip waited. Two men hidden in two different spots to make sure the saboteur escaped. Only, no one would know Richard was not in the departing car with Steven and the general.

If the authorities ever found out about the Kingsleys leasing the villa, the explosion would be good enough explanation for their quick escape. Charles could potentially go with his brother and the general.

"Too risky," Richard insisted. "We have to assume Yuri gave whatever info he had to your cousins. Which includes the location of this villa. We need to operate under the assumption the cops could show up any minute."

The authorities wouldn't have evidence of wrongdoing on their part, but they could—and would—detain everyone who was in the villa for some time. Which would include Phillip if he returned with Charles. El Peuchen would not find an escort waiting for him.

"Which also means *you* need to head out now, Major," reminded Potts. "Charles will have to stay with Phillip. No other option."

"Right," Richard said. "If the police do show up here..."

"I'll let them know you returned to Bilbao with Phillip and Charles," Potts said.

It took Richard fifteen minutes to reach his intended location. Trees, twigs crunching under his shoes, the distant sound of a dog barking... it wasn't easy even for a fit man like him to climb around the cliffside and squeeze into the space between two precariously positioned rocks. Which meant the chances of a casual hiker—or a refinery worker—happening on him were low.

Dumping the drag bag on the ground, he started setting up his rifle. Something rustled in the small bush to the right. In a fraction of a second, Richard swung toward the sound, the pistol from his ankle holster in his hand.

With a loud yowl, a wildcat streaked out of the shrubbery. Richard took a deep breath and let his pulse slow.

The phone rang in his pocket.

"Yeah?" he said into the device.

"JD called," said Steven. "We have a problem."

Two minutes later, Richard said, "Shit... we *knew* they were here. We should've made arrangements. Still, not a big deal. I doubt Alex and Victor's kids know what their daddies did to some tribe in South America. They're not going to recognize our boy."

Chapter 61

7:34 PM

(less than 2 ½ hours to sunset)

The smell of gasoline was unmissable, and of course, Michael heard the blaring siren long before he got to the restricted access section of the tarred road running through the hills. The entrance to the complex was guarded by a railway crossing contraption with a security booth right inside, and both gate arms were raised. Refinery workers were already huffing and puffing as they ran to safety. Birds squawked in the sky above.

Turning off his bike, Michael loped a few feet up the grassy hillside to get a better view of the terrain. Gabriel and Yuri followed. Scraggly bushes and clusters of wildflowers were scattered across the meadow, and farther up were trees—woods, really. There were in fact multiple such groves in all directions, beyond which Michael spotted a couple of houses. Perhaps the Kingsleys were in one of them, staring down at the chaos.

"How the hell do we find the manager?" Yuri shouted over the din.

"He should be at the exit," Gabriel yelled back. "At *one* of the exits."

"Or he could've bailed by now," said Michael.

He and Gabriel glanced at each other. "I'll talk to the fire crew," Gabriel said, nodding in the direction of a couple of men who seemed to be guiding the rest. "Let me—"

Out of the corner of his visual field, Michael saw the sky shimmer behind one of the tanks. A fireball shot up. The earth shook below his feet.

"Take cover!" he roared, slamming into Yuri and bringing him down. Gabe was already in a protective crouch on the ground, arms shielding his head.

A blast reverberated through the air.

Screams, terrified calls, thundering feet... more birds took wing from the trees and the bushes, all screeching in agitation. The siren continued to blare.

"Fuck!" Gabriel bellowed. "There are people still inside."

Michael scrambled around on all fours. Gabe was back in standing position, watching in alarm as the evacuating workers pushed and shoved each other in their hurry to get to safety. Many were scampering across the slope to get ahead of the rest, screaming and shouting nonstop.

Smoke, thick and black, rolled toward the meadow. Leaping to his feet, Michael tugged off the hoodie he used to disguise the festival clothes and handed it to Yuri. "Cover your face, please."

Michael twisted the red scarf around to cover his own nose and mouth. Gabriel was doing the same.

Only one of the tanks appeared to be on fire. "Will it spread?" Michael asked, blinking rapidly against the sting of soot and heat.

"There should be dykes around the tanks," said Gabriel. "Hopefully, it will be enough."

It took less than a second before another explosion rocked the terrain. All three of them dropped back to the ground.

"Dios mío!" someone shrieked from the crowd as a giant piece of equipment shot into the sky, landing somewhere unseen. More debris flew through the air, turning it dark and grimy.

More screams erupted. The crowd was completely out of control now.

"Help!" came a yell near where Michael and Gabriel stood. The panic in the voice made it impossible to say if it were male or female.

Turning, Gabriel shouldered his way through the stampeding mob and hauled someone up before he was trampled.

"Mike!" Gabe hollered, pointing his thumb toward the refinery. "I'm going in."

Michael raised a hand, asking his cousin to wait. "You need to get out of here," he said to Yuri.

"No way," said the man. "Harry said he and Alex will be here soon. All three of us need to return to the town and wait there."

Gabe had jogged back and heard what Yuri said. "It will be too late by then," said Gabriel. "These people need help *now*."

Yuri cursed. "Fine," he said. "I'm going with you."

"You'll only get in the way, mate," Gabriel said. "Let's go, Mike."

Without waiting for a response, they raced toward the gate. The two firemen at the location were too busy to notice.

Stopping for a moment, Gabriel said, "Damn. This looks bad." Human-shaped shadows could be seen through the black fog surrounding the tanks. "Hello!" he called to the fireman at the gate. "Gabriel Kingsley... I'm a firefighter back home. How many men do you have?"

"Nine," he yelled in response. "They're all inside."

"Jesus," breathed Michael. Nine people to fight a disaster this size? And it sounded like the ones at the gate weren't even part of the crew.

"Nine would be about the usual number for an outfit this size," said Gabe. "But they do need help." Taking a deep breath, he asked, "You think we'll make it?"

"Ma will kill us if we don't," said Michael.

With a short laugh, Gabriel made the sign of the cross and kissed his crucifix pendant. He took another moment to pat the Buffalo Woman bracelet around his wrist.

Michael took a deep breath and cleared his mind of all other thoughts. Something solidified inside... the resolve to rescue... the will to fight. Muscles bunched. His heart steadied, beating the rhythm of war drums. "Let's go," he said, voice hoarse from the smoke and the grit.

Bumping fists, they sprinted in.

#

8:40 PM

(1 hour to sunset)

Prone position in the space between rocks at the edge of the cliff should've given Richard reasonable visibility while providing adequate cover. If only El Peuchen did as he was told.

Sighting through the scope atop the Savage, Richard cursed. The second explosion had rendered the air thick and grimy even at this distance of a thousand meters. An *unplanned* second explosion.

There could be a natural reason behind the surprise blast, but somehow, Richard doubted it. He'd been the only one in the team to talk at length with Nate Bronco, and the boy didn't earn his street name merely for the occasional wheeze when he talked.

There was also too much damned chaos at the exits and on the roads for Richard to easily spot the Puelche boy. City fire trucks had arrived, and first responders were busy trying to put out flames and rescue those who were still trapped. The already acrid smell was worsening by the minute, and the shrill siren continued to ring across the landscape.

The second blast was likely why the siren was still on. Town authorities didn't know how many more they could expect, and every man, woman, and child was being told to stay the hell away. Not that it stopped idiot journalists from trying to get pictures. One or two had already been chased out, but there was a news chopper hovering in the distance.

"It ain't clear even with binoculars," Steven shouted over the phone which lay next to Richard's elbow.

Steven and the general were still at the villa. They'd waited for the explosion to give them cover for leaving. Unfortunately, the second blast meant Richard needed help spotting El Peuchen. So ignoring the evacuation siren, General Potts and Steven continued to watch through the field glasses.

"How's it looking at your end?" Steven asked for the umpteenth time.

"Nothing yet," Richard muttered. He had a straight-line view of the crude tanks and the closest exit. The poor air conditions might make identifying El Peuchen difficult, but he should've been visible once he got to the dirt path leading to where Phillip waited.

"Where the hell did the S.O.B. go?" Steven brooded. "My God! A second explosion!"

An investigation would've found traces of chemicals already present in the refinery. Chemicals which should've never been in proximity. The management would've been blamed for lax safety. No one would buy the explanation after a second explosion.

"Our first priority for now has to be to get the boy out," said Richard. "Then, we trigger plan B." It wasn't ideal, but Richard wasn't letting Steven lose no matter what. "Two possibilities on the kid. He got trapped by debris, or..."

"Or?"

"Or he's dead."

Steven hissed. "But Phillip can't leave, can he?"

Phillip would need to stay put until the boy either showed up or his death was confirmed. Charles would have to stay right along.

Not moving the rifle, Richard took his own binoculars to make certain the duo remained where they were supposed to. Phillip looked up suddenly as though aware of being watched.

He carried his handgun with him, but Charles was unarmed. It was Richard's job to make sure all three—Phillip, Charles, and the Puelche boy—got an unobstructed way out of the commotion.

"How long until Sheppard and Alex get here?" Richard asked. Getting the warrant for the Kingsley brothers had itself been risky. Not allowing the duo in Berlin to fly out was impossible without even more official involvement, which would raise suspicion of a conspiracy.

"Flight time from Berlin to Barcelona on the jet would be less than two hours," Steven said. "They left Berlin around seven-thirty according to Phillip's contact at the airport. Another hour for the helicopter to get them to Muskiz. That is if they're allowed to fly directly to the refinery heliport."

"We must work on the assumption they will be," Richard said grimly. "Expect them an hour and a half from now… right after sunset." More than enough time for El Peuchen to be spirited out. *If* he showed up.

"God," Steven murmured. "This is killing me. Where *is* the damn boy?"

"Major," General Potts broke in. "What about the other two lads? Steven's nephews?"

"Victor and Alex are not my brothers," Steven corrected immediately. "Their sons are not my nephews."

A jolt went through Richard. *No,* he said to himself. They weren't his nephews, either. Family wasn't simply about blood.

Moreover, it was Brad who ordered Michael into danger. JD said so. Gabriel followed his cousin. Richard had watched through the scope as the two idiots ran toward the fire. Yuri, too, tried to follow, but the city's emergency vehicles drove in before he could, and the firemen wouldn't allow him in. None of it was Richard's fault.

"If it's not clear outside the compound," Richard said out loud, "it's not going to be clear inside. How am I supposed to spot two specific people?"

Ignoring the impolite response, the general commanded, "Keep an eye out for them. I agree it's unlikely they know about El Peuchen, but they're still Victor and Alex's boys. Think back to what the dads were like at the same age."

Richard remembered quite well how young Michael Kingsley arrived at the clinic in Goa on a helicopter, rifle in hand. Gabriel was a firefighter and built along the same gigantic lines as his father. "Point is," Richard said, "the only way they could do damage at this time is if they recognize Nataniel as the machi's great-grandson."

#

9:05 PM

Somewhere over Europe

"God," muttered Alex, collapsing into yet another seat in the private jet. "My hands are shaking."

Harry didn't say a word, sitting still—very still—and staring straight ahead as he'd done since they boarded the plane. Except when he needed to use the air phone.

Alex didn't dare tell Sabrina where the two boys were. Harry didn't, either, only mentioning they were following orders.

Connection wasn't great, but Noah managed to convey how the sonuvabitch Drummond was still at the hotel, detaining four out of five Kingsley brothers. Dan and Shawn were on their way back from France, but they were delayed at the border thanks to the emergency security measures which went into effect after the explosions. The former attorney general had called the American consulate in Barcelona for help. Yeah, it would take time.

Time during which the boys would be alone at the site. Cell phone service was down in the disaster zone, but the refinery manager radioed to confirm the presence of the two young men. He didn't have further updates. The fire crew had escorted him out, leaving only emergency personnel and engineers to handle the disaster.

City first responders didn't initially realize two civilians were inside, trying to assist. The teens were assumed to be part of the refinery's own rescue team. The duo should've been sent out as soon as they were IDed.

Except, Steven and Armor were in proximity. The safest place for Michael and Gabriel would be with the cops guarding the perimeter until Alex and Harry got there. *If* Drummond hadn't managed to bribe the entire police force of Muskiz.

"Safety in numbers," Alex said to himself for the dozenth time. The refinery's team leader was asked to keep the boys amid the rescue crew but out of reach of the flames. Less chance of the enemy getting to them. The young men had already proven themselves useful, carrying a couple of injured workers to the road where ambulances waited. "Dammit, I don't like this at all," Alex brooded.

"Noah called the mayor again," Harry finally spoke.

"And?"

Shaking his head, Harry said, "No one at the house in Bilbao, but they can always claim to have been sightseeing. No available manpower in Muskiz to check out the villa. The evacuation siren has been going off for a while, and local police says everyone within a two-mile radius was supposed to have left already."

"Steven hasn't left," Alex said instantly.

"He hasn't," Harry agreed. "Charles, Major Armor, General Potts, and Major Potts... all five of them are still there. And El Peuchen."

"Six men," Alex brooded. "Against two unarmed boys. At least General Potts will... I don't know how he agreed to this, but there's a line he won't let Steven cross."

Chapter 62

9:23 PM

(30 minutes to sunset)

Michael slashed futile hands against the fumes of smoke, trying to see more than a couple of feet in front. Flames whooshing, electric power crackling, men shouting, and the siren—the shrill, unrelenting siren. Sweat plastering his tee to his chest, Michael strained to hear every faint cry, every feeble call for help.

He and Gabriel had been in the process of lifting a beam off someone's leg when city fire trucks rolled in. A first responder threw helmets and gloves at the boys and told them to follow directions— no ifs, ands, or buts. Still, they were pushed to the extreme periphery where there was little chance of getting into trouble.

The bomb squad was calling the shots since stopping further explosions was the number one priority. So far, they hadn't found more incendiary devices waiting to go off. Experienced professionals were trying to contain the blaze and put it out. Every spark outside the two burning tanks was stomped down instantly. Emergency shutdown was in progress, with engineers hurrying to power down systems, to close valves, to isolate tanks. Gabe was with them, standing on an aerial ladder between two giant tanks as he assisted a technician working on pipes.

Michael stayed with the rescue crew. Those trapped by rubble needed to be dug out, and ambulances waited to carry the injured to the hospital.

Three bodies had so far been retrieved from the periphery of the tanks which exploded, charred beyond recognition. It might have been a higher number if not for the warning given by Yuri. Still, three dead men. Who knew how many more were being reduced to ashes unseen? The smell of burning flesh was intense even over the stench of vaporizing chemicals. Michael gagged several times, and he wasn't the only one stopping now and then to take deep breaths.

At least three men were never returning to their families. Their sons wouldn't even have the hope of seeing their fathers after an exile.

A couple of crates of bottled water had been left near the ambulances. Grabbing yet another drink, Michael poured the warm liquid straight down his gullet, letting it soothe his insides.

"Check the office," the fire captain shouted.

The building was not burning, but part of a wall had collapsed, clearly thanks to the giant hunk of metal lying amid the wreckage. A few of the windows were broken.

"Anyone in here?" Michael called out again and again. He peered through whatever windows were available. *"Alguien aquí?"*

He was about to turn back when a faint yell reached him.

"Captain!" hollered Michael.

In ten minutes, he and a fireman were burrowing someone out from the bathroom.

"Gracias," the boy wheezed, coughing as he stumbled past them.

"Llévalo a la ambulancia," the fireman told Michael, instructing him to take the rescued kid to the ambulance.

"No, thank you," the boy said in accented English. "I'm all right."

Michael frowned. Not the accent of Spaniards. Something more familiar, closer to home. The voice sounded strange, making a sharp inflection at the end of the sentence. Before Michael could scrutinize the facial features, the boy turned away. It wasn't as if the light was enough to make a detailed study in any case. They were almost the same height, but the boy's frame was lean. His hair was dark, cut close to the scalp.

Keeping an eye on the departing kid, Michael jogged to where Gabriel stood mid-way up a tall ladder. "Yo, Gabe," he bellowed, gesturing at his cousin to come down.

Michael couldn't see Gabriel's expression, but his incredulity was clear in the stance, the upturned hands.

"Come down," Michael repeated. "It's important."

While Gabriel was clambering down, Michael sprinted to the ambulance parked a few feet away. "This guy needs to be checked," he yelled, grabbing the rescued kid by the arm and shoving him toward the medical technicians.

Snarling, the boy turned. "I told you I don't—"

"Legal requirement," snapped Michael. "Management insists."

While the medical crew was checking him out, Michael returned to the ladder. "What's up?" Gabe asked, tone low.

Michael inclined his head. "See that dude? Something about him... he could be our guy. El Peuchen."

"What's going on?" the fire captain shouted in Spanish. "Get back up there!"

"Shit," said Gabriel. Head swiveling, he eyed the ladder and the boy. "He's leaving. There are a couple of cops at the gate. Maybe we can have them hold him until Uncle Harry gets here."

The Kingsley brothers were still detained in the hotel as far as Michael knew. Dan and Shawn were still caught at the border. Harry and Alex were the only ones who even had a prayer of getting to the burning refinery tonight.

"You, there," bellowed the captain, gesturing at someone else. "Finish the job."

"Sorry, chief," Gabe called back. "It's an emergency. I need to talk to the police."

"You talk to the officers," Michael said. "My Spanish is not good enough to get them to understand."

Gabe ran ahead while Michael took care to keep a few feet behind El Peuchen. They didn't want the boy suddenly changing directions without anyone noticing.

The air was only slightly clearer close to the gate. Michael stood in the shadows next to the security station and watched as Gabe argued with the two cops in the only squad car present. There would be other officers farther up the highway, blocking entry to outside vehicles.

Whatever Gabe was saying didn't seem to make much impression. The other boy passed the squad car, making his way to the shadowed meadow where impending darkness would swallow him up.

"Hey!" Michael shouted. "El Peuchen!"

The boy swiveled, the slight hesitation when he turned revealing the realization of his mistake. The cops looked up but were plainly not convinced enough to intervene.

Michael ran toward the tarred road to apprehend the saboteur. Gabriel was already there, tackling El Peuchen.

The boy didn't tumble to the ground like Michael would've expected. El Peuchen aimed a kick at Gabe's crotch and threw an uppercut.

The cops yelled, asking the duo to cut it out.

Surprisingly, Gabe stumbled and fell to his knees.

Roaring, Michael pounced, but the boy slipped out of his grasp and ran backward a few feet. He appeared confused.

Before Michael could give chase, Gabriel groaned and collapsed on his back. "Mike, I think I've been shot."

\#

9:54 PM

(the beginning of civil twilight)

Hands shaking, Richard sat up on the ground. "Was it Victor?" he asked.

The face had not been clear in the smoke-tainted golden glow of the dying sun, but only El Peuchen had reason to go in the direction of the dirt path. Only the Kingsley brothers and their supporters had reason to stop the boy. The size of the fellow who tried to fight the Puelche kid... Richard hoped like hell it was Victor. The alternative...

The phone crackled. "Gabriel, I believe," said General Potts. "Victor's son."

"Let's make sure," Richard said rapidly. "General, please call JD. Maybe the cops let them go, and Victor got here."

"No," Potts said. "Victor's still in the hotel. It was Gabriel."

"Fuck," Richard spat out. A child. He'd shot a child.

Not just any child. Patrice's grandson. Richard's own flesh and blood. Scrambling to the bushes on his hands and knees, he heaved.

"Rich," Steven's voice came over the phone. "What's going on? Are you all right?"

"Gimme a minute," Richard said hoarsely. "I'm..." The killer of a boy he should've seen as a son. Richard's hair was suddenly wet with perspiration, his eyes blurry.

"Major," snapped Potts. "Get your act together. This is not the first time you shot an enemy soldier. I'm sure some of them were in their teens."

"Yes," acknowledged Richard, "but I didn't know them. God... Victor's son. He's eighteen." Or was. "Is he dead?"

"He was trying to fight afterward," Potts pointed out. "Also, the medical crew is right there. They'll take him to the hospital. Focus on what *we* need to do, Major. There's a bullet in Gabriel's back now. It won't be traced to us, but there's no longer any chance of passing off the explosions as accidents brought about by lax safety protocols. We need to switch to plan B."

"Right," said Richard. "Plan B." Careless security in an area with separatist activity. Which meant all of them needed to get out before the police swarmed the hills in search of the extremist who killed a—

The boy would live, Richard assured himself. Young Gabriel would've learned a lesson about leaving his back open to attack, but he'd live.

#

Same time

By the refinery gate

Michael collapsed to his knees next to his cousin. "Gabe... oh, my God... Gabe..." Looking up, he screamed, "Help! Man down!"

The two cops were also shouting, asking what happened. One of them skidded to a stop on Gabriel's other side.

"Gunshot," Michael said to the officer, glancing toward the hills.

"Upper back," said Gabe, voice strained. "In the middle."

The officer hissed. *"No te muevas,"* he ordered the injured boy, hollering, *"Necesitas ayuda!"* toward the ambulance crew.

The second cop was peering into the glowing hills as though he could tell where the bullet came from. He was simultaneously talking into a radio, coiled wire attaching the device to the interior of the squad car. Equipment in hand, the medical crew raced toward the wounded boy. Even a couple of firemen were running to the scene. El Peuchen was glancing wildly around as though unsure of his next move.

The siren continued to blare.

"What are you doing?" Gabriel asked Michael, tone urgent. Sweat was pouring down Gabe's temples, his chest heaving with obvious effort. "Don't let the S.O.B. get away!"

"Danos espacio, por favor!" snapped a sharp female voice, asking Michael to give the medics the room they needed to work.

He scooted back on his hands and knees.

"Go!" said Gabriel. "They're going to take me to the hospital. *You* have to keep El Peuchen here until Uncle Harry comes. This can end tonight, Mike. Go!"

Then, one of the medical personnel shifted, blocking Gabriel from Michael's view. There was a sharp pain in both his palms, the burning inflicted by squeezing the gravel on the road without even realizing it.

All attention was focused on the victim and on the shooter hidden in the hills. The second cop had joined his partner, both now staring into the rapidly deepening darkness. The few moments it would take Michael to remind the cops of El Peuchen would be enough for the saboteur to make his escape.

Breathing heavily, Michael glanced behind. El Peuchen was still there, staring at the scene. Their eyes met.

With a snarl, Michael leaped to his feet. This *would* end tonight. The enemy would pay for every drop of blood they shed. The dead would have their justice, from Liam's father and Harry's wife to the three men who were burned alive mere hours ago. There would be no more Lilahs getting assaulted, no Taras or Gabriels getting shot.

Chapter 63

Wheeling around, El Peuchen pushed through the men gathering to offer help.

Michael paused to take a quick look at the hills, gauging the shooter's likely location. Gabe had been hit in the upper back. Not the shoulders or the sides. And the distance... the shooter had to be hiding in one of the groves, most of them half a mile away or more. Or among the rocks. Major Richard Armor was a skilled sniper according to the military. It was him... had to be.

No one stopped Michael as he shouldered his way through the crowd around his injured cousin. Asking the officers for help yet again would be a waste of time for one more reason. The moment they tried to detain El Peuchen, Armor would fire a second bullet to make sure the saboteur never talked. The Kingsleys would get away with their crimes.

The fire captain was in the periphery of the crowd. El Peuchen shoved him aside, but the fellow simply shifted, continuing to gape at the wounded boy.

The saboteur was surely heading toward the men who paid him to do the job. Major Armor—if *he* got caught, his best buddy would go down with him. The Kingsleys would be finished.

As Michael reached the edge of the crowd, he crouched low. There—El Peuchen was running up the slope, peering over his shoulder now and then.

Bending double, Michael followed. The rapidly fading light would work in his favor, and the soot and smoke would make it even harder for the damned coward up in the woods to keep his target in sight. Nor would he have the advantage of a victim unaware of his presence.

#

"I can't see well enough," Richard stated. Too little light, too much smoke, too many people on scene. Shadows moved in every direction. Around him, there was the stillness of impending night. All the birds and animals appeared to have fled the woods. "Either our boy got away, or he's been detained. If the cops have him, he won't snitch right off the bat. If he managed to get away, he would take around fifteen minutes to get to Phillip. Let's say twenty. If the boy is not there by then, we will all leave and look for alternate ways to handle the complication."

If El Peuchen talked... well... only Richard had traveled to Argentina. The boy met only Major Armor and Major Potts. Steven would be safe. The network would remain in his hands.

"I have Phillip on my phone," said General Potts. "If he sees or hears something concerning, he and Charlie will leave right away. Steven and I will, too."

"What about you, Rich?" Steven asked.

"I will stay until Phillip and Charlie are out," stated Richard.

Changing positions on the ground, he redirected the Savage toward the small clearing where Phillip waited with Steven's idiot brother. The thermal riflescope offered just enough range to keep them covered.

#

The siren should've drowned out the wheezing sounds El Peuchen was making as he ascended the slope. Yet Michael could hear every tremble in the enemy's breath. A few stars were becoming visible in the still-golden sky, but it was as though Michael's vision sharpened, letting him see through the thick air, letting him spot every shrub he could hide behind as he followed the saboteur.

Michael kept a few feet to the right of the sonuvabitch as he got to the dirt path between the trees. The sniper would take care to keep El Peuchen in sight, and the shadow crouched low ten feet to one side would go unspotted. El Peuchen certainly didn't seem to realize he was being tailed. Fallen leaves and twigs hindered Michael's attempts to be quiet, but it didn't matter when the enemy himself was crunching dry foliage on his way up the hill.

El Peuchen came to a sudden stop. *"Gracias a Dios!"* the saboteur breathed.

Two men, Michael noted. One of them appeared military. Not Major Armor, although Michael thought he'd seen the fellow before. The military guy was holding a gun in his hands, peering behind El Peuchen as though to check for a tail.

The second man... Michael smiled in satisfaction. Charles Kingsley.

#

"Finally!" Richard agreed with Steven's muttered comment. Three hours after taking position in this spot, Richard's mission was at an end.

Almost.

Even through the scope, El Peuchen appeared flustered by his experience, the arrogance and the general hostility he exhibited until now nowhere in sight. Pistol in hand, Phillip waved the other two ahead.

A shadow flew across Richard's field of view. Phillip stumbled.

Before Richard could utter even a sound of surprise, the newcomer was rolling on the ground with Phillip, punching repeatedly. The other two appeared frozen in shock.

"What..." Steven shouted over the phone. "What's going on?"

"Lemme see," ordered the voice of General Potts. "Who the hell?"

Richard couldn't tell, either. The newcomer was moving too fast, not giving Richard a chance to zero in. "He knows where I am," Richard murmured in realization.

"Yes, he does," the general said grimly. "And it's Michael... Alex's son."

"*What?*" Steven shouted again. After a couple of seconds, he said, "God... what the hell is happening? Rich, shoot him!"

"I can't," Richard stated. "Not when they're moving around. I could end up hitting Phillip, instead."

Even if they weren't moving, the boy was seventeen! What was he trying to do? How did he imagine he would escape?

El Peuchen had gotten over his shock and was running up and down, trying to get the enemy off Phillip. Major Potts was no slouch at hand-to-hand combat, but the boy possessed the advantage of youth. Still, two-against-one odds—*four*-against-one if Richard and Charles were to be counted—did not look good for Michael.

A second or two... a rapid roll... Phillip was on top. Before he could use the position, Michael threw a kick. Not at Phillip. El Peuchen fell, clutching his stomach.

Another roll... Phillip was being pummeled again, but Michael took care to keep the enemy between him and the sniper's rifle. Charles just gawked uselessly.

Then, Michael was on his feet, Phillip's gun in his hands. Before Phillip could leap up, Michael's arm was around Charles's neck, the barrel of the revolver under his chin. The boy's back was toward the dirt path leading down, Charles a human shield in front.

Both Phillip and El Peuchen were blocking Michael, but this wasn't a basketball game, and they could do nothing without risking Charles.

"Rich!" screamed Steven. "Shoot the damn bastard! He's got Charlie."

"How—" started Richard.

"Go for the shoulder, Major," ordered Potts. "The boy is taller than the hostage, and he's keeping his head covered, but he's forgetting his weapon arm. It should be in your line of fire. You're skilled enough to do it without hurting Charles. Phillip will take care of the rest."

"Take care..." Shock went through Richard as he understood what Potts, Sr. meant. "Alex's son..."

"Yes, Alex's son," acknowledged the general, tone quite steady. "He's trying to take Charles to the cops at the refinery. Major, if the boy succeeds, we're all done for. The network will be the least of our worries. The charges will be terrorism. Even if Phillip and Charles escape, Michael will tell the cops what he saw. *Who* he saw. It will end up being his word against ours. Do you understand me, Armor?"

"I don't care whose son he is," Steven said wildly. "He has my brother!"

Richard couldn't. He simply—

A new sound added itself to the siren still blasting across the landscape. The familiar chop-chop-chop of a helicopter. There were no identifying marks to suggest media presence.

"Sheppard," Potts noted. "And Alex. I'm sure of it. Major, we're out of time. If they get close enough, they could spot Phillip and Charles. Shoot now or be prepared to spend the rest of your life in jail."

"For God's sake, Rich," said Steven. "Shoot! If you don't, I'll be the one getting killed... hanging from a noose. Do it for me."

Richard pulled the trigger.

#

A sudden pain... a hissing sound as an artery tore... a wetness down the shoulder. Michael looked in shock as his right arm fell uselessly to the side. The gun dropped.

Michael stumbled. He saw the kick coming, landing on his knees. His leg twisted. Something slipped out of place inside.

The dark sky tilted. The back of his head struck the ground. His vision swam, then cleared. Michael tried to scramble up, but his left leg wouldn't cooperate. Pain... so much pain. He managed to lift his torso only a few inches before tumbling a second time. Michael slid a few feet downhill along the path.

The military guy shouted something unintelligible. His gun was again in his hands, but he was looking up at the sky, at the approaching helicopter. Saying something else, he ran rearward into the protection of the trees.

El Peuchen followed, but Charles turned to one side. "Charlie!" yelled the military guy. "Let's go."

When Charles turned back toward Michael, it was with a small boulder in his hands.

Fingers of his left hand digging into the earth, Michael tried to roll out of the way, but his body took longer than usual to respond. Too long.

The helicopter got closer, its sounds louder.

The rock descended. Shock waves reverberated across Michael's skull. Something crunched. Liquid warmth slid down one ear.

Grunting, Michael fell onto his back again. He needed to—

"Charlie!" the military dude shouted again.

In a few more seconds, they were gone.

There was something Michael needed to do. What was it? His family... the Kingsleys... they couldn't be allowed to... so many people got hurt. But Harry was on his way. And Alex. They would... they would...

Michael looked up toward the heavens. The helicopter kept getting nearer. The half-moon was visible against the dusky blue of the sky. More and more stars were popping up between the clouds.

Stars—Michael smiled. Tara had said her name meant star in her language. What did she want to tell him when he returned to New York? She would have to tell Gabe, instead. He *had* to be okay. Ma would be heartbroken if both her boys got hurt.

Where was Michael's ma now? In their big castle in Panama? *No,* he tried to remember. They didn't live there, any longer. *Mama,* Michael called. *Where do we live now?*

Bright-green eyes crinkling with laughter, she said, *"I don't know, Mikey. Let's ask your daddy when he comes back."*

But Daddy wasn't at home. He was... was... Michael smiled again, watching the helicopter get bigger. There were two men inside, both of who called him son.

"Daddy," whispered Michael.

Then, he died.

THE END of Book 6

For a sneak peek at the last book in the series, please head over to <u>www.JayPerin.com</u>

Want to know what happens next to Harry, Lilah, and Alex? Order *The Capitol Showdown* today to continue with this exciting tale!

Afterword

In case you missed this info in prior books: the One Hundred Years of War series is an adaptation of the *Mahabharata*, the Indian epic mythology.

A few comments (some are repeats from prior books):

1.   Reception Day for West Point Class of 2004 was June 29, 2000, which meant Michael would've been living on campus by the events in Spain. I had to change it for the purposes of the story.

2.   As always, my thanks to the writers whose works on *Mahabharata* I've enjoyed and learned from and to fellow myth enthusiasts from various discussion groups. Thanks to my friends who have patiently sat through my arguments on various plot points.

3.   I did not use real characters except peripherally. That, too, only for things they were actually accused/guilty of doing.

4.   I tried to stick to historical facts throughout the story, including the minor details, but some changes were inevitable.

5.   Citations for the maps are in endnotes.

So that's it. See you again when *The Capitol Showdown* releases.

Sincerely,

Jay Perin

P.S. As always, if you liked the story, do tell others about it. Also, writers thrive on reviews. They help us figure out what worked and what fell flat. They help other readers make up their minds. Please do leave a comment on any of the sites.

472

Visit www.EastRiverBooks.com for a bunch of interesting stuff.

---

[i] *Attribution: **https://qms.nextgis.com/geoservices/2634/***
Map tiles by CartoDB, under CC BY 3.0.
Data by OpenStreetMap, under ODbL.
https://centrodedescargas.cnig.es/CentroDescargas/busquedaSerie.do?codSerie=MDS05
[ii] *Attribution: **https://www.ign.es/web/ign/portal/info-aviso-legal***